DEADLOCKED

JOEL GOLDMAN

PINNACLE BOOKS
Kensington Publishing Corp.
http://www.kensingtonbooks.com

PINNACLE BOOKS are published by

Kensington Publishing Corp.
850 Third Avenue
New York, NY 10022

All Kensington Titles, Imprints, and Distributed Lines are available at special quantity discounts for bulk purchases for sales promotions, premiums, fund-raising, and educational or institutional use. Special book excerpts or customized printings can also be created to fit specific needs. For details, write or phone the office of the Kensington special sales manager: Kensington Publishing Corp., 850 Third Avenue, New York, NY 10022, attn: Special Sales Department, Phone: 1-800-221-2647.

First Pinnacle Books Printing: January 2005

10 9 8 7 6 5 4 3 2 1

Printed in the United States of America

Chapter 1

Ryan Kowalczyk knew something few people ever knew: the exact time he would die. He had spent the last fifteen years watching each month melt away until only one month, July, remained. He lingered through those July days, indifferent to the merciless heat that claimed a dozen lives across Missouri, waking early on Sunday July 16th, his last day. His gut twisted. The hard floor cool to his bare feet, he sat on the side of his bed, head in his hands, wondering for the millionth time how it would feel when the drugs hit his veins at midnight.

Two kinds of people knew what he knew. Suicides and death row inmates. He couldn't kill himself. Not because he clung to the fantasy that some court more supreme than the one that had condemned him would grant him a new trial, though his mother promised him that each time she visited. Not because the governor might commute his sentence, the last chance his lawyer was still pursuing in the final hours of his life. And not because he lacked the courage. He had thought of plenty of ways to kill himself, beating the guards who were sworn to keep him alive until the prison's execution team could poison him.

Ryan Kowalczyk wouldn't kill himself because he was innocent. That's what he told the police when they came for him. That's what he told his mother when she clung to his bony shoulders, the jury's verdict a knife in both their hearts. That's what he told Father Steve, the priest who sat with him now in the death-watch cell, counting down the final sixty minutes of Ryan's life.

"Don't waste these last precious moments, boy," the priest said. "Confess your sins and go to God with grace."

Ryan ignored the priest, as he ignored his last meal, a thick steak swimming in bloody juice. What's the point, Ryan thought, rising from his bed, pressing his face against the small window cut in the door of his cell, the glass cool against his lips, a guard sitting on the other side, staring back at him. The guard checked his watch, impatiently tapping the crystal face with his finger. Ryan was already dead, numb to fear or regret, consumed by one question.

"What's it like?" Ryan asked Father Steve, not turning around, his breath fogging the glass.

"Heaven?" the priest asked, placing his hand on the condemned man's shoulder. "It's God's glorious kingdom, but it's reserved for those who accept God and come to Him with a clean heart. That's why you have to confess, Ryan. Before it's too late."

"Not heaven, Father. Dying. I don't believe in heaven or God or any of that bullshit. If all that were true, I wouldn't be here and you and I know that."

Ryan pivoted, facing the priest, his face inches from Father Steve. He could taste the sour scent of stale tobacco soaked into the priest's black clothes. Father Steve's lips twitched; he needed a smoke. Ryan was lanky and a head taller than Father Steve who was thick, his fat neck stuffed inside his collar, a trickle of sweat staining the white.

The death-watch cell was close, crammed with a cot, toilet, basin, and chair all made of steel. The floor was tile, the ceiling cast in concrete. Weak fluorescent light bathed the priest's face with a pale purple hue, reminding Ryan of faded vestments.

Ryan held the priest's eyes, catching a flicker of doubt that confirmed Ryan's certain disbelief in the deity.

"Your mother believes in heaven and a merciful God," the priest said, covering his own lapse. "She wants that for you."

Father Steve had known the family since Ryan was a small boy. His mother, Mary, was a regular at Mass. Ryan's earliest memories of the church were of the sweet fragrance of incense and Father Steve patting his head as Ryan clutched his mother's hand, a small boy in a strange place.

Growing up, Ryan never gave much thought to heaven or hell, putting more faith in his ability to hit a three-point shot from the top of the key with time running out, the memory of his last game winner still sharp. The ball spinning perfectly, dropping through the net as the gun sounded, his best friend Whitney King and the rest of his high school teammates mobbing him. He was seventeen then. Fifteen years ago. The last good thing he ever did.

"She wants it for her," Ryan said. "I'll be dead and buried."

"Then why not give it to her, boy?" the priest asked. "Is it such a hard thing for you to leave to your mother?"

Ryan looked at the priest, then through the narrow window to the long hall outside the death-watch cell. Two guards rounded the corner pushing a gurney toward him. Wrist and ankle restraints hung off the sides, leather slapping against metal, rough wheels clacking. The time-keeping guard stood and removed a pair of clear IV tubes from a cabinet marked MEDICAL SUPPLIES. Silver needles gleamed like minibayonets.

"No, I guess not, Father."

"Kneel with me then, boy."

Father Steve placed his hands on Ryan's shoulders. Ryan bowed his head, dredged his rote confession from childhood memory, admitted to sins against God and man, and begged forgiveness. His prayer was generic, silent about murder.

Ryan stumbled at first, his heart racing ahead, slamming against his chest, his words catching up, becoming a torrent as the door to the death-watch cell swung open. The guards cleared their throats. Harsh white light from the hall washed into the crowded space sharpened by a rush of cool air. The priest lowered his head and raised one hand against the advancing guards, holding them back. One guard scraped mud from the sole of his shoe against the frame of the gurney. Another softly thumped the IV lines against the mattress.

Father Steve rose first, drawing Ryan to his feet. Ryan blinked, not against the light, but against the involuntary steps he took as he was passed from the hands of his priest to the hands of his executioners. He looked at Father Steve over his shoulder with wild eyes, his throat tight, last words frozen in his heart.

"It's time," one of the guards told him.

"Go with God, boy," the priest said.

"How much longer?" Harry Ryman asked Lou Mason, drumming his fingers on the center console dividing the front seat of his Chevy Suburban.

It was Harry's car but he was sitting on the passenger side, letting Mason drive, Harry's concession to his fading eyesight. A retired Kansas City homicide detective, Harry was used to running his own show, not being chauffeured. Harry had dated Mason's Aunt Claire for the better part of Mason's life, the two of them filling in for Mason's parents who had been killed in a car accident when Mason was three. His long relationship with Mason was the only thing that made Harry's transition from driver to passenger a little easier.

"Fifteen minutes less than the last time you asked me," Mason told him. "Relax, Harry. It's just after ten o'clock. We'll be there in plenty of time to see Kowalczyk executed."

"I don't want to be late, that's all," Harry said, shifting his weight from side to side. Harry liked the Suburban because it fit his bulky frame, unlike a sedan that made him feel like he'd been shoehorned into the middle seat on a discount airline. "This damn thing with my eyes drives me crazy."

Harry shook his head, squinting against the night, trying to capture the stars. He sighed quietly with the knowledge that they now eluded him, taking little solace in the moon which had become a smudge against the sky. They had turned off I-70 a while ago, speeding down a succession of two-lane state highways lit only by the headlights of an occasional pickup going in the opposite direction. Harry felt more than saw the undulating, curving road, wondering if it was true that the loss of one sense heightened the others.

Patrick Ortiz, the Prosecuting Attorney, had invited Harry and his former partner, Wilson Bluestone Jr., a.k.a. Blues, to witness the execution since they were the arresting officers in the double murder for which Kowalczyk was to be put to death.

Blues declined Ortiz's invitation, telling him he didn't believe in the death penalty because he didn't trust the system to always get it right. Some rule, Ortiz had said, telling Blues he should apply it to himself, and Blues answering that he trusted himself just fine.

The system got it right this time, Harry thought, the big Chevy swinging wide on a curve, Mason over-correcting, making the chassis shimmy. Ryan Kowalczyk was a stone cold killer, beating that couple to death like he was taking batting practice. It was a goddamn miracle he didn't know their baby was in the backseat of the car or there would have been three bodies. Nobody ever deserved the death penalty more than that kid.

Trouble was, Harry conceded, the system got it wrong about Whitney King, Kowalczyk's buddy and codefendant. Harry rubbed his temples with his fingertips and ran his knuckles across his eyes, trying to clear his memory and his vision.

Graham Byrnes had been twenty-seven years old, his wife, Elizabeth, only twenty-five. Harry silently recited their names as he'd written them in his report of their murders fifteen years ago. Their baby, Nick, had been three and couldn't fall asleep. They had taken him for a drive because that always helped quiet him down. Worked too. The kid was sleeping in the backseat under a quilt. Slept through the whole thing. Imagine that. Harry couldn't.

It was near midnight. They were in a new subdivision. Roads were in but no houses or streetlights. The Byrneses had just bought a lot to build their first home. Nick had given them an excuse to go take a look. Kowalcyzk and King were out in Kowalcyzk's car, saw the couple, tried to rob them. Graham Byrnes fought back. Kowalcyzk and King killed them.

Harry tried focusing on the snaking road, headlights reflecting off the highway sign, cursing under his breath when he couldn't read the sign. June bugs splattered against the windshield.

"How far?" Harry asked Mason.

"Sign said ten miles to Potosi. The prison is just outside town."

Harry grunted, holding his watch to within an inch of his eye to check the time again, remembering how he and Blues had caught the killers. Usual brilliant police work, Harry had explained to his lieutenant. The killers were stupid and they caught a break with a witness who saw the suspects sideswipe a street lamp about a mile away, the lamp shining right on the license tag, the witness writing it down. They traced the car and found bloody clothes belonging to both boys in Kowalcyzk's basement. The only thing missing was the murder weapon. Harry assumed it was the tire iron from the couple's car. The coroner said the injury patterns were consistent with such a weapon. They had searched the murder scene, the surrounding area, the route to Ryan's house and both boys' houses, never finding it.

The boys told the same story, down to the punctuation. They played basketball on the same team and had won a big game that night. Partied afterward and were out driving around. Said they took a wrong turn, ended up lost in the subdivision. Saw the Byrneses and stopped to ask them for directions. Said the Byrneses were having car trouble, each kid saying he went looking for an all-night service station, couldn't find one, came back and found the people murdered. Claimed the kid that did the killing made the other one help hide the bodies. That's how they both ended up with blood on their clothes. All smears. No splatters. Harry could still see Blues shaking his head when they walked out of the courtroom, King acquitted, Kowalcyzk convicted.

Harry cracked his window, the hot night air too humid to cool even at highway speed. Mason slowed down, turned onto a county road, following the signs to the state penitentiary, finally easing the big Chevy into a visitor parking spot. A handful of cars were in the lot, only a couple of them from the press. Executions had become too common to make it off the back page.

Mason cut the ignition, pocketing the keys. "Any chance the jury got it wrong? That Ryan Kowalczyk was innocent?"

"Not a chance," Harry said.

Chapter 2

Mary Kowalczyk worried about what to wear to her son's execution and worried more that vanity at such a cruel time was especially sinful. Father Steve had heard her confession the day before, telling her that it was natural to think about such things, that it was her mind's way of holding on.

It was more important than that to Mary. She would be the last person her son would see in this life and she wanted him to remember her in an ordinary way, a smile on her face, wearing a nice dress, as if he'd just come home for a visit. She couldn't bear the thought of him remembering her in her grief, not after she fought so hard these last fifteen years to save his life, pushing the lawyers to file every appeal and re-file them when they were lost.

Vowing to mourn him after his death, not before, she chose a dark green dress she'd first worn on Ryan's sixteenth birthday. She and her husband, Vince, took Ryan out to dinner. Ryan admired the dress, telling her it made her look like an actress, what with her long black hair and slender frame, Mary smiling at her son's compliment, giving the fantasy a whirl.

The dress, like all her clothes, was old and fared better from a distance. She rarely bought anything new even before Ryan was taken from her. Vince was a carpenter who worked when the weather and his mood suited him, leaving little for frills. After the trouble, he began taking jobs out of town, staying away for longer and longer periods until one day he didn't come back. A dress had to last a long time.

Mary had been at the prison for hours, arriving with Father Steve for her last visit with Ryan. She was glad that the priest was with him in his final hour, tending to his soul. Father Steve had told her how important it was that Ryan confess his sins. She knew that he wanted Ryan to confess to the murders, charges he had denied from the start, never wavering, Mary never doubting his innocence. She knew he wouldn't admit to these unspeakable crimes even now as she prayed for his salvation in the next life.

She had asked the warden if she could spend some time alone in the witness room before the other witnesses arrived. The warden had told her that the witnesses usually did not go in until the prisoner was ready. She said she understood, but explained that it would be easier for her if she was familiar with the setting. The warden had showed her in, closing the door behind her. He was a considerate man in a hard place.

Two rows of six chairs occupied the rectangular room. A window filled the upper half of the wall looking into the execution chamber, a square space painted white with a concrete floor and a drain in the center. On the opposite wall there were two round openings through which she knew the lethal injection would be administered. Anonymous executioners would pump drugs into her son until he was dead. She would watch him die while his killers hid from her. Such men were cowards.

She stepped to the glass, pressing her balled hands against the unyielding surface, wishing she could break it, grab her son, and race away. Leaning her forehead on the middle of the window, her fingernails pinching her palms, she pounded on it. Softly, at first, then harder and harder until the glass shook, her blows rattling the frame, exhausting her so that she collapsed into one of the straight-backed wooden chairs, sobbing without tears, moaning. Her womb and her heart ached, one pain a memory of her son's birth, the other a harbinger of his death.

Of all the agonies she felt none was greater than the certainty of her son's innocence and the raw injustice of the jury's verdict, condemning her son while freeing Whitney King. Mary wasn't political, had never even voted. She accepted that some were rich and some were poor. God made Kings and He made Kowalczyks. She didn't complain. Envy was not among her sins. Yet she harbored such black bitterness knowing that Whitney King was living a grand life untouched by his guilt that it frightened her.

Her hatred was so deep that she kept it even from Father Steve, omitting it from her confessions, lest the priest think she might do the thing she talked of to herself and no one else. Mary admitted in her private moments of piercing despair that she could do it, gradually convincing herself that she must, recoiling at her sinfulness, praying for forgiveness and the wisdom to find another way.

She had always been puzzled, a bit unsure, about the boys' friendship. One thing Mary understood well was class differences and the gulf between her son and his friend was more than money. Hers was a family of laborers. The Kings were not monarchs, but they were Kansas City bluebloods. Only their common Catholic faith brought the boys together at St. Marks, the parochial school they attended. Ryan's family depended on the scholarships Whitney's family contributed. She had held her tongue instead of warning Ryan he shouldn't trust people like that, regretting forever that she had.

Nancy Troy, a public defender, had been Ryan's first lawyer.

She was a young woman who meant well and tried hard, but Whitney had a team of lawyers who attacked Mary's son from the outset in the press and in the courtroom, digging for dirt about her family, making it up when none was found. No one was more surprised than Ryan was when Whitney accused him of the murders from the witness stand. Mary wasn't surprised at all.

The door opened behind her, reflections of the other witnesses glancing off the window. She looked for one face, wondering if she would recognize him after all these years, a catch in her throat as he walked in. Tall and blond like his father, fine features like his mother. She hadn't seen Nick Byrnes since just after Ryan was taken from her. The boy's grandparents had taken him in and Mary had called on them to express her condolences. The grandfather had slammed the door in her face, the boy clinging to his grandfather's leg, peeking at her. Mary resisted the urge to stare though she was certain the boy would neither recognize nor remember her.

She had studied the list of witnesses. The big man with beefy hands and face was one of the policemen who took Ryan away, apologizing to her for her sorrow. Mary was glad his partner hadn't come, the Indian that had thrown her son against the wall in his bedroom. He was an awful man.

She counted the witnesses off in her mind: the woman from the governor's office, the doctor who would pronounce the moment of death, the prosecuting attorney, and the reporters, matching each face to a name except for one. A tall man with dark hair and steel eyes who glanced around as if he didn't belong. She listened without looking as the prosecuting attorney introduced him to the warden. Lou Mason, the prosecuting attorney called him. The name registered, but Mary was too distracted to struggle with the reason.

She hoped they would all ignore her. After all, what could

they say to her without being cruel? She closed her eyes and waited. Where was Father Steve? Where was Ryan?

Nick Byrnes was twelve when he learned that his parents had been murdered, not killed in a car accident as his grand-parents had told him when he was six and the vague story that they had gone to live with God was no longer persuasive. Truth was he never believed the God story. Nick couldn't imagine having parents so mean that they would leave him to live with anyone else, including God. And he refused to believe in a God that would let his parents leave Nick so they could move in with Him.

The car accident story worked pretty well until he was twelve. His parents didn't leave him on purpose. It was an accident. God didn't take them from him. He took them in. That's what his Grandma Esther had told Nick and it made sense.

One day, in seventh grade, Nick noticed kids at school whispering as he walked by, giving him weird looks like there was an alien arm growing out of the back of his head. His teacher, a flowery smelling woman, kept stopping at his desk, patting his hand and asking him if he was all right. Then one of the older kids, a newly muscled ninth grader named Alex, bumped him in the lunch line and asked him if he was going to the execution.

"What execution?" Nick asked.

"The guy that killed your parents, you dork. Don't you know anything?"

Nick mumbled something, and stepped out of the line, spending the rest of the lunch period in a bathroom stall, his pants down around his ankles and his stomach in his throat. He stayed after school, going to the library to read the newspaper, something he'd never done except to look at the comics. He found the article on the front page of the Metropolitan

section of the *Kansas City Star.* Ryan Kowalczyk was scheduled to die for the murders of Graham and Elizabeth Byrnes
committed nine years earlier.

Nick raced home, flush with embarrassment and anger.
His grandparents had lied to him again. Bursting into the
house, hot tears streaming down his cheeks, he caught his
grandmother wrapping a turkey carcass with the newspaper.

"I'm sorry you found out this way," she told him, rocking
him against her bosom. That was all she ever said, and it was
more than his grandfather would tell him.

A judge had spared Kowalczyk that night when he was
only six hours away from getting the needle; his grandparents learned about the stay of execution from a reporter
who called for their reaction while they were eating dinner.
His grandfather hung up on the reporter, stormed out of the
house, returning hours later, sloppy drunk and crying. His
grandmother retreated to her bedroom and didn't come out
for three days.

That night, Nick had the nightmare again. He'd had it for
as long as he could remember, though not in a while. It was
always the same. In the dream, he was sleeping, awakened
by an invisible, paralyzing fear, sensing that a horrible creature was hovering over him. Though awake, he couldn't see,
couldn't move, and could scarcely breathe. A woman cried
out, her voice familiar though he'd never heard it quite like
that, so terrified, exploding in waves. Men shouting, then the
woman screaming again, drowning out the men, drowning
out everything as if her whole life was that scream. Then it
was dark and quiet and cold, so cold that he shivered, waking
up for real, his teeth chattering, holding his knees to his
chest so tightly that he lost circulation in his arms and legs.

His grandparents wouldn't talk about the murders,
telling him that no good would come of it, leaving Nick to
find out on his own what had happened. The Internet made

it easy. Not only did he find articles on the *Kansas City Star*'s database, he found the court file on the Missouri Supreme Court's Web site, including the transcript of the trial. He downloaded everything, devoting endless hours to reading and rereading the story of his parents' deaths, at last understanding his nightmare when he learned that he had been in the car the night his parents were killed, his life spared by the quilt his mother used to cover him.

Ryan Kowalczyk was scheduled to die three more times and, each time, Nick wrote letters to the prosecuting attorney, the governor, and the Missouri Supreme Court urging them to carry out the death sentence. A victim's advocate from the prosecuting attorney's office called and thanked him for his letters, telling him to keep writing. A reporter from Channel 6 did a story on him and Kowalczyk's mother who was conducting her own letter-writing campaign to save her son. Nick's grandparents grounded him for a week for making such a public display.

Nick tracked developments in Kowalczyk's appeals on the court's Web site, struggling with matters of due process, laughing at the notion that the death penalty was cruel and unusual punishment. What's crushing his mother's face with a tire iron, he demanded to know in one of his letters, tearing up the empty, apologetic reply from the victim's advocate.

Nick's memories of his parents had faded long ago to gauzy images of faces kept familiar in photographs his grandmother hid in a box on a basement shelf. He felt guilty that he didn't remember his parents well enough to miss them, though he desperately missed having parents. His grandparents did the best they could for him, though they didn't have the energy to raise another child and he detected in their remoteness not only the pain of their loss, but their resentment at the burden they inherited, adding to his own guilt.

Nick hoped that Ryan Kowalczyk's execution would ease their burden and his, finding comfort in justice, no matter how long delayed. There would be no more appeals, no more last minute stays. This time Nick was certain that Kowalczyk would pay and it was only right that Nick should be there to witness his death. The world is round, his grandfather was fond of saying.

Nick had researched death by lethal injection. He knew that Kowalczyk would receive three drugs through the IV lines that would be inserted in his arms. The first drug would put Kowalczyk to sleep; the second would paralyze his diaphragm so that he couldn't breathe; the last drug would stop his heart. Death by lethal injection was supposed to be painless. Anything else would have been cruel and unusual punishment. Even so, Nick hoped for one thing. That in the moment when Kowalczyk's IVs were hooked up to the drug pump, in the instant the poison flooded his veins, in the last second of his life, Kowalczyk would scream.

Nick knew that Kowalczyk's death would not be the end of it. His mother's scream would continue to rupture his sleep. After tonight, there would be more work to do. Whitney King had gotten away with murder long enough.

Chapter 3

Lou Mason didn't know what to do. He had said yes when Harry asked for a ride, listened to Harry's rendition of the case against Kowalczyk during the three-hour drive, and gotten out of the car in the prison parking lot, a driver, not a witness, with no interest in watching someone die.

Harry lumbered ahead, chin down, broad shoulders rounded. Mason hung back, taking in the prison grounds. The main entrance led into the administration building, an unremarkable three-story, brick structure that could easily have been home to some insurance company in Kansas City. Dated, durable, and modest, except for the twelve-foot steel fence topped by razor wire surrounding the grounds, guard towers looming in the corners of the campus, stadium lights showering everything in perpetual daylight, and clouds of moths fluttering in the glare like summer snow.

Behind the administration building, four rows of squat dormitory-style buildings cast long shadows in the artificial light. Each one housed a segment of the prison population, the building farthest away segregated for death row inmates.

Though some of Mason's clients were tenants in the first three buildings, he had kept his clients out of the last.

Slapping at a mosquito drawn to the sweat rising on his neck in the thick night heat, Mason followed Harry inside, glad for the air conditioning. Space was limited, group functions not the prison norm: a couple of chairs, a vinyl-covered sofa, soft light from floor lamps and a weak ceiling fixture, thin brown carpet bearing the brunt of state budget cuts, a picture of the governor on one paneled wall.

The witnesses clustered according to their backgrounds. Cops and prosecutors exchanged biting verbal jabs, Harry joining them as if he hadn't been retired for a couple of years. Reporters tried to one-up each other, the doctor and the woman from the governor's office shuffled their feet, anxious to be anywhere else. The warden, an older man near Harry's age who was losing the battle with his gut, was the only one wearing a suit, bouncing between the groups, a good host at a bad party. Mason hung near the front door, ready to make his exit.

Mason guessed that the tall, blond-headed kid staring out the window at the parking lot was the son of the murder victims. Harry said his name was Nick. He was raw boned, all angles and no meat, blue polo shirt hanging over bone-colored chinos. A long face stretched by the shadows under his eyes, too dark for a kid but just right for the memories Mason was certain the boy carried. He looked to be the right age and Mason couldn't think of any other reason for the kid to be there. No one talked to the kid—another clue.

On the other side of the room, a petite woman with gray streaks scattered through black hair sat alone in a chair, rubbing rosary beads through her fingers, her hands tight against her dark green dress. Must be Kowalczyk's mother, Mason decided. Harry hadn't mentioned her name. No one spoke to her either.

Mason couldn't imagine a worse fate for a mother than to watch her child die. Stepping into her shoes for a split second was enough to spin Mason's attention back to Nick. Mason realized both he and the kid had lost their parents when each was three years old. Mason's parents had died in a car accident. He felt a strange kinship with the kid, both members of an exclusive club, one without a waiting list to get in.

The warden stopped to talk to the mother. The woman rose, asking the warden something Mason couldn't hear. The warden was shaking his head, the mother smiling grimly, her smile laced with steel. The warden dwarfed the woman. He shrugged his shoulders and turned his palms up, his body language saying he'd like to but he couldn't. The mother stiffened, placing her hand on the warden's arm, rosary beads draped across his sleeve, repeating her request. The warden shrugged again, this time in surrender, leading the mother through a doorway and into the prison. Mason admired the woman's tenacity, wondering what they were arguing about.

Harry peeled away from the cop group. "I talked to Ortiz. He says he'll add you to the witness list, if you want to come," he told Mason.

"Count me out," Mason said. "I don't like the prosecutor doing me favors and that's not much of a favor."

"Suit yourself," Harry said, heading back.

"Hold on," Mason said. "That the kid?" he asked, nodding at the boy next to the window, Harry nodded back. "Nick, right?" Mason asked, moving toward the boy, drawn to the kid by their common loss.

"I'm Lou Mason," he said, sticking out his hand.

"Nick Byrnes," the kid replied, shaking Mason's hand, his grip dry and firm, letting go quickly and staring again at the parking lot.

"Sorry for your loss," Mason managed, feeling like an intruder, but not ready to walk away.

"It was a long time ago," Nick said, not looking at Mason, the practiced response dry as his handshake.

"It's never over though, is it? I mean not even after tonight," Mason said, realizing he was talking about himself, wondering why he was telling the kid things he only thought about when he visited his parents' graves. "My folks died when I was three," he explained. "Just like you. It makes you different from everyone else, no matter what happens the rest of your life."

Nick turned to Mason, his gloomy eyes lighting up, his face guarded by a flat expression. "How did they die?"

"Car accident."

"Right," Nick said, shaking his head.

"Am I missing something here?" Mason asked.

"Sorry," Nick said, shaking his head again. "I didn't mean anything by that. It's just that my grandparents fed me the same story until I found out the truth."

"You were just a kid. They were probably trying to protect you," Mason said.

"That's what they said. So, who was trying to protect you?" Nick asked, the question knocking Mason back.

Harry stood in the doorway to the hall, the warden next to him as the other witnesses paraded past. He interrupted, saving Mason from having to answer.

"Lou. You coming or not? Ortiz says it's your last chance."

Mason looked at Nick, caught the caution in the boy's eyes, waiting for Mason to answer. Mason saw something else. A kid about to watch as the man who killed his parents is executed. The mother about to watch her son die had an edge on agony, but not much of one, Mason decided.

"Yeah. I'm coming," he said.

They passed through three security checkpoint X-ray scanners, emptying their pockets, standing with arms outstretched while a guard passed a metal detecting wand over their bodies.

"Now I know where the airlines learned how to do it," Mason said to Nick as they refilled their pockets.

The boy barely nodded at Mason's weak joke, shuffling his feet like a runner waiting to get down in the blocks, shaking his long arms, twisting his head from side to side, rolling his shoulders, and finally settling his limbs as the warden led them into the witness room. The mother was standing in front of the window looking into the execution chamber. She turned as they entered, a small gasp escaping her throat, her face pale, her eyes red, as her gaze settled on Nick. Just then, a priest wedged past them, crossing the room to the mother, embracing her. Mason overheard their brief exchange.

"Father Steve? Did he?" the mother asked the priest.

"Yes, Mary. Ryan made a confession," the priest said, the mother searching the priest's face with another unasked question. The priest answering. "To everything, Mary. To everything. I'm sorry. He did the right thing."

The woman buried her face against the priest's round chest for a moment, gathered herself, and returned to the window, her palms against the glass, her back to the rest of them. Mason glanced quickly at the witnesses, each of them nodding as they listened, satisfied that justice was about to be served.

The layout of the witness room and the execution chamber reminded Mason of a lineup, suspect and ringers arrayed on one side of a two-way mirror, cops and lawyers on the other. Mason wondered for an instant if Kowalczyk would be able to see them or whether the last image he would see would be his own. The warden answered his question.

"Mr. Kowalczyk can see us but not hear us. We will be able to hear him should he wish to make a last statement," the warden added, pointing to a speaker in the wall next to the window. "I am certain each of us recognizes the solemnity and difficulty of this occasion and will act accordingly."

The warden stationed himself next to the phone by the door, ready to answer if the governor called. No one spoke, a few of the witnesses taking seats in the back row, the others on their feet, holding their ground.

The silence was like an extra witness, crowding the small room, making everyone uncomfortable. The scrape of a chair by one, a cough by another, every sound grating on thin nerves. A round clock with a white face and black numbers mounted on one wall hummed with electrical current, seconds passing with a low buzz. Five minutes left.

Nick edged toward the left side of the window, leaving the right side for Mary and Father Steve, stealing glances at her, twirling a pen with one hand, the other drumming against his thigh. His breathing was shallow, turning rapid. Mason, worried that the boy might hyperventilate, stayed close to him.

Mary ran her beads through her fingers, praying in a soft, staccato whisper, the priest's hand on the small of her back. The door to the execution chamber opened, and Mary ended her prayers, forcing a smile as she let her beads slither to the floor.

Harry migrated to the window, filling the space between Nick and Mary, his jaw set, his eyes dark, his catcher-mitt hands gripping the ledge beneath the glass. His chest swelled as he took a deep breath, holding it as if it had to last forever. Four minutes left.

Ryan was on his back, head flat, no pillow, short brown hair matted, sweat reflecting the floodlights beaming from the ceiling. His wrists and ankles were strapped to the gurney, his thin white legs and bare feet sticking out from beneath his hospital gown. His palms were turned up, the blue veins in the center of his arms throbbed, impaled with IV needles, white tape holding the needles in place, a trickle of dried blood running toward one elbow, long clear plastic tubes dangling from each arm over the sides of the gurney. He raised his head, holding the angle as he found his mother, moistening his lips as he smiled. Mary smiled back. Ryan mouthed "nice dress," his mother nodding, her eyes glistening.

A guard pushed the gurney into position next to the far wall. Another guard threaded the IV tubes through the small openings until they were pulled taut from the other side by unseen hands. The two guards looked at the warden for a moment, then left, the door sealing behind them. The warden picked up the phone, flipped a switch on the wall, the speaker crackling. Two minutes left.

"Do you wish to make a last statement?" he asked, broadcasting the question into the execution chamber, a hiss of feedback spitting into the witness room.

Ryan craned his neck, whipsawing between the wall hiding his executioners and the window keeping his mother from him, watching for the first trace of death as it slid down the IV tubes toward him. His arms and legs trembled despite the straps, his chest heaved, his neck bulged with corded blood, his eyes widening as if someone had stretched his lids to their limit. He licked his lips again, swallowing to find his voice. One minute left.

Mary spread her hands wide on the glass, tilting her head a bit, her pained smile encouraging Ryan to be brave for both of them. Nick stopped twirling his pen, lacing it between his fingers and clamping down hard. Harry squinted, taking a short breath, his face turning red. The priest wiped his brow with a handkerchief, Mary touching her fingers to her lips, a last kiss.

Ryan let out a small cry, yanking his arms as he felt the burning sensation of the first drug. His head dropped to the gurney, lolling side-to-side, the drug working quickly. Mary turned to Father Steve, clinging to him, her eyes still locked on her son as Ryan lifted his head a final time, the words tumbling over his thickening tongue.

"I love you, Ma . . . So sorry . . . innocent."

And he was gone.

Chapter 4

Mason stood at the foot of his parents' grave two days after Ryan Kowalczyk's execution. His parents were buried in Sheffield Cemetery, a pious slab of land running down a long slope in an industrial district on the northeast side of Kansas City. Owned by an Orthodox congregation, it held the remains of hundreds of Kansas City Jews dating back to the early 1900s, taking its name from the steel company that once dominated the surrounding landscape. Mason's parents were buried high enough that he could see I-435 to the east and the railroad tracks that ran north and south not far from the bottom of the long slope. A train whistle split the morning, shaking the living even if it didn't stir the dead.

His parents' names were carved in a single block of black granite, John and Linda Mason. Their Hebrew names were entered beneath the English. Mason struggled with the letters, familiar only in their form, their sound and meaning unknown to him. Claire had not pushed him to obtain a religious education, telling him that all the rules paled after the

Golden Rule. Learn that one, she said, and you've learned enough.

Growing up, his Aunt Claire brought him to the cemetery on Memorial Day, though neither of his parents had served in the military. It was a good holiday for remembering people, Claire had explained. John was her older brother, Linda as close to her as any sister. Good people sorely missed was how she ended each of their visits.

Mason fell out of the routine of the annual visits when he left for college, returning to the cemetery only occasionally, the last time several years ago, the reason escaping him now. He didn't talk to his parents, as some people did when they visited the graves of loved ones. Mostly, he studied the headstone, hoping for an epiphany about what his life would have been like had they lived. He regretted nothing that had happened in his upbringing by Claire, though he missed every second of what his life might have been, the uncertainty never far from his mind.

Kowalczyk's execution prompted this visit. Nick Byrnes's odd question implying that someone had protected Mason from the truth about his parents' deaths hung over his image of Nick, Harry, and Mary as they had watched Kowalczyk die. Mason had never doubted the story Claire told him. That his father lost control on a rainy summer night, his car slicing through a guard rail, down an embankment, both his parents dead when rescuers reached them. Now Nick's question rose like a tide through Mason's memory, leaving him unsettled.

There was a rock on the center of the arched headstone, a smooth, flat oval that would have skipped forever across flat water. Leaving a small rock on a headstone was a Jewish tradition, a reminder to the deceased that they have not been forgotten, one of the few traditions Mason had picked up in his nontraditional upbringing.

Mason picked up the rock, rubbing his fingers across a

surface too polished for the rock to have been plucked from the ground. Whoever left the rock had brought it with them. Claire had never left a rock on the headstone to the Masons' memory, rejecting the practice as she did virtually every other religious ritual.

Claire was as strong an advocate of Jewish traditions of social justice as anyone could be, though she had no interest in the theology. God, she said, knew where to find her if He was looking for her. Mason doubted that Claire had mellowed in her antagonism toward spiritual faith, though he never quite understood its origins. He sometimes imagined Claire having a fight with God, calling it quits because God was a sore loser.

Who had left the rock, Mason wondered? He had no other family besides Claire and could think of no one who might have visited his parents' grave, leaving the rock behind as a calling card. He examined it again, turning it over in his hand as he turned over Nick's question in his mind, finding answers to neither, leaving the rock where he found it.

Several sections over from where he stood near the top of the slope a blue awning had been erected at the site of a fresh grave. The excavation complete, two gravediggers were setting up chairs for the mourners. They'd stuck two shovels firmly into the mound of dirt next to the grave so that mourners could sprinkle soil onto the casket after it was lowered into the ground, a final good-bye. It was not yet eight o'clock and the gravediggers were glad to be finished, the sun already bearing down at the start of another blistering summer day.

The city was roasting in a heat wave that had boosted temperatures into triple digits seven out of the last ten days. Humidity to match the temperature multiplied into a misery index that was off the charts. The sky was painfully blue. People were dying and the forecast was for more of the same. Mason had a feeling the gravediggers would be busy.

Curious whether the men might have seen someone deposit the rock on his parents' headstone, Mason ambled their way. The gravediggers, one black and one white, were sitting in the shade of the awning on the chairs they had just arranged, taking long pulls on water jugs.

"Bet you're glad this one's done," Mason said.

"You got that right," the white man said. "Funeral's not till eleven. You're early."

"It's not my funeral," Mason said. "I was just visiting my folks' grave. Back over there," he said, pointing. "John and Linda Mason," he added.

"Double plot," the black man said. "Don't dig too many of them. Most people, they go one at a time."

"How long you guys worked out here?" Mason asked.

"Me and Marty," the black man answered, "we been here ten years. Ain't that right, Marty?"

"You got that right, Albert," Marty said, wiping his wrist across his mouth.

"Don't suppose you might have noticed anyone else visiting my parents' graves. Someone left a nice rock on the headstone."

Albert shook his head. "Don't take this wrong, mister. I ain't got nothin' against your people, but I surely don't understand that rock business. What's a rock got to do with remembering someone anyway?"

"I couldn't tell you," Mason said, embarrassed that he couldn't. "Either of you see anyone?"

"We see lots of people visiting lots of graves. We too busy digging new ones to pay 'em much attention," Marty said, Albert nodding.

"Tell you what," Mason said, handing them each a business card and a twenty dollar bill. "Next time you see someone over there, pay enough attention to call me."

"All right, okay then," Albert said, pocketing Mason's

money and card. "Be lots of people here today. Probably be a whole lot of rocks left on this grave."

"Who died?" Mason asked.

"Name of Sonni Efron," Marty answered. "Woman got shot in the face standing in her own front door. Don't that beat all hell."

Mason recognized the name from the news reports. Sonni Efron had been murdered two days ago, front page news, the Kowalcyzk execution back-page filler. She was a prominent member of the Jewish community, active in philanthropic organizations and the arts. Claire knew her, though not well, and Mason not at all. Marty was right. There would be a lot of rocks left on Sonni Efron's headstone. The police had no suspects. Mason knew the cops would be in the funeral crowd, hoping her killer would be there too.

Mason had a different appointment at eleven that morning. He'd given Nick Byrnes one of his business cards, telling him to call if he needed anything, or if he'd just like to talk. Nick called the day after the execution, saying he had a case Mason might be interested in handling, though he didn't offer any details. Mason gave his parents' grave a last glance as he went to work.

Mary Kowalczyk was waiting for Mason when he pulled into the parking lot behind Blues on Broadway, a bar near Thirty-eighth and Broadway. The neighborhood was a stretch of Kansas City somewhere between run-down and uptown. Mason dodged potholes as he parked. His office was on the second floor.

The bar was owned by Harry Ryman's ex-partner, Blues, who played jazz piano or tended bar as the mood struck him. It was a long, strange trip for a full-blooded member of the Shawnee Indian tribe, a trip that included dispensing rough justice for Mason's clients and attitude adjustments for those who stood in the way.

Mary, dressed in black pants and a long-sleeved black blouse despite the heat, shaded her eyes against the morning sun that threatened to peel another coat of paint off the back wall of the building. Mason felt a knot in his chest, unable to separate her from her son, uneasy at seeing her again, uncertain how to console her. He hoped she hadn't come to see him, but couldn't think of any other reason for her to show up on his doorstep.

Mason didn't know whether her son was guilty. Harry's version of the case against Ryan Kowalczyk was convincing and Mason trusted Harry's judgment as much as anyone he knew. Still, he'd defended enough people accused of crimes they didn't commit to harbor a steady suspicion of the prosecution. Ryan's last gasp of innocence haunted him. What's the point of lying in that final instant?

Mason was less certain that Ryan deserved to die, his own feelings about the death penalty an ambivalent mush. He was opposed to it when he was defending someone on trial for his life in an imperfect system tainted by racial and class bias. A system dependent on the vagaries of recollection, often deceived by what the jury doesn't know. He was less certain when outrage at the perpetrator of an unspeakable crime swept over him.

Mason looked at his watch. It was eight-thirty. If Mary had come to see him, at least she would be gone before Nick Byrnes arrived at eleven. He'd been in the same room with them once before and didn't want to do that again. Mason slowed as he approached her, saying nothing, letting her make the call.

"Mr. Mason," she said. "I didn't meet you the other night. I'm sorry."

"It didn't seem like the right time for introductions. I'm

sorry for your loss," he added, hoping the sentiment was more comforting to her than it had been to Nick.

Mary looked around, craning her head up to the second floor. "Is this really your office?"

Mason grimaced, not usually embarrassed by his modest digs. "I'm up on the second floor. Are you here to see me?"

"If you have time for me. I mean, I didn't call for an appointment, so I understand if you don't."

"You're in luck," he said.

Mason led her inside, up the back stairway, down the hall past the open door to Blues's office. Blues sat at his desk reading his mail, not looking up. Mason continued on, unlocked his office, picked his mail up off the floor, and turned on the lights before he noticed Mary still standing in front of Blues's office, her eyes riveted on him.

"Mrs. Kowalczyk?" Mason asked.

Mary gave Blues a last hard look. "That man," she said as Mason closed the door behind her. "Do you know him? Did he use to be a police officer? A detective?"

"As a matter of fact, he did. That's Blues. His real name is Wilson Bluestone Junior. He owns the bar and this building," Mason answered, finally making the connection Mary had made.

"He is a terrible man," Mary said, leaving no room for debate. "He treated my son like he was the worst scum imaginable, throwing him against the wall like he was a dangerous criminal when all he was, was a boy taken advantage of by his friend."

Mary's words poured out, carrying venom that welled deep inside her. Mason knew that Blues probably did throw her son against the wall and treat him like a dangerous criminal because that's undoubtedly what Blues thought when he and Harry arrested the boy for double homicide. Blues was never gentle. A mother convinced that her son had been wrongfully executed would never forgive anyone who had a hand in his death. There was no point in defending Blues.

"Have a seat, Mrs. Kowalczyk," Mason said, pointing to the sofa. "What can I do for you?"

She sat, barely filling the corner of the sofa, her feet just touching the floor. "You mustn't discuss our business with that man," she said. "I won't allow it!"

Mason walked around his office, opening the blinds on the windows that overlooked Broadway, fishing two bottles of water out of the small refrigerator behind his desk, giving Mary time to cool down, not wanting to tell her that, so far, there was only her business, not their business. He handed her a bottle of water and sat in a leather chair at one end of the sofa.

"Everything we discuss is confidential, Mrs. Kowalczyk," he said, leaving out that Blues often worked with him when he needed special expertise in violence or protection. "How can I help you?"

Mary put her unopened bottle of water on the butler's table in front of the sofa, wiping the moisture from the bottle on her pants. Straightening her narrow back, leveling her chin at Mason, she told him. "My son was innocent. I want you to prove it."

Mason rolled his bottle of water between his hands, fumbling with the cap, taking a sip. He was never surprised by what people in trouble asked him to do. If their lives were on the line, they'd ask for the stars and settle for the moon. Mary Kowalczyk's trouble had come and gone. No celestial magic would change that, though he knew she wouldn't be convinced. He tried a different tack.

"Mrs. Kowalczyk," he began.

"Please," she interrupted. "Call me Mary," she said, forcing a smile over her grief.

"Mary," Mason began again, gently. "The other night,

there was a priest. I couldn't help but overhear what he told you. He said that your son confessed."

Mary waved her hand. "Father Steve is a fine priest, a good man. He was taking care of Ryan the only way he could. It was important that Ryan make confession before he was taken from me."

Mason was even less certain of Catholic tradition than Jewish tradition. "I'm sure that was the case. But the priest—Father Steve—said that Ryan confessed to everything. It sounded like he was talking about the murders."

"Nonsense," Mary answered. "My son was innocent. Father Steve thought it would be easier for me if I thought Ryan was guilty. Ryan never lied to me. I was his mother. I would have known. That boy was innocent and he was murdered no different than that poor couple, the Byrnes. Only the law killed my son."

"Are you asking me to sue someone for your son's death?"

Mary turned red. "Dear me, no, Mr. Mason. I don't want blood money. I owe it to Ryan, to let him rest easy in heaven. I can't have his life back but I'll have his innocence."

"Without some kind of trial to determine your son's innocence, the most I could do is investigate the case and tell you what I think."

"That's not what I want. I want the governor to pardon Ryan. I've read up on it. He can do it even after they took my son from me."

Mason sat back in his chair, looking at Mary Kowalczyk. She was a small woman made smaller by her thin, tired face, and the grief she wore like makeup. Her pants were worn at the knees, the cuffs and collar of her blouse frayed, the heels of her shoes scuffed flat. She wore a gold cross around her neck, though Mason was certain it wasn't real gold. Her dark eyes flashed, mirroring her determination. Saving her son's life had been her entire life. Saving his memory was all she had left.

"Is that it?" Mason asked.

"No. There is one other thing. I want you to prove that Whitney King killed those people. That boy should not be allowed to live another day pretending he had nothing to do with the killings!"

"I don't suppose I could interest you in the moon and the stars instead."

"Mr. Mason," she snapped, "I recognized your name when I heard the prosecuting attorney introduce you to the warden, but I couldn't remember why. It came to me yesterday. I've read about you in the papers. If you tell me you could get me the moon and the stars, I'd believe you. I only want justice for my son. I'll take it from you or I'll take it myself if I have to. Please don't make a joke out of that."

Mason rose, circling his office once again, passing the books on his shelves that laid out the law, the files for clients who depended on him, the dry erase board where he worked out the puzzles of his cases, stopping behind his desk. He rubbed his hand across his chest, feeling the scar left by the surgeon who'd saved his life after he'd been stabbed ten months earlier. He'd nearly died saving the life of Abby Lieberman, the woman he loved. Mary Kowalczyk only wanted him to save the memory of the son she loved. That didn't sound so tough. He looked at her again, wondering if there was more than grief behind her threat to take justice in her own hands.

"I'll start with the court file. See where it goes," he said, not wanting to over promise.

"I can pay you," Mary said. "My husband bought a life insurance policy for Ryan when he was born. It was for ten thousand dollars."

Mason shook his head. "You keep that money."

"I'd sooner burn it than spend it on myself, Mr. Mason. Either you take it and do the job right or I'll give it to the church."

"You don't give up, do you Mary?" he said.

"Not when I'm right, Mr. Mason."

"Please," he told her. "Call me Lou."

Chapter 5

"Who was that woman?" Blues asked, walking into Mason's office unannounced, his tall, muscled frame shrinking the space between the door and Mason's desk.

Mason stood in front of his dry erase board, studying the names of Ryan Kowalczyk and Whitney King written in blue connected by red lines to the names of Graham and Elizabeth Byrnes. Mason was a visual thinker, preferring to chart the progress of a case on his board, crisscrossing the connections between people, places, and things until he found the pattern that tied them all together. He wrote Mary Kowalczyk's name, circled it in green and tied it to Ryan, doing the same with Nick and his parents.

"Mary Kowalczyk," Mason said. "She doesn't like you."

"She was staring at me from the hall. I thought I recognized her. That's one mean woman."

"Mary?" Mason asked, plopping into his desk chair, leaning back, feet propped on his desk. "That woman doesn't have a mean bone in her body."

"You try arresting her son," Blues said. "Forget the bones. Her whole body is mean." Blues sat in the middle of the sofa, spreading his arms out, nearly covering its length.

"Mothers are protective," Mason said.

"She's way past that. Called me a dirty Indian. Came at me with a butcher knife. I wanted to take her in too, but Harry talked me out of it."

Mason dropped his feet to the floor, unable to conjure a picture of Mary as a bigot or attacking a police officer. Blues was tough enough to ignore ethnic slurs in emotionally charged situations. He was less forgiving of assault.

"She says you threw her son against the wall."

"Damn right I did. Harry found both the kids' clothes in the basement. They were covered with the victims' blood. I found the Kowalczyk kid trying to climb out his bedroom window. Mary came running in the kid's bedroom, screaming like a banshee, ready to open me up with that knife."

"You're a foot and a half taller and outweigh her by a hundred and fifty pounds. Don't tell me you were scared?"

"I'll tell you something, Lou. Every time I went into someone's house I was scared because I never knew what I was going to run into. Nicest house, nicest looking people. Sure as hell, some asshole throws a brain clot and comes out shooting. A little woman like that catches you from behind, puts that knife in your ribs. Trust me, you'd be scared too. No doubt in my mind she'd have done it if she could have. What's she want from you?"

Mason shook his head. "She made me promise to leave you out of it."

Blues stood, crossing to the dry erase board. "Don't say as I blame her if it's got anything to do with those murders," he said, turning to face Mason, his coppery skin and jet black hair offset by the white board. "That boy was guilty. Fact is both of them were guilty."

"You think I can prove Whitney King was guilty?" Mason asked.

Blues smiled. "I thought you were supposed to leave me out of it."

"Hypothetical question," Mason said.

"The prosecutor couldn't get the job done and he was a damn good lawyer. Forest Jones. Patrick Ortiz was just starting out, carrying Jones's briefcase into court every morning. You're good enough. Trouble is you're fifteen years too late."

"Feel like helping me?"

Blues looked at him, chewing his lip. "Is this just about King?"

Mason stood, measuring himself against his friend. "No," he answered. "She wants me to prove Ryan was innocent. She wants her son pardoned."

Blues raised his hands. "Figured it was something like that. Count me out."

"Why?" Mason challenged him. "Because you arrested Ryan? Now he's dead and you might have been wrong?"

Blues dropped his arms to his sides, his face slack, eyes hard. Mason knew that look. It was Blues at his most dangerous, sizing up a situation, deciding whether to wade in or walk away. If he waded in and wasn't on your side, you were in big trouble.

"That kid was guilty as sin. Bank on it," he said and left.

"Shit!" Mason said, angry with himself.

He had jumped Blues without reason. Yet the accusation

gave voice to the thing that had gnawed at Mason since Ryan Kowalczyk uttered his last words. What if Ryan was innocent? What if Mason had stood by watching an innocent man be put to death? That he couldn't have done anything to stop it changed nothing. He was there. He was a witness. Blues might be able to walk away, certain of both guilt and justice, unwilling to question either. Mason couldn't.

The phone rang, jarring Mason. "Yeah?" he answered.

"Good morning to you too, Sunshine," his Aunt Claire said. "Who stepped on your toes so early in the day?"

Mason took a breath. His aunt was the antidote for whatever ailed him. Too lazy and she kicked him in the ass. Too cocky and she took him down a peg. Too moody and she lightened him up.

"An old case that I'm going to take another look at," Mason said, explaining about his new client.

"You're all right. I don't care what anyone else says," Claire told him. "I may even be proud of you one day," she teased.

"Thanks for the vote of confidence," Mason said. "What are you up to?"

Claire sighed. "I'm going to Sonni Efron's funeral this morning. Care to come along?"

"No thanks. I didn't know her and I've already been to the cemetery today."

"Really? What for?"

Mason ran his hand through his hair, stalling for time, knowing that was a mistake with Claire. "I hadn't been in a while. The grave looks nice. They keep it trimmed up."

"Uh huh," Claire said. "That's nice."

"I didn't know you were close to Sonni Efron," Mason said, changing the subject.

"We belonged to some of the same organizations. We

weren't close friends, but I knew her well enough to pay my respects. What an awful thing. Shot to death like that in her own home."

"The paper says the cops don't have any suspects yet. Harry hear anything?" Mason knew that Harry kept his lines of communication humming with his former colleagues.

"Just that they don't have a clue. Her house is between Ward Parkway and State Line, set way back from the street with landscaping like a wall around the front door. No one saw or heard anything and it happened in broad daylight."

"Hell of a thing," Mason said.

"Yes it was. Now tell me why you were at the cemetery since you obviously don't want to talk about it," Claire said.

"It's crazy really," Mason said, unable to resist his aunt. "I met Nick Byrnes at the execution the other night. His parents were the murder victims. I told him my parents were killed when I was three, just like him. I was making small talk, if you can do that at an execution."

"Passes the time," Claire said.

"Anyway, he asks me how my parents died and I tell him they were killed in a car accident. He says that's what his grandparents told him until he found out the truth. I told him they were just trying to protect him because he was just a kid and . . ."

Claire interrupted, "He asked you who was trying to protect you and your devious, suspicious mind wasn't satisfied with the obvious answer that no one was, so you went to the cemetery to ask your parents. Am I right?"

Hearing her say it made it sound all right and silly at the same time. She was telling him that she understood and that he shouldn't worry about it. "On the money," he answered, relieved.

"I loved your parents dearly," Claire said. "They're gone and they've been gone a long time. Visit them as often as you like, but leave it alone. Life is for the living. I've got to get ready for the funeral."

Mason expected Claire to reassure him about the car accident, not tell him to forget about it. Her response sent a tremor through him.

"Good advice," he lied. "By the way, someone left a rock on the headstone. A nice one, all polished and smooth. I'm sure it wasn't you."

"No," she answered too quickly, unable to keep the caution from her voice. "It wasn't me."

"Any idea who might have left it? I mean who visits their grave besides you and me? And why now?"

"I don't know," she answered. "Maybe it was someone visiting another grave that had an extra stone and thought it would be a nice gesture."

"Makes sense," Mason said, not believing it did. "I've got another client at eleven. I'll let you go."

Mason had settled into a funk by the time Nick Byrnes arrived. Crumpling junk mail into tight wads, he riffled them through the hoop nailed to the back of his office door, letting the door sweep the pile away the next time someone opened it. He'd taken on Mary's case as much out of misplaced guilt as conviction, pissed off his best friend in the process, and gotten the runaround from Claire, the one person who never ran him around in his life.

Mary Kowalczyk charmed him with her poignant strength, while Blues left her one step short of assault with intent to kill. As for Blues, he'd never walked away from Mason before. And Claire had never lied to him, though he couldn't shake the suspicion that she had at least dodged the truth this time. Mason felt like he was slipping into an *X-Files* episode where everyone turns out to be someone else.

Adding to his irritation, Mickey Shanahan, his legal assistant, was late again. Mickey had spent the summer working as a volunteer on Josh Seeley's campaign for the U.S. Senate. Abby Lieberman did public relations work for Seeley and hooked Mickey up with the campaign. Mickey's life ambition was PR and politics, shoving his day job to the bottom of the priority list. The primary was three weeks away and Mason had seen less and less of Mickey as the summer wore on.

Nick Byrnes's arrival did nothing to lift Mason's mood. The kid came in pulling a handcart loaded with three banker's boxes. Mason knew what was in the boxes before he saw the neatly printed lettering on the sides—*State v. Kowalczyk and King.*

"How ya doin', Mr. Mason," Nick said, standing in front of Mason's desk, breathing hard from carrying the boxes and the handcart up the stairs, a sheen of sweat dampening his hairline and wetting his upper lip.

"I'm good, Nick. How 'bout you?" Mason asked.

"Hot, man. This weather is a killer. They say it's gonna be like this for another couple of weeks."

"Stay cool, son. No heavy lifting," Mason said. "That your file on your folks' case?"

"Yeah," Nick smiled sheepishly. "I know it looks like a lot of stuff, but I've organized everything. I've got the police reports, the trial transcript, and the exhibits. Well, except for stuff like the clothes. The cops still have that in storage. They don't throw anything away."

Mason nodded, wondering why he ever thought Nick had a case for him that didn't involve the murders. It was the nature of solo practice. Every day began with the hope that a homerun case would walk through the door, landing in his lap like a winning lottery ticket. Mason doubted that Nick wanted him to get a pardon for Ryan Kowalczyk.

"Have a seat. What do you want me to do with all that?" Mason asked, pointing to the boxes.

Nick didn't hesitate. "I want you to sue Whitney King for the wrongful death of my parents," he began, holding up his hand before Mason could answer. "I was a minor when they were killed. That means the statute of limitations didn't start to run until I turned eighteen. I have a year after that to sue him. My time runs out two weeks from today. I've been all over town looking for lawyers to take my case, but everyone turned me down. They all say that I don't have a case since King was acquitted. I ask them about O.J. Simpson. He was acquitted too and the families nailed his ass for big bucks on a wrongful death deal. They don't care. They're only interested in the sure thing. You're my last chance."

Mason leaned back in his chair, hands clasped across his middle. "Do you need the money?"

Nick furrowed his brow. "Nah. My folks had life insurance. It's in a trust fund that will pay for college and get me started when I finish school. I don't need the money."

"Then why do it?" Mason asked.

Nick stiffened. "Come on, Mr. Mason. That asshole killed my parents and he got away with it! Nobody gives a shit about that, I guess. Everybody says the system isn't perfect; it was a long time ago, leave it alone, life is for the living. What a load of crap! Son of a bitch, Mr. Mason, I thought if anyone would get it, you would!"

Mason grinned. "Oh I get it all right, Nick. I just wanted to make sure you did. There's just one problem."

"What's that?" Nick asked.

"Mary Kowalczyk beat you to the punch. She hired me this morning to get a pardon for her son."

"A pardon? What good will a pardon do him? Besides, he was guilty."

"She doesn't think so. She wants me to clear his name and prove that King killed your parents. I can't represent both of you unless you both agree."

"As long as you nail Whitney King, I don't care what you do for Kowalczyk. He's dead, so it won't matter anyway."

"Maybe or maybe not," Mason said.

Chapter 6

The hottest part of a summer day in Kansas City is late afternoon. That's when asphalt streets and brick buildings are at their oven best, soaking up the deepest cool spots, wringing out the shallow ones. That's when the cottony air swells with heavy humidity drifting in from the Missouri River, settling in the city's lungs like the croup, squeezing the air out of anyone foolish enough to go outside and draw a breath. That's when power plants wheeze and grind, pushing current to air conditioners and ice machines, borrowing hot air, cooling it with interest.

Kansas City Power & Light warned of brownouts and power failures, making good the threat in staggered outages that hopscotched across town, knocking out the power in Mason's office at 5:15 P.M. Mason was deep into the trial transcript—not noticing when the refrigerator quit humming and the ceiling light disappeared, finally catching on when the air started to clot.

The transcript provided the facts but didn't tell the whole story. Why would one or both boys, neither of whom had any prior history of violence, suddenly go on such a rampage? The prosecutor's version was robbery, a crime of opportunity that spun out of control. Graham Byrnes's wallet was found next to his body. There was no cash in it, but there was no evidence of how much cash, if any, had been in it before he was killed.

Mason sensed something more primal in the murders. He agreed it was a crime of opportunity but doubted that the perceived opportunity had been robbery, not if Whitney King had been the killer. Whitney was rich so he didn't need the money. The opportunity was the chance to get away with murder. A thrill killing. Exercising the power of life and death was the ultimate rush for a thin slice of twisted souls. The trial transcript didn't open that window into either defendant. Insanity was not pled as a defense. No psychiatrist testified to a lifetime of abuse or chemical imbalance that stoked the killer's rage.

The most common motives for murder—greed, jealousy, love, and hate—were nowhere present in the facts laid out for the jury, leaving Mason with an inescapable conclusion. One of those boys—or both—was a natural born killer who came of age that night. If he was right, and Whitney King was the killer, Mason knew one other thing. It may have been his first time, but it wouldn't be his last.

He'd just finished reading the testimony of an auto mechanic who inspected the Byrnes's car, testing Kowalczyk's and King's alibis that it had broken down, each defendant pleading that the murders were committed by the other while he went for help. The car had been towed from the scene, examined by the mechanic the following day. Worked fine, the mechanic testified. A lot better than the defendants' alibis, Forest Jones, the prosecuting attorney, noted in an aside that drew an objection and the judge's impotent instruction to the jury to disregard.

Nancy Troy, Ryan's court appointed attorney, scored on cross-examination when the mechanic admitted that he'd found a short in the alternator that could have caused the car to fail to start one time but not another. Mason wasn't surprised at the testimony. It was like everything else so far in this case. The truth depended on which side you were on and who asked the last question.

The dry record of the case made Ryan Kowalczyk's conviction inevitable. His car. His clothes soaked with blood from both victims. The undisputed facts forecasted King's conviction as well. King was with Kowalczyk. King's clothes were as bloody as Ryan's clothes. The only thing missing was the murder weapon. The cops assumed the boys had used the tire iron from the Byrnes's car, since it was gone. Yet King got off.

Their mutually exclusive alibis ranked low on the squirrel-came-in-the-window-and-ate-my-homework credibility scale, particularly after the mechanic testified. There was an all-night service station two miles away. The employees never saw either boy that night. It was as if the defendants agreed to blame one another in the hope that the jury, unable to decide which one did it, would acquit both of them. Mason knew that criminals were rarely as clever as they gave themselves credit for being, but this last possibility pegged the stupid meter.

Though both boys were athletic, it seemed unlikely that one of them, acting alone, could have beaten two people to death without a struggle. There was no evidence that either Graham or Elizabeth Byrnes had fought back, neither defendant showing any bruises, cuts, or scratches. Neither victim had the blood, skin, or hair of one of the defendants under his fingernails.

Mason was growing confident that King was guilty, unable to find any explanation for the jury's decision to set him free. The explanation lay outside the facts. Maybe King had better lawyers. Maybe the jury just believed King's unlikely story. Maybe Kowalczyk had a nervous tic when he testified. The collective mind of a jury was a strange and mysterious place, decisions hatched as compromises, born of indigestion and other human vagaries.

His best chance of understanding what had happened in the courtroom would come from talking with the lawyers, the judge, and the jury. Even that was an uncertain prospect. Lawyers justify their wins and losses with increasing clarity as time goes by, attributing the former to their skill, the latter to insurmountable bad facts. Judges lose track, one case blending into another. Jurors just forget.

Another jury, looking back on the same facts fifteen years later, might well come to the right decision, finally holding Whitney King accountable for that murderous night. While that would serve one of his clients, it wouldn't serve the other.

Mason had called Mary Kowalczyk after his meeting with Nick Byrnes, explaining the nuances of representing two clients in the same case. Mary enthusiastically endorsed Mason's proposal.

"Anything that will prove Whitney King is guilty is fine by me," she said.

"That won't prove that Ryan was innocent."

"Then you'll just have to do both," Mary told him, ending the discussion.

Mason cranked open the windows behind his desk, opening his door, hoping to generate a breeze, instead getting a dose of traffic exhaust, car horns, and more hot air than a campaign commercial. He tolerated the mix while he made a quick scan of the boxes Nick Byrnes had left him, each one sealed with heavy packing tape. Mason fished through his desk drawers looking for a utility knife, found it at the bottom of the bottom drawer next to a gun Blues had given him when he first moved in above the bar. It was a .44 caliber semiautomatic with a nine-shot magazine.

"You better learn to use it," Blues had told him, "if you're gonna keep pushing hot buttons on people that don't have any cold buttons."

Mason had killed one man, though not with a gun, and shot another who hadn't died. He had nightmares about the first man, but not the second, and that bothered him enough to give the gun back to Blues.

"You hold onto it for me," Mason said. "I'll let you know if I need it."

After the Gina Davenport case, Blues gave it to him again. "Any man gets stabbed in the heart and lives to tell about it, damn well better carry a gun. Even a fool only gets so many chances," he said. "Register it and get a permit to carry it."

Mason didn't argue, registering the gun, getting the permit, and burying it in the bottom drawer, forgetting about it. He took the gun out, hefting it in his palm, liking the solid feel more than he cared to admit. He worked the action, confirmed the magazine was loaded and set the gun down on a stack of papers about to be blown off his desk by the breeze. Picking up the utility knife, he sliced the boxes open, looking for something short and simple for a last look, settling on a thin file labeled JURY.

The file contained a single sheet of paper, the verdict form signed by all twelve jurors, each signature telling its own story. Four were left handed, judging from the slant at which they wrote. Some signed in small letters, hiding among the others as they probably did in the jury room. A couple used bold strokes, penning their names with the certainty of founding fathers. A few were feminine, given to soft strokes. One of these caught his eye as he said it aloud: Sonni Efron.

Mason stared at the verdict form, pacing around his office, waiting for the letters to rearrange themselves into the name of someone who hadn't been murdered two days ago and buried that morning. He stopped in front of the dry erase board, a siren from the street shrieking into his open window as an ambulance raced by, the coincidence of Sonni Efron's murder and Ryan Kowalczyk's execution occurring on the same day more stunning than the siren.

Mason didn't believe in coincidence any more than he believed in King Tut's curse. Legend had it that those who entered Tut's tomb were cursed to die horrible deaths, many of them doing so, their deaths serving the legend if nothing else. That a juror who condemned Ryan Kowalczyk to death for murder would suffer the same fate couldn't be the result of jury duty, a modern equivalent of Tut's curse.

Mason knew that. He knew that many crimes were random, the victim and the perpetrator connected by nothing more than fatal coincidence. Bad timing, nothing more. Yet Sonni Efron's murder felt like another shift in the earth beneath his feet, another small tremor rippling under him, adding to the aftershocks of Ryan's execution, the stone on his parents' grave, his aunt's admonition to forget about his parents' deaths, and Blues's refusal to help Mary Kowalczyk. Feeling the heat, Mason added Sonni's name to the board, closing the cabinet doors, shutting the questions about her murder inside.

"Done for the day?" Sandra Connelly asked.

Mason turned around. Sandra was framed in the doorway to his office, one hand on a cocked hip, the only woman he knew who looked good in this weather. They had been partners at Sullivan & Christenson, ridden out of the firm on the same rail, tied together in a killing spree that nearly claimed them both. Afterward, Mason retreated to a solo practice, shunning the limelight even when his cases shined the spotlight on him. Sandra sought out the beacons, leveraging her notoriety to land big clients with big cases, delivering victories, crushing the opposition.

Her hair was shorter now, a shade darker, her body sleek and full at the same time, her mouth still turned in a smug twist that promised a rough ride you'd thank her for. A ride she had offered to Mason that he had declined, though just barely. Horses sweat, men perspire, and women glow, Claire once told him. Sandra had the glow, beating back the heat. A purse on one shoulder, a briefcase slung from the other. A knife in both, Mason bet, counting on Sandra not to have changed that much.

"All in and all done," Mason answered. "Grab a deck chair, enjoy the ocean breeze," he said, retrieving two bottles of Boulevard Beer from his refrigerator, glad the chill hadn't left the glass.

Sandra chose the sofa, kicking off her heels, leaning against the cushions, rubbing the bottle against her neck, beneath her chin. She was wearing wheat-colored linen slacks with a pale pink blouse, open at the throat, a chunk of diamond dropped on a thin gold chain perched just above the swell of her tanned breasts. Mason chose the neutral zone behind his desk, feet on the floor, bottle unopened.

"Nice office," Sandra said, taking a quick inventory, then a short draw on the beer, Mason not answering, letting Sandra take her time. "Cute paperweight," she said aiming the bottle at the gun on his desk.

"Cigarette lighter," Mason explained, putting the gun back in the drawer. "You still carry a knife wherever you go?" he asked.

She opened her purse, pulling out a three-inch, pearl-handled knife, blade closed until she pushed an invisible button on the side, and the blade snapped to attention. "No. Just this letter opener," she said.

Mason laughed, remembering how Sandra's fascination with knives had once saved their lives. He hadn't seen much of her in the last several years; her practice focused on well-heeled corporations, his on down-at-the-heel individuals. She was a star at McKenzie & Strahan, the city's biggest law firm. The last he'd heard, she was defending tobacco companies, convincing juries that people were responsible for the addictions they chose, not the companies that sucked them in.

She studied him, testing Mason's nonchalance, giving up after a moment when he didn't melt at her feet. "Okay," she said, taking a sheet of paper from her briefcase. "I hear you've got a new client."

"Things must be slow downtown for a piece of news like that to hit your corner office," Mason said.

"Nick Byrnes hit my office," Sandra said. "Or, more precisely, his e-mail did after Whitney King forwarded it to me," she added, handing Mason the hard copy. Nick's message was right to the point.

YOU'VE GOTTEN AWAY WITH MURDER LONG ENOUGH. I'VE GOT A LAWYER. HIS NAME IS LOU MASON. WE'RE COMING AFTER YOU. BE AFRAID. BE VERY AFRAID.

"I should have that printed on my business card," Mason said, noting the e-mail identified Nick Byrnes as the sender, Whitney King as the recipient. Time of message, three o'clock A.M. that morning, hours before Mason had agreed to represent Nick.

Sandra pulled a file folder from her briefcase, dropping it on the table in front of the sofa. "Your client is fond of sending e-mails in the dark of night. Take a look. They're all variations on a theme. You killed my parents. I'm going to get you if it's the last thing I do. Yadda, yadda, yadda."

Mason refused the bait, annoyed with Nick, but just as annoyed with Sandra. Mason accepted his clients as they were. Some guilty. Some innocent. Some eccentric pains-in-the-ass. They may be jerks, but they were his jerks, and he didn't hesitate to protect them.

"Nearly as I can tell, Nick's right. Your client killed his parents. That must be why Whitney has never tried to stop Nick from sending e-mails reminding him about what he did. In case Whitney forgot, that is."

Sandra tapped her bottle against the side of the table, slipped her shoes on, and stood. "My client was acquitted by a jury. The same jury that convicted Ryan Kowalczyk, whose conviction was upheld by every state and federal court that reviewed the case. Your client's obsession is understandable, but tell him to move on. Life is for the living."

"You know," Mason said, coming around from behind his desk. "This life is for the living crap is getting on my nerves. It's a lousy excuse for letting someone off the hook. Nick Byrnes has a good case against Whitney King for his parents' wrongful death. It won't mean jail time, but it will mean a lot of money, not to mention a new jury saying what the last one didn't have the balls to say. Whitney King killed those people."

"Are you telling me you are actually going to sue Whitney?"

"Nick's statute of limitations runs in two weeks. If Whitney wants to make a deal now, maybe we can work something out without a lot of noise," Mason said.

"Right. Why don't I just cut off my arm and beat myself senseless with it instead. Save my client the trouble. You don't have a case, Lou. Your client is a screwed-up kid. A whack job. File that lawsuit against Whitney and you'll draw a counterclaim for harassment and those e-mails are exhibit A."

"Your client is a murderer. I'd watch your back. Cutting off your arm may just be the beginning," Mason said.

Sandra shook her head, back in the doorway. "You haven't changed a bit," she said. "Into the breach."

"Beats the hell out of crushing widows and orphans."

Sandra drew her lips back. "You don't want to take me on, Lou. I'll carve you up."

"Funny," Mason said. "I thought your client was the killer. Not you."

Chapter 7

Mason and Abby Lieberman lay in bed late that night, windows open, begging for a breeze, the crickets too hot to make much noise. Electric power came and went, the mayor broadcasting an appeal for people to turn up the thermostat on their air conditioners to ease the demand for electricity. Mason's air conditioner went the mayor one better. It quit. He found a fan buried behind boxes in the attic, dusted off the blades, and set it on a TV table at the foot of his bed.

"It's an oscillator," Mason explained to Abby with due reverence, the fan pushing warm air at them. "Says so on the label."

"My favorite kind," she said, kicking the sheet off of the bed.

"We could go to your place," he offered.

"This is good," she murmured, snuggling close. "It reminds me of summer camp."

"You never went to camp," Mason said.

"I saw a special on the Discovery channel."

They were naked, glistening from lovemaking, Abby tracing the path of the scar on Mason's chest with her fingertip. It was an eighteen-inch raised track, pink, smooth, and shiny, short zipper scars bordering each side. He'd been stabbed in the heart, lost his pulse in the ambulance, dead on arrival. A surgeon opened his chest in the ER to stop the bleeding, massaging his heart, bringing him back before hypoxia cooked his brain. Half a day of open-heart surgery repaired his wounds.

"Does it ever hurt?" she asked him, the fan drying them.

"Nope," he told her. It was the same answer he gave her each time she asked, even though there were days when his chest was filled with a dull ache that pressed against his ribs. Normal, give it time, his surgeon said. Abby gave him a T-shirt featuring a beat-up biker scarred from stem to stern promising that chicks dig scars. He counted on that.

They'd been together almost a year, their relationship igniting when Claire invited Abby to Harry's birthday party the day after Labor Day. Abby owned a public relations firm, Fresh Air. Opportunity and crisis management she called it until the phone stopped ringing after she was caught up in the Gina Davenport case. Then she turned off the lights.

Josh Seeley bailed Abby out when he hired her to help with his race for the United States Senate, his first run for elective office, the primary scheduled for August 1. He was one of Kansas City's moneyed elite who decided that his balance sheet qualified him for office. Abby guided him through the fallout from murky business deals dug up by his primary opponent, Congressman Delray Shays. Abby accepted Seeley's offer to work full time for the campaign, shut down Fresh Air, and recruited Mickey Shanahan as an unpaid volunteer.

The loss of her business festered like a low-grade fever in her relationship with Mason. They told each other it was neither of their faults, more the rule of unintended consequences. No hill for their love to climb, Mason assured her, Abby nodding through gritted teeth. Abby told him that her credibility would be restored if Seeley won. Then she would reopen Fresh Air.

Mason propped himself on one elbow, Abby on her side facing him. She'd let her hair grow to cover the scar on her neck left by the same knife that had lacerated his heart. She recoiled whenever he touched her scar, the closed wound still raw. It was shorter than his, no more than a couple of inches, but jagged. It was a cut made as much to disfigure as to kill. Abby wore high collars, scarves, and turtlenecks year round.

Mason told her about his two new clients, gauging her reaction. He had promised her that he'd stay away from cases with deadly retainers, the kind of case that appealed to what she called his death wish. Not that he wanted to die, she explained. It was that he wanted to find out how close he could get to death to prove he was really alive. She'd been there with him the last time and had made it plain that she wouldn't go back.

Mason didn't argue with her. He called his knack for getting in over his head diving into dark water. He used to rationalize that it was a by-product of trying to find the kind of law he wanted to practice—big firm, small firm, good pay, or good works. That was part of it, but not the part that drove him to take chances they didn't prepare you for in law school.

Something was missing in his existence and he kept looking for it in close encounters between life and death. With Gina Davenport's case, he'd come as close to the line as he dared, risking not only his life, but also Abby's, chips he vowed not to play again. This case, he told her, would be different. It was only about money and memories.

"It's still murder," she told him. Mason didn't argue or complain when she held him so tight he thought his scar might tear open. He didn't tell her about Sonni Efron or the stone on his parents' graves, two wild cards he didn't have a grasp on. "Are you going to sue Whitney King?" she asked.

"If I don't fire my client first. I chewed Nick out about the e-mails he sent to King and I told him that he was on his own if he didn't stop."

"How did Nick take that?" Abby asked.

"About as well as any eighteen-year-old takes getting yelled at by an adult, but he got the point. He's not a bad kid and he hasn't had it easy, so I cut him some slack."

"So, are you going to file the lawsuit?"

"Sandra Connelly didn't give me much choice. If I don't file in the next couple of weeks, Nick's case will be barred by the statute of limitations. He's got a good enough case against King that I can't take that chance."

"What about Mary Kowalczyk? Can you get a pardon for her son?"

Mason flopped back on his pillow. "The case against King is tough enough. Finding witnesses fifteen years later won't be easy. Even if I find them, their memories may not stand up under Sandra's cross-examination. Plus the two investigating detectives are my closest friends. Sandra will make us look like coconspirators. That's a cakewalk compared to the pardon. All I have to do is convince a governor running for reelection to admit that he ordered the execution of an innocent man."

"Will you make it dangerous?" she asked, rolling away from him.

"No," he promised, stroking her side, feeling her muscles tense at his touch, both of them wanting to believe him. He wanted to tell her that it wasn't all up to him, but he knew Abby believed in a different kind of free will.

Abby got up, closing the bathroom door behind her. Mason slipped on a pair of boxers and stepped over his dog, Tuffy, a German Shepherd–Collie mixed breed, sleeping on a pillow under the window. He padded down the hardwood hall from the bedroom on bare feet to turn on the attic fan, stopping at a window on the front of the house, raising it open. A full-bodied oak tree, its leaves an early brown from lack of water, rustled in the thin current of air passing through its limbs. The branches fragmented his view of the street. A moonless sky had dropped a black curtain on the city.

A car crept down the block. An expensive sedan. Japanese or German, Mason guessed. The driver doused the headlights, slowing to a crawl when it reached Mason's house. The passenger window slid down. A sharp flash exploded from inside the car, the spit of a bullet barely heard. The first floor window directly beneath where he stood shattered along with his promise to Abby, setting off his house alarm.

Abby burst from the bedroom, clutching a towel over her body with one hand, her other hand clamped over her scar. Mason wanted to tell her that it was nothing, that it wasn't his fault, and that he was sorry. He stood in the hall looking at her shake, not saying a word because he knew it wouldn't matter.

The alarm company sent the cops. Mason and Abby were just getting dressed when they arrived, Mason in gym shorts and a T-shirt, no shoes. Abby marched down the stairs, past the cops toward her car parked on the street as she tucked her sleeveless turtleneck into her cargo shorts. Mason followed her, his bare feet slapping the concrete walk. Tuffy trailed both of them, her tail on high alert.

"Don't go," he said, catching her arm as she reached the curb.

"I'm not doing this again, Lou! I told you that."

"It was probably just some kids. There's no proof it has anything to do with this case."

"Are you delusional?" she demanded. "You're hired to

prove Whitney King murdered two people, his lawyer tells you to back off, and someone tries to kill you. All in less than twenty-four hours. If it's not connected, you're the king of bad luck!"

"No one tried to kill me, Abby," Mason pled. "The house was dark. It was the middle of the night. The shooter was counting on no one being on the first floor of the house."

"Fine," she said, pulling her car door open. "Whoever did it wasn't trying to kill you. It was just their way of saying hello. You can live that kind of life, Lou. People killing and getting killed. You and Blues pretending it's all water off a duck's back. Well, it's not water. It's blood. I know. I killed somebody and the blood didn't wash off my back. It stuck. I can't do this any more," she added, her hands raised in protest. "I can't."

Abby drove away, her parking spot taken by an unmarked police car, two detectives joining the four uniformed cops already securing his house. Mason tugged at the rough growth on his chin, clawing heat-stunted grass with his toes as Tuffy rubbed against his thigh. The dome light came on as the detectives opened the door. Samantha Greer stepped out from the passenger side.

"My luck," Samantha said. "I come out here at two o'clock in the morning for a busted window. You're not even shot."

Mason and Samantha had dated intermittently, for hormonal reasons as far as Mason was concerned. He broke it off when Samantha said she wanted something more and Mason told her he was fresh out of anything else. Mason met Abby shortly after that. Samantha gave up any hope of getting him back.

Samantha had shoulder-length blonde hair, green eyes, and a compact body that he hadn't thought about in months. Facing her in the dark, flush from the heat and sex, his memories of her surfaced like the twitch of an involuntary muscle, compounding his guilt about Abby.

"You get paid the same whether or not I got shot, so don't complain," he told her.

"That Abby?" she asked, pointing to the car disappearing at the end of Mason's long block.

"Yeah. Shootings make her jumpy. She went home. You can talk to her tomorrow if you need to, but she didn't see anything. She was in the bathroom."

Samantha asked him, "How about you? What did you see?"

Mason told her, Samantha writing it down. Her partner, a rumpled, overweight, middle-age guy with a bad comb-over stood back, letting her handle the interview.

"What's it all about, Lou?" she asked him.

Mason ran both hands through his hair, shaking his head. "Beats the hell out of me, Sam."

"It usually does, Counselor. Go after any bad guys lately? Piss off any good guys with bad tempers?"

Mason grinned, one reaction Samantha could count on from him. She understood him and didn't try to change him. Then again, they weren't sleeping together anymore. Maybe, Mason thought, she'd be less casual about his capacity to find trouble if they were.

"You remember the King and Kowalczyk case, the two high school kids convicted of killing that couple, Graham and Elizabeth Byrnes?"

"Sure," Samantha said. "That was Harry's and Blues's case. I was just out of the academy. Ryan Kowalczyk was executed the other day, wasn't he?"

"That he was."

"What's that got to do with you?" she asked. As Mason told her, Samantha listened. This time her partner was taking notes. When he finished she said, "Are you telling me Whitney King was using your front window for target practice?"

"No. Like I told Abby, I don't buy the connection. It's probably some kids just horsing around."

"You think they borrowed Daddy's Lexus or BMW for a drive-by shooting at your house instead of picking up a dozen Krispy Kremes and calling it a night?"

"You think only poor kids get bored eating donuts all the time? he asked her.

Samantha nodded. "That work for you?"

"Has to," he said. "Mind if I switch gears?"

"This one isn't going anywhere," she said.

"Are you working the Sonni Efron case?"

"Matter of fact, I am. Why?" she asked.

Mason asked her, "Any leads?"

Samantha glanced over her shoulder at her partner. "Lou, say hello to Al Kolatch, my partner." Mason and Kolatch exchanged nods. "Al, remember this. Lou Mason never asks whether you've got any leads in a fresh murder case out of idle curiosity. Isn't that right, Lou?"

"Would it do me any good to lie?"

"No," she told him. "We've got nothing official yet, but we're following a number of leads. Why the interest?"

"Nothing special," he said. "Just one thing. Sonni Efron was a juror in the King and Kowalczyk case. She was murdered the same day Ryan Kowalczyk was executed. Interesting coincidence, don't you think?"

Samantha looked at Mason, the corners of her mouth flattening out. "Real interesting," she said. "Let us eliminate Kowalczyk as a suspect. Thanks for the tip. Go back to bed."

Chapter 8

An early morning run through the Country Club Plaza did nothing to clear Mason's head or pound the kinks out of his body from lack of sleep, the last punishing uphill mile on Wornall Road payback for sins not yet committed. The shops and restaurants on the Plaza were dark and quiet, the sun glinting off the Spanish-tiled rooftops, casting morning shadows on the outdoor sculpture that adorned the wide sidewalks. Swans in the Loose Park pond south of the Plaza glided through the shallow mist hanging at the edges of the water, unruffled by passing cars and early runners.

Mason made it back to his house two blocks south of Loose Park before the sun put the city on the spit for another day. He stood in front of the wide, rectangular window that looked into his living room, pockmarked by a single bullet, a minicrater on the pane of glass. The police had found the bullet on the living room floor and dropped it into a plastic evidence bag, assuring him that they would run ballistics on it and check it against other drive-by shootings. It was a .22 caliber slug, lacking the punch to do much besides break the window. A vandal's ammunition, not a killer's. Mason doubted whether Abby would appreciate the distinction.

He'd grown up in the two-story, dusky brick house Claire gave to him and his ex-wife Kate as a wedding gift. It was as familiar to him as a second skin, though it, like him, had become a target too many times. Neighbors had quit talking to him and instructed their children not to ring his doorbell on Halloween. Anna Karelson, the one neighbor who'd stuck by him, moved away, confirming his isolation. The shooting nearly convinced him that it was time to move on as well before the neighbors had him thrown out and the house torn down as a public nuisance.

Anna had sold Mason her husband's TR-6. Mason had sold the car for scrap after it was stripped by carjackers, the carcass recovered by the cops. He put the money into a new Road Runner, a rock-solid truck masquerading as a car. Mason liked the higher view, the solid ride, and the wall of steel around him, attributing the change in his tastes more to midlife than nightmare memories.

Tuffy ran from the back of the house, glad to see him, happier that he didn't take her on his run. She sniffed at his feet and crotch, removing any doubt of his identity, and shoved him toward the house so he could feed her. Mason was glad to have someone in his life whose needs were so easily met and whose affection was so unconditional. Maybe, he thought, all he needed was another dog.

Mickey Shanahan's office was between Blues's and Mason's. It was more of a one-room efficiency apartment since Mickey had no other known address. The only other office on the floor had been vacant since the last tenant, a CPA, moved out. Mickey had quickly occupied it, referring to the offices as his rooms. The door to the CPA's office was open, the first sign he'd seen of Mickey all week.

Mickey was in his early twenties, a skinny scammer with an engaging smile. He had a wild shock of brown hair and a patchy mouse in the cleft of his chin. He walked into the bar one day soon after it had opened and convinced Blues to rent him an office for a PR shop that had yet to see its first client. Blues traded Mickey rent for part-time bartending and pretended not to notice that Mickey lived in the one-room office.

Mason hired Mickey as his legal assistant a couple of years ago, a title Mickey loosely interpreted to mean running the store when Mason couldn't, and covering Mason's wing when things turned ugly, Blues usually taking Mason's back. Mickey claimed that politics was his real meat and that he would one day walk the halls of the powerful, whispering in their ears, making things happen. Abby gave him a taste, landing him a spot on Josh Seeley's volunteer staff.

"Welcome back," Mason told Mickey.

Mickey was throwing clothes into an olive drab duffel bag. "Hey, Lou. What's up, man?"

"The usual," Mason said. "A fight for truth and glory as our clients define it. We've got a new case. A lot to do," Mason added, pointing to the duffel bag. "You coming or going?"

Mickey zipped the bag, hefted it onto his shoulder. "Going. Josh Seeley put me on the payroll for the rest of the campaign. Said he'd take me to D.C. if he wins. Isn't that great! I tell you, Lou, Seeley's train is pulling out of the station and I'm riding in the first car."

Mason kept his poker face, not wanting to step on Mickey's moment, telling himself that he got by without Mickey before and would do so again.

"When did you talk to Seeley?" Mason asked, clearing his throat instead of asking Mickey to give two weeks' notice.

"Well, I haven't yet, not really anyway. Abby called me this morning and said she'd talked to Seeley and it's a done deal. She said Seeley wants both of us to travel with him at least through the primary. It's going to be nonstop, man. A hand-shaking, rubber-chicken-dinner, baby-kissing extravaganza."

Mason nodded, waiting for Abby's kick in the head to stop ringing in his ears. He wondered if Abby would call to say good-bye.

"When do you leave?"

Mickey checked his watch. "Couple of hours. I've got to get down to the campaign office. I put the mail on your desk plus something Claire dropped off. You can hold my last check until I get back. Either that or send it to the nation's capital. Later man," he said, his kid-in-the-candy-store smile hanging off his face. He brushed past Mason, pulling the door closed and leaving Mason alone in the hall.

Mason propped open his office door and his window, offering refuge to the bugs that flew in, a fair price for the chance of a breeze. He checked his voice mail and e-mail for a message from Abby. Nothing. That Abby had pulled strings to get Mickey his job was plain to Mason. The question was why. To get back at Mason or to protect Mickey from what she was certain lay ahead in Mason's newest case?

Mason decided to ask her if she called to tell him she was leaving for the next two and a half weeks or forever. Whichever came first. If she didn't call, neither the question nor the answer would matter.

He opened the dry erase board, grabbed a bottle of water from his refrigerator, and studied the names he'd written on the board the day before. The names didn't tell him anything because he didn't know enough about the people.

Though he had watched Ryan Kowalczyk die, all he knew was that Ryan had been convicted but died claiming he was innocent. He had met Ryan's mother and Nick Byrnes. Heard and seen conflicting portraits of both. The pictures of Graham and Elizabeth Byrnes in the file Nick had given him were of good-looking, vigorous people. They were the bred-to-succeed type who would have sent Nick to private school, lived in a big house, and traveled. At least he knew what they looked like.

Mason didn't even have a current picture of Whitney King. He knew nothing about him except that his life was the opposite of Ryan's. He was acquitted, though Mary and Nick claimed he was guilty. He was alive while Ryan was dead. The rest was a one-dimensional year-book summary. Whitney had been a decent student at St. Mark's, a parochial school on Main between Westport and the Plaza. He was a basketball player who had never been in trouble before that night. He could have been anybody.

Brandon Potter, King's lawyer at the trial, had been in his prime then, more committed to the courtroom than the pint of scotch he now carried in his briefcase. Even then, Potter had been expensive. Mason guessed that the defense ran at least a quarter of a million, plus the expert witnesses who had testified that the fatal blows were struck by someone taller and stronger than Whitney, someone fitting Ryan's build. So the King family had money and, Mason knew, defendants with money spend less time in jail than those represented by public defenders.

There was nothing in the little he knew about King that explained the murderous rampage against Graham and Elizabeth Byrnes. He had to say the same for Ryan Kowalczyk. Working-class family. Same good grades. Same school. Same basketball team. No red flags like torturing small animals, pulling the wings off of flies, or even sending threatening e-mails in the middle of the night.

Juries want to know what happened and who did it. Those answers often came more easily than the one they most wanted to know in a case like this one. Why? Why did one or both boys—good boys from good families—go crazy and kill those people? If Mason could answer that question, he'd have a chance of getting his clients what they wanted.

Normally, he would have told Mickey to run an Internet search on all three families, the Kings, the Kowalczyks, and the Byrnes, picking up data on houses, cars, and neighbors, the dull stuff that sometimes led to the good stuff. Mason promised himself that he'd get around to that, picking up his phone instead. Rachel Firestone answered on the second ring.

"Buy you dinner," Mason said.

"Wouldn't blame you if you did. Company like mine is hard to come by. Especially for a man."

Rachel was a reporter for the *Kansas City Star,* a self-described lipstick lesbian who gratefully extended the term *sister* to describe her close relationship with Mason. She and Mason had an understanding about what was on and off the record that let them both do their jobs.

"Company like mine comes at a price," Mason said.

"No free lunches or dinners, huh? What do you need?"

"Background on Whitney King."

"Name's familiar. Wait a minute. The other kid, what was his name, Kowalczyk or something like that? They were tried for murder. One was convicted, the other got off. Which was it?"

"Kowalczyk was executed the other day. That help any? Or are you only covering the society pages these days?"

"Easy, cowboy. You're the one that wants the freebie here," she told him. "What's the story and when can I write it?"

"Bring me the freebies and I'll lay it out for you. There's a new place at Eighteenth and Vine I want to try. Camille's. Meet me there at seven."

"The Jazz District," she said. "A straight shot east on Eighteenth from the paper. Even I can't get lost. See ya."

Mason thumbed through the day's mail, stopping at a thin envelope with his name written on it in Claire's sharp-edged script. A time-yellowed news clipping from the *Kansas City Star* was inside. The photograph above the story was a grainy, black-and-white of a car dangling from the back of a tow truck, its front end mangled, the passenger side caved in, the windows blown out. In the background, a gash in the guard rail cut by the car on its way into the gully below. Wet pavement reflected the glare of the camera's flash. The story below the picture was brief, the camera telling it better.

> John and Linda Mason were killed last night when their car spun out of control on a wet roadway in south Kansas City late last night. Police officers at the scene described the conditions as treacherous.

Mason checked the date on the clipping. August 1. The fortieth anniversary of their deaths was less than two weeks away. Tucked behind the clipping was another, this one of his parents' obituary cut out from *The Jewish Chronicle,* the weekly newspaper focusing on Kansas City's Jewish community.

The obituary featured a picture of his parents, probably from their wedding or engagement, judging from the unabashed joy they showed in their broad smiles and electric eyes, their heads millimeters apart. Mason held the clippings, one in each hand, not able to match his parents' faces to their collapsed car. His hands shook so that he dropped the clippings on his desk. He pressed his palms flat on the hard surface, locking his elbows to restore order in his limbs.

Mason had never seen the clippings, never thought to ask if there were any, Claire never hinting she had them. He picked up the envelope, and a handwritten note from Claire slipped out, settling on top of the clippings.

It's all here. Let it go.

Claire had never shrunk from any confrontation on any subject no matter how uncomfortable. She taught him about sex, drugs, race, religion, and politics. Not just the sterile, public consumption versions. Telling him there were no stupid questions, just stupid people who were afraid to ask questions. She talked to him about masturbation and wet dreams, not easy topics for a twelve-year-old boy to cover with his aunt. She answered his questions about drugs, admitting her dope-smoking days, telling him she hoped he would be smarter than she was. She fought for the underdog, battling fiercely, never backing down.

Sending him the clippings instead of sitting down with him to talk it through was not just unusual. It was the anti-Claire and it told him one thing. It wasn't all there and he couldn't leave it alone. Nick Byrnes's question echoed in his mind. *Who was protecting you?*

Chapter 9

Mary Kowalczyk lived in a cramped house off of Van Brunt Boulevard, a northeast pocket of the city built before World War II and not much improved since. Small homes and apartment buildings, more tenement than residential, mixed with low-slung businesses that fixed leaky radiators, sold pagers, and rented appliances.

Though old and modest, the house was well maintained, the front porch furnished with a swinging bench suspended beneath a pitched roof. The front of the house was made of stone, the sides covered in clapboard, giving it a sturdy feel. The narrow concrete steps leading up the sloped yard to the front door were lined with summer flowers that were holding their own in the heat, no doubt because Mary was ignoring the emergency ordinance restricting watering.

A white Kia sedan, the front fender creased, was parked in front of her house when Mason pulled up behind it shortly after lunch. A bumper sticker on the rear fender identified the owner as a fan of the St. Mark's Mustangs.

He had to learn as much about Ryan as he did about

Whitney, not from the sterile court record, but from the people in their lives. He didn't expect Mary to be an objective historian, but she was the logical person to start with.

Sitting in his car, Mason checked his voice mail for a message from Abby. He snapped the lid of his cell phone shut like it was the phone's fault that Abby hadn't called. He cut the engine letting the car heat up along with his mood, then getting out before he boiled over.

Mary was at her front door, but not because she was waiting for him. Mason hadn't called to say he was coming, preferring the unprepared responses he got when he dropped in on clients and witnesses. Mary had another guest who was leaving. Shading his eyes against the sun, Mason recognized the short, squat figure of the priest who'd been with Mary at Ryan's execution. Father Steve, Mason remembered. He waited for the priest as Mary watched from the porch.

Father Steve, his black pants and short-sleeved black shirt sucking in the heat, took his time, sweat oozing from his temples when he reached Mason. He extended his hand, squinting against the harsh sunlight. Mason caught the sour scent of sweat and cigarettes.

"Mary says you're the lawyer," the priest said.

Mason shook the priest's moist hand. "Lou Mason," he said.

"I've seen your name in the papers," Father Steve said, wiping his hand on his trousers. "Mary's been through quite a lot. I'm not certain she needs your kind of help just now. She needs to grieve for her son and move on. That's what I've told her."

"She believes her son was innocent," Mason said. "Some people can't move on until they know the truth."

"And you, Mr. Mason, you think you can find the truth for Mary?"

"I don't know, Father," Mason answered. "Sometimes the truth gets wrapped up in so many different versions it's hard to separate what people want to be true from what is true. But, maybe you can help me."

Father Steve folded his arms over his middle. "How so?" he asked.

"At Ryan's execution, you told Mary that Ryan had confessed to everything," Mason said. He held up one hand as Father Steve narrowed his eyes and tightened his jaw. "I know confessions are confidential and I wasn't eavesdropping. Everyone in the witness room heard what you said. It made them feel better, hearing a priest say that Ryan had confessed to murder. Is that why you told her that? So she would feel better about watching her son die. Or did he really confess to the murders?"

"A confession is a sacred trust, Mr. Mason. As is the counseling I give to my parishioners. Whatever you may have heard was not intended for your ears and I won't discuss it now."

"The reason I ask, Father," Mason said, "is that Mary didn't believe you. That's why she hired me. Which makes me wonder why a priest would lie about someone confessing to murder? I don't suppose you can help me out with that theological dilemma."

Father Steve tried to hold Mason's eyes, looking away instead as he fumbled in his pocket for a pack of cigarettes. He pulled one out, raised it to his mouth then crumpled it, flecks of paper and tobacco sticking to his palm.

Mason took advantage of the priest's discomfort. "Tough habit to kick, Father. Good for you."

"We all have our struggles, Mr. Mason."

Father Steve left him on the sidewalk. Mason watched as the priest wedged himself behind the wheel and shook another cigarette from the pack, a trail of smoke escaping from his window as he drove away.

* * *

Mary opened the door for Mason. A weak front of cool air greeted him. The house was dimly lit, shades drawn against the sun, a window air conditioner barely holding its own against the heat, cooling the front room of the house.

"I wasn't expecting so much company," Mary said.

"I should have called," Mason said.

"Oh, that's all right," Mary said, waving her hand. "I don't drive, so I don't get out a lot. Visitors are nice. I made some ice tea. Would you like a glass?"

"Sounds great," Mason said, following her into the kitchen.

A fan sat on the floor, blowing warm air across the room. A portrait of Jesus hung on the wall above a small table with two chairs and a plastic floral arrangement in the center of the table.

"It's cooler in the front room," Mary said, pouring them each a glass of tea, leading him back. "I don't have air-conditioning upstairs, so I've been sleeping on the sofa," she said. "I don't know how the poor people are getting through this heat."

Mary sat on the sofa, while Mason took in the room. The green carpet was worn thin. The walls were paneled to look like wood, the synthetic texture unmistakable. A large crucifix adorned one wall next to a framed high school photograph of Ryan, a shrine within a shrine.

A rectangular aquarium, the water bubbling, housed a handful of colorful striped fish. Mason bent to get a close look. A miniature deep-sea diver was suspended in the water, perfectly weighted to hold his position while the fish swam around him, detouring through a coral reef and a sunken ship half hidden by plastic plants.

"Ryan begged and begged for that aquarium. We finally got it for him when he was ten," Mary said. "I keep it up. I know it's foolish, but there are some things I can't let go of. They remind me of when things were right."

Mason sat in a chair across from the sofa, taking a drink of his tea. "Father Steve thinks you shouldn't have hired me."

"Father Steve has been my priest for thirty years. I know what he thinks," Mary said. "The man can be a comfort, but he's no port in a storm. You told me that Nick Byrnes brought you his file on Ryan's case. Have you looked at it? What do you think?"

She had a mercurial manner, shifting like quicksilver from a soft-spoken invitation for tea to a hard-edged dismissal of her weak-willed clergyman.

"I think there's enough evidence there for me to file a wrongful death case against Whitney King, which is what Nick wants me to do. I don't know if there's enough for me to prove that Ryan was innocent, which is what you want me to do."

"Did you come here to tell me that you're giving up on my case? Because if you are, I'll see this through by myself. My son is dead because of that King boy, just like that poor couple. I'll not rest until that's put right."

Mason shook his head, having no doubt that Mary would leave him behind. "No, I don't give up that easily. I need to know what isn't in that file. I need to know why you are so certain Ryan was innocent."

"You think it's because I'm his mother, don't you?"

"If that's not part of it, you wouldn't be his mother. You sat through the trial and heard all the evidence. There has to be more."

Mary drew circles in the moisture that gathered on her glass of iced tea, not looking up as she answered. "Ryan was a good boy. My husband and I raised him right. He was not capable of killing anyone," she said with a certainty that defied contradiction.

Mason put his glass down on the low table between the sofa and the chair. "Tell me about that night, Mary."

Mary shifted her vision to a middle distance, aiming at the past, not at Mason, speaking so softly Mason had to lean forward to hear.

"They were both on the basketball team at St. Mark's Academy, Ryan and Whitney. Best friends as far as Ryan was concerned. I never believed it. Kings and Kowalczyks don't mix. The Kings lived in a big fancy house. Society people. We were dirt to them. Whitney would come over here looking down his nose at our house. Ryan couldn't see it. Ryan didn't make friends real easily, so I didn't say anything to him. I just knew he'd be sorry if he ever had to count on a boy like that Whitney."

"Had there been any trouble between Ryan and Whitney before that night?" Mason asked.

"If there was, Ryan never said anything. As far as he was concerned, Whitney King hung the moon. Ryan was always talking about Whitney doing this, doing that. Like the boy was some kind of celebrity when all he was, was a snotty kid with a rich daddy."

"Was Whitney with Ryan when he came home that night?" Mason asked.

Mary shook her head, biting her lip. "I was in bed. I worked at Truman Medical Center then and had to go in at five in the morning. Vince, my husband, was working an out-of-town job. I didn't hear Ryan come home."

Mason knew all that, had read Mary's trial testimony, but wanted to hear her tell it, listening for anything that didn't fit. "The police came the next day?"

"Dinnertime," Mary said, her voice rising, her shoulders shivering. "They had a search warrant and they asked for Ryan. I said what's this all about. They wouldn't tell me. There were two detectives and some other officers in uniforms. They swarmed all over my house like locusts," she said, brushing her arms, wiping away the memory like a stain.

"Where was Ryan?" Mason asked.

"In his room. I called up to him. I told him the police were here and wanted to talk to him. He didn't answer. Detective Bluestone, that horrible man at your office, he went upstairs. I could hear Ryan screaming from the kitchen. I don't know what came over me, but I grabbed a butcher knife and ran upstairs, I was so scared. Another policeman grabbed me. They were going to arrest me too, but the other detective, Mr. Ryman, the one you were with at the execution, he made them let me go."

She held her arms tightly against her sides, elbows cocked. It was as if she could feel the cops hands on her again, keeping her from her son.

"Mary," Mason began. "Ryan's clothes were covered with blood from both of the Byrneses. The police found the boys' clothes hidden in your basement. I know the story both boys told. One of them has to be lying. I've got to have something more to go on. How can you be so certain Ryan was innocent?"

Mary looked at Mason, not a trace of doubt on her face. "He had no reason."

"What about Whitney King?" Mason asked. "What reason could he possibly have had?"

"The rich are different, Mr. Mason. They don't need a reason."

Mason looked around the drab room. Mary Kowalczyk, wearing a faded shift that had seen too many hot summers, sat rigidly against the tired cushions of the sofa she slept on. Jesus gazed down at them from his cross. The air conditioner wheezed as the room was shrinking. Mason understood at last. Mary Kowalczyk believed her son was innocent because she hated rich people.

Chapter 10

Mason picked Harry Ryman up in front of Union Station an hour later. He wanted to run through the facts of the case with Harry. Mason was troubled by the missing murder weapon. The prosecutor didn't need it to prove that the Byrneses had been murdered or that both boys had committed the crime. Mason needed it to prove that Ryan was innocent. Even after fifteen years, there could be fingerprints or DNA evidence that would prove who had swung the tire iron.

Mason had another problem that was also dependent on the murder weapon. He hoped that Harry would help him with this one even though he knew Harry had an arresting cop's bias.

There was no evidence of a struggle between the victims and the killers. If Ryan was innocent, Whitney King had managed to kill both victims before either could resist or flee. Whitney may have been a spoiled rich kid, but that didn't make him a ninja.

With his deteriorated eyesight, Harry didn't trust himself to drive outside Red Bridge, his neighborhood in south

Kansas City. When he couldn't stand being cooped up any longer, he walked two blocks from his house and caught a bus that took him all the way downtown and into the River Market area along the Missouri River. He'd wander around the shops, grab lunch, sometimes taking a walk through River Front Park, catching a southbound bus back home, getting off if something else struck his fancy along the way. When Mason called his cell phone, Harry was sitting next to the fountain in front of Union Station.

Once the second largest passenger rail terminal in the country, Union Station had been abandoned, boarded up— an eyesore that was too big to be forgotten. Saved by the vote of people living on both sides of the Missouri-Kansas state line in favor of a tax to raise money for its restoration, the station had been returned to its glory days, once again delivering passengers to the center of the city. The station was on Twenty-fifth Street between Main and Broadway.

Just to the south high on a hill above Union Station, stood the Liberty Memorial, a towering obelisk honoring those who had died in World War I. It too had recently been restored.

Mason parked next to a granite pillar with a bronze plaque that commemorated the spot in the Union Station parking lot where Pretty Boy Floyd and his gang had gunned down four lawmen in an effort to free their friend Frank Nash, who was killed in the effort. It was Kansas City's answer to Chicago's St. Valentine's Day Massacre.

Mason stopped to read the summary of the bloody business that had taken place on June 17, 1933. Nash had escaped from the Kansas State Penitentiary nearly three years earlier where he was serving a twenty-five-year term for assaulting a mail custodian. Finally captured in Arkansas, two FBI agents and a local chief of police escorted Nash by train to Kansas City where he would be transferred back to the prison in Leavenworth, Kansas.

When the FBI agents and Nash got into their car, Floyd and his men opened fire on them and their police escort. Floyd escaped the botched rescue only to be killed in a shootout in Ohio in October 1934. Bloody as the massacre had been, the books had been balanced with the same red ink. At least, Mason thought, no one had second-guessed Floyd's fate. Looking up the hill at the Liberty Memorial, Mason was struck by the City's impulse to honor its dead when the cause was noble or the death dramatic. There would be no monument for Ryan Kowalczyk.

"Hot enough for you?" Mason asked Harry when he joined him at the fountain.

"I don't mind the heat," Harry answered. "Besides, the fountain helps. I'll bet it's ten degrees cooler next to that water."

The fountain was an array of high-powered jets, the sprays choreographed in a kaleidoscope of patterns that never seemed to repeat, sometimes set to music. Kansas City bragged about its fountains. They may be baking in a heat wave, but the city wouldn't let the fountains run dry.

"It's great that you can see it well enough to enjoy it," Mason said.

"Hell, I can't see the patterns worth a damn," Harry said. "About all I can see is when one spray starts and another stops. But, I can feel it, like the water vibrates around me. That's something."

"How about I give you a ride home?"

"Cheaper than the bus," Harry answered. "What are you up to besides running a taxi service?" he asked when they'd settled into Mason's car.

"Mary Kowalczyk and Nick Byrnes hired me. Mary wants me to get her son a pardon and Nick wants Whitney King's head on a pike outside the village gates."

"I know. Blues told me."

"You okay with that?" Mason asked. "I mean the part about proving Kowalczyk was innocent."

"None of my business," Harry said, looking out the passenger window, his left hand balled into a fist, drumming against his knee. "We all gotta eat, but you ought to find another way to pay for your groceries. Kowalczyk is dead. You can't un-ring that bell and I'm not losing any sleep over it. He was guilty. Plain and simple. You want to have your head handed to you, be my guest."

Mason drove, neither of them talking. Harry never said anything trite to Mason, like telling Mason he thought of him as a son, though he had treated him that way since Mason was a small boy, Harry's relationship with Claire dated back that many years. Harry took him to ball games, slipped him a few bucks for a date, and gave him a stern eye if his grades slipped. In recent years, he cut corners and pulled strings for Mason when he needed help from the police department.

Growing up, Mason had idolized Harry, making it tough for him to take Harry on, though he'd done it once before when Blues's life was on the line. Blues and Harry had been partners until Blues was forced from the police department. Harry had carried a grudge against Blues that was almost fatal when Mason was caught in the middle years later. Blues was the brother Mason never had. This time, Mason was taking both of them on. Long odds.

"Why do you think the jury acquitted Whitney King?" he finally asked Harry.

Harry shook his head. "The jury was deadlocked for two days. Then they split the baby. I've never been in a jury room, but that's one I'd have paid for admission. We had those boys dead to rights. Their alibis were bullshit. They both should've gotten the needle."

Mason sighed. "I've got a feeling Kowalczyk was innocent."

"A murder case isn't a prom date, Lou. Feelings got nothing to do with it. It's all about the evidence and the evidence in this case was overwhelming."

"There's something that bothers me about the facts," Mason said.

"What's that?" Harry asked.

"Graham and Elizabeth Byrnes were young and healthy. His parents testified that they ran marathons, worked out all the time."

"What's your point?"

"The murder weapon was never found. Everyone assumed that it was the tire iron from the Byrnes's car since it was missing. If that's true, the killers had to hit them one at a time."

"So what?" Harry asked.

"So, if the husband got it first, why didn't the wife run away? If the wife got it first, why didn't the husband put up a fight? If both boys were there when the murders took place, the one not swinging the tire iron would have had to hold the other victim down. There were would have been a struggle. One of the boys would have ended up with bruises or cuts. One of the victims would have had the killer's skin under their fingernails. Something would have happened, but nothing did. It's like the victims stood still while they were killed."

Harry said, "The wife wouldn't have run and left her baby in the car. Who's to say there wasn't a fight? Besides, that doesn't prove one of those kids was telling the truth and it doesn't prove there was only one murder weapon. Could have been two and we didn't find either one of them."

"Maybe not," Mason said. "But it doesn't add up. If Ryan Kowalczyk was innocent, we need to know that."

"Why?" Harry asked. "So his mother can sue the state of Missouri and wooly some boo-hoo money out of the taxpayers? So you can prove that Blues and I caused an innocent kid to die? How's that gonna help anybody? Especially us?" Mason had no answers to Harry's questions. "Pull over," Harry said. "I'll take the bus the rest of the way home."

Chapter 11

Nancy Troy was a public defender, spending her days and nights fighting off a better staffed, better equipped, better financed foe. The State. She was handicapped by another small problem. Most of her clients were guilty and there were too many of them to keep track of, let alone do the exhaustive job of preparing a defense that Mason did for a client that could pay the freight.

She was a miniature bulldog, barely cresting five feet, carrying an extra fifteen pounds of midlife, sandy hair half gray, not vain enough to care. She snapped and snarled at cops and prosecutors, walking the tightrope in a system that balanced overcrowded criminal dockets with overcrowded prisons. Her definition of success was squeezing justice out of the process when she could. Ryan Kowalczyk had been one of her clients.

Her office was in a one-story brick building on the east side of downtown, across the street from what used to be the bus station, an empty building now on the city's list of things it didn't know what to do with. Nancy had been a public defender for twenty years, getting one of the few perks of her practice, a private office; the walls were covered with her kids' artwork and a handful of framed letters of thanks from grateful clients. She offered Mason a seat, closing the door behind him.

"You're lucky you caught me in the office," she told him. "I'm usually at the courthouse or the jail. Or I've got a waiting room full of clients. Sometimes this place is more popular than a public health clinic passing out free condoms."

Mason liked Nancy. It was hard not to. She defended the worst of the worst, making less money in a year than he sometimes made on a single case, doing it because she loved it, giving Mason a hard time about what she called his limelight practice.

"I'm on a tight schedule," Mason explained. "If I start making appointments to see people, I'll run out of daylight."

"What's up?" she asked. "*People* magazine waiting for you back at the office?"

"Yeah. They're doing a feature on lost causes. Mary Kowalczyk hired me to get a pardon for her son."

"Ryan Kowalczyk? Isn't that a little late?"

Mason shrugged. "Not for a mother who has nothing left but memories. She wants me to clear her son's name."

"So what's the rush? Ryan's gone."

"He's not pushing me. I'm also representing Nick Byrnes, the son of the murder victims. He was three when his parents were killed. He wants me to sue Whitney King for their wrongful death. His statute of limitations runs in less than two weeks."

Nancy took a deep breath, letting it out like a slow leak, leaning back in her desk chair. Mason was certain her feet didn't touch the floor. "Okay," she said. "No pressure. Ryan was my first capital murder client. Not exactly what he or his mother wanted to hear, but like my first boyfriend said, who wants to go second anyway."

"You were ready for trial," Mason told her. "I've never known you to be anything but ready."

Nancy let her chair come forward, pulling herself up to her desk. "You don't have to suck up that much, Lou. Even if you're right. Ryan's mother—your client—was a royal pain in the ass. Second guessed everything I did at the trial. I was glad to turn the case over to our appellate guys."

"She's convinced her son was innocent."

"Lou, all mothers are convinced their sons are innocent. Daughters too."

Mason laughed. "I know. Same with my clients. I've read the trial transcript. You didn't have much to work with. The alibis sounded like a bad idea for a TV movie."

"Tell me about it. The other kid, Whitney King. He had Brandon Potter and Potter was still pretty good in those days. Potter sold the alibi to the jury and I didn't."

"Was there anything in either kid's background that would explain why they did it?" Mason asked.

"No child abuse or satanic cults, stuff like that," Nancy said, leaving it open.

"But?"

"But Whitney was a strange kid. Not jump-out-at-you strange. I picked up bits and pieces. There were rumors among some of the kids at school that he had hit on a few girls a little too hard, maybe even raped one. I could never substantiate anything."

"What was Ryan doing hanging out with a kid like that?" Mason asked.

"Ryan was a nice, geeky kid who wouldn't say shit if he had a mouthful. Whitney was practically his only friend. Whitney liked being worshiped."

"Did you buy Ryan's alibi?" Mason asked.

Nancy pursed her lips, nodding. "Enough to let him testify to it. I mean I had no reason to believe he was lying when I put him on the stand, but I couldn't corroborate it either. It made sense in a funny kind of way."

"Meaning?"

"The coroner said that the first blow to both victims was to the face. That means they saw it coming. Neither one fought back; at least near as we could tell. Nothing on the victims or the defendants to show they fought. The cops couldn't come up with a murder weapon, but they assumed there was only one. I didn't argue because the one weapon theory was better for Ryan. Unless the boys took turns, it made sense that there was only one killer."

Mason was relieved that someone else had picked up on the failure of the victims to resist. "If both boys were there when the murders took place, one of them would have said he saw the other one do it, and was too scared to try and stop him. Take a chance on a conviction for being an accessory, not a killer. That makes more sense than each one saying that he left and it was over when he came back."

"Exactly," Nancy said. "I pressed Ryan about that. Gave him every chance to tell that story. The kid was consistent all the way through. Wasn't there. Didn't do it. Didn't know squat about any murder weapon."

"Did you talk to the jury after the trial?"

"You know," Nancy answered. "That was weird. They were deadlocked for two days. I would have settled for a hung jury. Then we could have tried the case again or made a deal."

Mason asked, "What broke the deadlock?"

"I never found out. The jury sent a note to the judge saying they didn't want to talk with the lawyers after the case was over. Only time that's ever happened to me. I tried talking to them anyway, just in case there was any jury misconduct that would get Ryan a new trial. I called some of them. Went to see some others. Nobody would say a word. It's like they made a secret pact."

Chapter 12

Eighteenth and Vine is an oasis on the east side of Kansas City, a part of town known more for being neglected than celebrated. The block had been restored to its 1930s heyday when it was a chamber in Kansas City's jazz heart. The refurbished Gem Theatre hosted new and old talent touring the country, reminiscent of the days when Basie, Ellington and their brethren blew sweet sounds and blue notes from its stage. Negro League Baseball, and Kansas City's jazz heritage split space in a museum across the street from the Gem. The strip is a stark contrast to the depleted blocks surrounding it, giving the whole place the feel of a Hollywood back lot.

"A secret pact?" Rachel Firestone asked Mason, sitting across from him at Camille's, their corner table giving Rachel a view of the rest of the room while Mason's view was limited to Rachel.

Mason preferred his view. Rachel was a redhead wonder, a beautiful woman whose flashing green eyes matched her effervescence. He felt better when he was with her. There was a time when he thought that meant he was in love. With Rachel, he'd learned that it meant she was a friend he could count on.

Camille's was a down home soul food restaurant, drawing on another tradition of Kansas City's African American community. Fried chicken and chops, ribs, ham hocks and beans, collard greens and corn, potatoes fried and mashed. Cakes, pies, and ice cream, all homemade. No little red hearts on the menu for the healthy selections. Plenty of cold beer, iced tea, and lemonade. It was the perfect cure for heat that rose like the tide from the streets to the rooftops, swamping the city.

"That's what Nancy Troy called it," Mason answered. "A secret pact."

Rachel asked, "How long did the jury deliberate?"

Mason said, "Three days. Both Harry and Nancy said the jury was deadlocked for the first two days. Then, something happened to break the logjam."

"If the jury took a vow of silence, how do Harry and Nancy know they were deadlocked?" Rachel asked.

Her question stumped Mason for a moment; the obvious contradiction had escaped him. He shrugged his shoulders. "It's an assumption, I guess. A jury doesn't deliberate for two days without being deadlocked."

"Yeah, I understand that," Rachel said. "But how did they know the jury was deadlocked? And why did they both tell you it was two days and not three? How do they know the jury wasn't just taking their time going over the evidence until they finally reached a verdict?"

Mason looked at her with the wide-eyed wonder of someone who'd just seen a magician pull a rabbit out of his ear but couldn't believe it even though he'd seen it with his own eyes.

"Maybe," he conceded. "Here's one thing I know for certain. One of the jurors, Sonni Efron, was murdered the same day Ryan was executed. I hate coincidences," Mason said. "But that's the kind I really hate."

Rachel's eyes switched from flashing to focused, her reporter's instinct boring in. "You think there's a connection?"

Mason shrugged. "Don't know. I'm going to track down the rest of the jurors and find out if the secret pact is still a secret. What did you dig up on Whitney King? I don't even know what the guy looks like."

"He's good looking," Rachel said. "If you like the rugged, muscled look. Which, I admit, is my kind of woman," she added, handing Mason a clipping. "He likes triathlons, extreme sports, that kind of thing. And he likes to win."

The clipping included a picture taken at a fund-raising triathlon, King holding his trophy in one hand and an oversize copy of his donation check in the other, the caption explaining that he'd come in first both as a competitor and a contributor.

"Which came first? The check or the trophy?" Mason asked.

"According to my friend who covers the society beat, he pays to win. The charities need the money. On this one, Whitney got help from a friendly stopwatch."

"Women?"

"He collects them. None of them last long. Word has it that he likes it rough. He's had a few complaints, but they always get settled quietly."

"What's he do for a living?" Mason asked.

"Runs the family business," Rachel said. "King Construction Company. Whitney's grandfather started it. Over the years, they've built everything from subdivisions to high-rise office buildings."

"When did his father die?" Mason asked.

Rachel slid another clipping across the table. "Week after

the trial. Tragedy strikes again. Newspapers love stuff like that."

Mason read Christopher King's obituary, a litany of private club memberships. "How did he die?"

"Fell down the stairs," Rachel said. Mason's eyebrows bounced in astonishment. "No kidding," she said. "Number one cause of accidental deaths in the home. Falling down. I ever buy a house, it's gonna be a ranch. No two-story death traps for me."

"What about Whitney's mother?"

"The son's trial and the husband's death were too much for her. She fell apart. Whitney got her the penthouse at the loony bin. Golden Years Psychiatric Hospital in Lenexa. She's been there ever since."

Lenexa was a suburb of Kansas City across the state line in Johnson County, Kansas.

"Nice family," Mason said. "I can't wait to meet him."

"From your lips to God's ears," Rachel said, looking past Mason. "He's on his way to our table."

Mason took Rachel's word for it, resisting the temptation to turn around, catching Whitney's reflection off a parabolic mirror mounted in the corner of the ceiling, the distorted image squashing Whitney, doing the same to Sandra Connelly who followed a step behind.

King was dressed in black, just like Father Steve, except for the collar and the build. Father Steve was soft rolls and paunch. King was bounce-a-quarter-off-his-pecs buff, his silk shirt stretched across his chest, short sleeves straining against his biceps. Sandra, her toned and sculpted arms rippling from linen sleeves, was the perfect accessory.

"I understand you're looking for me," King said, standing at Mason's shoulder, forcing Mason to turn or stand. Mason did neither, leaving the newspaper clippings spread before him.

"Nope," Mason answered, watching King's funhouse image in the elevated mirror. "If I want you, I know how to find you. That's what your lawyer is for."

King glanced at the mirror. Mason ignored him, locked onto Rachel's green eyes, as Rachel bit her cheek. King flexed his fingers, wanting to make Mason turn and face him, the entire encounter all about who blinked first.

"Let's go, Whitney," Sandra said, her hand on his arm. King shook it off, laughing lightly.

"Mason," he said. "You sue me for those murders and I'll wipe your ass all over the courtroom."

"If I don't sue you, will you wipe my ass anyway? I could use the help," Mason said, keeping his back to King.

"Sandra told me all about you, Mason," King said, conceding the first skirmish, stepping between Mason and Rachel. Mason pushed back from the table, hands in his lap.

"Like I said," Mason told him. "That's what your lawyer is for."

"She said you were a smart-ass. Won't back down. Too stubborn to live. That sound about right?"

"Close. She got the stubborn part wrong. That's too stubborn to die."

King smiled, his perfect white teeth giving the grin its ice, his eyes narrowing. "On second thought, Mason, you go ahead and sue me. I'm going to enjoy cleaning your clock."

"Gosh, Whitney," Mason said. "Do you think you'll have as much fun as when you murdered Graham and Elizabeth Byrnes?"

King cut the short distance between him and Mason in half, his chest and neck swelling, the move a threat, not a plea. "You're forgetting the jury said I didn't do it."

Mason finally stood, measuring himself against King's shorter frame, sensing that King's coiled power offset his own height advantage.

"Then you can clean my clock and wipe my ass. Sandra is expensive, but at least you'll get your money's worth."

King closed the distance between them again. Sandra slid in front of him, her back to Mason, her hands on King's shoulders.

"Bell's rung, boys. Round one is over. No blood on the floor. Just lots of testosterone. Come on, Whitney," she told him. "You bought the most expensive table at the Jazz Museum fund-raiser tonight. Don't waste it trying to prove you've got a bigger dick than Lou. You probably do, but Lou doesn't think size matters."

Sandra wrapped her arm around King's shoulder, pulling him to her breast. King smiled again, this time like a wolf, pointing his fingers at Mason like an imaginary gun, dropping the hammer.

"Take my advice, Counselor. Stay away from windows," King said.

Sandra rolled her eyes, pretending King and Mason were just little boys having a play date, all of them knowing that neither of them was playing. King gave Sandra a shove, leaving her a step behind.

"You make friends so easily," Rachel told Mason after King and Sandra left.

"Really," Mason said. "I didn't think he liked me that much."

"Liked you?" Rachel said. "He wanted to kill you."

"I guess old habits die hard," Mason said.

"His or yours?" Rachel asked.

Chapter 13

Dinner ran long. Mason was in no hurry to go home, checking his voice mail while Rachel went to the bathroom. There was no message from Abby, though he had left one for her. Call when you can. He bet that she wouldn't.

Mason lingered outside Camille's after Rachel left, eyeing the Jazz Museum across the street. A pack of valets hustled cars from the front of the museum to a vacant lot a block away, bringing them back when people began to leave. Young guys sprinted for the lot when a guest handed them a claim check like it was the baton in a relay and they were running the anchor leg. The owners pressed tips into the valets' hands when they returned with the cars, the valets palming the bills, checking them on the sly, grunting at the cheapskates, saluting the swells.

He had no place to go and nothing to do when he got there, so he returned to Camille's, took a table in the front window, picked at a piece of pie, and waited for Whitney King to leave. Whitney had either admitted to the drive-by shooting at Mason's house or teased him with the knowledge that he knew about it. The shooting hadn't made the paper, but that didn't mean it was a secret.

Sandra Connelly left before King did. Mason was glad they were traveling separately, having a hard enough time thinking of Sandra as King's lawyer. Not wanting to add consort to counselor. It wasn't jealousy. Sandra could ignite Mason's lust, but she couldn't sustain his romantic affection. He looked past her sharp-edged, hardball style and saw someone he didn't want taken down by her client. They'd been through enough together that he owed her that much.

Summer light surrendered slowly, the heat sticking around, the valets dripping with each dash to the parking lot as the sky purpled, then blackened. The neon street lit up, the honky-tonks honked though not with the wild abandon they must have had when Kansas City was a wide-open town in the days between the World Wars. The people on the street tonight were there to look at the past, not make the present.

King left just after ten o'clock, the lucky valet clicking his heels when King tipped him, turning to his mates before King pulled away, flashing a bill and a grin to match. King drove a BMW 7 series sedan, black, the windows tinted. Mason squinted, crunching his eyes to match the car with his memory of the one on his blacked-out street. It was a definite, tentative maybe.

Mason had gotten lucky when he arrived at Camille's, finding a parking place on the street across from the restaurant, allowing him to fall in behind King, separated by a short string of cars creeping west on Eighteenth Street back to the donors' side of town. Mason didn't plan to follow King. It just happened that way, Mason having no reason other than curiosity, confident that King wouldn't spot him.

King took Eighteenth Street west to Main, turned south on Main, then west on Forty-seventh, cutting through the Plaza, then south on Wornall and west onto Mason's street before it dawned on Mason that King had not only spotted him but was pimping him. King glided to a stop in front of Mason's house.

Mason turned into his driveway, this time not able to ignore King. He parked, got out of his car and leaned against the passenger side, waiting. The driver's door on King's car swung open, King stepping out. They stood silently in the dark, King making his point. He knew where Mason lived.

King broke the silence. "You're out of your league, Mason. Give it up."

"Lucky for me, this is a neighborhood watch area," Mason said.

"Then you better hope your neighbors are watching you all the time," King told him, pointing at Mason's house. "When you get that window fixed, I'd recommend bulletproof glass."

Mason watched King drive away, looking too long at his house before heading for the garage. Mason wasn't hard to find. His address was in the phone book. King could have driven by out of the same curiosity that prompted Mason to follow him, unaware that Mason was behind him, taking advantage of Mason's arrival to jack with him. Or, he could have seen Mason in his rearview mirror, stringing Mason along just to play tough guy one more time. Mason wondered which scenario gave King too much credit.

He wanted to dismiss King's threats, but couldn't. Not if he was going to prove that King murdered Graham and Elizabeth Byrnes, then let his boyhood best friend die for his crimes. King had emerged from the murders without blood on his hands, building a life on a foundation of money, the first floor of a penthouse he inherited. King wouldn't let go easily. He'd fight to keep that life, even if someone else had to die.

Maybe, Mason thought, King was right. Maybe Mason was out of his league, especially with Blues and Harry sitting this one out and Mickey on the road. The clincher hit him as he pulled into the garage. Innocent people let their lawyers deliver threats. Killers don't pass up the pleasure.

Abby was right to leave, he realized. He didn't want her to call, afraid that she would come back before it was over.

Tuffy was pacing in the kitchen, her tail down, greeting Mason with a low whine.

"A hungry dog is not a happy dog," Mason told her, filling her dish, going outside with her when she was finished eating.

Mason took a slow tour of his house, treading in the shadows the brick walls cast on the grass, picking up the dusty smell of parched ground and the sickly sweet decay of wilting flowers. There was a story in the paper that day of an elderly couple overcome by the heat, not found until the smell gave their death away. The mayor reminded everyone to check on their neighbors and not water their grass or flowers. Weather forecasters said they were sorry, but there was no end in sight. Mason touched the wall of his house, still radiating the day's warmth, bricks and mortar the only things that could stand up to the weather. Living things were out of their league.

He rattled his first-floor windows to make certain the locks were secure, knowing that the protection they offered was illusory. He'd had an alarm system installed a few years ago when thugs broke in and redecorated; giving in to Claire's insistence that he wasn't Superman. The alarm system was down until the living room window was replaced and the motion sensor reinstalled.

"Be another week," the guy from the alarm company had told him. "They don't make your system anymore, so we had to find the part on E-bay."

"Why did they quit making it?" Mason asked.

"Didn't sell enough. People wanted something with a louder siren," the alarm guy had told him. "Keep your doors locked in the meantime," he had advised.

Mason slid around the overgrown shrubs that wrapped

around the house, making a mental note to find a neighborhood kid to trim them back, remembering Claire's description of Sonni Efron's house. Shrubs like a wall, giving her killer all the cover he needed. Mason stood in his front yard, absently rubbing the scar on his chest, sweat lubricating the raised flesh.

He was chasing middle age, worrying about bushes, locks, and alarms, trading trash talk with a killer ten years younger. The smart way out was to quit. Let someone else or no one else represent Mary Kowalczyk and Nick Byrnes. Prove to Abby that he'd changed. Reassure Blues and Harry that he didn't blame them for an innocent man's execution. Take the advice everyone had given him. Move on. Let it go. Give it up.

He was alone and he was scared, but he couldn't quit. It wasn't about testing his limits or tempting the fates. It was about the voice he kept hearing. Ryan Kowalczyk's last gasp. *Innocent.*

Mason dragged his rowing machine up from the basement, shoved his dining room table into the living room and ducked the equipment where the table had been. He'd moved the rowing machine into the basement in deference to Abby's conventional views on interior decorating, bringing it back now that he was more likely to get that kind of advice from Martha Stewart than from Abby.

He changed into gym shorts, shoes, no shirt, and brought the fan downstairs from the bedroom. He opened the dining room window and turned the lights off. He settled into the seat of the rowing machine, losing himself in the half-light. He started out with a long, slow series of strokes, driving back with his legs, pulling the handle into his gut, letting the flywheel carry him forward, starting again. Rowing was monotonous, almost hypnotic, the rhythm soothing. Breaking him down, building him up.

The fan whirred behind him, drying his back and neck, leaving the rest of him soaked, picking up the pace as his muscles found their groove. Meters and minutes passed, Mason trying to out run Kowalczyk and King, grunting with each stroke, his calves burning, his chest aching, his arms trembling when he finally quit nearly an hour later. Staggering off the machine, sucking air, Mason walked laps around the first floor, betting Tuffy whether she would outlast him, the dog anxiously sticking her nose in his hand.

Grabbing two bottles of water and his cordless phone, Mason led the dog onto the patio where he collapsed into a vinyl lounge chair, his body temperature finding equilibrium with the night, both overheated. His breathing was still ragged. He gagged on the humid, musk air like it was bad medicine. He started to call Abby, tell her she was right, don't come back. Please come back. Instead, he drank one bottle of water, pouring the other over his head, closing his eyes, the phone on his belly, Tuffy at his side.

A few hours later, Tuffy barked, a short burst like shots fired, waking him. The dog was on point at the foot of the lounge chair, her hair bristling. Mason sat up, straddling the chair, the phone in his lap. Peering into the darkness. Listening. Nothing there. Not convinced, the dog edged toward the far corner of the house, growling.

The phone rang. Mason snatching it, answering on the first ring. "Hello."

Dead air. Mason slapped the phone against his thigh.

"Asshole!" the best he could do.

Jumping from the chair, he raced to the front of the house, the dog beating him by a step. The block was deserted. The phone rang again.

"This is your neighborhood watcher. You can go inside now," Whitney King told him.

Chapter 14

Mason finished proofreading the lawsuit against Whitney King, increasing the amount of compensatory damages sought from five million dollars to ten million, doubling the prayer for punitive damages from fifty million to one hundred million. He'd spent the morning drafting the papers, coming to the office early, giving up on sleep after King's wake-up call.

King wanted to shake Mason up. Not a problem, Mason muttered, double-checking the lawsuit a third time. King would be more than shaken up when Mason served him with the papers. Mason looked forward to delivering King's invitation to the courthouse party in person. Look for the story in the *Kansas City Star,* Mason would tell King on his way out the door, another copy under his arm for Rachel Firestone.

"Come on in, Nick" Mason said when someone knocked at his office door close to noon.

"How'd you know it was me, Mr. Mason?" Nick asked, leaving the door open. He was wearing baggy cargo shorts, a T-shirt, and sandals. Sunglasses were perched on top of his head.

"You're on time. I told you to be here at noon, and you're

here at noon. Have a seat," he said, pointing to the couch and taking the chair next to it.

Nick settled into the couch as Mason handed him a copy of the lawsuit. "Is this it?" Nick asked, eyes wide.

"You bet it is," Mason said. "I wanted you to see it first. I'm going to file it this afternoon."

"Wow," Nick said softly, taking his time, reading each numbered paragraph on each page, Mason watching, smiling, taking pride in his authorship.

"The law is a beautiful thing, Nick. It holds people accountable. It makes them answer for what they've done and it gives people like you the chance to see justice done. The money won't bring your parents back. Nothing can do that. But Whitney King will pay for what he did and the rest of the world will know him for what he is. A murderer."

Mason had rehearsed the speech in the back of his mind as he drafted the lawsuit. It was what he believed. It was what kept him from calling the cops or picking up the gun in his bottom desk drawer and going after King. Whatever else he was, Mason was a true believer in the system of law. King could threaten him, and wake him up in the middle of the night, but Mason could drag King into court, cut off his head, and put it on a pike outside the village gates as a lesson to anyone else who thought they could intimidate him.

"Nice speech," Blues said, standing in Mason's doorway. "Bad idea, but nice speech."

Mason had been so focused on delivering his closing argument to Nick that he hadn't noticed Blues, a big man to overlook, loose fitting slacks and shirt disguising his power build, soft-pedaling his capacity for sudden violence. Blues had bailed Mason out of more than a few jams, using a mix of rough justice and hard muscle that filled the gaps left by the niceties of the law.

Blues's presence was a swift reminder to Mason that his

speech sometimes looked better on paper than it did when the other guy refused to play by the rules. Mason wanted the rules to be enough this time, but Blues's comment was a reality check.

Mason hadn't talked to Blues about the King case, or much else, since Blues told Mason he wouldn't help him. While drafting the lawsuit, Mason had convinced himself that he didn't need Blues's help after all. He would win this case the old-fashioned way: in front of a jury. It might not be enough to bring Abby back, but it felt right.

He wasn't surprised at Blues's attitude, though he didn't want Blues to share his doubts with an eighteen-year-old kid who would be easy to shake up.

Nick looked at Mason. "Who's he?"

"Wilson Bluestone Junior," Mason answered, punctuating the name with a reluctant sigh. "He's a piano player and my landlord. People call him Blues because he's got such a positive outlook on life."

Nick jumped to his feet. "You were one of the detectives who caught Kowalczyk and King." He stuck out his hand, Blues taking it. "I never got to thank you for everything you did. I mean I was just a kid then. I didn't realize you two knew each other."

"Oh yeah," Blues said. "We know each other real well. Let me see that lawsuit you're so excited about."

Nick handed Blues his copy, standing between Blues and Mason, hands on his hips. "Wow! What a team! Mason and Bluestone. We're going to kick Whitney King's ass, man!"

Blues tossed the papers on the table in front of the sofa. "So long as he doesn't kill you first, Nick."

Mason started to protest, Blues holding up his hand, Nick interrupting, his jaw dropping. "What are you talking about?" Turning to Mason, "What's he talking about?"

"I'll tell you what I'm talking about," Blues said. "Are your grandparents still alive?"

"Yeah," Nick answered.

"What do they think about you filing this lawsuit?"

Nick rolled his shoulders, shaking his head, looking at the floor. "They don't want me to do it. They say it will only stir up bad memories."

"They could have filed the lawsuit for you anytime you were growing up, but they didn't. Whitney King knows that. He knows without you, there's no case," Blues explained.

"What are you are trying to say?" Nick asked.

"You hired the best lawyer in town, as far as I'm concerned," Blues said. "But if you file that lawsuit, you're going to need a bodyguard, not a lawyer. If King is the bad man you think he is, he's bad enough to kill you, son, maybe even go after your grandparents to make sure they don't have any second thoughts. The way a killer thinks, that's a lot simpler than letting Lou kick his ass in the courtroom. Cheaper too. Like I said, Lou. Good speech. Bad idea."

"Kill me and my grandparents?" Nick asked. "You've got to be kidding, man! If I file this lawsuit and anything happens to us, King is the first one the cops are going to come after."

Blues nodded. "That's the way you and I think, but not King. He's been down that road already. He beats one murder rap, he starts thinking he can beat them all. Killing people isn't a risk to someone like him. It's the way to solve problems."

"So what am I supposed to do?" Nick pled. "Let him get away with it? Forget about it? That's bullshit, man!" Nick said, hands at his sides, fists clenched, eyes flaring, bouncing between Mason and Blues. "Come on, Mr. Mason! Help me out, here!"

Blues cut Mason off again. "It's not a perfect world, son. A lot of bad things happen and some of them can't be put right. Getting you or your grandparents killed would just be another one."

"That's enough, Blues!" Mason said, standing, putting his

hand on Nick's shoulder. "No one is going to get killed over a lawsuit." Mason stepped in front of Nick, shielding him from Blues's warning, ignoring his duet with King the night before. "If we have to, we'll get a restraining order to keep King away from Nick and his family."

"That so? How many pieces of paper does it take to stop a bullet?" Blues asked. "Rachel called me this morning. Said you and King had a little dust up last night at Camille's. Said she was worried about you. Said King threatened you if you filed that lawsuit. Rachel said he would've killed you on the spot if he could have figured how to get away with it. Lou, you want to do the dance with Whitney King, that's your business. Dragging this innocent boy into the mix, putting him in harm's way. That's something you should think twice about."

Nick crossed his arms, pressing his fists against his chin, blood flushing his face. Mason reached out to him. Nick turned away. Mason couldn't believe Blues was trying so hard to torpedo his case. He'd understand if Blues had voiced his concerns privately, but doing it in front of his client had only one purpose: frighten Nick into walking away. Blues had his own reasons for discouraging Mason, but Mason wouldn't let him hide behind concern for Nick's safety to sabotage the case.

"It's kind of late for you to be worrying about putting innocent boys in harm's way, don't you think, Blues," Mason said. "Or are you just trying to balance the books. Scare the piss out of Nick to make up for what happened to Ryan Kowalczyk."

Blues gave Mason a hard stare, his unblinking eyes erecting a wall between them. "The past is past, Lou. The dead don't need anybody else to die for them."

"Well, I'm not going to die for fucking Whitney King!" Nick said. "He might die, but not me!" He stormed out of Mason's office.

Blues shook his head and followed him.

Chapter 15

Mason slammed his office door, hoping the knob caught Blues in the back, wincing from the advice Blues had given Nick. Mason marched to his desk, ripped a handful of steel-tipped darts from a drawer, and let them fly at the circular target on the opposite wall, not satisfied until the darts punctured the rubber and fractured the plaster behind it.

Mason wasn't angry at Blues just because he'd interfered. He was mad because Blues was right and Mason had ignored the obvious danger to Nick the lawsuit would bring. He had gotten wrapped up in a personal fight with King, making the case about him and not about his clients. Killers didn't play by the rules. Mason was kidding himself to think that King would let him control the battlefield, choosing one where the only ammunition was words.

He had to admit that Mary Kowalczyk could be in danger too. A pardon for Ryan meant a public admission that King was the killer. It wouldn't matter to King that Mary didn't want any money. All King cared about was squelching any effort to resurrect the case against him. Mason couldn't blame him for that. Admitting the possibility that King would settle both cases by killing his clients underscored Mason's belief in King's guilt.

Mason called Mary, but her answering machine told him to leave a message. Mason told her to call as soon as she got home, that it was important.

Though he was concerned for their safety, Mason wasn't ready to quit. Not that easily. If he could put the case against King together before Nick's statute of limitations expired, he'd take his proof to Samantha Greer and get police protection for Nick and Mary.

If Samantha turned him down, he'd go to Blues. Blues was a hard man, living by his own often violent code. Mason had all but accused him and Harry of being responsible for Ryan's death, a charge more emotional than accurate. Harry and Blues had investigated a crime, taken the evidence to the prosecuting attorney, and let the system take over. A system Blues was the first to criticize for its failure to find the truth.

If Ryan Kowalczyk shouldn't have been put to death, it wasn't Blues' fault. Everyone except Blues would agree with that. He would hold himself responsible. That's the way his code worked. If Mason could convince Blues that Ryan was innocent, Mason would take his chances with the code, counting on Blues to pay his debt.

He opened the dry erase board, his eyes immediately drawn to Sonni Efron's name. The jury had a secret pact, Nancy Troy had said. It was time to talk to the jurors.

Shuffling through the boxes Nick had left him, Mason found a list of the jurors with a quick summary of their backgrounds. Holding the page in one hand, he added the information to the board.

Iver Clines   George Tasker
White, male, age 63   White, male, age 40

Retired machinist
Lives in Raytown
Married, 2 kids

Miguel Bustillo
Hispanic, male, age 36
Truck driver
Lives on west side
Divorced, no kids

Troy Apple
Black, male, age 22
Student,
Lives on east side
Single, one kid

Andrea Bracco
White, female, age 27
Secretary
Lives in Gladstone
Single

Judith Dwyer
Black, female, age 50
Nurse
Lives in Red Bridge
Divorced, no kids

Frances Peterson
White, female, age 36
Sells real estate
Lives in Brookside
Divorced, 1 kid

Insurance salesman
Lives in Romanelli
Divorced, 3 kids

Nate Holden
Black, male, age 44
Owns restaurant
Lives in Grandview
Married, 1 kid

Sonni Efron
White, female
Housewife, age 38
Kansas City
Married, 2 kids

Martella Garvey
Black, female
Teacher, age 38
Lives on east side
Married, 4 kids

Lisa Braun
White, female
CPA, age 41
Lives North KC
Single

Janet Hook
Black, female
No job, age 24
Lives east side
Single, 3 kids

The list looked like any other jury he'd ever seen. Blacks, whites, Hispanics. Married, divorced, single. White collar, blue collar, and unemployed. Nothing to suggest why they would have taken an oath of silence. At least one of them, Sonni Efron, was dead, another murder victim. Mason hoped her death would prompt the others to talk.

He opened the phone book, looking up each juror's name and realizing that his information was fifteen years old, jotting down the list of phone numbers that could belong to each. The hope that they all still lived in Kansas City, or that they were all alive, defied actuarial wisdom, but he didn't need all of them. He only needed one who would tell him the truth.

He got lucky with the first name on the list. Iver Clines was in the book, still listed in Raytown, a small city in eastern Jackson County.

"Is Mr. Clines home?" Mason asked the elderly woman who answered on the second ring.

"I'm sorry," the woman answered. "My husband passed away."

"Then I'm the one who is sorry," Mason said. "I hope you don't mind me asking, but when did he die?"

"Almost fifteen years ago. Hit and run. They never found the driver," she added, anticipating Mason's next questions.

Mason thanked her and hung up, imagining a wife who so missed her husband that she kept his name listed in the phone book fifteen years after his death. Equal parts devotion and denial, Mason guessed, the ache of Abby's departure simmering beneath his scar. He squeezed the phone, as if to force it to ring with Abby on the other end. She was too compulsive not to check her messages, too stubborn and angry not to ignore his.

Mason worked the phone into the late afternoon, leaving messages, crossing out numbers that didn't match, adding new names and numbers that might lead him to the jurors. He found George Tasker's brother who told him that George was dead, killed four years ago when someone accidentally shoved him off a crowded curb into the path of a bus, whoever it was disappearing in the confusion, never caught.

Miguel Bustillo's mother added her son's name to the list of deceased jurors, telling Mason her son had been shot in the face a year ago while parked at a truck stop, eating his dinner in the dark, the case still unsolved. Mason felt a jolt of his own when she said her son had been shot in the face. Sonni Efron had died the same way. He offered his condolences as Miguel's mother sobbed.

Mason couldn't confirm the fate of any of the other jurors, but he didn't like the trend. Two jurors killed in accidents that didn't sound like accidents. Two jurors shot in the face. Using a red marker, he wrote *dead* on the dry erase board across the names of Clines, Tasker, Bustillo, and Efron.

The odds that a third of the jury would die violently were too stunning to contemplate. The chances that their deaths were not connected to their jury service defied Mason's rule against coincidence. The likelihood that Blues was right about the danger of the lawsuit stuck in Mason's throat, prompting another call to Mary Kowalczyk and another message left on her machine.

Taking a break, he straightened the papers on his desk, coming across the obituary for his parents. He read it again, this time aloud, giving voice to the short story of their lives, trying to draw these distant relatives closer to him. His voice quivered at the end when he read the names of the six pallbearers: Jake Weinstein, Michael Rips, Randy Allenbrand, Doug Solomon, Frank Roth, Jeff Sanders.

They were names he'd never heard before. How could that be, he asked himself. Pallbearers were chosen for their close relationship to the deceased. Yet he'd never heard nor seen their names in his entire life. How, he wondered, could Claire omit them from his upbringing? If they were so close to his parents, why didn't they take an interest in him? It was as if another door had opened into his past, and darkness was the only thing on the other side.

Mason wrote the names on a piece of paper, tacking it to the cork on the inside of the dry erase board door. He opened the phone book again, anxious to learn whether pallbearers had a better survival rate than jurors.

Chapter 16

Mason closed the phone book without writing down a single number. He knew what the King case was about and what he wanted to ask the jurors. He didn't know what he would say to the pallbearers. Tell me about my parents, he could ask them. Another question: why don't I know you? Is there anything I should know about my parents that my aunt, my closest living relative, the woman who raised me, left out of the family history, because if there is, I would really like to know. And, while we're at it, do you have any idea why Claire kept the truth about my parents from me?

Real ice breakers, Mason admitted. Should warm these old folks right up. They would at least be older folks. Mason did the math, guessing they had been contemporaries of his parents then in their thirties, adding forty years, dividing their memories by the passage of time. The remainder a mix of what was and what should have been. He came back to the central question, cast in the tones of political scandals. What did Claire know and when did she know it? Mason wasn't ready to investigate his aunt, at least not until he gave her the chance to answer his questions first.

Linwood Boulevard is an east-west commercial artery that would have been called Thirty-third Street if the city hadn't named it after Mr. Linwood. Main Street runs north and south from the Missouri River through midtown, an entrepreneurial stretch that dwindles into a residential track south of the Country Club Plaza.

Claire's office was on Linwood, just east of Main, in a pre–World War II whitewashed stucco house, grand in its day, with a broad front porch, bay windows, and a gabled roof. The house had been bought, sold, and abandoned. Restored and subdivided into apartments, neglected by its tax-deduction driven owner, abandoned again. Claire bought it at a tax foreclosure sale, rehabbed it with Harry's help on weekends until she was ready to hang her shingle from the front door, her office on the first floor, her home on the second. She'd lived and worked there for a year.

"I lived in that house of yours for so long, I just got itchy. I'm glad you got married so I could give it to you and get rid of it," she said when she explained to Mason why she had bought the new house. "Though I'm just as glad you got it in the property settlement with Kate."

"What was the matter with the place you had downtown?" Mason had asked her.

"The loft was fine for a while. I liked being around the young people who lived there until they started calling me their house mother. The older I get, the more I need to keep changing things to keep life interesting."

The neighborhood was a mix of rough and rehabbed, box stores and liquor stores, down-and-outers and up-and-comers, midway between downtown and the high-rise condo gold coast of the Country Club Plaza. Claire's clients, she explained to Mason, felt comfortable there, finding encouragement in her ability to make something out of nothing, a task often too difficult in their own lives.

Claire was at her desk, working her way through a stack of papers. Glancing up with a smile when Mason walked in, she took off her reading glasses, leaving them dangling from a beaded chain around her neck. She had a big frame, adding an imposing physical dimension to the passion she brought to her causes, offering warmth to those who needed her, presenting an immovable object to those who opposed her. Claire ignored convention more than she defied it. She paid little attention to her white hair, wore no makeup, and was a fashion disaster, proving the last with the brown Capri pants and orange blouse she was wearing.

"Slow day?" she asked Mason, as he looked around her office.

Mason pursed his lips. "So-so," he answered.

"Well, mine isn't," she said, holding up a thick document. "Look at this," she said, shaking the papers. "This brief is two inches of utter crap. A crooked contractor duped my client into borrowing thirty thousand dollars to make improvements on a house that wasn't worth thirty thousand to begin with, did a lousy job, and left the house uninhabitable. That crook hooked my client up with a crooked finance company that loaned her the money and wants to foreclose because she can't pay and she shouldn't pay them a nickel. I sued the bastards for a hundred and one violations of every federal and state law I could think of and their weenie lawyers are trying to bury me in a paper blizzard."

"I wouldn't want to be those weenie lawyers or their crooked clients," Mason said.

"Neither would I," Claire agreed. "Now you didn't come here to listen to me rant. Sit down and talk to me."

Claire loathed beating around bushes. Mason took a chair opposite her desk, handing her his parents' obituary, the names of the pallbearers highlighted in bright yellow.

"Tell me about these men," he said.

"There's nothing to tell. They were pallbearers at your parents' funeral."

"Did you know them?"

"Of course I knew them. I chose them."

"Why haven't I ever heard their names before? They must have been my parents' closest friends."

Claire fingered the obituary like it was sharp-edged glass, studying the names. "I gave you this, and the newspaper article, so you could read for yourself what happened to your parents. I should have known that answering one question for you would only lead to another."

"More than one other question," Mason said. "The real question is why you've never told me any of this before and why getting anything out of you now is like pulling teeth."

"Tell me something," she said, leaning forward, elbows on her desk. "Did I do a bad job raising you?"

"No," he answered.

"Did you ever want for anything? Did you ever feel unloved, even for a second?"

"You know I didn't. But that's not the point."

"It is exactly the point," Claire said, stabbing the air with the side of her hand. "It's why you never asked, not once, about any of this. I told you what happened to your parents as soon as you were old enough to understand. I told you that your parents were good people and that was true. That was all you wanted to know. I took you to that damn cemetery so you wouldn't forget them."

She was right. Mason had never pushed Claire for more details. He'd only thought of his parents when he wondered what his life would have been like had they lived. He had no memories of their voices, touch, or love to make him miss them in anything but the abstract. He'd never explored their lives, content to grow up in a world that began with him and his aunt, as if he'd materialized out of the ether on her front step. Never wanting to know about the past, it was easy for Claire to keep him focused on the future and what he would make of it.

"I may not have asked then," he said, "but you didn't want me to ask either. Well, I'm asking now."

Claire held his stare, not answering. She was, he knew, incapable of lying to him, choosing silence instead. Mason finally nodded and stood, taking the obituary from her and leaving, neither of them saying another word.

Chapter 17

Mason hit the street. Waves of heat radiated off the sun-baked pavement, humidity rising in his path like a city swamp. He waded through it to his car parked around the corner a block away, his shirt sticking to his back like a poultice.

Three young black kids, barefoot, wearing shorts, no shirts, struggled with the plug on a fire hydrant, tiptoeing on the searing curb. An elderly black woman sat on her wooden stoop wearing a sun-faded flowered shift, begging shade from a bent tree. She fanned herself, watching the kids, a dog flat out on the brown grass next to her. The chrome door-handle on his car sizzled, the leather steering wheel too hot to hold, air inside the car stiff. Mason was oblivious to the kids and the woman who stared at him as he passed.

He jerked the key in the ignition and banged on the gas. The car jumped out from the curb, windows down, hot air escaping as the air conditioner played catch-up. Heading east on Linwood toward Mary Kowalczyk's neighborhood, he tried to make sense of Claire's silence, deciding that Nick

Byrnes had been right. Claire was trying to protect him from something.

Nick's parents had been murdered, the story of a car accident a thin cover for the brutal truth. There was no doubt Mason's parents had been killed when their car left the road. Was that it, then? Was his parents' accident not an accident at all? Did the person who left the rock on his parents' headstone do so out of guilt? Mason wouldn't let the questions go unanswered.

He called Mary again as he drove, hanging up on her answering machine, uneasy that she'd been gone all day. For a woman who, by her own admission, had few places to go, she'd been gone a long time. Mason pulled up in front of her house just as the temperature inside his car was approaching the no sweat zone.

Taking the steps two a time, he found no signs that Mary was at home. The curtains were drawn as they had been on his last visit. The house was silent, no footsteps answering when he rang the bell and rapped hard against the door. Her mailbox was mounted next to the door, the day's slim offerings still there—a catalog, an electric bill, and a sweepstakes offer.

Mason jiggled the doorknob but a deadlock bolt held it firm. Leaning into the picture window on the front of the house, he couldn't find a seam in the curtain to see inside. He dialed Mary's number again from his cell phone but her recorded voice repeated the instructions to leave a message.

He circled around to the back of the house where the gate on the chain link fence hung open on rusted hinges. A worn path led to a small screened-in porch, its door unlocked, the fine mesh black screen giving Mason cover as he tried the back door to the house, giving it his shoulder, the door yelping as the weak lock surrendered. Stepping into the kitchen, he called her name, softly at first, then loud. No one answered, the house was deaf.

He'd feel like a fool if she suddenly came home, trying to explain that he'd broken and entered because he was afraid that Whitney King might do her harm. He'd feel worse than a fool if he found her stuffed in a closet, his fears too real, his timing too late.

The house was small, the first floor cool, the second steamy, as she had said. The basement was dank and musty, the floor an unfinished slab, no signs of a freshly dug grave. Mason made fun of himself at the thought. The whole place was empty. It was clean and tidy, her clothes in closets and drawers. Her suitcase was under the bed and food for a week was in the refrigerator. It was the way she would have left everything if she was coming back.

Mason didn't know what else to do, so he sat in her front room and waited, searching the closets again when he got impatient, listening to her answering machine, his message the only one. He checked his voice mail for a message from Mary. Finding none, he paced in the small house until the sun retreated, then drew back the curtains and watched the street. An occasional car passed by; the street was quiet. The night wore on as Mason sat in the front room, kept company by the fish in the aquarium.

He turned off the lights and sat in the dark, thin illumination leaking in from the street. His eyes adjusted to the interior dusk, shapes and shadows visible in silhouette. He imagined Mary sleeping on the couch in the only cool room in the house, wondering how the poor people got by.

He thought about what she had done for Ryan. How she had given him life, then tried to save it and, when she couldn't, insisted on saving his memory. He thought about Elizabeth Byrnes and how she had saved Nick's life by covering him with a quilt and how he had honored his parents' memory by demanding justice for them. Last, he thought about his parents and their violent deaths. He had accepted their fate, demanding nothing, not even the truth. When he measured himself against Mary Kowalcyk and Nick Byrnes, he came up short.

The night passed as he took inventory of his life and those of his clients. The darkness didn't conceal a thing.

He held Mary's phone in his lap. It didn't ring. No one knocked at the door. She lived by herself. People left her alone. She was gone and no one would miss her. Except for him.

Chapter 18

It was one-fifteen on Friday morning when Mason woke Samantha Greer, rousting her out of bed. Samantha peered through the peephole of her front door, opening up, hair tousled, lips tight. She stood in her entry hall, keeping Mason outside, a purple tank top barely covering her panties, a pistol in one hand, close against her thigh.

"Who died?" she asked. "And it better be someone important, like the president."

Mason stared at her without meaning to; her breasts were escaping from her top, one ankle locked behind the other, her gun hand up on her hip, the other hand cocked against the door frame. Samantha caught his look, covering up with her arms, squaring her legs as Mason glanced away.

"Sam," a male voice called from upstairs. "What's going on? Who's there?"

"Nothing and nobody. Go back to sleep, Phil," she said over her shoulder, leaving the gun on a table in the hall, joining Mason outside as she pulled the door closed behind her.

Samantha lived in a neighborhood north of the Missouri

River. The river came down to Kansas City from Omaha, bending east toward St. Louis. The Kansas River cut across the plains, pouring into the Missouri at the river's bend. The two rivers were geographic quirks that divided the region into thirds. One-third was Wyandotte County and Kansas City, Kansas. Kansas City south of the Missouri, together with the suburbs of Johnson County, Kansas, made up the second slice. The part of the city north of the Missouri, called the Northland, was the last piece. In a tribute to tribalism, each region looked down on the other like a stepchild.

Samantha's subdivision was off of North Sixty-fourth Street, middle-class split levels and ranches. Not the kind of neighborhood where women hung out on their front steps in the wee hours, dressed only in their underwear, with or without guns.

"Thanks," he said.

"For what? Calling you a nobody?" she asked.

"No. For not shooting me. This is important."

"I'm listening," she said.

Mason explained, "I've got a missing client."

"And I've got office hours," she answered, turning around.

"Don't, Sam. Not so fast," he said, his hand on her arm. "Hear me out."

Samantha looked at him, shaking her head. "Okay. *Reader's Digest* version." Mason told her about Mary Kowalczyk. Samantha shook her head again, drawing figure eights with her toe.

"Your client give you a key to her house?" she asked Mason.

"Not exactly," he answered.

"This isn't a commercial for Hertz, counselor. Representing someone gives you permission to overcharge, not break and enter."

"You find Mary and ask her if she wants to file a complaint," Mason said. "I'll plead guilty."

Samantha puffed her cheeks, letting out the air, not hiding her annoyance. "Lou, you know how these things work. No one is a missing person for at least twenty-four hours. Adults with no history of mental illness or disability who don't come home are not missing persons for a lot longer than that. You're not giving me anything to get excited about. Who would want to hurt your client?"

"Whitney King. He knows Mary hired me to get a pardon for her son."

Holding up one hand, reaching for the door with the other, Samantha said, "Do you have any idea how crazy that is? A jury found King innocent. Getting a pardon for someone who was just executed for two brutal murders from a governor who denied him clemency and is running for re-election isn't exactly something Whitney King would lose any sleep over. Besides, he's probably a big campaign contributor and the governor cares a whole lot more about money from the living than he does pardons for the dead."

"I'll tell you what's crazy, Sam," Mason said, grabbing the handle on the door. "The jurors in King's case take a vow of silence and then start turning up dead."

"What are you talking about?" she said, sharpening her question.

"I'm talking about four out of twelve jurors who are dead. Two of them in accidents that probably weren't, and two of them shot in the face, including Sonni Efron. I haven't tracked down the rest of the jury yet."

"You may be certifiable this time, Lou, if you want me to believe that Whitney King fixed the jury in his murder trial fifteen years ago, then turned around and started killing the jurors to keep them quiet."

Mason smiled. Samantha's scenario fleshed out his own ill-formed suspicions. "Doesn't sound so crazy when you say it out loud."

"It's stupid!" Samantha said. "In the first place, the kid

was seventeen at the time. How's he going to fix anything, including his lunch? In the second place, why kill the jurors after all these years if they've kept quiet. And, if they haven't, once he kills one or two of them, the rest are going to fall all over each other talking so we'll protect them. None of which has a damn thing to do with your client, I might add."

"Sure it does," Mason said. "If Mary and Nick are out of the picture, I've got no reason to stir things up. It all stays quiet."

"So now you're telling me that Nick Byrnes is missing too?"

The door opened before Mason could answer. Phil, the voice from upstairs, handed Samantha a cordless phone. He was a few inches shy of Mason's six feet, soft in the middle, losing his hair. He was wearing an open terrycloth robe over boxer shorts and house slippers.

"It's for you," he said. Samantha took the phone, walking into her front yard, cupping her hand over the mouthpiece. Phil turned to Mason, "Phone rings more in the middle of the night than it did with my ex-wife, and she was a doctor, but at least no one knocked on the door."

"Sweet dreams," Mason told him as Phil trudged up the stairs, scratching his backside, the back of his robe bobbing like a tail.

Samantha cut small circles in the yard, Mason not able to hear her end of the conversation, moon shadows dancing through a red oak, splashing at her feet. Her call finished, she tucked the phone under one arm, chewing her lip, eyes narrowed, like she couldn't decide what to do with Mason. Thank him or smack him.

"We found your client," she said, arms folded over her chest again.

Mason crossed the short distance to Samantha, his shadow enveloping hers, his pulse jumping, knowing that cops didn't call each other with good news in the middle of the night.

"Where is she?" Mason asked.

"Not Mary. Nick. He's in the hospital."

"What happened?"

"Whitney King shot him."

Chapter 19

Nick Byrnes was at St. Joseph Hospital in south Kansas City, twenty miles and a lifetime from Samantha Greer's house. The light and siren on Samantha's car brushed aside what little traffic there was at that hour. Mason followed Samantha south on I-29, merging into I-35, crossing the Paseo Bridge over the Missouri River, all night gamblers still hitting on sixteen at the riverboat casino docked next to the bridge.

They picked up the Bruce R. Watkins Memorial Freeway on the east side of downtown, cresting a hill with a panoramic view of the skyline to the west and the Channel 5 television tower farther south, an exoskeleton patriotically illuminated in red, white, and blue that dominated midtown. Mason replayed what little Samantha had told him about the shooting.

"Looks like self-defense," she had said. "There's at least one witness who vouches for King, says Nick came after King with a gun. King tried to take it away from him and it went off."

"How many times?" Mason had asked, the question rising in his throat like bile. He couldn't forgive himself for letting Nick race out of his office, threatening King. Mason didn't take the threat seriously. He knew better, but blamed Blues anyway for inciting the boy.

"Once. In the chest. It's bad, but St. Joe's trauma docs are good. He's got a chance."

Mason had a lot more questions, but they would have to wait. They covered the twenty miles in fifteen minutes, their cars racing in tandem. Mason was a step behind Samantha as they passed through the ER on their way to the surgery waiting area. A uniformed cop picked them up, whispering an update to Samantha, glancing warily at Mason.

Samantha's partner, Al Kolatch, was already there, sitting with an elderly couple Mason guessed were Nick's grandparents. The woman rested her head on the man's shoulder, both of them white haired and slight, his arm around her. Both sets of eyes were red, the woman's face crumpled, the man's face hard. Kolatch fidgeted with his notepad, stirring a cup of coffee, forcing himself to stay in his chair. Comforting the unconsolable was not one of his strengths.

Samantha joined Kolatch, shaking hands with the man; the woman lifted her head for a moment, no strength for more questions. She motioned Kolatch to the other side of the waiting room, their conversation an exchange of murmurs and nods out of Mason's earshot. Samantha took Kolatch's place with the couple, coaxing a few more answers out of them while Kolatch briefed Mason.

"Your boy's in bad shape," Kolatch began.

"So I'm told," Mason said. "What went down?"

Kolatch looked at his notepad. "About eight o'clock last night, your client assaulted a Mr. Whitney King in the parking lot of his office building in the Holmes Corporate Centre just off I-435."

Mason knew the area. I-435 was the beltway around Kansas City. Holmes Corporate Centre was only a couple of miles east of the hospital. Office towers with an outer skin that reflected like mirrors.

"I know where it is," he told Kolatch. "What do you mean my client assaulted King?"

"Assault, Counselor. Threatening bodily harm. It's a Class B felony. Only since your client had a gun and threatened to kill Mr. King, it's assault with a deadly weapon and attempted murder. Both of which are Class A felonies. That's what I mean."

"That doesn't tell me what happened," Mason said. "Did Nick say anything? Was there an argument? Or am I supposed to believe Nick just walked up to King, stuck a gun under his nose, and King took the gun away and shot Nick?"

"Sorry, Counselor. Your client did better than that," Kolatch said without any sign of regret. "He was screaming at King about King killing his parents, that he wasn't going to let King get away with murder any more, crap like that. Same kind of threats it turns out he had been making by e-mail, only this time he delivered in person. King grabbed for the gun, it went off. End of story."

"King tell you about the e-mail?" Mason asked, remembering the copies Sandra Connelly had given him.

"Nope. His lawyer did. Good-looking gal, too, but I'm guessing she'd cut your nuts off for sport. King called her before we got to the scene. She was waiting for us downtown when we brought King in."

"Did you charge him?"

"With what? Self-defense is the law, Counselor. It isn't against the law."

Mason looked past Kolatch to Samantha. "Are those people Nick's grandparents?"

Kolatch nodded. "Martin and Esther Byrnes. Nice folks.

Don't seem right, though. Having their son and daughter-in-law murdered, then their grandson pulls a stunt like this. Some kids got no gratitude."

Mason wanted to assault Kolatch for his charitable disposition. "You don't cut any slack for a kid who's sleeping in the backseat of the car while his parents are beaten to death outside the car, then grows up knowing that the guy who did it is walking around everyday laughing in his beer about getting away with murder?"

"Whitney King was acquitted. That means he was innocent," Kolatch said.

"No, that means he wasn't found guilty. That's all it means," Mason answered. "How long has Nick been in surgery?"

"About four hours. One of the docs came out a while ago, said they'd be done pretty soon one way or the other."

"Where'd you learn your bedside manner, Kolatch?" Mason asked. "A meatpacking plant?"

"Wise guy," Kolatch said. "Sam told me."

"Yeah. She told me there was a witness. Who was it?"

"Can't beat this one," Kolatch said. "A priest. Name of Father Steve Ramsey."

Mason did a double take; his hand on Kolatch's shoulder, betting against an outbreak of priests in Kansas City named Father Steve. "Short guy, kind of heavy? Smells like an ashtray." Mason asked. "Tell me the name again?"

"Father Steve Ramsey," Kolatch said. "Hey, you know the guy. Am I right?"

"You've got a keen mind, detective," Mason answered. "Sam told me."

A doctor pushed open the door, pulling his surgical cap off his head, wadding it in his hands, his face as long as *War and Peace,* pulling up a chair next to the Byrneses. Samantha threw her arm around Esther Byrnes, layering it on top of Martin's. Mason sidestepped Kolatch, getting as close to the grandparents as he could without Samantha or Kolatch hustling him away.

"He's going to make it," the doctor said. Esther erupted in tears as Martin clamped down harder. "But we don't know how fully he will recover. The bullet fragmented and part of it is pressing up against his spinal cord. We can't get it out, at least not yet. It's too risky until he's a little stronger."

"Are you telling us he's going to be a cripple?" Martin Byrnes asked.

The doctor took a deep breath. "Your grandson is paralyzed and on a ventilator so he can breathe. The next forty-eight hours are critical. If we can keep him stable, go back in and get the rest of the bullet out, and if the cord is only bruised, he'll be okay. If not," he paused. "We've got some very good rehabilitation people. Advances are being made every day. I'm sorry," the doctor added, patting them both on the shoulder as he left.

Samantha motioned Mason out into the hall. "They don't want to talk to you," she told him.

"The grandparents?" Mason asked. "They don't even know who I am."

"I told them. They think this is all your fault."

"My fault?" Mason asked. "Whose gun was it? The grandfather's?"

"He kept it locked up. Nick found the key. Doesn't change anything for them. They said Nick hadn't been able to find a lawyer to take his case until he ran into you at Kowalczyk's execution. They were hoping the statute of limitations would run out and Nick would finally let it go. Then you told him what a great case he had."

"He does have a great case," Mason insisted.

"Save it, Lou. I'm not your audience. They said Nick came to see you yesterday. When he came home, he was really upset but wouldn't tell his grandparents why. What happened?"

"Sorry, Sam. You know that's privileged."

"Bullshit, Lou! Nick told his grandparents someone else was there besides the two of you. Who was it? Blues? Because if it was anybody not on your payroll, there is no privilege."

Mason knew she was right. The attorney-client privilege only applied to communications between him and Nick. If someone else was present who wasn't part of Mason's legal team, there was no privilege. Still, Mason wasn't going to incriminate his own client. He'd make Samantha work for that.

"Take it up with the judge," Mason told her.

"That kid is lying in there hooked up to a breathing machine with a bullet stuck against his spinal cord," Samantha hissed. "Talk to me!"

"Why? So you can charge him with a couple of felonies, and send him off to a prison hospital for rehabilitation with the rest of the disabled inmates. I'll pass," Mason told her. "Sorry I woke you."

Chapter 20

Mason added Blues to the list of people he woke up in the middle of the night. Only Blues wasn't asleep. He answered on the third ring, an Oscar Peterson CD playing in the background and a woman saying, "C'mon on, baby."

"Mary Kowalczyk is missing," Mason told him.

"She's not over here," Blues said.

Mason one-upped Blues with his own punch line. "Nick Byrnes went after Whitney King with a gun he stole from his grandfather. King shot him. Nick's going to live, but there's a good chance he'll be paralyzed."

"Why you bothering me up with all the good news?" Blues asked.

"Samantha Greer wants to talk to you about what Nick said when you dropped in on us yesterday. She thinks you'll tell her that Nick threatened to kill King. The prosecutor is going to give King the self-defense merit badge, charge Nick with a couple of felonies, and send him to the crippled kid's prison for rehab. That conversation isn't privileged unless you're working for me. I just thought you'd like to know."

"I hear you," Blues said, hanging up.

Mason hoped Blues would get off the sidelines. He knew Blues believed that Ryan Kowalczyk was guilty. Any regrets Blues may have had about Kowalczyk's execution focused on doubts about the system, not about Kowalczyk. Mason counted on Mary's disappearance to change Blues's calculus.

Blues had warned Mason about putting Nick in harm's way. Mason hoped Blues would realize he'd given the boy a shove of his own. He knew that Blues wouldn't make any concession speeches or humble apologies. He'd just show up.

Mason caught a few hours' sleep when he got home, stopped at the office to see if it was still there, and tried Mary's house again. It was still empty, the morning paper on the driveway. Mason took it inside, letting himself out the back. He walked the block, knocking on neighbors' doors, asking if anyone had seen Mary.

One man said he saw her leave the house around nine o'clock the morning before, watching her from his garage. He lived across the street and two houses closer to the corner, the route Mary would have taken to the bus stop. She was carrying a purse, the man said, nothing more. The man invited Mason in. Mason gagged on the odor of expired kitty litter; half a dozen cats lounged on the furniture, fur balls rolling across the floor like mini-tumbleweeds. The man didn't notice, giving Mason a yellow-toothed grin, glad for the company.

Mason called the bus company and worked his way through a bureaucratic minefield, finally reaching someone who claimed to know the names of the bus drivers and their routes.

"I'm sorry, Mr. Mason," the woman said. "We don't give out that information."

Mason hated bureaucrats almost as much as he hated having a tooth pulled slowly. He struggled with people who were trained to say no with more conviction than a captured spy reciting name, rank, and serial number.

"Tell me your name," Mason said.

"Why is that important?" she asked.

"Because I'm a lawyer investigating my client's disappearance and I want to spell your name correctly on the subpoena when I sue the bus company for obstructing my investigation and putting my client's life in danger."

"You don't scare me," the woman said.

"Good for you. I'll tell you what," Mason said, not up for the battle. "You can keep your name a secret. Just give me the bus driver's name. He might have been the last person to see my client alive and that scares me."

The woman hesitated, measuring her victory in how long she made Mason wait. "Gaylon Dickensheets," she said, breaking her convent vow of silence.

"Is that you or the driver?" Mason asked, pushing his luck.

"Stick to scary. Funny doesn't work for you. He gets off at four. Game over," the woman said.

Mason returned to the hospital early in the afternoon, feeling slightly hung over, a throbbing at the base of his skull and a buzz in his ears from lack of sleep. A crowd had gathered outside the hospital, a ring of television and radio news minivans hugging the perimeter. The shooting had made the local news. Each station carried footage of Whitney King leaving the police station accompanied by Sandra Connelly who kept repeating that King had no comment. Mason had expected the press to show up at the hospital, but he didn't expect the crowd.

Walking toward the entrance from the parking lot, he realized the crowd wasn't there because of the shooting. They worked at the hospital, many of them wearing surgical greens, nurse's uniforms, and white coats. They were milling around waiting for something to happen, reporters sharing in their impatience, the afternoon heat making them restless.

A caravan of sedans pulled up as Mason reached the curb, all heads turning to the cars. U.S. Senate candidate Josh Seeley popped out of the lead car, working the crowd as if he had four hands, shaking and back-slapping his way to a lectern decked in Stars and Stripes bunting near the entrance. Mason had a brief view as the crowd parted for the candidate. The doctors and nurses greeted Seeley with the sedated enthusiasm reserved for someone they knew would promise to respect them in the morning even if he wouldn't call again until the next election.

Abby and Mickey poured out of the second car. Abby reached the lectern seconds before Seeley, tap-testing the microphone, ducking out of view as the candidate raised his hands to quiet the crowd. Mickey stood off to the far side, counting votes, Mason guessed.

Mason held his ground, separated from Abby by the street that passed between the hospital and the parking lot, watching as she scanned the crowd, waiting for her head-to-head search to find him. She seemed to hold her breath when she saw him, brushing invisible lint off her suit before regaining her composure, making her way to his side of the street.

Mason watched her—smiling at everyone, her chin up, her eyes radiating confidence, her dark hair swept back—feeling the same jolt he had the first time he saw her. And the second time and every time since. She owned him. When she left town without telling him, it was like she had opened his chest again. He was running on fumes, one client down, another missing. Knowing she was back, but not for him, left him raw.

"I was going to call," she said, standing close enough for Mason that he could smell her perfume and hair, scents that hurt.

"When," he asked, "after the primary or the general election?"

Abby crossed her arms, the muscles in her neck tightening. "Don't turn this around. This is about you, not me. I can't live my life with someone who keeps painting a target on his back."

"What about Mickey?" he asked. "Did you tell him you got him the job with Seeley to punish me or to protect him from me?"

"You don't need to be punished," she said. "But the people who care about you need protecting."

Mason had no answer. He'd made and broken his promise to Abby, and wouldn't make it again. The scarf around Abby's neck was reminder enough that he couldn't keep it. Standing next to her, he felt like he was drowning. She was a lifeline just beyond his reach. Fragments of Josh Seeley's speech drifted back to them. Something about limits on malpractice lawsuits, the audience finally clapping like they meant it.

Abby broke their silence. "I don't want you following me around like this."

"I'm not following you," he said. "I didn't know you were going to be here."

"Then why are you here?" she asked, suddenly anxious, her eyes wide. "Is it Claire? Is it Harry? Are they all right?"

"They're fine," he told her, taking a deep breath, knowing she would find out anyway. "My client, Nick Byrnes, is here. Whitney King shot him. The police are calling it self-defense."

Abby swallowed hard, her mouth a silent cry, her eyes

filling. "And what do you call it? Diving in the dark water or self-destruction?"

She left him on the curb. Mason watched her wade into the crowd, joining in their cheers, taking her place behind Seeley, Mickey at her side. Mickey looked across the crowd, finding him and lighting up when Mason gave him a salute. Abby tugged at Mickey's sleeve, forcing him back to their business. Together, they ushered the candidate into his car, directing the troops to their next destination, gone again.

Mason found Esther Byrnes in the food court on the lower level of the hospital, the first floor rotunda giving him a view below. She was by herself, a tray of uneaten food in front of her. She was wearing the same blue slacks and pale green blouse she'd had on the night before. Trying to gauge her mood, Mason watched her for a moment before going downstairs.

"Mrs. Byrnes," he began when he reached her table. "I'm Lou Mason, Nick's lawyer."

She looked up at him, her face a clouded patchwork of wrinkles and sorrow, his name registering in the deepening downturn of her mouth. "Nothing's changed," she said. "They've got him sedated so he doesn't move around. Otherwise the bullet might press more against his spinal cord."

She gave him the news with flat, rote precision, looking away as if that should be enough to satisfy him and leave her alone. Mason forced a weak smile and pulled out a chair.

"You know, Nick's a strong kid. He'll pull through just fine," Mason said, her blank stare saying she knew no such thing. "Is your husband with him?"

She shook her head. "He went home. He can't take it. He couldn't take it when Graham and Elizabeth were . . . when they died," she said, choosing the easier explanation. "It's different for a mother, I think. We're used to the pain our children bring us. It starts when they're born and keeps on hurting with every scraped knee and broken heart. Fathers, I just don't know. Martin is like a lot of men. They're so full of their feelings they don't know what to do with them, so they just get all balled up and mad all the time."

"I've seen pictures of your son. Nick looks just like him," Mason said.

She nodded this time. "I don't know what to make of that," she said. "It's a bitter comfort, I suppose."

"I know you didn't want Nick to hire me, Mrs. Byrnes," Mason said. "But Nick wants Whitney King to be held accountable for what he did. That's really important to him and I think he's right to want to do that."

Esther looked at him, studying him as if she was only just then aware of his presence. "My son and daughter-in-law are dead, Mr. Mason. For no reason other than Whitney King decided to kill them. Now he's ruined Nick, maybe left him worse than dead. There's no way to hold him accountable for that. It's a debt that can't be paid."

Mason asked her, "What about Ryan Kowalczyk? Wasn't he guilty too?"

Esther shook her head, a rueful smile easing the burden on her face for a moment. "I never believed that. Never did," she said, clasping her hands together, her arms stretched out in front of her.

Mason pulled his chair closer to the table, leaning toward her. "Why not?"

"Ryan was a lost boy. You could see it in his eyes. He was sweet, tender. Good to his mother. I could tell, watching them in the courtroom. He could never have hurt my children."

Mason sat back, disappointed but not surprised that Esther had no proof of Ryan's innocence, just a grandmother's intuition. "What about Whitney King?"

Her face darkened. "He has the devil's cruelty," she answered. "And an ugliness about him that I've never seen. He killed my children because he could, no more than swatting a fly. I truly believe that, Mr. Mason. All through the trial, he acted like it was a lark, a high school field trip to the courthouse, like he knew he was going to get off. Sometimes he'd look at me, his eyes so black it made me cold."

"Then why didn't you and your husband sue him? It's easier to win a civil suit for wrongful death than it is to get a murder conviction."

Esther stood, putting distance between her and Mason's suggestion, waving one hand in front of him, the other shielding her heart. "No, no it isn't. Not with that one. You see what he's done. He's taken enough from us. That boy is a killer."

Chapter 21

Gaylon Dickensheets parked his bus in the company lot at exactly four o'clock. Mason had been there for fifteen minutes, marking the time as he waited in his car, knowing it was Gaylon's bus by the number on its side, 451, which corresponded to the legend in the route map he had picked up.

Gaylon drove an east-west route, covering the city's eastern border with Independence, Missouri, reaching into the west side along Southwest Boulevard, all the way to the Kansas state line. The route kept him south of the Missouri River and north of midtown, navigating an urban artery, a straight line distance of some thirty miles, longer with the zigs and zags of city streets.

Mason had found a picture of Mary when he returned to her house earlier that day, taking it with him to show people who might have seen her. It was a snapshot of her sitting at her kitchen table holding a cup of coffee, not posed for the camera, her sober expression hiding the vitality Mason had detected in her. The date was superimposed on the print, the picture taken in the last year. He found it in the kitchen, beneath the glass covering a small desk, along with other pictures, one of her, Ryan, and her husband, the rest pictures of Ryan before he was arrested.

Gaylon climbed down from the bus, a small, slender man with a button face, barely five-five, dwarfed by the rig he drove. Mason got out of his car, cutting across the lot.

"Mr. Dickensheets," Mason called out. The driver turned, shielding his eyes from the sun.

"Sure I am," Gaylon said as Mason approached.

"I'm Lou Mason," he said, extending his hand, the driver wiping his own against his pants, taking Mason's.

"Sure you are. The dispatcher said you wanted to talk to me about a passenger. That right?"

"That's right," Mason said, showing him Mary's picture. "Do you recognize this woman?"

"Sure thing. That's Mary Kay."

"Mary Kowalczyk?" Mason asked.

"The same. I like to give my regulars nicknames, you know. Makes the ride a little friendlier. I tease her about being that cosmetics lady. Tell her she should be driving one of them big pink Cadillacs instead of riding the bus. She always gets a kick out of that one."

"Did you pick her up yesterday?"

"Sure thing. On my morning run, nine-o-five."

"Where'd she get off?" Mason asked.

"Downtown, like she always does. Tenth and Main. Transfers to a southbound."

"She didn't happen to say where she was going, did she?"

"Didn't have to," Gaylon said. "Yesterday was Wednesday. She goes to the church every Wednesday. St. Mark's."

"What's she do there?" Mason asked.

"Volunteers. Helps out one of the priests, I think. Father Steve, she calls him. Mary's a real sweet little lady. Had a hard time, she has, but you'd never know it. Always has a nice word for me."

"Does she ride your bus on the way home?"

"Depends on when she goes home. Could be mine, could be one of the other buses. There's six of us drive this route. We all know Mary."

"You wouldn't mind checking with the other drivers, would you? Ask them if they gave her a ride home yesterday," Mason said, handing Gaylon a business card. "Call me and let me know what they say, will you?"

"Sure thing. Say, she's okay isn't she?"

"Yeah," Mason answered. "Sure thing."

St. Mark's Catholic Church was at Forty-first and Main, a limestone cathedral, a parsonage, and a high school on ten acres of ground surrounded by a high wrought-iron fence. Mary had attended the church for thirty years, she had told Mason. Ryan Kowalczyk and Whitney King had attended the high school, and played their last basketball game in its gym.

A bronze dedication plaque set in stone at the entrance marked the cathedral's completion in 1937. The school building was a mix of old and new, the most recent addition still under construction, a brightly painted sign promising it would be ready by the start of the fall semester.

It was late in the day. Parishioners arrived for mass and Mason followed them into the church, not certain where to go. Most people gave him a friendly nod though a few gave him wary looks reserved for strangers. Mason was suddenly aware of being Jewish.

He rarely attended synagogue services, not even belonging to a congregation, another sore point with Abby, who had extracted his promise to attend services for the Jewish

New Year and Day of Atonement, the High Holidays coming in the fall. That was before Abby hit the campaign trail. Though he was certain a dose of atonement would do him good, he doubted whether Abby would save him a seat.

Mason's experience in Catholic churches was limited to weddings and funerals. He'd never attended mass; the prospect of doing so now just to track down Father Steve made him feel like he was trespassing.

He stood at the door to the sanctuary for a moment as a young priest greeted people as they came in, sunlight fracturing into rainbow rays as it cut through stained glass. People took their seats on wooden pews with red velvet cushions matching the thick carpet. Mason retreated outside to wait for the end of the service, figuring to ask the priest where he could find Father Steve.

Father Steve was Mary's priest. He was also a priest to Whitney King and his family. Two families. One rich and one poor. It made sense that Father Steve would maintain his relationships with both Mary and Whitney, even after all that happened.

Still, Mason was troubled by the priest's insistence that Ryan had confessed to murdering Graham and Elizabeth Byrnes, a confession that was unsupported by Ryan's last words, Ryan's mother, or Mason's gut feel from reading the trial transcript. Now Father Steve was the sole witness to Whitney's claim that he had shot Nick in self-defense. Adding the priest as the last person who may have seen Mary Kowalczyk put Mason's trust in coincidence to a real test. He wasn't ready to accuse Father Steve, but he had questions for the priest and he wouldn't accept the answers on faith.

Chapter 22

Mason wandered over to the school, skirting the construction site, getting a close look at the artist's rendering of the structure being built. The main entrance to the school was blocked off. A sign announced the new administrative wing made possible by the Christopher King Trust, Whitney King, Trustee. Another sign identified King Construction Company as the general contractor. Mason decided Whitney was building a stairway to heaven.

The construction crew had fashioned a temporary entrance to the school. A lax workman had left it unlocked at the end of the day. Mason took advantage, ducking inside, the hallways stuffy, air-conditioning being saved for the school year. The lights were off, but sunlight made its way from tall classroom windows to rectangular-shaped windows laid end-to-end like dominos along the interior wall above rows of lockers, painting the halls a smoky gray.

Mason had graduated from Southwest High School, a mile or two south of his house, a big city public school with big city public school problems—not enough money, motivated students, or interested parents. Mason managed to get a decent education anyway. Claire told him that four years spent with people who didn't look, live, or think like he did was his enrichment program.

The gym was tucked onto the back of the school, an addition made in 1955. A trophy case displayed accumulated hardware; basketball team rosters were engraved on plaques hung on the wall outside the gym. Mason traced the ten-member teams through the years, finding Ryan Kowalczyk's and Whitney King's team, Whitney's name was preserved along with those of eight other boys. Ryan's name was missing—a blank spot in its place.

"It was easier for the school to pretend he'd never been here than to try to forget what happened," Father Steve said. Mason spun around, finding the priest behind him. The priest apologized, "I'm sorry. I didn't mean to startle you, Mr. Mason. They teach us to walk quietly at the seminary." He smiled at his joke and Mason smiled back.

"Makes it easier to sneak up on the sinners," Mason said.

"Oh, I don't have to worry about that. God catches all sinners eventually," Father Steve said. "Like me and this dirty habit of mine," he continued, taking a pack of cigarettes from his pants pocket. "I can't sneak a smoke in the church, so I sneak one at the school. How about that?"

Mason couldn't help smiling again. Father Steve was short, stocky, and willing to make fun of his shortcomings. A benign, soothing combination Mason was certain put congregants at ease. Father Steve hadn't shown such self-effacing charm at Ryan's execution or in their last prickly exchange in front of Mary's house. Since then, Mary had disappeared and Nick Byrnes had been shot right before his eyes, jolts that should rattle, not calm.

Maybe, Mason thought, the priest was just more comfortable on his own turf, enjoying an ecclesiastical home-court advantage.

"I imagine there are worse sins," Mason said.

"Would you like the complete list?" Father Steve asked.

"No thanks. I've got my hands full with murder."

Father Steve pulled a cigarette from the pack, tapped the end of it against his palm, lighting it, drawing hard, the smoke working its way through him, thin vapors escaping from his mouth and nose. "You've chosen one of the greatest sins, taking another's life."

"When Graham and Elizabeth Byrnes were killed, it was murder. When Ryan Kowalczyk was executed, it was justice. Sin is a tricky thing."

"Not really, Mr. Mason. Killing is killing. The church opposes capital punishment unless executing the offender is the only way of protecting society against an unjust aggressor, a circumstance the pope says is virtually certain never to exist. There's always a way to protect people. That's what jails are for."

Mason asked, "Is it a greater sin if the state executes an innocent man?"

"No life is more valuable than another, though Ryan Kowalczyk was not innocent. He confessed to me, as you heard me tell his mother."

"I believe Ryan was innocent," Mason said.

"Then we're both men of faith, Mr. Mason. We just believe different things to be true. In my world, faith is proof enough of the existence of God. In yours, belief in a man's innocence doesn't overrule a jury's verdict."

"Juries make mistakes. That's not a matter of faith. It's a matter of fact," Mason said.

"This jury struggled with the truth until they found it.

Whitney's father told me they were deadlocked for two days before they reached a verdict on the third day. You're entitled to your own struggle."

Mason studied the priest for some sign that he knew the significance of what he had said. Ryan's lawyer, Nancy Troy, knew about the deadlock, as did Harry Ryman. Father Steve had added himself and Whitney's father to that inner circle. Rachel's question about how Nancy and Harry had known took on added significance.

"The jury refused to talk with anyone about their deliberations. How did Whitney's father know what had happened?"

The priest flicked the ash from his cigarette, an involuntary twitch that matched his stuttered answer. "He didn't . . . say. Maybe . . . he just assumed," he said, looking down the hall to avoid Mason's stare.

"Did you attend the trial? Did you talk with the jurors?" Mason asked, homing in.

Father Steve's shoulders sagged. "I ministered to both Ryan and Whitney, and their families."

Mason stepped toward the priest, backing him against the wall. "I'm sure you were a comfort to them, Father. I'm more interested in the jury and why you're trying so hard not to answer my question. The jury was deadlocked for two days. Something happened that made them convict Ryan and acquit Whitney. What do you know about that?"

"The jury found Ryan guilty. He confessed to me," the priest said dully as if he was repeating a catechism.

"Ryan was innocent. I'm going to prove that."

"And then what?" Father Steve asked, glancing at Mason.

"You tell me, Father. Is it a sin to let an innocent man die?"

The priest drew on his cigarette. "If you know he's innocent and you remain silent, that's a grave sin."

"The sin of silence. Where does it rank on your list?" Mason asked.

"It's one of the worst," the priest said, his voice steeped in sadness. He moved away from the wall, putting space between him and Mason. "Our sins reflect our weaknesses as human beings. Many of them come from the things we want. Sex, money, power. The sin of silence is different. It comes from fear and it condemns the innocent whom the guilty are afraid to save."

"Is that what happened when Whitney King shot my client, Nick Byrnes? Were you afraid to save him?"

The priest took a final drag, the tobacco glowing red, the smoke slithering off his face. "I thought Mary was your client."

"They both are and they both want the same thing. To prove that Whitney King killed Graham and Elizabeth Byrnes."

"And now you would add the shooting of Nick Byrnes to Whitney's list of crimes?"

"Nick was no match for Whitney, even if he had a gun. You were there. Tell me what happened."

"Oh, with that gun, that boy was more than a match for anyone," Father Steve said. "He was screaming at Whitney, threatening to kill him. I was a witness and he would have killed me as well. If Whitney hadn't stopped him, both us would be dead."

"Describe what happened, Father. Give me the blow-by-blow."

Father Steve sighed. "I don't do play-by-play commentary, Mr. Mason. Especially when I'm scared to death."

"Give it a try, Father," Mason said.

The priest took a deep breath, his cigarette down to a stub. "All right. We came out of the office building. The boy was there, like he was waiting for Whitney. He was waving the gun around at first, carrying on, as I said. I recognized him from the execution. I told him that I understood his pain but that he was making it worse, not better. I tried to calm him, but he wouldn't be calmed. He just got more upset. Then he pointed the gun straight at Whitney. Whitney grabbed his arm. They struggled. The gun went off."

Mason didn't know enough yet about what had happened to argue. He just wanted to get the priest committed to a version he'd have to live with. "Why were you with Whitney King last night?"

"You ask me that question as if I was somehow a suspect too. Do you include me in your conspiracy, Mr. Mason? Is that why you asked about those who stood by silently and let Ryan be executed? A boy I baptized? The child of a woman who has been at my side for thirty years?"

"I've known people to do worse, Father. With or without God on their side. I don't apologize for doing my job. You can tell me now or tell me in court."

The priest's jaw hardened for an instant, his eyes narrowing; then a small smile crept into the corners of his mouth as he relaxed. "Money, Mr. Mason. The church needs it and Whitney has it. My job is to ask him for it. It's demeaning but necessary. Is that all?"

"Almost. That woman who has been at your side for thirty years has disappeared. Do you know anything about that?"

"Mary's disappeared?" Father Steve asked, hands at his sides, mouth open. "What do you mean?"

"She's missing. She left home yesterday, got on a bus to come here and see you. She never made it home."

"Am I supposed to have spirited her away? Come now, Mr. Mason."

"Was Mary here yesterday?"

"Of course she was. She volunteers every Wednesday, helping out in the office, whatever needs to be done."

"You saw her, then?"

Father Steve dropped his cigarette to the floor, grinding it beneath his heel. "Yes, Mr. Mason," he answered with diminished patience. "I saw Mary. I spoke with Mary. I saw Mary leave. Now what do you mean she didn't go home?"

Mason studied the priest, thinking of him as any other witness, evaluating his demeanor, his motive for telling the truth or not, his interest in the outcome of the case, conceding that his collar enhanced his credibility.

"Just that," Mason said, still pressing, "she's disappeared and you're the last person to have seen her alive."

"I hope you are not such an alarmist with all of your clients," Father Steve said. "Mary told me she was going away for a few days. She said she might go visit her husband. They never divorced, you know. He called her after Ryan's death."

"Did she say where her husband was living?" Mason asked.

"Omaha, I believe she said."

"Well, then. I'm sure she'll be back soon," Mason said, his sarcasm lost on the priest.

"Of course she will," Father Steve said. "I've got to get back. If you'll excuse me."

"One last thing. Something you said bothered me," Mason said.

Father Steve stuck his hands in his pockets, rocking back on his heels, his smile and his patience flattening out. "Try me, Mr. Mason. I'm a priest. I specialize in things that bother people."

"Why do you suppose Mary would go to Omaha for a few days and leave her suitcase under her bed?"

Father Steve stopped rocking, tilted his head to one side, biting the corner of his mouth. "I suppose," he answered softly. "She had two suitcases."

Chapter 23

Certainty is the sum of need and faith. Wisdom is the remainder of living. Knowledge is the division of doubt by facts. Truth is the product of them all, Mason repeated the math Claire had taught him when he was growing up as he jogged toward the Plaza on Saturday morning before most people were out of their houses. The sky teased the city with the promise of rain, the sun burning through a low layer of gray clouds like dry kindling.

Mason was certain that Ryan Kowalczyk was innocent and Whitney King was guilty, though his certainty was the sum of need and faith, as was his belief that Claire was hiding the truth about his parents. He rejected the wisdom of Harry and Claire who said leave well enough alone. He had yet to find the facts that would divide their doubts. The truth still eluded him.

He ran east along Brush Creek, a landscaped tributary of the Missouri River that defined the southern border of the Plaza. He looped back, finding Tuffy waiting for him, thumping her tail for breakfast as he carried the morning paper inside. The headline read "Hot Streak Breaks Record," nothing selling better than bad news turned into a spectator sport.

The toll was charted in a sidebar column with numbers followed by the calamity they represented. Forty-two days without measurable precipitation. Nineteen days above ninety-five degrees. Eleven power outages due to high demand for electricity. Eighty-three people admitted to area hospitals for heat exhaustion. Sixteen people dead throughout the state from heat-related causes, five of them from Kansas City.

Mason took the paper with him to his office, posting his personal tally for the week on the dry erase board. One execution witnessed. One client missing. One client critically wounded. One girlfriend lost. Two best friends pissed off. One closest living relative maybe not so close. His numbers were smaller, but the toll bore down on him like a personal heat wave.

What made it worse was how little he had to show for it, getting pimped by a priest the highlight. I suppose she had two suitcases, Mason repeated the punch line, throwing another dart across his office, taking little satisfaction in the puff of plaster as it stuck in the wall, tail feathers vibrating. Maybe she did. Mason didn't think so.

He tried directory assistance for Omaha. There was no listing for Vince Kowalczyk. Mickey had convinced him to subscribe to an Internet service that promised to find anyone, anywhere in the United States for twenty-five dollars, as long as you had a Social Security number. Otherwise, the most you could hope for was a list of people with the same name. Mason booted up, striking out on Vince, the Web site practically accusing Mason of making up the name.

He did the same with a few of the jurors' names, shooting craps each time, cursing Mickey until he figured out how to cancel the Internet service. At least he was back on track with the one approach that made sense. Find a juror. One that was alive. One that would tell the truth.

Giving the computer another chance, Mason logged onto the city's Web site, clicking his way to the vital records page, certain he could do a quick search of death certificates for the jurors. They had lived in Kansas City at the time of the trial. If they had died in Kansas City since, the city would have a record of it. The city did, but he had to mail in his request with the date of death and the deceased's Social Security number, and wait four to six weeks for a response. The Web site was a cyberspace version of you can't get there from here.

He left a message for Rachel Firestone who called him back ten minutes later. "What's going on?" she asked.

"How far back do the paper's obituary records go?" Mason asked.

"Like everything else. To the beginning of time. You should read Moses's obit. It takes up five books."

"Jewish newspaper humor must be an acquired taste," Mason told her. "If I give you a list of names, can you check to see if they made the obituary page?"

"As long as I can write about it if it's a good story."

"I've got eight names. They all show up, you can write a book," he said, giving her the information.

"Okay. I surrender. Who are they?" Rachel asked.

"They were jurors on the King and Kowalczyk case. The other four jurors are dead. Two of them in accidents that don't pass the smell test. Two of them shot to death. In the face. Sonni Efron was one of them."

Rachel whistled. "What are the odds?"

"Don't try to figure the over-under. Just run down the names. Let's see who's vertical and who's horizontal."

* * *

Mason wanted to talk to Whitney King. He wanted to hear King's story about shooting Nick Byrnes. He wanted King to explain his relationship with Father Steve. He wanted to watch King's reaction when he asked King about Mary Kowalczyk's disappearance. He wanted to talk to King in private, off-the-record, counting on King's arrogance to tell him more than he would in front of witnesses, even if he were under oath. Especially under oath.

Mason threw another dart at the wall, knowing he couldn't talk to King. Knowing that he couldn't drop in on King at his office, arrange to run into him at the gym, or invite him over for dinner. Not because King wouldn't talk to him. Mason bet he would. Mason couldn't talk to King because the Model Rules of Professional Conduct for lawyers prohibited a lawyer from communicating directly with an adverse party that the lawyer knows is represented by counsel.

Any communications had to be in the presence of the adverse party's lawyer unless the lawyer agreed otherwise. Sandra Connelly was King's lawyer and would never agree to let Mason go one-on-one with Whitney King.

Mason plucked the darts from the wall, paced off ten steps, turned, and fired again, this time hitting the center of the dart board and laughing. Not at his lucky shot, but at the absurdity of worrying whether talking to a killer without his lawyer violated the Model Rules of Professional Conduct. Killers should have such problems, Mason thought. Rule number one of the Model Rules for Murderers. A murderer shall be prohibited from killing members of more than one generation of a family.

Each state had a disciplinary committee that reviewed complaints against lawyers for violating the Model Rules. Mason imagined a similar body for murderers, made up of the best and the brightest killers, admission by secret handshake, no doubt bloody. A liberal-minded committee certain to extend the prohibition to include kidnapping and crippling family members of prior victims because if killers started hoarding their victims, there wouldn't be enough for everyone else.

Mason unleashed his last dart, wondering where he could get a radar gun to clock his speed. He picked up his phone and punched in Sandra Connelly's number, not surprised to find her in her office on Saturday.

"I want to talk to your client," Mason said. "Without you."

"Lou?" Sandra asked.

"The one and only," he answered.

"Are you drunk or just out of your mind?"

"Do you have a preference?" he asked her.

"If you're drunk, you'll sober up. If you're out of your mind, there's not much I can do for you."

"I'm serious, Sandra. I want to talk to Whitney King alone."

"What possible reason would I have to agree to that?" she asked.

"I want to know what happened with Nick Brynes. I don't want a sanitized version that passes through your filter and gets me nowhere. I want the truth."

"In the first place, I'll ignore the implication that I would let a client lie to you or anyone else. In the second place, if I agreed, I'd be committing malpractice and you know it. In the third place, who the hell do you think you are that the rules don't apply to you?"

Mason took a deep breath. Sandra was right and he knew it. "Okay, okay. I'll tell you what. Just let me talk to him. You can sit next to him and tell him to shut up anytime you want."

"You know, Lou. There's a procedure for this. It's called filing a lawsuit. Then you can subpoena my client to give a deposition and ask him anything you want. Why should I give you two bites at the apple?"

"Because there isn't time. Mary Kowalczyk is missing. I need to know what King knows about that too."

"Why would you think he knows anything about it? You can't blame him for everything that happens to your clients. If you lost your client, call the police, not me."

"Listen, Sandra. I know it's your job to defend Whitney, but let me give you a game summary so far. He killed Graham and Elizabeth Byrnes. Four out of the twelve jurors who let him get away with it are dead, the last one shot to death this week. Whitney shot Nick Byrnes and my money says he did it because he could, not because he had to. Mary hired me to put a legal beating on your boy and then she disappears. And I'm leaving out the potshots at my living room window and late night heavy breathing phone calls, both courtesy of your client. Are you getting the picture here?"

"I'm getting a picture of someone who I used to think was a pretty good lawyer who needs to get a grip. When you get one, call me," she said, hanging up.

Chapter 24

That went well, Mason said to himself, hands on his hips, surveying his office. He was stuck and didn't have the traction to get moving. Even if he did, he had no idea which direction to go. The phone rang and he grabbed it, hoping Sandra had reconsidered.

"Hello?" Mason asked.

"This here is Albert from the cemetery. I'm looking for a fella name of Lou Mason."

"Hi, Albert. I'm Mason."

"You the one what gimme twenty dollars to call you if someone visited your momma and daddy's grave?"

"That's me," Mason said. "I was there the other day. Asked you about someone leaving a rock on their headstone. You told me about Sonni Efron's funeral. I gave you a business card with the money."

"Okay, then," Albert said. "I guess it's you."

"It's me. What do you got for me, Albert?"

"Someone come by this morning. Left another of them

rocks, a real smooth one, shiny too. But I left it alone. I'm not messing with nobody's grave. I just dig 'em."

"Did you get a look at the person?"

"No, sir. I surely didn't. They was too far away. Looked like a woman though, course you can't really tell the way some people dress and all, and the sun was kinda of in my eyes."

Mason sighed. Albert's call was another wisp of information that evaporated without adding anything. "Thanks for calling, Albert. She shows up again, there's another fifty if you get a name."

"Now hold the phone there, Mr. Lou-fifty-dollar Mason," Albert said. "Marty, he was working down along the wall near the street. I hollered down at him, did he get a look at her. Marty says at who, and I holler back at him, that woman what put a rock on the Mason headstone. And Marty, he hollers back there's a woman pulling out from the curb right then, must be her on account of there ain't nobody else around there but him and me. So Marty, he writes down her license plate."

Mason grinned for the first time in a week. "Albert, you and Marty are going out for the biggest steak dinner my money can buy. Give me the tag number."

Albert recited it, telling Mason he liked his steak well done. Mason thanked him again before making another call.

Harry Ryman picked up on the second ring.

"Harry, it's Lou. Can you get someone in the department to run a plate for me?"

Harry hesitated, clearing his throat. "The chief is clamping down on that sort of freelancing since I retired, from what I hear."

Mason didn't know whether that was true or not, but he knew that Harry could get the plate run in a heartbeat even if the chief had to do it himself. Harry was no more in the mood to help Mason prove Ryan Kowalczyk was innocent than he had been the last time they'd talked.

"It's got nothing to do with the King case, Harry. It's something else. Something personal. I'd really appreciate it," Mason added.

Mason listened to Harry breathe. Harry finally said, "Give it to me. I'll see what I can do."

"Thanks, Harry. One other thing," Mason added, not wanting Claire to know what he was doing. "Keep this between you and me, okay?"

"Sure, Lou. I can do that."

"Wait a minute," Mason said before Harry could hang up.

"What?" Harry asked, his meter running.

"You remember telling me that the jury in the Byrnes murder trial was deadlocked for two days before they reached a verdict on the third day?"

"Yeah, so what?" Harry asked.

"Nancy Troy told me that the jury refused to talk to anybody after the trial. How did you know they were deadlocked?"

"Because, Clarence Darrow, they hadn't reached a decision."

"That doesn't mean they were deadlocked. They could have been working through the evidence, talking about it. You and Nancy said the same thing. The jury was hung up and then something happened. How did you know that?"

Harry was silent for a moment, Mason visualizing him as he called up his memory of the trial. Harry remembered the details of every case he ever worked. Mason waited patiently.

"It was the priest," he said at last. "You remember the priest at the execution?"

"Father Steve. He's practically my new best friend," Mason said.

"He didn't miss a day of the trial. He was the one who told me."

"Father Steve says that Whitney's father told him about the jury," Mason said.

"Whitney's father didn't know squat. He never got within a mile of that courtroom."

Mason rode the surge of energy he always got when he put things in motion. It wasn't much but it was better than whining and throwing darts at his defenseless wall. He drummed a pen against his desk, shuffled stacks of paper, wiped off the dry erase board and started a new mosaic, linking names with lines, broken and solid. He was ready to try anything to nurture his rekindled momentum.

He stood back from the board, the pattern plain. Father Steve was at the center of this new universe. The Kowalcyzks and the Kings were his parishioners. He was the last one to have seen Mary and the one witness to the shooting of Nick Byrnes. His church depended on Whitney's money.

The latest flake of suspicion was even more intriguing. Father Steve knew that the jury had been deadlocked, though he shouldn't have known anything about their deliberations. His claim that he had learned that fact from Whitney's father didn't wash with Harry's memory.

Mason conceded the vagaries of fifteen-year-old memories; he'd won enough cases by convincing juries that memory had an accurate half-life of minutes, not years. Unless it was Harry's memory. None of this made the priest guilty of anything, but all of it made Mason wish for a seat next to Father Steve the next time he made confession.

Mason asked himself what angles he wasn't working, what rocks he was stepping over instead of turning over. Vince Kowalczyk, he realized, might not be in the Omaha

DEADLOCKED 171

phone book, but Mary said he was a carpenter, which meant he could be in a union. Mason got the phone number of the Omaha local from directory assistance. A human being answered his call instead of an artificial voice telling him their options had recently changed.

"I'm looking for someone who may be a member of your union. His name is Vince Kowalczyk. I am an attorney representing his wife, Mary. It's very urgent that I talk to him," Mason explained.

"Hold on," a man said, asking someone named Jim if it was okay to give out membership information. Mason eavesdropped from his end of the conversation. Jim said to take the guy's name and we'll give the message to Vince, let Vince call the guy if he wants to.

"Works for me," Mason said, leaving his phone number when the man repeated the message.

His paper shuffling brought the clipping about his parents' accident back to the surface, Mason picking it up again, asking himself the same questions. What was he missing? The article told only part of the story: how the car went off the road. Mason wanted to know why. The article said nothing about witnesses, but that didn't mean there weren't any. Their names would be included in the police report. Mason picked up the phone again.

"Detective Greer," Samantha said.

"What's the best way for me to beg a favor?" Mason asked.

"Dial another number," she answered.

"Too late. I'll settle for the second best way. I need an accident report."

"A car accident? You've got to be kidding. Get off your ass, go to the records department, pay your ten dollars, and wait for the mail. Just like everybody else."

"I would, except for one thing. This accident happened

forty years ago. No records clerk is going to lose any sleep tracking that down unless it's an order instead of a request."

"What's so important about an accident that happened forty years ago? A little late to file a lawsuit, isn't it?" Samantha asked.

"It's my parents' accident," Mason answered. "They were killed. I never knew the details. Now I want to know."

"I'll buy that if it will keep you out of trouble for a while," she said. "Friday afternoon is no time to ask someone to start a search like this. Can it wait until Monday?"

"Monday would be fine. And, thanks, Sam."

Mason wondered if the accident report would tell him why someone was visiting his parents' grave now. The accident happened on August 1 forty years ago. Today was July 19. There was no way to know when the rock Mason had found had been left there. It could have been a week, a month, or a year.

Mason couldn't remember when he'd last visited his parents' grave or whether there were any rocks on the headstone. But someone had left another rock today. Mason knew the question, writing it on the board, even if he didn't know the answer. *Why July 19?* Then, Mason added another question. *Who left the rock?*

Mason didn't have answers, but at least he had questions. He'd kick-started his case and peeled open his past. Now all he could do was the one thing he hated to do most of all. Wait.

Chapter 25

There's only so much heat a city can take. Some people shrug it off at first, declaring over cold beer and barbecue that it augurs for a hard winter and pass the beans, please. Like they'd written *The Old Farmer's Almanac*. Others claim to like the heat, thumping their chests as they jog or paint the house while the sun is at its zenith, their faces rigid with surprise when the rest of their bodies wilt, somebody calling an ambulance for them if they're lucky. Then there are those who go to the mattresses, cranking up the air-conditioning, watering their lawns at noon, flying their I'll-be-goddamned-if-anybody's-going-to-tell-me-what-to-do flags every time the mayor invokes another emergency heat ordinance.

But stoke up the blast furnace long enough on people who struggle every day to hold their lives together in the midst of money problems, job problems, family problems, and the heat starts burning them down like a wildfire on a New Mexico mountain. Short tempers get shorter, disappearing in a swallow of whiskey or in the crack of an insult. And people start killing each other.

A local shrink said as much on the Channel 6 evening news Monday night, a week and a day after Ryan Kowalczyk was executed, a legal killing that didn't offend the laws of nature or cause the distress that an outbreak of weekend fights and domestic disturbances had generated.

Two Hispanics in a bar on Southwest Boulevard fought over whether one had insulted the other's girlfriend, both of them too drunk to know for certain. The fight ended with the boyfriend's throat ripped open by the jagged edge of a broken bottle of tequila. The boyfriend bled out. The girlfriend grabbed a table knife, snapping the blade off between the other guy's ribs. One dead, one wounded. The girlfriend in jail.

North of the river, two brothers fought over a gold cap for the younger brother's tooth. He'd left it in the older brother's car and the older brother offered to sell it back to him for thirty dollars. The younger brother decided it was cheaper to cap his brother with a .38.

On the east side, rival black gangs cruised up and down Prospect Avenue, trash talking until respect and disrespect turned into guns and knives, the cops firing tear gas and busting heads. Two dead, eight injured, two of them cops.

In Mission Hills, a part of town where only the hired help spoke Spanish and the only cruising was done on a ship, a bank president grilling steaks dumped hot coals on his drunken wife when she confronted him about his latest mistress. The banker told the cops his wife was screaming so loud, he thought he'd give her something to scream about.

Mason half listened to the news, finishing a cold beer and short end of ribs as he leafed through part of the King file he'd brought home from the office. Setting the file aside, he replayed his weekend. Tuffy nudged his thigh until he shared the ribs with her.

Friday night, he'd found Josh Seeley's campaign Web

site, clicking on the candidate's itinerary, toying with the notion of showing up at one of Seeley's events despite Abby's insistence that he stay away. Mason wasn't willing to give up. His ex-wife, Kate, had cut off their relationship one day with the dispassionate news that she was finished with him. So long. It's been real. Let's be friends. Or not.

Abby hadn't said that. The hurt in her eyes said she loved him too much to live the life he'd chosen. She would come back to him if he could find his way back to her. It was one of those how-did-I-get-here moments for Mason, wanting her back but not knowing how to make it work and knowing he couldn't walk away from Nick and Mary.

Seeley was campaigning in Cape Girardeau, a small town in the Missouri boot heel, more Tennessee than Missouri, the first stop on a swing through the southeast part of the state. Mason watched a streaming video feed of the candidate climbing down from his chartered plane, catching a glimpse of Abby behind him, her hair swirling around her face in the prop wash. She could have been Neil Armstrong walking on the moon, she was that far away.

Mason spent Saturday catching up on his other cases, writing a brief to convince a judge his client lacked criminal intent when he sneaked out the bathroom window at Best Buy with a thousand dollars worth of computer software stuffed down his pants. It was an exercise in legal gymnastics that ended when he launched another dart assault on his office wall.

He stopped by the hospital to visit Nick, not getting past Nick's grandmother. She told him that the doctors were going to operate on Tuesday to remove the bullet fragment. Progress of a sort, Mason told her, asking her to tell Nick he'd been there. She grunted in reply, leaving the interpretation up to Mason.

On Sunday he took another pass at Mary's house. Newspapers had accumulated on her driveway, mail filled the mailbox. The fish in the aquarium were listless. Mason found a container of fish food on a shelf beneath the aquarium and sprinkled some on the surface. After a moment, the fish woke to their meal, darting after the morsels, knocking over the deep-sea diver. Mary wouldn't have left the fish unattended. He knew her that well. She would have asked a neighbor to pick up the papers and the mail and feed the fish while she was gone.

He stopped to talk to the neighbor across the street, glad to catch him outside. Cats peered at them from the front window.

"Any sign of Mary?" Mason asked.

"Nope. Not a peep," the man said. "But you're not the only one been looking for her."

Mason straightened. "Who else has been over there?"

"A woman. Driving a silver Lexus. Came by Friday afternoon, late in the day. Knocked on the door and left. That was it."

"What did she look like?" Mason asked.

"Dressed to the nines, that's all I can say," the man told him. "Real pretty. Dark hair. I wandered down to the curb, said hello to her. She give me a look like to cut right through me. I said fare-thee-well my lady to you too, if you get my meaning," he said flourishing his hands like a hula girl.

"That I do," Mason said, recognizing Sandra Connelly.

After hammering him for not playing by the rules, Sandra had gone Mason one better by not bothering to ask him for permission to talk to his client. Maybe she just wanted to find out for herself if Mary was really missing. Either way, Mason was primed for his next conversation with her.

Vince Kowalczyk called Mason Sunday night, saying no, he hadn't talked to Mary in two years. Mason thanked him, adding Father Steve to his Monday call list, anxious to hear the next dodge the priest had for him. He wasn't surprised Monday morning when a secretary at the church told him Father Steve wouldn't be in, apologizing that she didn't know where he was or how to reach him.

Mason had no better luck with Sandra Connelly, leaving her a voice message, following the recorded instructions to press the number two if his message was urgent.

Late Monday morning, he went downtown to police headquarters and filled out a missing persons report on Mary Kowalczyk, telling the desk clerk to deliver a copy to Detective Samantha Greer. The desk clerk, a skinny kid with slicked back hair and a T-bone nose, wearing a civilian uniform, playing cop dress-up, gave Mason a look that translated as I'll-get-around-to-it. Mason left Samantha a message, convinced that the rest of the world was observing Don't Answer Your Phone Day.

He didn't hear from Harry about the license plate on the car at the cemetary and forced himself not to push. Harry was reluctant to trace the plate and, as much as Mason wanted to know who was visiting his parents' grave, he had to let Harry do it on his own schedule. It was one more piece of his past that hung out of reach.

Rachel Firestone had wrapped up Mason's Monday with a scouting report on the King jury.

"I've tracked down five of the eight names you gave me. You're not going to like this," she told him over the phone.

"Give it to me," he said, putting her on the speaker phone, standing at the dry erase board, red marker in his hand.

Rachel began. "Nate Holden dropped dead of a heart attack nine years ago."

Mason read from his notes on the board. "He was forty-four at the time of the trial. That makes him fifty when he died. I can buy that. Shit happens when you turn fifty," he said.

"Another juror, Troy Apple, was shot coming out of his house early one morning. Cops suspected it was drug related."

"Apple was black, twenty-two years old. Back then. Single, lived on the east side. Who needs proof when you've got a good stereotype? Any arrests in that one?"

Rachel answered, "Nope. But, you'll like the trend. He was shot in the face."

"Why am I not surprised? I'd rather hold out for the heart attack," Mason said.

"Check this out," Rachel said. "Martella Garvey and Judith Dwyer are both dead. Garvey disappeared one day. Her body was found six months later, beaten to death. Same story for Dwyer. But, you'll be glad to know that Lisa Braun died of cancer two years ago."

"Son of a bitch," Mason said. "Aren't the cops paying attention? Doesn't anybody notice that this jury has a worse survival rate than a new sitcom?"

"No reason to. Martella Garvey was killed in Kansas City. Judith Dwyer moved to Chicago and was killed there. Besides, nine deaths spread out over the last fifteen years in different cities won't attract any attention. And the odds are against the cops finding out the victims served on the same jury since people generally don't include jury service in obituaries."

"Still," Mason said, "nine out of twelve jurors are dead. Only two from natural causes. That leaves Janet Hook, Frances Peterson, and Andrea Bracco."

"It's hard to believe," Rachel said. "But, who would want to kill those jurors? Ryan Kowalczyk was in jail. Whitney King was found innocent. I don't get it."

"Remember, Nancy Troy said the jury made a pact not to talk about the case."

"You told me. It still doesn't make sense. Why would they have needed a pact?" Rachel asked.

"If the jury was fixed, they'd have to keep it quiet."

"You mean the entire jury was bribed to find Whitney innocent? That's nuts! How are you going to bribe all twelve people and keep it quiet?"

"I don't know how you bribe all twelve of them, but I do know how you keep it quiet. Kill them. I've got to find the last three jurors."

On Monday evening, Mason had picked ribs up on his way home from the office. Tuffy gave him another nudge, earning the last rib, trotting off to enjoy it alone. The Channel 6 reporter recapped the victim list from the weekend's violence, adding them to the day's top story about a residential real estate agent lured to an unoccupied house and shot to death. The woman's name was Frances Peterson. Police have no suspects, the reporter said.

Mason nearly choked on his rib. He grabbed the list of jurors from the file he'd brought home, running his finger down the page. Frances Peterson. White. Age thirty-six. Lived in Brookside. Divorced. Two kids. Residential real estate agent. Fifteen-year-old information that he bet was still accurate.

Mason reached for the phone, catching Samantha Greer at home.

"Who's working the Frances Peterson case?" he asked her.

"Don't you ever say hello anymore? Or even I'm sorry to bother you at home again? And, by the way, I got the report on your parents' accident and faxed it to your office. You must have already left or I'm sure you would have thanked me."

"Thank you and hello. I'm sorry to bother you at home again. Nine out of twelve jurors in the King case are dead.

Only two from natural causes. Frances Peterson is the tenth. Was she shot in the face like Sonni Efron?" Mason asked.

Samantha didn't answer, Mason hearing her catch her breath. "Jesus Christ, Lou," she said. "I'll get back to you."

The phone rang as Mason set it down.

"Lou, it's Sandra. We need to talk."

"You've got that right," he told her, smiling grimly. "I'll be at my office."

Mason pulled out of his driveway. The sun was setting but the heat was rising.

Chapter 26

By the time Mason got to his office, the sun was melting the horizon, long shadows advancing in its wake, an orange volcanic rim around the sky. The pale blue neon spelling out Blues on Broadway above the door to the bar was faint competition for the celestial light. Cars were lined up in front, the bar's cool, dark comfort calling people in off the street.

Blues was playing his baby grand when he came in the back way. The clear notes rode over the bar chatter, air-conditioning for the soul, before slipping out the door. Mason paused for an instant, trying to place the tune. Blues jammed with the bass player, trading riffs. Blues had bought the bar when he got tired of playing someone else's gigs; he now played as much for himself as for the people who paid for the pleasure.

Taking the stairs two at a time, keeping the pace down the hall, fumbling with his key, Mason pushed the door to his office out of the way, not bothering to turn on the light. The pages of the accident report quivered in the fax machine, rippled by the breeze from the open door, Mason's hands trembled as he picked them up.

It was a Missouri Uniform Traffic Accident Report. Said so in large print across the top of the first page. The report was divided into sections, beginning with the names, addresses, phone numbers, sex, race, and age of the driver and passenger. John Mason. White, male, age thirty-three. Linda Mason. White female, age thirty. Next there were a series of boxes to be checked off for every detail. Road conditions—wet. Weather—rain. Time—11:00 P.M. And on it went, Mason scanning and double-checking the multiple choice rendition of life and death, disappointed when he saw that the box for witnesses was empty.

The second page ended with a narrative description by the investigating officer and another box labeled Cause. Mason repeated the officer's conclusion, slumping onto the sofa, not believing the sound of his own voice.

"Intentional," Mason said. "What the hell is that?"

"A word that means on purpose, not an accident. A necessary element of every major felony," Sandra Connelly said from the doorway to Mason's office.

She was wearing slacks and a blouse that passed for business casual during a heat wave, the blouse open at the throat, veins in her neck taut against her skin. Mason looked up, forgetting that he'd told her to meet him at his office.

Dead jurors and missing clients had suddenly become nuisances, as had Sandra's appearance on his doorstep. The meaning of the accident report sliced through Mason. "Intentional," the investigating police officer had concluded, meaning that Mason's father had driven through a guard rail and into a ravine on purpose, the only possible purpose being to kill himself and Mason's mother.

For a moment, he didn't blame Claire for not telling him. Nothing she could have said would have softened the blow. She cast life's harsh realities as the brutal truth, shielding her clients from things that would only curse them, no matter how true they were. That's what she'd done for him.

In the next instant, he rejected her, resenting her for cutting him off from a truth he couldn't have imagined. The man that had given him life had taken his own life and his mother's. The fantasy images he'd conjured as a boy of his grand and glorious pop haunted him in a flash of humiliation.

The scar on Mason's chest tightened, like he was being stabbed again, only this time from the inside out. He slipped his hand between the buttons of his shirt, massaging the scar.

"Lou," Sandra said. "Are you all right? I've seen CEOs doing the perp walk that looked better than you do."

Mason folded the pages of the accident report, and put them in the top drawer of his desk. He was burning up, flushed with shock, anger, and shame. The obvious questions banged inside his head, making him dizzy. How could his father do such a thing? What had happened between his parents? What did it mean for him all these years later?

He took a bottle of water from the refrigerator behind his desk, and drank half of it, stalling for time. The last thing he wanted to do was talk to Sandra, or anyone else.

"It's the heat," he said, wiping his mouth with the back of his hand, tasting the sweat. "I know you wanted to get together, but something's come up. I'll give you a call in the morning. We'll have lunch."

Sandra crossed the room, standing on the other side of the desk. She clutched the strap of the purse strung over her shoulder like it was a ripcord on a parachute, her other hand palm down on the desk, steadying herself. The tremors at the corners of her mouth looked like fault lines.

She shook her head. "Whatever you just shoved into that drawer will have to wait until morning. We need to talk now."

Mason took a deep breath. His parents had died forty years ago. Sandra was in trouble or headed there in a hurry. That was plain. Putting her and his clients on hold while he figured out what had possessed his father wouldn't bring his parents back. He could leave the accident report in his drawer and never take it out again. Or he could try to make sense of it. What he did about his parents and when he did it wouldn't change a thing. Besides, from the look of her Sandra wasn't going anywhere.

"Okay," he told her. "You called this meeting. What's so important?"

"Whitney King has agreed to meet with you."

"Alone?" Mason asked.

Sandra swallowed. "Yes. I'll be there, but in another room."

Mason finished his bottle of water. "Why didn't he take your advice and tell me to pound sand?"

"Because he's got more testosterone than sense. Going one-on-one with you appeals to his puerile instincts. He wants to do it tonight at his office," she said, coming as close to begging as he'd ever heard her.

Sandra carried a knife in her purse. Unlike a lot of women who carried weapons for self-protection, she knew how to use it and wouldn't hesitate. She didn't rattle easily, but she was barely able to stop from shaking.

"You don't have to represent him," Mason said. "You know that. You can quit. Let him find someone else."

"I don't quit, Lou. You know that. Besides, Whitney has a certain charm that comes from having enough money to get into enough trouble to make getting him out of it worthwhile," she said.

"Then why do you look more swept away than swept off your feet? And why were you checking up on my missing client after giving me the lecture on ethics?"

"I didn't break any rules," she snapped. "Mary wasn't home. If she had been, I would have told her to call you."

"But you had to see for yourself, didn't you?" Mason asked her.

"Yeah," Sandra answered. "I always do and sometimes I don't like what I see. Let's get going. I'll drive. I'm parked in front."

Chapter 27

Mason followed Sandra through the club. Blues was back behind the bar, polishing a glass, listening to a guy on a stool spin a story, watching them pass. Mason met his look, both of them wearing masks. Blues poured his customer a drink, not spilling a drop, not taking his eyes from Mason's back until the door closed behind him.

Sandra pulled out into traffic and whipped around a driver that had slowed down in front of the Uptown Theatre, an art deco remnant from the fifties with a wraparound marquee above the doors. Mason had gone there as a kid to watch monster movies. It had been rehabbed into a venue for rock bands, Bar Mitzvah parties, and book signings, one of each advertised for the coming week.

Sandra was dodging traffic and Mason's questions. He wasn't going for a ride with her without pushing harder for answers.

"Eight of the twelve jurors who acquitted Whitney are dead," Mason said. "One was named Sonni Efron. She was shot in the face last week. Frances Peterson was another one.

She was shot in the face today. Dress it up all you want, Sandra. Whitney's a bad man and you know it."

She gave him a sharp glance that said she'd considered the possibility enough to worry about it. "You think he's bad enough to kill the people who acquitted him?"

"I do," Mason said. "Especially if he fixed the jury and didn't want anyone to find out."

"Whitney was seventeen years old when the trial took place," she said, the words a last plea with herself, not an argument with him.

"So he was a child prodigy," Mason said.

Sandra slipped through traffic, winding through the shops and restaurants on the Plaza. She stopped for a string of tourists crossing the street aiming for the Cheesecake Factory, gunning her Lexus past the last straggler. Someone pulled out of a parking space on Ward Parkway along Brush Creek. Sandra cut off another driver to snag the spot. She got out of the car, slammed her door, and walked to the edge of the creek, arms folded over her heaving chest.

Brush Creek was a quiet canal, broad grassy banks sloping up to the street on either side. The Plaza was on the north shore, its Spanish-inspired architecture and outdoor sculpture lending a cosmopolitan backdrop. Postwar brownstone apartment buildings converted into condos lined the south shore. People jogged on paths alongside the water, ignoring the heat. Gondolas floated past, carrying passengers who had nothing better to do with twenty-five dollars. The last fingers of sunlight laid golden tracks on the water.

"Daniel Boone trapped beaver on this creek in the early eighteen hundreds," Mason said, standing at Sandra's shoulder. "Can you believe that? Tom Pendergast paved it with concrete in the nineteen thirties. Some people think he tossed a few of his political opponents into the cement before it dried."

"You'd make a great tour guide," Sandra told him, biting her lip, not looking at him.

"I can't help you if you don't talk to me," Mason told her.

Sandra turned to face him, her hand on his cheek, a quiver rippling along her jaw. "Good old Lou," she said. "You'll be using that line on women until you're too old to remember why."

Mason took her by the wrist, pulling her hand away. "If it's about Mary, where she is, what's happened to her, you've got to tell me."

"I don't know anything about Mary," she said, sticking her hands under her arms, studying Mason, arguing with herself, giving in. "Look, my firm represented Whitney and his family for a long time before I was hired. I spent the weekend reviewing the family files."

"You need to get a life," Mason told her with a teasing smile.

"I know you, Lou. You're going to sue Whitney and you're going to dig up every rock the family laid down before and after Graham and Elizabeth Byrnes were murdered. I was just getting ready."

"What did you find?"

She raked her fingers through her hair, tugging on the ends. "The more money a family has, the more twisted things get. I may have tumbled onto something that puts me in a very bad spot."

Despite what many people assumed, lawyers are governed by complex ethical rules that try to balance more than one right thing at a time. A lawyer can't disclose a prior crime by a client revealed in confidence but must disclose a client's intent to commit a crime in the future. If disclosing the future crime would reveal the prior crime, things get complicated. If the disclosures could get you killed, survival becomes more important than ethics. Mason read Sandra's dilemma in the flutter of her eyes.

"Whitney's past runs all the way to the present," Mason said gently, "and you can't cut one off from the other."

She nodded, adding, "It's not just Whitney."

Sandra's cell phone rang. She took it off the clip on her belt, answering and listening. Her chin was on her chest, her shoulders slack. "Okay. I understand," she said with a grim voice. She closed the phone and started toward her car. "Come on," she added over her shoulder. "We're late."

"Was that Whitney?" Mason asked, barely closing his door before Sandra was back in traffic.

"No. It was Dixon Smith. He's a former federal prosecutor who's on his own now. We're representing defendants in the same case," she answered, keeping her eyes straight ahead, enforcing a brittle calm.

"Okay," Mason said. "Let's get back to Whitney and his family's files."

She tossed her head as if she was shaking off the tremors, giving him a weak smile. "Later," she said. "Let's see how it goes with Whitney."

Mason couldn't tell whether she was concentrating on the cars in front of her or whether she just didn't want to look him in the eye when she lied to him. Mason knew Dixon Smith, had banged heads against him when he was in the U.S. attorney's office. Smith usually defended people accused of violent crimes, leaving the white-collar variety to lawyers like Sandra. Sandra's lie was that Dixon had called her about another case. She was about to tell Mason what she had found in the King family files until Dixon called.

Sandra continued south, cutting east a few blocks then south again on Holmes Road, an artery that would take them to Whitney's office some fifty blocks away.

"Why is Whitney working late? Just to talk to me?" Mason asked.

"Hard as it may be to believe, he might prefer that to going home to a big empty house."

"Where does the lonely rich boy live?"

"Burning Oak, that new golf course project in Lenexa," Sandra answered.

The metropolitan area was bifurcated by the state line between Kansas and Missouri, wealth accumulating in a string of cities that ran together in Johnson County on the Kansas side. Lenexa was one of them, wedged into the western part of the county. Burning Oak offered golf course lots priced at a quarter million on which buyers could build a house for a million-five more and lay down fifty grand to join the country club.

"So what's he doing at the office? Counting his money or stalking jurors?"

Sandra banged her hand on the steering wheel. "Damn it, Lou! Give it a rest!"

He did, keeping his mouth shut the rest of way, his thoughts staggering back to his parents, shredding fabricated images of their lives while Sandra parked outside Whitney's office building. She didn't move for a moment, finally turning the ignition off and taking a deep breath.

"Okay, then," she said. "This is it."

The parking lot was empty, no sign of Whitney's car. Mason assumed there was underground parking or that Whitney had parked on another side of the building, which was one of several in an office park ringed by mature trees with a jogging path laid among them. Park benches and picnic tables were scattered along the outer wall of greenery.

The building was ten stories, packaged in reflecting glass that made it impossible to see inside. It was past nine o'clock, dark, and no one was working late. They were at the entrance to the building when Sandra's cell phone rang again.

"Yes," she said, pausing. "Hello, Whitney. We're outside your building now. Where are you?" Mason tried the door, jiggling it so Sandra could tell that it was locked. "We're locked out," she said. "How long before you'll get here? Fine. We'll wait."

"What's the story?" Mason asked as Sandra stowed the phone and looked around.

"His mother is in a nursing home. He took her out for dinner and has to take her home. He'll be here in about twenty minutes and he wants us to wait. Let's try the bench over there," she said, pointing to one in the shade of the trees lining the jogging path.

"I thought she was in a psychiatric facility," Mason said.

"It's both, really," Sandra said. "Nice place for crazy old people. They have an Alzheimer's unit. Whitney says his mother has a reservation."

The bench was made of a forgiving heavy plastic or light metal. Mason couldn't tell which, only that it was more comfortable than it looked. They sat for a moment, Mason picking out stars. He turned to Sandra.

"You remember the first case we worked on together?" he asked her.

"Hard to forget," she said. "Both of us almost got killed."

"Because we didn't trust each other," he reminded her. "Let's not make the same mistake again."

Sandra pivoted toward him, tucking one leg under the other. "I do trust you," she said, her mouth opening wide at the same instant he felt something sharp and hot pierce the back of his shirt. Her scream was swallowed by his as a jolt of electricity fired a paralyzing spasm through his body.

Mason tried to turn but couldn't make his muscles respond. He was suddenly aware of someone standing behind him, feeling a hand on his shoulder, smelling something familiar, his brain not processing the odor. Seconds unfolded in slow motion.

Sandra raised her hands in front of her face. An ear-splitting crack from a gun rocked him as her hands flew away and her face exploded in a spray of blood and bone. Her body splayed across the bench. The shooter grabbed Mason's right hand, wrapped it around the gun, and laced Mason's finger against the trigger with his own, firing the gun again, another burst of blood flowering from Sandra's chest.

Sensation oozed back into his limbs, his movements slow, like he was swimming in molasses. He struggled against the gun that now inched upward across his chest, the hot barrel searing his neck, pressing hard beneath his chin. His hand was more jelly than muscle. His finger was still looped around the trigger, pulling it back against his will, about to leave him a dead puppet when his hand and the gun suddenly dropped in his lap and a hard shove put him on the ground in a heap.

He opened his eyes, rolling over on his back, staring up at Sandra's body. He heard footsteps, someone running toward him. He tried to cry out but couldn't make a sound. He tried to get up, collapsing when his legs refused to move, thrashing his head against the next assault.

Strong hands slipped beneath his shoulders, scooping him up, framing his face, holding him until he stopped shaking.

"I've got you, man," Blues said.

Chapter 28

Mason sat in a patrol car in the parking lot less than a hundred feet from where Sandra Connelly's body lay draped across the park bench. The center of her face was a bloody, pulpy mush, the bullet ripping through her hands, barely slowing. Her neck lay at an uneasy angle across the top edge of the bench, her head dangling off the back, blank eyes turned to heaven. Her arms were spread, one leg still tucked beneath the other; the blood pooling from her chest wound dripped onto her lap.

A cop sat next to him, another in the front seat, neither of them talking. His shirt was splattered with Sandra's blood. He reached over his shoulder to a sore spot above his left shoulder blade, the skin irritated, his shirt torn. Petty wounds. He'd regained his coordination within minutes of Blues's arrival. He tried to explain what had happened, but Blues told him to save it.

Mason understood why. Blues had been a cop long enough to size up a murder scene and this one looked simple. Sandra was dead, shot to death with a gun that Blues found next to

Mason. Mason was the obvious suspect and Blues didn't want to be forced to testify to anything Mason told him.

"Let the cops figure it out for now," Blues had told him. "You'll have plenty of time to tell me about it. Get your head straight and keep your mouth shut."

Samantha Greer and her partner, Al Kolatch, were running the scene. Samantha gave him one look, the pain in her eyes like another gunshot. He was standing in the parking lot surrounded by three cops when she arrived while two others interviewed Blues.

"You want to tell me about this?" she asked him.

"Later," he said.

She bit the inside of her cheek, pointing to two of the cops. "Put him in a car and keep him there. And no visitors, especially that one," she said, pointing at Blues who was talking to Kolatch.

Forensic cops searched the area under the glare of bright lights set up to illuminate the scene. They shot video, took still photographs, scraped blood, tissue, and bone from the bench and the ground. They scoured the area for bullets, fingerprints, and footprints. They measured distances and angles, building a case against Sandra's killer. The coroner arrived, examined Sandra's body, giving a silent signal when he was finished. An ambulance crew slipped her body into a black zippered bag, then quietly left the scene.

Samantha motioned to the cop in the backseat to trade places with her. "You want a lawyer or do you want to talk to me?"

Mason didn't blame her for treating him like a suspect, but he was innocent. Blues had given him the same advice he would have given any client, even though he knew that silence could be as incriminating as any confession. He had a lot to explain, but nothing to hide.

"I don't need a lawyer and I know my rights. You can put

that thing away," he said as she took her Miranda card from her purse.

"You're covered with the victim's blood. You know I've got to read it to you, Lou," she answered, putting the card away when she finished. "Still want to talk?" Mason nodded. "Okay, what were you and Sandra doing here?" she asked him.

"We were supposed to meet Whitney King. His office is in that building," Mason answered, pointing across the parking lot.

"What were you going to talk about?"

"The murders of Graham and Elizabeth Byrnes. The shooting of Nick Byrnes and the disappearance of Mary Kowalczyk," he answered.

"I got your message and a copy of the missing persons report you filed. Whose idea was the meeting with King?" she asked.

"Mine. I told Sandra I wanted to talk to Whitney alone. At first she told me no, then she talked to Whitney and he said he'd do it. Whitney set the meeting for tonight."

"Where was Whitney?"

"He called Sandra just as we got here and said he'd be late and asked us to wait. He was taking his mother back to the nursing home."

"So you just decided to pass the time on the park bench?"

"That was Sandra's suggestion."

"Tell me what happened," she said.

"Someone came at us from behind the bench, probably from the other side of the trees. I never saw his face. He must have used a stun gun on me. I couldn't move. He shot Sandra in the face, then put the gun in my hand and pulled the trigger again. Then he tried to make me shoot myself with the gun. I guess he wanted it to look like a murder-suicide. He had the gun jammed under my chin when he just let go and knocked me to the ground. Blues must have scared him away."

"Is that it?" Samantha asked.

"That's it."

She reached across to Mason, holding his right hand close to the dome light inside the car.

"Powder burns," she said, letting go.

"I told you," Mason said. "The guy put the gun in my hand and made me pull the trigger. That was the second shot, the one in her chest. I'm sure the first one killed her. The second one was to set me up."

Sandra scratched the side of her face, brushing her hair out of the way, looking at him, then out the back window of the car. "Where'd he get you with the stun gun?"

"Back here," Mason said, pointing to his left shoulder.

"Let me have a look," she said.

Mason was wearing a polo shirt. He hiked it up around his neck, letting Samantha run her fingers across his skin.

"Looks like a couple of red marks, could be a rash. Could be pimples. I don't know."

Mason pulled his shirt down, facing her. "Sam? What's going on? I mean I know how it looks, but it's me, Lou. You don't really think I killed Sandra?"

She motioned to a cop standing outside the car who handed her an evidence bag. She held the bag by the edge, a gun snug against the bottom. "Do you recognize this?" she asked him.

"It's the gun," he said.

"We ran the registration. It's yours."

More than once, Mason had told a client there were worse things than spending a night in jail. Lying on his bunk, prisoners snoring in the cells around his, he didn't bother making a list. The county followed the mayor's heat warnings to a fault. The air in the cell block was warm and ripe. Each time he shut his eyes, he saw Sandra's face in the last instant before the bullet struck her. He heard her say that she trusted him, then watched as her face split open, her head knocked back, her life evaporated.

He felt his hand squeezing the trigger for the second bullet, rubbing his hands together, kneading the skin, unable to shake the sensation. It was like an amputee's phantom pain. He was certain that the first shot had killed Sandra, knew that he'd been made to fire the second shot, but couldn't escape the fear that he had killed her. What if the first shot wasn't fatal? What if he'd fought harder or just enough to alter the aim?

He forced himself to concentrate on what had happened, to resurrect each detail, no matter how trivial, knowing that his freedom and his life could depend on it. He'd had no answer for Samantha when she told him his gun was the murder weapon. She'd handcuffed him and left him in the patrol car, her eyes red and wet. Replaying each second in his mind, making a mental list of each sound and sensation, he knew what trouble he was in because even he doubted the story.

A mysterious assailant appeared out of the woods, incapacitated him with a stun gun, shot Sandra with Mason's gun, and then made him shoot her a second time, escaping when Blues showed up. It was an explanation that threatened Ryan Kowalczyk's story on the *Ripley's Believe-It-or-Not* scale.

The only way he could explain the use of his gun was that someone had stolen it from his office. The last time he'd seen it was when Sandra first came to his office to tell him about Nick Byrnes's e-mails to Whitney King. That was almost a week ago.

Security wasn't tight at Blues on Broadway. A thief didn't have to break in. He could just get lost in the crowd, then wander to the back and up the stairs. The lock on Mason's office door wasn't issued by the Department of Homeland Security. He'd jimmied it open a few times himself when he'd misplaced his key.

The thief would have had to know that Mason kept a gun in his desk. Blues, Mickey, and Sandra were the only ones who knew that he did. Blues knew because Mason had told him. Mickey had also seen the gun, but he was a lifetime away with Abby. Sandra knew because she'd seen the gun and seen him put it away. Sandra might have told Whitney and Whitney may have stolen the gun, but Whitney's mother was his alibi.

If the shooter wasn't Whitney, who could it have been? Someone Whitney trusted enough or paid enough to do the job. Mason clinched his eyes tightly, the jolt of the stun gun leaving him with gaps in his memory. There was something familiar about the shooter, something lurking on the edges of his recollection, playing keep-away with his mind.

He breathed deeply and sat up, the paper slippers they'd given him scraping like sand paper against the cement floor of his cell. He stood and stretched, pacing the eight steps from the bars to the back wall, six steps side-to-side, his finger-tips stroking the ceiling as he reached overhead. Pressing his face against the bars, he could barely see a clock at the end of the corridor that ran between the two rows of cells. It was just past four in the morning. He lay back on the bunk, his arm over his eyes, and went through it again.

Chapter 29

Two guards ushered Mason into a conference room at eight o'clock Tuesday morning, each of them squeezing his arms hard enough to leave tattoos. Handcuffs chafed against his wrists, while a pair of ankle bracelets slowed his walk to an old man's shuffle. The windowless room one floor beneath his cell was equipped with a midsize table, seating for six, the surface scarred, legs on the chairs uneven. The county didn't have money for new furniture, but the air-conditioning worked fine, cooling the room. The contrast with the cell block punctuated the difference between life on the inside and life on the outside.

Claire Mason stood as he entered, taking a short sharp breath. She was wearing one of the severe gray suits over a white blouse with a high collar that she wore year-round when doing battle, indifferent to weather and fashion. His aunt was broad-backed and pushing six feet; her outfit reminded him of body armor. Today, he liked her style.

"You look like hell," she told him.

His hair was ratty, his face unshaven, and his jail jumpsuit didn't cover the smell of sweat, blood, and guts. "Tuesday is casual day at the county jail," he said.

Patrick Ortiz, the prosecuting attorney, came in through the same door. "Take off his cuffs and ankle bracelets and wait outside," he told the guards. "Sit down," he told Mason when the guards left.

Mason remained standing and rubbed his wrists as he and Ortiz studied one another, Ortiz tossing a hand in the air saying have it your way. They had battled in the courtroom more than a few times, Mason always careful not to underestimate him. The prosecutor was an Everyman, unassuming, with a thrown together, soft-bellied look that deceived inexperienced lawyers. He talked to jurors like they were on the same bowling team, putting them at ease, making them like him, knowing that a verdict was often a popularity contest between the lawyers. He left nothing to chance and had filled a lot of vacancies on death row.

Ortiz had gone after Mason in the past, trying to link him to an arson, not making it stick. They respected each other as adversaries, but they weren't friends.

"Patrick," Claire began. "You're not going to question my client. I haven't even had a chance to talk to him yet. I want to see a judge about bail. What time is the arraignment?"

Mason was weary, off-balance, but not enough to make the mistake of representing himself again, mindful of Abraham Lincoln's admonition that a lawyer who did so had a fool for a client. He also wasn't ready to be cross-examined by Ortiz and he was glad Claire was there to keep Ortiz off his back, though he knew she couldn't represent him past this meeting. She wasn't a criminal defense lawyer and, even if she was, she lacked the objectivity he needed. Still, seeing her square off against Ortiz, her spine straight, her attitude unmovable, he felt well protected and well represented, his doubts and suspicions about his parents' deaths shoved aside.

Ortiz smiled. "Lou, you better not stiff Claire on her bill. She was on me last night and first thing this morning and worked over the investigating officers in between."

"What time, Patrick?" Claire asked again.

Ortiz looked at his watch. "One o'clock. Judge Pistone."

"I want to see the detective's reports before then," Claire said. "And I want to know your position on bail. Lou is obviously not a flight risk or a threat. Make it reasonable and I won't fight you on it. We'll be ready to post bail by this afternoon."

"Claire," Ortiz said, "you'll get the reports before the preliminary hearing, just like everyone else. Your client is charged with first-degree murder with aggravating circumstances. Bail is tough to come by in a death penalty case. Judges don't like it when lawyers kill people, even if the victim is another lawyer. Neither do I. Take your time. We'll get him cleaned up before he sees the judge," he said, leaving them alone.

Mason embraced his aunt as she worked her fingers against the back of his neck. They held each other tightly, Mason carried back for an instant to days when such a hug meant everything would be all right, knowing that this time it might not be so.

"Blues called me," she said, letting go of him, taking a seat at the table.

"I'm glad he did," Mason said, pulling out a chair next to hers. "He must have followed Sandra and me when we left the bar, but I don't know why."

"He told me that from the look on both of your faces, you weren't going dancing. Harry says Blues has a cop's instinct for trouble."

"If he hadn't shown up when he did, I'd be dead," Mason said, telling Claire what had happened.

"That's not much to go on," she said when he finished. "Don't you remember anything else?"

"I didn't get a look at the killer. I can't prove he used a stun gun and I don't know how he got hold of the .44 I kept in my desk. I know that I shot Sandra, but I didn't kill her. The first bullet did." Mason pounded the table with the flat of his hand. "Christ!"

"It's not that bad," Claire said.

"Not that bad?" Mason asked. "It's worse than that. Now I know how Ryan Kowalczyk felt when he told the cops his story. Ortiz can't wait to hear me try mine out on the jury."

"So we've got a lot of work to do," Claire said. "Harry and Blues will help."

"Claire," Mason said, "you're the meanest son of a bitch in the valley, but this isn't your valley. You haven't handled a criminal case in years, let alone a death penalty case. I need you more than ever before, but I need a different lawyer."

She wiped her eyes with the back of her hand, clearing her throat. "Exactly what I would have said. Well then, who do you want?"

"Dixon Smith," Mason said. "As fast as you can get him here."

Dixon Smith met Mason in the basement of the courthouse, joining him on the elevator with Mason's escort of three sheriff's deputies. Mason was clean, shaved, and dressed in a new jumpsuit, the bright orange color labeling him guilty, the cuffs and ankle bracelets tagging him as dangerous.

"I understand you'd like to talk to me," Smith said, grasping Mason's cuffed hands, smiling broadly. The deputies flinched as the two men shook hands.

"Thanks for dropping by," Mason said.

He'd spent the morning pacing in his cell, expecting Smith to show up in time to prepare for his arraignment.

More than once, Mason had raced to court at the last minute, meeting a client for the first time, reassuring the client that he was ready, soothing his client's impatience with a confident smile and a good result. Mason chafed at being on the other end of the last minute and resolved never to be late again.

"I got tied up. Sorry, but you know the drill," Smith said.

Mason told him, "We're due in court in ten minutes. That enough time to figure out how to get me out on bail?"

Smith had a shaved head and a narrow face with a dark goatee dressing his chin, accenting his deep brown skin. He had a fat-free runner's frame with the forward lean of a man in a hurry, and he was nearly Mason's height. He wore a navy, chalk pinstripe suit, pale blue shirt, power red tie, gold coin cufflinks, and black shoes with a blinding shine. He tapped his fingers against a thin brown leather briefcase, keeping time against a tightly wound internal clock. The elevator was hot, jerking its way up seven flights. Mason felt the sweat against his back. Smith was cool and dry, his steady eyes holding Mason's, both men deciding whether this was going to work.

"You think I was just sitting by the phone with nothing better to do than hope your auntie would call?" Smith asked.

"No," Mason answered. "From what I've heard about you, I think you're up to your asshole in alligators defending gang bangers and dope dealers. I appreciate you squeezing me in, but I don't like being squeezed."

Dixon laughed. "Get used to it, man. Once you get a set of those orange threads, all you get is squeezed. I've got a full docket, but your auntie is a force of nature. She doesn't understand the word no."

The elevator stopped at the eighth floor and the deputies led Mason and Smith to a witness room. Smith cut between the deputies and Mason, turning to face them as Mason stepped into the room.

"Knock when it's time," Smith told the guards, closing the door. He tossed his briefcase on a small table against the wall. "Claire and Blues filled me in. Samantha Greer gave me a quick look at her report, though I couldn't tell whether that was because of me or you. I got a dollar in my pocket says there's some heavy history between the two of you. Ortiz would crap sideways if he found out she showed it to me, but that's the way the game is played. No law says we got to go into this arraignment blind."

"What do you think?" Mason asked.

"I think I got gang bangers and dope dealers hustling crack on the sidewalk outside City Hall that have a better chance than you do. You and your mysterious stun gunner are going to give Dr. Richard Kimball a run for his money the next time they remake *The Fugitive*."

"Are you this optimistic with all your clients?"

Smith flashed a grin. "Just the ones that can write a check and the check for murder one is a hundred thousand dollars. Up front. We get down to fifty grand, you put in another fifty. We keep going like that until the money runs out or the jury comes back."

Mason stood against the wall, shackled hands hanging in front of him. He sometimes apologized to clients when he told them about his fees. Smith's were no different than his. The difference was in the delivery. Mason felt like he was being hustled, but that he didn't have a choice. He'd gotten what he'd asked for.

"I don't have my checkbook with me," he said.

"Don't you worry," Smith said. "Like I told you, your auntie is a force of nature." One of the guards knocked at the door. "Let's go ask Judge Pistone what he had for breakfast. That way, we'll know what kind of mood he's in."

* * *

Judge Joseph Pistone was a small man with a heart to match, hunch-backed from years spent on the bench looking down at the papers in front of him, looking up at lawyers and litigants only if provoked. Mason had made the judge look up more often than most lawyers, a distinction that served his clients but not himself.

Pistone was an associate circuit court judge. His days were spent listening to an endless parade of minor disputes that earned decent ratings for TV judges, but offered no entertainment value to the people who came before him. When he wasn't handling the adult abuse docket, the deadbeat dad docket, or the landlord-tenant docket, he heard criminal arraignments. Veteran lawyers understood that the bail he set rose or fell depending on which side incited his chronic indigestion.

The preliminary hearings he conducted to determine whether a defendant should be bound over for trial in the circuit court were models of efficiency. The result rarely deviated from his monotone recital that the state had established reasonable grounds to believe that the defendant had committed the crime with which he was charged.

Arraignments were equally perfunctory. Defense lawyers usually waived a formal reading of the charge, entered a plea of not guilty, and hoped that the bail bondsman was in a generous mood. Judge Pistone's courtroom was small, his docket rarely attracting a crowd, arraignments no different. A handful of defense attorneys waited their turn as an assistant prosecutor worked her way through a stack of files; the judge exercised his gavel, mumbling "next case."

Mason heard the buzz before one of the deputies opened the door to the courtroom. It was the chatter of the lawyers and reporters that had elbowed their way into the courtroom, a seat at his arraignment being the hottest ticket in town. Mason had never sought the limelight. His cases had shoved him into the glare. He was good copy for the media and tough competition for his brethren.

Reporters had packed the courtroom, certain of a good story for the six o'clock news or the morning edition. His competitors were there to watch him go down. Some were sympathetic, the kind who knew that everyone took their turn in the barrel. Some silently cheered, the kind who watched NASCAR races hoping to see a wreck.

The noise stopped when Mason entered, the last sound a collective gasp. He stutter-stepped toward the counsel table on the far side of the courtroom. His hands and feet were manacled, and deputies were at his side. Claire, Harry, Blues, and Rachel Firestone were in the first row of spectator seats behind his table. He nodded to them, mouthing his thanks, taking his seat, wishing Abby was there. He knew why she wasn't. She had begged him too many times to show up now and tell him she told him so.

Patrick Ortiz sat at his table, an assistant nervously drumming a pen until Ortiz took it from her. He pretended not to notice the crowd or Mason as he walked past.

Dixon Smith leaned over the rail, whispering to Blues, when the judge's bailiff instructed everyone to rise. Smith turned and cupped Mason's elbow as Mason stood.

"Be cool," Smith told him.

Chapter 30

"The court calls the case of *State v. Mason*. Counsel, state your appearances," Judge Pistone said, his chin aimed at his lap, scribbling notes on the docket sheet.

"Patrick Ortiz for the state, your Honor."

"Dixon Smith for the defendant, Lou Mason. We waive reading of the charges and enter a plea of not guilty."

"Bail?" Judge Pistone asked.

"We ask that the defendant be released on his own recognizance," Smith said before Ortiz could answer.

Judge Pistone looked up, leaned back in his chair and held up his hand as Ortiz started to reply. "You're slow off the mark today Mr. Ortiz, but you'll get your turn. Mr. Smith," the Judge continued, "have you ever known any judge to release someone charged with capital murder on their own recognizance?"

"No sir," Smith answered.

"Then why would you make such a ridiculous request, knowing that I'll never grant it?"

"It's no more ridiculous than what the prosecutor is going to ask for, especially if he opposes any bail."

"I've denied bail in many murder cases," the judge said. "Why will the prosecuting attorney oppose bail in this case?"

Smith moved from behind his counsel table to the center of the courtroom, placing himself between the judge and Ortiz, blocking out his opposition. Elbows angled out from his hips, hands open, he filled the stage he had set.

"Mr. Ortiz is going to tell you that this was a heinous crime—that Mr. Mason is a lawyer and that lawyers are held to some higher standard because they are officers of the court. He is an officer of the court but that doesn't mean he gets any less justice or due process than the lowest born. The prosecutor is going to tell you that there's overwhelming evidence of Mr. Mason's guilt and that that makes him a flight risk and a danger to the community. Mr. Ortiz is going to tell you all of that and then ask you to set bail so high Mr. Mason can't possibly post it or deny it outright."

"Mr. Ortiz," Judge Pistone said. "Sounds like Mr. Smith has heard you make that speech before, as have I."

Ortiz rose, strolled past Smith, and rested his forearm on the shelf beneath the judge's bench that lawyers used during trial when they wanted to tell the judge something they didn't want the jury to hear. He turned toward the audience, ignoring Smith, and smiled, covering his irritation that he had let Smith get out of the box ahead of him.

"Your honor, it was true the first time I said it and it's even truer today," he said, pivoting back toward the judge, both hands on the shelf, shrinking the courtroom to an intimate box that excluded Mason and his lawyer. "This was a cold-blooded, premeditated murder. The defendant lured Sandra Connelly to an office park at night when no one would be around to interfere with his plan. He has admitted shooting her with his own gun and has made up the biggest fish story since Jonah and the whale to blame it on some mysterious assailant. There's a very good argument to be made that bail should be denied."

"If there is, Your Honor, that's not it," Smith said, joining Ortiz at the bench, crowding the prosecutor. "We're not here to try this case. If we were, you'd hear evidence that the killer disabled Mr. Mason with a stun gun, fired the fatal shot, put the gun in Mr. Mason's hand, pulled the trigger a second time to frame Mr. Mason, and then tried to make Mr. Mason kill himself."

Smith returned to his counsel table, then paused enough to let the scenario he'd painted sink in. He drew the judge's attention away from Ortiz who was forced to turn his back to the judge so he could hear the rest of Smith's argument. Standing behind Mason, his hands on Mason's shoulders, he continued.

"If the killer had succeeded, Mr. Ortiz would say it was a murder-suicide and call it a day. The killer didn't succeed because Wilson Bluestone, a former homicide detective, chased the killer away. The court knows Mr. Mason. He's a well-respected lawyer who has lived in this community all of his life. Sandra Connelly was his friend and former partner. There's nothing more important to him than clearing his name and finding out who killed her. He's not going to flee and he's not a threat to anyone. Mr. Ortiz hasn't got a motive for Mr. Mason to have killed Ms. Connelly and he hasn't got a reason for Mr. Mason to be a threat to anyone else," Smith said, leaving Mason for the podium between the counsel tables.

"Are you asking the court to deny bail, Mr. Ortiz?" Judge Pistone asked. Ortiz took a breath, buying a moment, stuck between the judge's bench and the podium. "Mr. Ortiz," Pistone snapped. "Make a decision."

"Yes," Ortiz answered, facing the judge. "The state opposes bail."

"On what grounds?" Smith demanded.

"Mr. Smith," Judge Pistone said, "sit down. This isn't your courtroom and Mr. Ortiz isn't on the witness stand."

Smith unbuttoned his suit jacket and smiled as if he'd received an invitation, not an order.

"We have reason to believe that Mr. Mason poses a serious threat to others," Ortiz said.

"What others?" Smith asked from his seat, drawing Judge Pistone's glare. "Sorry, Your Honor. My mistake."

"What others, Mr. Ortiz?" Judge Pistone asked, pretending not to hear the muffled laughter from the audience.

Ortiz shot a glance at Smith, angry that he'd let Smith trap him. Smith had goaded the judge into making Ortiz reveal more of his case than he was ready to. Ortiz knew he either had to fold on Mason's bail or tip his hand. Having committed himself to opposing bail, he would lose too much credibility with the court if he didn't back it up. Smith didn't return Ortiz's look, watching the judge instead.

"Your Honor," Ortiz began. "Sandra Connelly was representing Whitney King. The defendant had two clients, Nick Byrnes and Mary Kowalczyk, who were threatening to sue Mr. King. Mr. King will testify that the defendant had followed him and threatened him. Ms. Connelly had tried to talk the defendant out of filing a lawsuit. Mr. King's office is at the Holmes Corporate Center. We believe that the defendant used Ms. Connelly to lure Mr. King to his office where he intended to kill both of them. Mr. King didn't show up, so he killed Ms. Connelly anyway."

"Why didn't King show up?" Smith asked.

Judge Pistone hammered his gavel. "Once more, Mr. Smith, and both you and your client will need lawyers! Understood?"

Smith raised both hands in surrender. "Understood. Yes sir. Understood."

"Well, Mr. Ortiz," Judge Pistone said. "Why wasn't Mr. King there?"

"Your Honor. As Mr. Smith said, this isn't a trial. It's premature to lay out all the evidence at this stage of the case."

"Not if you expect me to deny bail because of a threat to Mr. King."

Ortiz nodded, blood creeping up his neck as he returned to his seat, his assistant shrinking into her chair. "Mr. King didn't know about the meeting. That's all I'm prepared to say at this time," he said.

Mason looked at Smith, who smiled back, waiting for the judge to call on him.

"Now it's your turn, Mr. Smith. What do you have to say?"

Smith rose slowly, taking his time to the podium, resting his elbows as he looked at Ortiz, shaking his head like a disappointed parent, then straightening and giving his attention to the court.

"Whitney King was tried for the murder of Nick Byrnes's parents fifteen years ago in this courthouse. He was acquitted. His codefendant was Mary Kowalczyk's son, Ryan, who was convicted of the murders and executed last week. Nick Byrnes and Mary Kowalczyk both hired Lou Mason to prove that Whitney King was guilty of those murders and that Ryan Kowalzcyk was innocent. Since King's murder trial, eight out of the twelve jurors who acquitted him have died violently. Two of them were shot to death in the last week. Both were shot in the face, just like Sandra Connelly. Last week, Whitney King shot Nick Byrnes. Although Nick survived, he may be crippled. No charges have been filed in that case. Mary Kowalczyk has vanished. Yesterday, Mr. Mason filed a missing persons report on her and the police are investigating her disappearance.

I'd say that if anyone needs protection, it's Lou Mason, not Whitney King."

Judge Pistone rested his chin on his fingertips, looking back and forth from the defense to the prosecution.

"Bail set at one hundred thousand dollars. Next case."

Chapter 31

Claire and Harry picked up Chinese food, joining Rachel Firestone, Blues, and Mason at Mason's house. Mason caught Harry alone for a moment.

"You get anything on that license plate?" Mason asked him.

Harry fixed him with a bewildred stare. "You don't have enough problems?" Mason didn't answer, holding Harry's look with his own. "I'm working on it," Harry finally said.

They gathered at the dining room table that Mason had shoved into the living room to make way for his rowing machine. Tuffy patrolled the perimeter, sniffing out morsels that landed on the hardwood floor.

Television trucks had lined the curb in front of Mason's house since he got home, broadcasting live reports of the day's events. Mason didn't tune in, disconnected his phone, and let Blues answer the door when reporters knocked. After Blues turned away the first two reporters with a look that said don't come back, the rest retreated to the other side of the street, searching for neighbors who would say they knew all along something was wrong with Mason, which was why they wouldn't let their kids play in his yard or ring his doorbell on Halloween.

By seven o'clock, the last broadcast truck had pulled away. Claire had turned up the air-conditioning, saying they'd had enough heat for one day.

No one talked about the charges against Mason or the rest of the case. No one exchanged high-fives to celebrate the judge's order setting bail at a manageable level. They were having dinner, not a party, sticking close to Mason. They finally ran out of food and small talk, unable to avoid the day's events any longer.

"It's a good thing the bail bondsman likes you," Harry said to Mason.

"I've done enough business with Carlos Guitteriz to support all three of his ex-wives and his six kids," Mason answered.

Harry said, "Carlos cut his fee in half and took an unsecured promissory note for the bail. That's loyalty."

"I thanked him," Mason said. "But I haven't thanked you for taking care of Dixon Smith's retainer," he told Claire. "I'll pay you back."

"I have no doubt," Claire said. "And, if you don't, I know where you live."

"I don't get the part about the stun gun," Rachel said. "How do those things work?"

"It's pretty simple," Blues said. "A stun gun uses compressed nitrogen to fire probes connected to a wire. The probe carries fifty thousand volts and the current lasts for around five seconds after it hits. The victim is incapacitated as long as the charge lasts, but it takes most people a few minutes to recover completely. That's plenty of time for the killer to do what he did. Effective range is about fifteen feet for commercial models you can buy on the Internet."

"Can Lou prove that's what happened? Does it leave a mark on the skin?" Claire asked.

"Usually not," Blues answered. "Maybe a red mark like a small burn, but that will fade pretty quickly. The big drawback is the wire. The killer had to reel it in like a fishing line. When he saw me coming, that probably saved Lou's life. Either I would have caught him or he would have had to leave the gun behind, which would have corroborated Lou's story."

The doorbell rang. Mason's shoulders sagged as he looked at Blues, who eased out of his chair, flexing his hands like he was ready to hang a reporter from the nearest street light. The entryway to Mason's house was an arched vestibule that was not visible from the dining room. Conversation stopped as Blues swung the wide oak door open, closing it with a decisive thud before leading Dixon Smith into the living room.

Smith, still wearing his suit, his tie cinched tightly against his neck, and carrying his briefcase, surveyed the room. Rachel had gathered the empty food boxes, building a pyramid in front of her.

"How come the lawyer never gets invited to the party?" Smith asked.

"You know the answer to that, Dixon," Claire said. "We're only wanted when we're needed. Lucky for you, you're both. Have a seat."

"I may be both wanted and needed, but the Kung Pao chicken is wanted and eaten. Is that it?" he asked, laughing and poking a hole in Rachel's pyramid.

Rachel scooped the remains from one box onto a paper plate, sliding it across the table to Smith.

"No thanks," he said. "I make it a rule never to eat off of paper unless I'm having a picnic, and this case definitely doesn't qualify. Come here, dog," he said, holding the plate for Tuffy who inhaled the scraps, licking Smith's hand when the food was gone.

"So, Dixon," Rachel said. "Don't sugarcoat it. What do you think about Lou's case?"

"If I tell you, am I going to read about it in the morning paper?"

"Not unless you tell someone else," she said. "The paper quit letting me cover Lou's cases a long time ago."

Smith looked around the room, stopping at Mason who nodded his permission, Smith nodding in return.

"Most cases, the defense attorney's job is to make the prosecutor prove his case, not prove the defendant is inno-cent, just convince the jury that there's reasonable doubt the defendant is guilty. If there's reasonable doubt about guilt, the jury is supposed to acquit. The prosecutor has it easy since most defendants are guilty anyway. Even if juries don't know that, they believe it. And people pay a whole lot more attention to what they believe than what they know."

"That's how most of us go through our whole lives," Claire said.

"Exactly," Smith said. "People don't change when they get into the jury room. Lou already told the cops he shot Sandra and they know the gun was his. So the prosecutor doesn't have much to prove, which means I do. I've got to try Lou's case, Nick and Mary's case against Whitney King, and the original murder case against King and Ryan Kowalczyk."

"Why do you have to do all that?" Rachel asked.

"Juries hate the I-don't-know-who-did-it-but-it-wasn't-me defense. They expect the defense attorney to give them someone else to pin it on. Whitney King is the only choice. If I prove he killed Nick Byrnes's parents, rigged the jury to acquit him, then spent the last fifteen years knocking off the jurors to keep them quiet, then shot Nick and disappeared Mary Kowalczyk to shut them up, the jury will buy that he killed his lawyer and set up Lou to take the fall for the same reason."

"You have any idea how over the top and out of sight all that sounds?" Harry asked.

"That's why I take my fee up front," Smith said. "No offense, Lou," he added.

"Harry's right. It doesn't make sense," Blues said. "King was acquitted of the Byrnes murders. He could take out an ad on a billboard admitting he did it and never do a day in jail. A civil case is just money and he has enough to make that go away."

"Dixon, are you trying to make me feel better?" Mason asked.

"Nope," Smith said. "I'm trying to get you ready for work. Party's over," he said to the others. "It's time for my client to come to Jesus."

Chapter 32

"Nice job today, Dixon," Mason said after his company left. "You got a lot of mileage out of Ortiz. You ripped a chamber out of his heart with every question."

They remained in the living room, seated on opposite sides of the table while drawing on cold bottles of Fat Tire Beer Mason had retrieved from the kitchen. The dog was lounging on the floor beneath the picture window that had been punctured by a bullet a week before. It was the first shot fired in what had become a guerrilla campaign. The wind was picking up, whistling through the hole in the glass.

"You know Patrick as well as I do. I snuck up on him today. That won't happen again."

"We'll see what happens at the preliminary hearing," Mason said.

"Not going to be any preliminary hearing," Smith said. "Ortiz called me late this afternoon. Said he was taking the case to the grand jury instead. They meet again this Friday and they're going to indict you for murder. Speedy trial and all that. We'll get a jury by Thanksgiving and a verdict by Christmas."

Mason sucked in his breath. Smith watched him, not blinking, put together like a high-fashion puzzle, callous and cool. Mason had been impressed by how Smith handled the arraignment, satisfied with his choice of counsel even though he hadn't picked Smith for his skill. Mason knew the importance of managing a client's expectations, especially a criminal defense client whose life was on the line. Smith took it to another level, wringing any sentiment out of the equation.

"It's Ortiz's call," Mason said. "He can take the case to the grand jury or have a preliminary hearing. He picked the grand jury because it's secret and you made him look bad today. It killed him to tell the judge that Whitney King denied that he was supposed to meet Sandra and me at his office."

"It may have killed Ortiz, but it's worse for you. King's not going to back up your story."

"There's got to be a record of Sandra's phone call to King. When we get the phone records, no one is going to believe King. Getting that piece out of Ortiz was almost worth the price of admission," Mason said.

"We'll see. I subpoenaed Sandra's and Whitney's records today. I should have them by Friday. But, like I said, Patrick isn't going to let me sneak up on him again. He'll subpoena every one of the people you had over for dinner tonight."

Mason said. "Then we have to get them ready to testify. Let's divide up the work. There's plenty to go around."

"That's not the way I work. I don't divide things up," Smith said. "Besides, I don't want you interviewing witnesses. Every time you open your mouth, you'll create another witness to testify against you. You're the client this time, Lou, not the lawyer. Nothing you say is privileged anymore unless you say it to me."

In a week of tectonic shifts in his world, this was the latest harsh reality to hit Mason. Being the lawyer meant being in control, running the show. Being the client meant finding religion, putting his future in the hands of a stranger. Mason was a true believer in himself and not much else.

"Fine," Mason said, taking a deep breath, trying to hold onto something. "I'll do the legal research and write the briefs. I'll hide out in the library. You'll get all the glory."

"Sorry, Lou. I can't let you do that. You know the law. I'm not worried about that. But no one on trial for murder writes or thinks as clearly as they think they do. You've got one job. Point me in the right direction and I'll do the rest. That's how I earn my fee."

Mason stood, slamming his chair against the table, hands on his hips. "That's bullshit! You think I'm going to sit on my ass and wait for the judge to tell Ortiz to call his first witness? I'm looking at the death penalty. I've witnessed one execution and that was enough for me!"

Smith tilted his chair back on the rear legs, hands folded in his lap. "When was the last time you let a client work up his murder case?"

"This is different. I'm not one of your street thug clients. I know what I'm doing and I'm damn good at it!"

"Then you don't need me. You can represent yourself. I'll refund the unused part of my retainer to your auntie in the morning," Smith said, standing as Mason glared at him. Smith held the stare, his face flat, indifferent.

Mason raised his hands, waving Smith off. "Okay. You made your point. But what am I going to do?"

"You've got other clients besides yourself," Smith answered.

"Not after today. There's no way I can represent a criminal defendant when I'm charged with murder. I'll have no credibility with the prosecutor or the courts until this is over.

I've got a few civil clients, but they won't stick around to see how this comes out. I'm shut down," he said, slumping back into his chair.

"You can take up golf," Smith said, returning to his seat.

Mason managed a small laugh. "You charge extra for the jokes?"

"Depends on how many I have to tell. You ready to get after this?"

Mason put his hands on the table. "Yeah, I'm ready. I don't have a choice."

Smith took him through it, starting with Ryan Kowalczyk's execution, breaking down every conversation, taking notes, and writing down names in the margins. He jumped around, interrupting Mason's narrative, asking what King was wearing when Mason talked to him at Camille's, asking the make and model of the cars that the valets retrieved before they brought back King's car. He tortured Mason for details.

"I didn't count King's molars if that's what you're going to ask me next," Mason said after a couple of hours.

"I was getting to that," Smith said. "The details don't matter as much as whether you remember them. It's all about credibility. Do you remember everything, or just the part that helps you? Did you forget everything or just the part that hurts you? You know the drill."

"I do," Mason said. "But not from this side of the table."

"Get used to it," Smith said. "I think I've worked you over enough for one night."

Mason said, "You left out the one question I thought you would ask."

Smith pried apart the last crab Rangoon, spooning the cold filling out, leaving the fried wrapping. "So ask it yourself," he said, washing the crab down with warm beer.

"Why did I hire you?" Mason asked.

"You tell me," Smith said. "Has to be more than my good looks and charm."

"Sandra had found out something about Whitney and his family that she wanted to tell me but she hesitated because it may have been privileged and because I was on the other side. She was about to tell me when you called her. After that, she shut up."

"You think it had something to do with Whitney King, so you hired me because you think I'll tell you," Smith said.

"Sandra said you were working together on another case. I don't buy that."

"Why? Because she worked downtown and represented big corporations and white-collar crooks and I work on the east side representing people who get collared instead of wear collars? Or maybe it's one of those what's-a-good-looking-white-woman-doing-with-a-black-man things."

"Neither," Mason said, ignoring the bait. "Because I knew Sandra well enough to know that she didn't scare easily and she was shaking. She trusted me. That's the last thing she said to me before she was shot. She wanted to tell me something but didn't know how to do it. Whatever you said to her shut her up. I paid you a hundred thousand dollars to find out."

"Correction," Smith said, pushing back from the table. "Your auntie paid me." He walked into the dining room and tapped his foot against the flywheel on Mason's rowing machine. "Waste of time," Smith said, pointing to the machine. "All that work and you're right back where you started when you finish."

"You look like a runner," Mason said, following Smith into the dining room. "You do the same thing."

"Wrong. When I'm running, I'm always going someplace even if I always come back. Sandra was like that. Always going some place. Fact is we were working on another case.

One of her clients was a doctor with big-time gambling debts who'd gotten in too deep with a private lender. He was overcharging his Medicare patients to pay off his debts."

"And you represent the private lender who uses a bent-nose collector to pick up the weekly installment?"

"Her doctor rolled over on my lender as part of a deal with the feds," Smith said.

"Gang bangers, dope dealers, and loan sharks," Mason said. "Quality clientele."

"Don't give me that crap, Lou. You're right down there with the rest of us. Most of the people we represent are guilty. They know it, the prosecutors know it, and we know it. Sandra knew it, too. She knew I had contacts. People that could find out things that other people couldn't."

"She told me that she'd spent the weekend reviewing her firm's files on Whitney King's family. Did she find something that made her ask you for help?"

"She didn't say anything about any files. All she asked was if I would look into something for one of her firm's clients."

"Whitney King?"

"Close. His mother."

"She's in some kind of psychiatric nursing home," Mason said.

"They're separate facilities actually. A nursing home and a psychiatric hospital. Same company owns them. It's called Golden Years. Sandra wasn't sure which one the mother was in, but she wanted to know if the mother belonged in either one," Smith said.

"Don't tell me," Mason said. "You're not a doctor even though you play one on TV."

"You charge your clients for the jokes?" Smith asked.

"Depends on how many I have to tell. What's your nursing home connection?"

"Like you said, I've got a quality clientele. Not all of it is gang bangers, dope dealers, and loan sharks. There's a lot of money to be made taking care of old people. Those Medicare care regulations are a bitch. Going after doctors, hospitals, and nursing homes is easy money for the feds. Damon Parker owns Golden Years. I've kept him open for business a couple times when the feds had other ideas. He liked the fact that I had good contacts in the U.S. attorney's office from my days as a prosecutor."

"So, if Sandra wanted to know something about King's mother, why didn't she ask her or ask King?"

"You said she was scared," Smith said. "Maybe she didn't want King to know she was asking."

"What did you find out?" Mason asked.

"Nothing. I put out a feeler and Parker fired me. That's what I told Sandra when I called her."

"Ask a question and get fired. That makes the point," Mason said.

"Not like getting shot in the face," Smith said.

Chapter 33

It was close to ten o'clock when Dixon Smith left. Mason and Tuffy walked him to the curb, the dog stretching as Smith drove away. Mason kneaded the back of the dog's neck. The wind came in gusts, raising the rest of her coat. Thick layers of indigo clouds had rolled overhead, blanketing the stars and promising a storm powerful enough to shatter the heat wave.

He lingered at the curb, the dog nudging him to go inside, uneasy at the weather. At least one of them had the sense to avoid the storm.

"C'mon," he told the dog, who leaped out ahead of him. Mason followed slowly, hands jammed into his pockets.

He did a few slow laps around the first floor, cleaning up in the haphazard way of someone who has no one to clean up for, too restless to sit, reviewing the list of things he'd told Dixon Smith to do.

Run down Sandra's cell phone records and Whitney King's. Check local suppliers of stun guns for sales to King. Forget about Internet suppliers. There were too many and they don't employ real people anyway having figured out how to run a business entirely on e-mail and voice mail.

Find Janet Hook and Andrea Bracco, the last two jurors before they turn up dead. If they were still alive. And find Mary Kowalczyk.

Talk to Whitney King's mother, Victoria. Test her son's alibi. Figure out why Sandra questioned whether Victoria King belonged in either a psychiatric hospital or a nursing home and why Smith got fired for asking if she did.

Smith had nodded while Mason rattled off his checklist, not taking any notes.

"Thanks," Smith had told him when Mason finished. "Never would have thought of any of that."

"No charge," Mason said. "I appreciate your courtesy," he added, returning the jab.

"A hundred thousand dollars buys a lot of courtesy," Smith had replied. "Let me handle this, Lou. I know what I'm doing."

"Do I have a choice?"

"You've always got a choice. Not a good one, but you've got it."

Mason sat on the rowing machine's sliding seat, rolling forward and back a few times. He got up, a stationary workout not what he needed. Smith was right to keep him on the sidelines, but Mason didn't know how long he could stay there.

He grabbed his car keys and a moment later was southbound on Wornall Road heading for St. Joseph Hospital. Nick Byrnes was supposed to have had surgery earlier in the day. Visiting Nick wasn't meddling in Smith's handling of his case, Mason rationalized. The kid was probably still sleeping off the anesthetic anyway. It was something to do and that's what Mason needed.

The hospital lobby was brightly lit, though the lack of foot traffic and the faintly antiseptic air gave it an abandoned feel. No one greeted him from the information counter. He leaned over the rail above the food court looking for Nick's grandparents, finding only a young couple hunched over a table, the woman comforting the man.

Large signs directed him toward the Surgical Intensive Care Unit. He passed a few nurses on the way, but no one stopped to tell him that visiting hours were over. He found the double doors to the ICU, passed through them, and ran into his first resistance.

"May I help you?" a nurse said from her seat behind a circular workstation with a raised countertop that hid the desk where she was sitting. She was a stout, middle-age woman whose question wasn't a question. It was an order to get out.

Mason stepped up to the workstation, leaning over as the nurse straightened stacks of patient charts. "I'm a friend of Nick Byrnes. I just stopped by to see how he's doing," Mason said.

"Family only," the nurse said.

The ICU was designed in an outer ring of rooms with curtains instead of doors, the curtains drawn halfway. The nurse's station was an inner circle, giving the nurses a view into each room. The rooms were half-dark, lighted by the glow of monitors tracking vital signs. Patients' names were written on dry erase boards mounted at the entrance to each room. Mason scanned the names, finding Nick's on the far side, the words "Family Only" written beneath his name in red.

"How's he doing?" Mason asked.

"All patients in the ICU are considered to be in critical condition," the nurse said.

"Details only for the family?" Mason asked.

"That's correct, sir."

"I'm not family, but I think I qualify for an exception. My name is Lou Mason. I'm Nick's attorney."

The nurse's eyes fluttered as she caught her breath. He was not only in the news, he was bad news. Dropping his name had the opposite effect he had intended. She picked up the phone, holding the receiver to her breast. In her haste, she pushed several patient charts onto the floor.

"Family only," she repeated. "Please leave or I'll have to call security."

"It's all right," a woman said from behind Mason.

Mason turned, finding Esther Byrnes at his side. She looked up at him, her face worn with worry.

"Are you sure, Mrs. Byrnes?" the nurse asked. "I can call security."

"That won't be necessary," Nick's grandmother said. "I'm not afraid of Mr. Mason."

She slipped her arm around Mason's, tugging him gently. "Let's go see Nick," she said.

Mason smiled at the nurse, who held tightly to the phone, her finger poised, ready to dial if he tried anything funny.

"Was the surgery successful?" Mason asked Esther as she pulled the curtain back and they stood at the foot of Nick's bed. He was asleep, an oxygen line clipped to his nose, IV lines plugged into both arms, heart monitors glued to his chest.

Esther clutched Mason's arm with one hand, her other on the rail at the end of the bed. "The surgeon says he got the rest of the bullet fragments."

"Then he'll be okay," Mason said.

"I don't know what that means anymore, Mr. Mason. The surgeon said Nick's spinal cord was bruised, but that should heal and he'll be able to walk. It just takes time."

She squeezed Mason's arm again. Mason covered her hand with his. "Thanks for not being afraid of me," he said.

"You're no more a killer than that other boy, Ryan Kowalczyk," Esther said. "I can tell. It's that Whitney King. He makes everyone else look guilty. That's who I'm afraid of, Mr. Mason."

Chapter 34

The rain had begun while Mason was visiting Nick, blistering the pavement as he ran across the parking lot. He drove home, his clothing soaked, humidity inside the car fogging the windows. Thunder bellowed and the sky jumped with arcs of lightning. Pea-size pellets of hail snowballed into nickel and quarter-size rounds, bouncing off his car like automatic fire. By the time he pulled into his driveway, the front lawn was salted with hail.

Tuffy ran to greet him when he walked into the kitchen from the garage, planting her front paws on his belt, as afraid of the storm as a small child. He dropped to a knee, hugging the dog, stroking her coat, laughing at her name.

"You're more chicken than dog," he told her.

The wind roared outside, fighting the thunder for domination, muffling the rain as it beat against the house. Thunder exploded like a bomb dropped on his roof, shaking the windows. The interior walls glowed in the shadow of an electric blue lightning bolt, knocking out the power to his house.

The dog stayed close as Mason fumbled in the dark

kitchen for a flashlight he kept in a drawer. The question was which one. Mason cursed when he pulled one drawer out too far, dumping the contents at his feet. He found the flashlight in the next drawer, shining it on Tuffy who whined and shoved her wet nose into his hand.

Mason looked out his dining room window at the rest of his block. The streetlights were out and the other houses were dark. Peering between the houses across the street to the next block, he couldn't see any lights. The power failure wasn't his problem alone.

A car crept cautiously down the street, its headlights illuminating the rain that continued to fall in sheets. Mason stepped back into the darkness of the room, remembering the last time he'd watched a car come down his street late at night. This car turned into his driveway, the driver getting out, head covered with a jacket, racing to his front door.

Mason reached the door as the heavy brass knocker on the other side smacked against the strike plate. He pulled the door open, shining the light in his visitor's face.

"Nice night if it doesn't rain," Abby Lieberman said, stepping inside.

Mason lowered the light, the beam catching the water dripping from her coat. He took her hand, drawing her closer. She didn't resist, wrapping her arms around him, Mason holding on, not knowing what else to do. They stood like that, the door still open, the storm blowing past them, until the rain began to puddle at their feet. Tuffy circled them, rubbing against their legs, not willing to be left out of the reunion.

Abby finally let go, easing Mason's arms to her side. She crouched next to Tuffy, brushing back the dog's coat, not minding the paws on her shoulder. Standing again, she took the flashlight from Mason and shined it up and down him.

"At least Tuffy knew to come in out of the rain.

"You're a mess," she said. "What were you doing? she asked, closing the front door.

"I was out late. I got caught in the storm when I went to my car," he said, not wanting to tell her he'd been to see Nick or anything else that might send her away. He didn't know what was safe to say or not say, why she was here or whether she would stay. He was still raw from her sudden departure. Their chance meeting at the hospital had salted the wound, not healed it. He didn't know what to make of her return.

"I drove up from Jefferson City," she said. "We had a fund-raiser there tonight. I couldn't get away any earlier."

"I'm glad you came," Mason said.

"Then why don't you invite me into the living room like a proper guest?" she teased.

Abby aimed the flashlight past Mason into the living room, the dining room table casting a shadow against the wall, the bullet hole in the front window whistling with the wind. She gave Mason a sharp look, aiming the light into the dining room, outlining the rowing machine.

She let out a sigh. "Well, that didn't take too long."

"You said you weren't coming back," Mason answered, trying to keep his tone neutral.

The furniture wasn't important to either one of them. It was what it represented. Life with Abby was orderly and proper. Dining room tables belonged in the dining room. Exercise equipment belonged in the basement. Life with Mason was disorderly. Orderly was predictable and safe. Disorderly was unpredictable and dangerous.

Abby shook her head, the flashlight hanging limply from her hand, spotlighting their feet. She stepped past him, running the light along the wall and up the stairs as if she was retracing her route from when she'd last been there. She sat on the bottom step, knees drawn to her chest. Tuffy lay at her feet.

"I said there wasn't a place for me in your world. That didn't mean we couldn't be together in a different world. One where there's a sofa in the living room and the windows have screens instead of bullet holes."

"I'm sorry if that's the way you see it," he said.

"Is that supposed to be an apology?"

"Would an apology change anything?" he asked.

"Not that one. You're telling me that you're sorry I feel the way I do, not that you're sorry about the choices you've made. I call that an apology with a tail. I'd expect that from Josh Seeley because he's a politician, but not from you."

Her accusation stung, reminding Mason of a judge who increases a defendant's sentence for failing to take responsibilty for his crimes. Conceding her charge, he joined her on the stairs, the flashlight between them. The beam that bounced off the far wall kept them in the shadows.

"Then why did you drive two and a half hours in a monsoon in the middle of the night?"

"You're in trouble," she said. "Did you think I wouldn't come?"

He shook his head. "You told me why you left and nothing's changed, except for the worse. That's not much of a reason to come back. Besides, it's obvious how much Seeley and his campaign mean to you."

Abby leaned back against the wall. "Pour one cup of guilt, mix with equal amount of jealousy, and stir. You don't make this easy."

"I'm not much good at easy," he said.

"Does it matter that I cared enough to drive through the storm in the middle of the night just to make certain you're all right?"

"Not if you don't stay. I'm not a patient in a hospital. I don't need visitors."

Abby sprang to her feet, the heat in her eyes visible even

in the dark. She crossed her arms over her heaving chest. "What do you need, Lou? Someone to watch while you destroy yourself? I won't do that."

Mason rose. He wanted to put his arms around her again but she shrank against the wall when he stepped toward her.

"What am I supposed to do? You think I applied for the job of accused murderer?"

Abby chose her words carefully, measuring them as she spoke. "I think you don't care enough about what happens to you, which means you don't care enough about what happens to me or to us."

Mason didn't have an answer. Platitudes about the glory of the law, the duty to protect the innocent rang hollow in his mind. Pleading that he was a victim of events out of his control was weak, stupid, and untrue. No one had held a gun to his head when he said yes to Mary Kowalczyk and to Nick Burns. He had taunted Whitney King, dismissed Sandra Connelly's warnings, and ignored the advice of his own attorney as if he was checking each move off a list of ten things to do to ruin your life. Whatever he truly cared about, it was hard to prove Abby was wrong.

"I didn't mean it to be this way," he said.

Abby came to him and cupped his face with her hands. He held her wrists, feeling them both tremble.

"I love you. That's why I came back."

He lowered her hands, holding them at his sides. "Then stay," he said.

She looked down, tears rolling off her face. Mason raised her chin toward him, his hand caressing her neck, brushing against her scar.

"I can't," she whispered, grabbing his hand, pulling it from her neck, turning up the collar of her jacket, holding it to her throat. "It's why I came back, but it's why I can't stay."

Abby wiped her eyes and opened the door, her back to him.

"I'm innocent," he said.

The wind had died down, the rain slowing to a light shower. The thunder rumbled in the distance, the storm moving on.

"I believe you," she said, walking out without looking back.

Chapter 35

Innocence is, for some, simply the blessed ignorance of reality. For others, it's a state of grace, a pass into this world revoked on the way to the next. It's the first defense of the accused and the last words of the condemned: a protective mantle thrown over their shoulders by a system that rips apart its fabric in the pursuit of justice. It was a threadbare comfort to Mason when he considered how little his innocence mattered if it couldn't be proved.

Patrick Ortiz was readying his case against Mason for the grand jury. Ortiz would put forth all the evidence of Mason's guilt he wanted the jurors to hear. Mason would not be permitted to confront his accusers, offer evidence of his innocence, or be represented by a lawyer before the grand jury. Ortiz would call Mason to testify, forcing Mason to choose between answering questions, or refusing to answer on the grounds that his testimony may incriminate him. The right against self-incrimination carried the burden of exercising it, taking the Fifth Amendment a wink shy of a confession in the minds of many.

That the grand jury would indict Mason for the murder of Sandra Connelly was certain. Grand juries were often little more than rubber stamps wielded by prosecutors who loved the grand jury for its secrecy, for their ability to control the agenda, and for the gratification of announcing indictments returned by the people, like Moses coming down from the mountain.

Mason understood that Patrick Ortiz had other reasons for choosing the grand jury over a preliminary hearing. The prosecutor knew that a trial began long before the jury was selected, the opening rounds fought in the press. Ortiz had lost the first round in the coverage of Mason's arraignment and had decided to play catch-up with a swift indictment that would dominate the headlines.

Mason knew that potential jurors who swore to their ignorance and impartiality about a case in order to be selected had often read every scrap of news they could find. Even after they were selected to serve and the judge admonished them not to read or listen to any news reports about the case, or talk about the case to anyone, many did. They weren't liars in the willful way of CEOs and their accountants. They believed in their neutrality and they wanted to serve. But they couldn't resist the news. So unless they were out of the country until the moment of their selection and were sequestered thereafter, they lapped up press coverage like a cat laps up cream.

Sitting in his office late on Wednesday afternoon, Mason admitted that Ortiz had made the right play. Mason wouldn't complain, having used the media on behalf of his own clients if he needed the edge. Besides, he couldn't do anything about Ortiz's decision except practice saying that he respectfully declined to answer the question on the grounds that his answer might incriminate him. He was glad to have the constitutional right to refuse to answer, though he couldn't shake the weasel out of the words no matter how many times he repeated them.

He'd spent the day referring his clients to other lawyers. The criminal defendants understood, treating him with a new kinship that Mason couldn't embrace. A few of his civil clients protested, saying they would stick by him. Mason thanked them for their loyalty but explained that he had to devote his attention to his defense and that they would be well taken care of by their new lawyer.

Between phone calls, he reviewed his financial situation. The data were neatly organized on his computer.

He had ten thousand dollars in his law firm bank account and another seventy-five thousand in accounts receivable. With luck, he'd collect most of that over the next sixty days. He tallied up his unbilled time on the cases he was referring out, deducting those amounts from the retainers he'd been paid. The net was another twenty-seven thousand dollars. If everyone who owed him money paid up, he'd have enough to pay Claire back plus enough left over for lunch money.

He'd managed to save a few dollars since he'd opened his own practice though he'd taken a beating in the stock market. His portfolio was so thin it was invisible when he turned it sideways.

The house was his only other asset. He'd borrowed against it to even out the irregular cash flow of a one-man law practice, eating into the equity. He wasn't certain what the house would appraise at now but had the gnawing certainty that any remaining equity would be sucked out as soon as Dixon Smith ran through his initial hundred thousand dollar retainer. Without an income to repay the loan, he'd likely have to sell. His neighbors would probably help him pack.

He'd had this conversation with many clients, the financial impact of being charged with a crime often as devastating as the charge itself. At least a convicted spouse didn't have to worry about where his next meal was coming from even if it was only served with a spoon. The family that lost their breadwinner often paid a debt to society they didn't owe.

Telling himself the new financial facts of his life was another out-of-body experience for him. Each day another piece of his life broke off and washed away. He couldn't stop the erosion, knowing that he could bottom out on death row praying for a phone call from the governor. Patrick Ortiz and Dixon Smith would fight over his legal carcass, leaving him picked clean when it was time for the next case. It was nothing personal, they would say. It was just business.

"But I'm innocent," Mason muttered, turning off his computer, wishing it mattered.

He called Dixon Smith, getting his voice mail, leaving a message asking for an update on his case. Hanging up, he cringed with the recognition that he was quickly becoming the worst kind of client—the pain in the ass that calls every day expecting a miracle.

His practice shut down, Mason resorted to throwing darts at the board hanging on the wall across the room. He tried different techniques—the high lob, the underhand, the side arm toss. After five minutes and no hits close to the inner ring, he gave up, leaving the darts scattered across the wall.

He opened the cabinet covering his dry erase board and wiped it clean, needing to take a fresh look at his case. Dixon Smith didn't want his help. Good for Smith. Mason wouldn't help Smith. He'd help himself. Start at the beginning, build the case, find the thread that would tie it together. Put it in a nice package and deliver it to Smith. If Smith didn't like it, Mason could find another lawyer. Although by that time, he'd probably qualify as one of Nancy Troy's public defender clients.

He listed the key players on the board—Graham and Elizabeth Byrnes, their son Nick; Ryan Kowalczyk and his mother, Mary. Whitney King and his mother, Victoria. And Father Steve. He added the names of the jurors from the King and Kowalczyk trial, drawing circles around the names of Janet Hook and Andrea Bracco, the two still unaccounted for.

With a red marker, he added Sandra Connelly's name to the board, feeling again the jolt from the stun gun, recoiling from the gunshots that struck Sandra, sensing the killer's hand on his, squeezing the trigger. His memory let loose the scrap of the killer's familiarity that had eluded him that night, teasing him ever since. The killer smelled but not like someone who'd missed a bath. Like someone who'd smoked enough to be stained with tobacco. It was the same smell that permeated Father Steve, as if his confessional was in the church's smoking section.

Mason stepped back from the board. The priest had been with King when King shot Nick. The priest was the last person to have seen Mary, giving Mason a line that Mary had gone to see her estranged husband. Father Steve had told Mason that his job included soliciting contributions to the church from King. Maybe, Mason thought, he was more bag man than fund-raiser, hiding behind his clerical collar. Still, Mason couldn't imagine a reason for Father Steve to kill Sandra. Then again, he couldn't shake the memory of that moment and his certainty that the killer was dipped in smoke. The priest was still the center of the wheel, everyone else a spoke.

The phone rang, Mason answering it, half-listening as he stared at the board.

"Lou, it's Dixon," his lawyer said.

"Yeah," Mason answered. "What's up?"

"You called me, man," Smith answered.

"Right. I did. I just wanted to know if you had anything new. I'm sorry. I'm not going to be one of those clients that make you wish you'd doubled the retainer. I know you'll call me when you have something to tell me."

"Hey, don't apologize," Smith said. "If it was my life, I'd be calling you every fifteen minutes. I was going to call you anyway. It's been a busy day."

Mason sat at his desk, turning his back to the board. "I'm listening."

"Ortiz has subpoenaed Blues, Whitney King, and Father Steve to testify before the grand jury. And you. I told him I'd accept service of your subpoena. He wants you Friday afternoon at three o'clock."

"Who else is going to testify?"

"The cops and the coroner," Smith answered.

"When do you want to get together to talk about my testimony?"

"There's nothing to talk about, Lou. You say anything in there except your name and the Fifth Amendment, you might as well check in to the penitentiary now and save the taxpayers their money. I'll meet you there."

"You're right. I've been practicing my lines. Is that it?"

"No. I talked to Whitney King. He said he didn't know anything about a meeting with you and Sandra."

"That's no surprise. What about the phone records?"

"If the phone companies didn't have lawyers, I'd have gotten the records today. Should still have them by Friday."

"It is what it is," Mason said.

"There's something else," Smith said. "It's the kind of thing Ortiz will leak to the press so get ready."

Mason's gut chilled. "What?"

"The coroner says the first bullet didn't kill Sandra. When she put her hands up, it deflected the bullet. The first shot did a lot of facial damage but exited through her cheek."

"The second shot?" Mason asked.

Smith said, "Fatal. Blew a hole in her heart." He paused, letting the news sink in. "Don't worry, Lou. It's all expert witness jive. There's a pathologist in New York who testifies in all the high-profile cases on the East Coast. I'll call him tomorrow. He requires twenty-five grand up front before he'll even look at a case, but I think we're going to need him."

"Sure. Whatever you say," Mason said, dropping the receiver in his lap, not hearing Smith say good-bye. He swiveled his chair back toward the board. All he could see was Sandra's name written in red.

Chapter 36

The minimum qualifications for the grand jurors who would decide whether to charge Mason with murder were that they had either registered to vote or had licensed a car. Those were the lists from which the grand jury was chosen to serve for a six-month term.

Mason knew that selecting a jury was one of the most critical parts of a trial. It was his chance to question potential jurors about anything that could reveal their bias against his client. Billed as a way to select a fair jury, it was, in reality, a way to de-select jurors who were likely to favor the other side.

When he selected a jury, Mason tried to learn as much as he could about each potential juror: where they lived, where they went to school, what they did for a living, what they thought about legal issues such as the death penalty and the burden of proof. He observed their body language, thought about the clothes they wore, and wondered if they watched PBS or *American Idol* and whether they read *USA Today* or *The Wall Street Journal*.

The grand jury was different, chosen at random from the

county's master list of jurors. Neither Mason nor his lawyer had any right to question them or to object to their selection. His fate was in the hands of twelve strangers whose names had been plucked from the public rolls.

On Friday, Mason chose a navy blue suit for his grand jury testimony, rejecting the black as too funereal and the gray as too bland. He picked a white shirt and a pale blue tie, hoping the ensemble shouted his innocence in muted tones. He was in the bathroom down the hall from the courtroom used by the grand jury studying his appearance in a mirror, only minutes left before he would testify. He caught a tic in the corner of his left eye, an involuntary betrayal of his less than steely nerves. Worried that the grand jurors would read the minispasm as a guilty plea, he massaged the spot, hoping it would pass.

That his life might depend on such trivial matters sent the tic momentarily into overdrive. He loved the courtroom arena, always getting juiced by the battle, never shrinking from the challenge. He embraced nervousness, knowing that it was born of anticipation, not fear. Beneath it all, he had an inner calm nurtured by his trust of the system. He believed in its fundamental fairness and he never doubted the wisdom of leaving life and death to a jury of one's peers.

Until today. Hearing his name called as the defendant and not the counsel of record changed everything. Now every weakness in the system jumped out at him like bogeymen at a haunted house. Prosecutors dealt from a stacked deck. Jurors had hidden agendas, waiting for a chance to star in the ultimate reality show. Defendants were presumed innocent but must have done something wrong to have been charged in the first place.

Grand jury proceedings were more frightening because they were secret. The jurors were prohibited from disclosing the witnesses' testimony or their vote on whether to indict.

Witnesses, however, were free to discuss their testimony after their appearance.

Whitney King had been the first witness that morning, holding a brief televised press conference afterward on the courthouse steps. Mason had watched from his office. The storm had left behind a city with temperatures in the low eighties, Mother Nature's apology for the brutal heat wave. Morning was even cooler, giving King a crisp appearance, the sun smiling over his shoulder.

"What did you tell the grand jury?" a reporter asked King.

"The truth," King answered. "When I was charged with a crime, I put my faith in the truth and I wasn't disappointed."

"At the arraignment, Lou Mason's lawyer said you were supposed to meet Mason and Sandra Connelly at your office. Is that true?" another reporter asked.

King shook his head. "No. I told the grand jury that I don't know anything about that."

"Why would Mason say that if it was so easy to prove he was lying?" a third reporter asked. The camera panned to the reporter. It was Sherri Thomas from Channel 6, no friend of Mason's. She had chased Mason throughout the Gina Davenport case, Mason refusing to feed her habit of distorted reporting aimed only at boosting her ratings. The camera swept back to King for his answer.

"Desperate people do desperate things," King said.

"Like Nick Byrnes trying to kill you?" Thomas asked.

King pursed his lips. "Nick Byrnes and I have more in common than you think," he said. "We've both been hurt by the murders of his parents. I understand that and that's why I'm not pressing charges against him. The doctors say he's going to be okay. I'm glad for that. It's time for both of us to move on."

"What about the disappearance of Mary Kowalczyk and the suspicious deaths of all those jurors who found you innocent? Why do so many people connected to you end up shot, missing, or dead?" yet another reporter asked.

The camera remained locked on King, but Mason recognized the reporter's voice. It was Rachel Firestone. Mason knew she wasn't covering the story. She was covering him. King's jaw tightened, his eyes narrowing for an instant as he fought with his composure.

"Life is a fragile thing, Ms. Firestone. You'd do well to remember that," he answered.

Moments from his grand jury appearance, Mason repeated King's answer, rolling it around in his mind, testing it for elements of confession and threat. He owed Rachel a bottle of her favorite wine for taking the shot at King, especially since he knew her editors at the *Kansas City Star* would probably kick her to the classifieds for butting into a story that was off limits to her because of her friendship with Mason. He was grateful for what she had done, but didn't want her on Whitney King's short list of problems to be solved.

He took a last look in the bathroom mirror. The tic had submerged for the moment. He splashed cold water on his face, wiped it clean and winked at himself for luck.

The grand jury met in a courtroom on the sixth floor of the courthouse guarded by sheriff's deputies who kept out the curious. Dixon Smith was waiting for Mason outside the courtroom, greeting him with a firm handshake and a clap on the back. Smith guided him to a quiet alcove.

"I got the phone records this morning. There's no record of a call from Whitney to Sandra."

Mason leaned hard against the wall. "Maybe Whitney stole a cell phone so the call couldn't be traced to him."

"Negative," Smith said. "All of Sandra's incoming calls are accounted for except one that fits with your time frame.

There's no information identifying the source of that call, only that it was received."

"How can that be?"

"I don't know yet. But, if Whitney used his phone, there would be a record of it. If he stole a cell phone, there would be a record on that account and on Sandra's bill. We can show Sandra received a call, but we can't prove who made it."

"Swell. Who am I following?" Mason asked.

"The priest," Smith answered. "Father Steve. I think Ortiz is going to use the shooting of Nick Byrnes as part of your motive. He'll tell the grand jury that you decided to take the law into your own hands or some bullshit like that."

"Were you here when Father Steve came out? Did you get close to him?"

"Not close enough to make confession. Why?"

"Did he smell like he'd been smoking?"

Smith thought for a moment. "Yeah, I guess he did, now that you mention it. So what? Even a priest has to have a few vices."

"Remember I told you that there was something familiar about the killer but I couldn't put my finger on it? Well, I remembered. It's that smell."

Smith rolled his eyes. "Lou, you don't have enough problems, you want to accuse a priest of killing Sandra Connelly because he smokes?"

"It's all I've got," Mason said.

"Then we damn well better get something else. Now, remember the magic words—Fifth Amendment—and you'll be out of there in five minutes," Smith said.

"If I'm not, send in a search party," Mason said.

Smith gave him another pat and opened one of the heavy, double doors for Mason who stepped inside the courtroom, the door silently closing behind him, a small rush of air swooshing out of the room. Mason stood still for a moment, surveying the scene.

The courtroom was big, suitably grand for the stature of the jury. The judge's raised bench was vacant, flanked by the state flag on one side and the Stars and Stripes on the other. The Great Seal of the State of Missouri hung above the bench, two bears surrounding the inscription "United We Stand, Divided We Fall." It was a curious choice for a state that had been more slave than free when that phrase meant something.

Without a judge, it felt to Mason more like a movie set with the grand jury rehearsing their roles. They were dressed for summer, wearing short-sleeved shirts, slacks, and jeans. Even Patrick Ortiz had taken off his suit coat and rolled up his sleeves as if their production wasn't even a dress rehearsal. Though he knew it was real, Mason still couldn't believe the part he was playing.

The jury box was cut from dark walnut, as were the judge's bench, counsel tables, and pews. There were no windows, the only light coming from a constellation of fixtures planted in the high ceiling, bulbs shaded by opaque milky glass, diffusing cool light, leaving the room gray and cold.

The grand jurors were seated in the jury box, legal pads poised on their laps for the notes they were taking. They were a mix of races and ages, all staring at him. He wanted to study them, do a quick and dirty jury analysis, pick the strong leaders to focus on, the weak followers to ignore. But he knew there wasn't time. Hesitation, even at taking his seat, could give the wrong impression.

Mason smiled at them, nodding, drawing a handful of smiles and nods in return, pleased that he'd made a connection, even if it was only a reflex courtesy. He strode toward the witness stand, paying no attention to Patrick Ortiz who stood at his counsel table, head down, gathering his notes. One assistant prosecutor arranged stacks of exhibits while another hurriedly scratched questions on a legal pad. The flurry of activity would be wasted as soon as Mason invoked the Fifth Amendment.

The court reporter seated at her steno machine raised her right hand as Mason approached the witness stand.

"Raise your right hand and be sworn," she told Mason who faced her, his hand up, palm out, level with his face. "Do you solemnly swear that the testimony you are about to give in this proceeding shall be the truth, the whole truth, and nothing but the truth, so help you God?"

Mason looked past her to the grand jurors, answering in a loud, clear voice. "I do."

"Be seated," the court reporter said.

Patrick Ortiz sauntered to the podium in the center of the courtroom, sighing as he put his papers down. He was a working man doing the people's business. Without a judge, it was like playing a ball game without an umpire. Every pitch would be a strike.

"State your name," Ortiz said.

"Lou Mason."

"Mr. Mason, this grand jury has been convened in the matter of the death of Sandra Connelly," Ortiz began. "You understand that you have been summoned here to testify in connection with that crime?"

The witness chair could swivel and rock, adding more spin to an evasive witness. Mason leaned against its wooden back, planted his feet firmly on the floor, hands folded in his lap, bracing the chair with his feet.

"I do," he answered.

"Mr. Mason, were you with Sandra Connelly when she was killed?"

The question was a simple one. The answer would place him at the scene of the crime, the first step in convincing the grand jury that he should be charged with murder.

Mason couldn't answer the questions he liked and invoke

the Fifth Amendment to avoid the questions he didn't want to answer. The privilege was absolute, not elastic. If he answered any question about what happened that night, his privilege was gone forever. If he declined to answer, Ortiz would ask a few more questions to make the point that he was refusing to testify, then kick him loose.

His case was a marathon, not a sprint. The smart play was to take the Fifth. He'd take his lumps today and be ready for trial. The privilege was for his protection. He had never let a client waive it, making the prosecutor earn his money. It would be a mistake to break that rule in his case.

Still, Mason wanted to answer. He wanted to put his faith in these people, not the system. He wanted to talk to them the way he knew Ortiz would. Like they were having coffee and he was telling them what happened. They were reasonable people. They would understand. They would believe him.

The grand jurors were sitting twenty feet away, holding the power to indict him for murder or set him free. He knew that they wanted to hear what he had to say as much as he wanted to tell them and that his refusal, no matter how well grounded in the law, would turn them against him.

He looked at them again. They were sitting up straight, edged forward in their chairs, a few holding their breath without knowing it.

"Mr. Mason," Ortiz said, stepping around the podium, holding a plastic evidence bag containing his handgun. "Would you like me to repeat the question?"

Mason squared his shoulders and turned toward the grand jury, the mantra of his right not to testify forming in his mind, the words never materializing, shoved aside by what seemed like common sense.

"I didn't kill her."

Chapter 37

Mason emerged from the courtroom four hours later surrounded by a half-moon gauntlet of reporters, cameras flashing and questions exploding in his face. The reporters swarmed over him, knowing he'd been inside too long just to have refused to testify. He spotted Dixon Smith behind the crowd, leaning against the wall, his arms crossed like he was wearing a straitjacket; his head was tilted back, eyes roaming the hallway for an emergency exit.

Sherri Thomas pushed to the front of the pack, her cameraman poised at her shoulder. She wore her blonde hair cut close to her chin and her suit cut close to her implants, aiming her looks at her key demographics.

"You were in there a long time, Mr. Mason. Does that mean you didn't refuse to testify?" she asked.

Dixon Smith knifed through the crowd, grabbing Mason by the elbow, raising his hand and flashing a smile before Mason could respond.

"Mr. Mason is cooperating with the process," Smith replied, not giving Sherri anything she could use.

"You mean he didn't take the Fifth?" Sherri asked.

"I mean he's cooperating with the process," Smith answered.

"Then let him answer our questions. We're part of the process too," Sherri said.

"Mr. Mason is innocent," Smith said. "We'll try his case in the courtroom, not the press. That's all we have to say at this time."

Holding onto Mason, Smith shouldered through the pack of reporters who followed them to the elevator, blocking them from coming along for the ride down, waiting for the doors to close before he unloaded on his client.

"Tell me what happened in there," Smith began, as he punched the button for the basement floor and paced inside the car. "And make it good because I've spent the last four hours telling myself that you aren't stupid enough to have really thought you could convince the grand jury that you were innocent."

Smith stopped moving, hands on his hips, daring Mason to disagree. Mason took a deep breath, looked away and let the air out, his answer evaporating in the silence.

Smith squeezed his chin like he'd rather rip it off than cut Mason any slack. "Tell me," he continued, "you didn't look at those twelve people and convince yourself that everything would be okay if you just told them what happened since they looked like fair minded, reasonable people who would believe you because it was so obvious you were telling the truth and the prosecutor was full of shit to have even taken up their time with his bogus story that you shot Sandra Connelly with your own fucking gun! Tell me that you didn't do that!"

Smith banged his hand against the elevator wall as the door opened. Mason walked past his lawyer into the basement corridor that led to the exit reserved for attorneys and courthouse personnel. Smith caught up to him, planted his hand on Mason's shoulder and whirled him around.

"Tell me!"

"It seemed like a good idea at the time," Mason said quietly, biting off the words.

"Really?" Smith asked. "A good idea? Why?"

"Because," Mason answered, "I didn't kill her."

"Like that makes a damn bit of difference, man," Smith said, releasing his grip on Mason's shoulder. He straightened Mason's lapels, the exaggerated gesture helping him calm down. "So," he continued as if they were talking about their golf game, "how did it go?"

Mason pursed his lips, stuck his hands in his pants pockets and shrugged his shoulders. "Shitty. I fucked up. It was a bad idea. Ortiz worked me over pretty good. He punched enough holes in my story that I was ready to indict me. I think the only reason he quit was that he got tired. I'm sorry."

"Don't apologize to me, man," Smith said. "I've still got a life."

Mason slumped against the wall. "Do I need a new lawyer?" he asked.

"Not until your money runs out."

Mason asked, "What do I do now?"

"I'd tell you to go home and clean out your sock drawer and let me do my job, except I know that you won't. I'd tell you to get a rabbi and start praying, but you won't put your faith in anyone but yourself. So the only thing I can tell you is whatever you do, don't make it any harder for me," Smith said.

Mason perked up at Smith's suggestion. "Maybe I'll get a priest instead of a rabbi."

"You planning on converting to the pope's religion or meddling some more in my case?" Smith asked.

"Just hedging my bets in case there's more than one way to get to heaven."

* * *

Mason was resigned to his coming indictment for murder, his testimony sealing the deal for the prosecutor. At least Dixon Smith had given up trying to keep him on the sidelines. He was caught in the middle of a mess he'd made and he was the only one who could clean it up. As good as Smith was, waiting to be vindicated at trial wasn't an option. Ortiz's conviction rate was better than 90 percent. Adding in Mason's testimony boosted Ortiz's chances even higher. Relying on those odds made him feel like a patient with a terminal disease hoping for a miracle.

Whenever a case closed in on him with suffocating confusion, he started over. He'd done that when he wiped his dry erase board clean, putting the players back on the board. That exercise ignited his suspicion of Father Steve, fueled by his recovered memory that Sandra's killer had smelled of smoke. Dixon Smith had doused that theory, reminding Mason that paranoia and desperation revealed paranoia and desperation more often than they revealed the truth.

On the other hand, he conceded as he power walked to his car, paranoia and desperation were damn good motivators to get out of his office and back on the street where he could find some real answers. He rolled the windows down, letting his thoughts circulate with the breeze, and drove while he clicked off what he knew, what he believed, and what he didn't know but had to find out.

He knew that Graham and Elizabeth Byrnes had been murdered by either Ryan Kowalczyk or Whitney King, or both. He believed that Ryan was innocent and King was guilty; one boy executed, the other free. He didn't know how to prove it.

He knew that Father Steve had told Mary Kowalczyk that her son had confessed to the murders minutes before his execution. He believed that the priest had lied to Mary. He didn't know why.

He knew that ten out of the twelve jurors who had acquitted King were dead, only two of them dying in their sleep after a life lived well and full. He believed that King had killed the other eight. He didn't know why.

He knew that the last two jurors, Janet Hook and Andrea Bracco, were unaccounted for. He believed they knew why the other jurors had been killed. He didn't know where they were.

He knew that Whitney King had shot Nick Byrnes. He believed that Father Steve was covering up for King, corroborating King's claim of self-defense. He didn't know why.

He knew that Mary Kowalczyk was missing and that Father Steve was the last person to have seen her. He believed the priest had lied to Mason when he said he didn't know what had happened to her. He didn't know why.

He knew that Sandra Connelly had been killed with his gun. He believed that she was killed to prevent her from telling him something about Whitney King that would have answered at least some of Mason's questions. He didn't know what that was.

The litany snaked into territory Mason hadn't expected. He had hired Dixon Smith because he believed that Smith had known what Sandra was about to tell him. Smith had denied knowing, giving Mason a story about whether King's mother belonged in a nursing home. Replaying Smith's story, Mason remembered one of the first lessons his aunt Claire had given him about practicing law.

"It's not that people lie to you," she said. "It's that they mix the truth up with lies until they can't tell the difference and neither can you."

Smith had pushed Mason to the sidelines and told him to keep his mouth shut to the grand jury. It was the same advice Mason would have given if Smith had been his client. It didn't matter. Paranoia and desperation were circulating in the air like night riders on a raid. A cold current whipsawed Mason. He didn't trust his lawyer and he didn't know why.

Mason parked in front of Mary Kowalczyk's house, the setting sun painting the picture window a burnt orange before giving way to a dusky violet shadow. It had been several days since Mason had stopped by. Newspapers soaked by the storm had disintegrated on the driveway; weeds sprouted through the cracks in the sidewalk. The house seemed to sag as if it missed Mary.

The mailbox was full, the contents kept dry by overhanging eaves. He shuffled the envelopes, checking the return addresses for any hints of what might have happened to her. There were no postcards or ransom notes. Her life was captured in a thin string of credit card solicitations, discount coupons, and utility bills that kept coming, indifferent to her fate.

He knocked on the front door and jiggled the knob, a combination of pretense and wishful thinking that roused no one. The back door was still unlocked, the air in the house musty and stale. He moved slowly through each room, looking for things he hadn't seen before, finding only his images of Mary.

He first saw her at her son's execution, a slight woman compressed by her grief. Two days later, at his office, she had shown a lock-jawed determination to see justice done for her son. The last time he'd seen her had been in this house surrounded by her memories, an ordinary woman in an ordinary place carrying an extraordinary burden.

She had asked then if he was going to drop her case. He promised her that he wouldn't. He had made the same promise to Nick, though he wasn't sure he was keeping either promise. Walking through Mary's house, he realized that he hadn't dropped their cases. He'd been kicked off of them by Sandra's murder, forced to worry more about saving himself than serving his clients.

Perhaps, he thought, Sandra hadn't been killed to keep her quiet. Maybe she'd been nothing more than a pawn in a deadly strategy to eliminate Mason as a threat. It would have been simpler just to kill him, though setting him up to take the fall for her murder would do just that. The state would kill Mason, making him the second innocent man to be executed for a murder committed by Whitney King. If Mason was right, Whitney King had redefined what it meant to work the system.

Everything in Mary's house was as it had been on Mason's first visit. Nothing was out of place. Her bed was made. Her clothes were undisturbed. The copy of *People* magazine was where Mason had left it after he had spent an evening waiting for Mary to come home. It all appeared as he had left it until he stopped at the aquarium to feed the fish, staring at the water until he realized the fish were gone.

"What the hell?" Mason said out loud.

The deep-sea diver stared back at him, alone in the tank.

Chapter 38

Mary was alive. That was the only conclusion Mason could reach. No one else would have bothered to retrieve the fish. He discounted the possibility that the fish died and someone else threw them away. He raced through his reasoning, checking for flaws, hitting one head on. If the police were investigating Mary's disappearance, they could have gotten a warrant to search her house, discovered that the fish were dead and disposed of them.

He paced back and forth in front of the aquarium, flipping open his cell phone and calling Samantha Greer on hers.

"Sam, it's Lou."

"How could you be so stupid?" she asked.

"About what?" he asked, stunned by her vehemence.

"The grand jury!" she said, unable to hide her exasperation. "Ortiz couldn't wait to tell me. Honest to God, Lou. What were you thinking?"

"That I'm innocent. That I've gotten nothing to hide and that the system protects the innocent."

"Fractured fairy tales and you know it as well as anyone does," Samantha said.

"Hey, you're supposed to be on Ortiz's side, not mine."

"I know," she said. "I am on his side. I investigated the crime scene. I found your gun. But I don't want you to be guilty and, even if you are guilty, I don't want you to make it so easy for Ortiz to nail you."

"I had to spot him a few points to make it a fair fight," Mason said.

"Don't even try that crap with me, Lou," she said. "Ortiz is very good and you're not defending yourself. You're the defendant. Dixon Smith is your lawyer."

Mason forgot about Mary's fish for the moment. "You make being defended by Dixon sound almost as bad as being arrested. What do you hear about him?"

Samantha hesitated, cleared her throat. "Nothing. Forget it," she said. "He's fine, from what I hear."

"Okay," Mason said. "Now get back on my side and tell me what you really hear."

"He's your guy," Samantha said. "Why did you hire him if you're worried about what I've heard?"

"Remember me? I'm the guy charged with murder who waived my right against self-incrimination. You think I'm smart enough to pick the right lawyer to defend me?"

Samantha laughed. Mason was pleased at the sound of her voice. In spite of their luckless romantic history, he and Samantha had been able to hold onto their friendship. He needed that now.

"Good point," she said. "Okay, I hear that he practices at the edges. Maybe gets too close to his clients."

Mason knew what she meant. Criminal defense lawyers were not immune to the temptations sometimes offered to them by their clients, especially those whose illegal operations generated wholesale amounts of cash, drugs and women—or men—depending on the lawyer's gender and inclinations. A lawyer who got too close to his clients could end up in business with them whether he liked it or not.

"Any particular client?" Mason asked. Samantha hesitated again, Mason pressing her. "C'mon Sam," he said. "If I've got a problem, I need to know now, not when I'm writing appeals from death row."

"Damon Parker."

"The guy who owns Golden Years, the nursing home guy?" Mason asked, the muscles in his neck tightening.

"Yeah. That Damon Parker. He's made a fortune developing something he calls Life Care Communities. He builds condos, assisted living apartments, nursing homes, and psychiatric hospitals with Alzheimer's disease units. All under one roof. Signs people up for the last part of the downhill slide. All the way from independent living to the graveyard. When their insurance or Medicare kicks in, he moves them back and forth from the hospital to the nursing home as each round of coverage runs out."

"What's illegal about that if the insurance companies or Medicare are supposed to pay for the care?"

"That's not the problem. The problem is billing for care that isn't given, like therapy given to dead patients, or care that isn't needed, like claiming that everyone over the age of seventy has Alzheimer's. It's a federal investigation so I only know what I hear."

"Then how do you know anything about it at all?" She didn't answer, Mason filling in the blanks. "Ortiz told you after Dixon Smith waxed him at my arraignment. Ortiz has friends in the U.S. attorney's office. They must have told him. Smith used to be an assistant U.S. attorney until he quit and started his own practice."

"He didn't quit, Lou," Samantha said softly. "I'm sorry, but that's all I can tell you and I shouldn't have told you that much."

"I'm glad you did," he said. "You have to admit, though, he did a great job for me at the arraignment."

"So what? He got you out on bail so you could hand Ortiz your head in front of the grand jury!" she snapped, before apologizing. "I'm sorry, Lou. You've got enough problems without me yelling at you too, but it's not too late to hire someone else."

"I'll keep that in mind," Mason answered, remembering that he'd given similar advice to Sandra Connelly, telling her she could quit representing Whitney King. Sandra wasn't ready to let go of King and he wasn't ready to fire Smith.

Smith's story that Sandra Connelly had asked him to look into whether Whitney King's mother belonged in a nursing home was suddenly more interesting to Mason. Especially the part about Smith's client firing him when he made the inquiry. His Aunt Claire's lesson about mixing truth and lies reverberated again. If he fired Smith, he wouldn't be able to separate those facts from fiction.

"You didn't call to get a reference for your lawyer," Samantha said. "What do you want?"

He'd stopped pacing without realizing it, finding himself staring again at the aquarium. "Has anything happened with the missing person's report I filed on Mary Kowalczyk?" he asked.

"I talked to the detective on the case today. Her name is Barbara Wilson. She's got a stack of reports and yours is on it."

"At the bottom?" Mason asked.

"Dead last," she answered. "She's got more to read than she'll ever have time for. She does a great job with the cases she gets to, but she's overworked and underpaid."

"That's great!" Mason said.

"You're kidding," Samantha said. "How can that be great?"

"It's a real fish story. Remind me to tell you later," Mason said.

* * *

The online world was open for business every second of every day, converting distances formerly measured in miles to download times measured in seconds. Mickey Shanahan had convinced Mason to buy a laptop with a wireless Internet connection to use at home, explaining to Mason that he could be online whether he was working at his desk or sitting on the toilet.

"I've got the *Kansas City Star* if I need something to do with my hands when I'm on the can," Mason had told him.

"Think globally," Mickey had said. "You could read the *New York Times* and the *Washington Post* instead."

"I'm a creature of habit. My bowels are used to the local paper," Mason told him.

"Be careful, boss," Mickey had said. "Once you start planning your life around your bowels, you're doomed. You'll skip middle age and go straight to a soft food diet. You'll end up with one of those seven-day pill packs filled with fiber pills, vitamins, and stool softeners. You won't be able to shack up away from home because of all the crap you've got to take before you go to bed each night."

It was easier to buy the laptop than argue with Mickey about his future. He and Abby had stocked each other's bathrooms with travel sets of their toiletries. It had been a gradual process, a few things added at a time, proving Mickey's point that spontaneous sleepovers became more difficult after the age of forty. After a while, he'd cleared a dresser drawer for her night things and underwear and she'd done the same for him. They had been easing toward living together while avoiding a decision whether to move into his place or hers. Mason had left her things where they were, unable to pack them up.

Mickey taught him how to use the laptop and Mason had become a proficient surfer. He logged on while seated in his living room at the dining room table. He'd picked up Greek carryout on the way home, washed it down with a cold beer, and shoved the remains to the center of the table to make room for his computer. He kicked off his shoes, rubbing Tuffy's belly with his bare foot.

Rachel Firestone's sources had said that King's mother, Victoria, had been a patient at the Golden Years Psychiatric Hospital since the death of her husband, Christopher King, his death coming on the heels of Whitney's acquittal in the Byrneses murder trial. Mason could understand how the combination of those events could fracture a sound psyche, though Victoria King's must have been eggshell thin to have left her institutionalized for the last fifteen years.

Mason found the Golden Years Web site touting its caring staff and comfortable surroundings at its nursing homes and psychiatric hospitals located in Kansas, Missouri, Iowa, and Illinois. He clicked on the button for locations, selecting Lenexa, Kansas.

The hospital and nursing home were located on a twenty-five-acre campus that included condos and assisted living apartments. A map showed directions to Golden Years, Mason noting that it was only a short distance from Burning Oak, the exclusive development where Whitney King lived. It was hard to fault a man for living close to his mother.

Mason returned to the Golden Years home page, clicked on a link titled "About Us" and learned that the privately owned company was founded thirty years ago to—according to its mission statement—"provide special care for special people with special needs."

There was a message from Damon Parker, the president of the company, spreading good cheer and compassion for the elderly and those suffering from mental illness and Alzheimer's. Parker's picture was pasted in the upper-right-hand corner of the Web page, a thin-faced man with a

Marine brush cut, black-rimmed glasses over narrow, hawk-ish eyes, and a smile that Mason was certain had been digitally enhanced. Parker looked to be in his late sixties, maybe early seventies, and Mason wondered whether he'd reserved his own Golden Years suite.

After reading Parker's message, Mason clicked on the word "more" scripted in bright blue at the bottom of the page. The following Web pages recited the company's history and included photographs of the groundbreaking ceremony for the Lenexa location. Mason double-clicked on those photographs, enlarging them one at a time to fill his computer screen. He held the laptop up so he could study the pictures more closely, setting it down again when he saw what he was looking for.

"Son of a bitch," he said, pressing too firmly on Tuffy's stomach, the dog snapping at Mason's toes. "Sorry, dog," Mason said, patting her on the head, "but you aren't going to believe this."

Mason carried the laptop to the office he kept in one of the upstairs bedrooms. He attached a printer cable to the laptop, put a sheet of photo quality paper in the printer, and clicked print. A moment later, he had a glossy image of the groundbreaking ceremony, a sign reading "King Construction Company, General Contractor" clearly visible in the background. Mason had no trouble picking out Damon Parker. He had had the birdlike face, geek glasses, and flattop haircut a long time. Equally obvious was Christopher King, a dead ringer for his son Whitney. Both men were grinning, holding gold-tipped shovels and wearing spotless hard hats.

A woman and a little boy stood behind Christopher King, the woman draping her hand across the boy's chest, the boy grasping a miniature shovel, gold-tipped like his father's. Mason savored the irony that Whitney's father had built a home for his wife without even knowing it.

He carried the picture of little Whitney and his parents into his bedroom, comparing it to one of him and his parents Claire had given to him when he was a boy. It was more snapshot than portrait, a five-by-seven showing Mason on a swing set, his father pushing him from behind, his mother pretending to catch him. Claire had taken the picture a week before his parents were killed, the date written on the back. Mason kept the picture in a Plexiglas frame on the nightstand next to his bed, space shared with a framed picture of Abby.

He sat on his bed, laying the King family picture aside, thinking of his fragmented past and his uncertain future. The phone rang, saving him from dipping too deeply into those waters. He let it ring twice before picking up.

"Hello," he said, his thoughts still distant.

Harry Ryman said, "Lou, I finally got the story on that license plate you asked me to run. Sorry it took all week, but like I told you, the chief has made it tough. The son of a bitch says the department isn't in the favor business."

Mason stood, not taking his eyes from the picture of him and his parents. "You mean the license plate from the cemetery?"

"What cemetery?" Harry asked. "You didn't say anything about a cemetery."

"Sorry, Harry," Mason said. "What did you find out?"

"The car is a Mercedes SUV registered to a woman named Judith Bartholow."

"Did you get an address?" Mason asked, grabbing a pen.

"I'm full service," Harry said reciting the address. Mason wrote it down on the back of the King picture. "Her name mean anything to you?" he asked Mason.

"I hope so," Mason answered.

Chapter 39

There were times in a case when Mason knew he was on the verge of making sense out of the contradictory, indifferent, and depraved impulses that led people to lie, cheat, and kill. It was an urgent, irresistible sensation that reminded him of when he used to fly down the long, steep, sweeping curve of Ward Parkway from Fifty-fifth Street to the Plaza.

It was the summer before his junior year in high school when the only thing he could drive was a ten-speed bike. In those days before the Plaza went upscale, Sears occupied a four-story building on the west end of Nichols Road, the shopping district's main drag. Mason worked on every floor and in every department from electrical to women's hose, setting a record for the most men's cologne sold the day before Father's Day.

Ward Parkway was a wide boulevard divided by a lush, green median. South of Fifty-fifth, it carried traffic on a level plane to the homes of the urban landed gentry. North of Fifty-fifth Street it became a bike rider's bobsled run, fast and furious. Mason would kick his bike into high gear just before he crossed Fifty-fifth Street, churning the pedals, making his spokes blur as he launched himself down the stretch he called "The Chute."

He hunched over the handlebars, molding his body to the frame, elbows tight to his sides like a jockey on the home stretch. His necktie whipped over his shoulder, the wind digging tears out of the corners of his eyes as he leaned into the curve, pounding the pedals, shooting past cars on his left. He flew, skinny tires spinning over the pavement, teasing gravity and fate, knowing that a misplaced pebble or an unseen crack in the pavement could throw him under the tires of the cars chasing him.

When he came out of the chute and the road flattened again, he straightened in his saddle, his arm raised, his fist clenched in triumph, as he slowed for a leisurely finish alongside Brush Creek. It was his first memory of testing himself against things that threatened him.

The need to measure himself, the need to feel the heat, the urge to raise his clenched fist in victory had driven him to take chances others wouldn't. Sometimes it made the difference for a client threatened by a more powerful adversary—the state. Sometimes it made the difference when the adversary was personal and threatened him. Sometimes it raised the stakes too high, as it had with Abby.

When a case was about to come together like a double helix, he felt like he was flying down that hill again—that if he could only pedal a little faster, he'd come out of the chute like a rocket. He couldn't resist that sensation. Harry's call should have kicked him into high gear. Instead, it left him at the top of the hill, backpedaling and afraid.

He was afraid of what he might learn from Judith Bartholow. The accident investigation report had all but accused his father of killing himself and Mason's mother. How could his father have done such a thing, not just to them, but to him? Mason's throat filled as he searched the picture of his family for answers, finding none. He searched himself for anger, pity, and pain, finding only fear. What would he learn and what would it matter?

He turned the picture of the groundbreaking over, looking at it again. Whitney King was two years old in that picture, his father building for his future, his mother depending on it. He propped the picture alongside the one of him and his parents. Were they so different then? Neither picture hinted at any future calamities. They were, after all, only snapshots.

Saturday morning dawned bright and muggy, the humidity making the sky fuzzy. The heat wave may have broken, but it was still summer in Kansas City which meant that each day could turn ugly. The heat and humidity could make the air stand still or it could whip it into wild storm cells filled with tornadoes and microbursts that pulverized anything in its path.

Mason and Tuffy compromised on morning exercise, settling on a walk in Loose Park. In spite of their easy pace, he was dripping and she was panting when they headed for home.

A neighbor from across the street stood at the end of her driveway, dressed in her bathrobe, the morning paper clutched under her arm, glaring at Mason as he and the dog made their way up the block toward her. Her last name was Irwin. Her first name was something or other. She and her husband had two small children she had forbidden to enter Mason's yard and she had eagerly offered her opinion to the press that it was terrible to live so close to a killer. Her uncombed hair looked like snakes in flight, highlighting the fierceness in her pinched face and burning eyes as she waited with crossed arms for Mason to reach her.

"Mr. Mason," she said, stepping onto the sidewalk.

"Good morning, Mrs. Irwin," he answered. Mason wasn't much for formality, especially with his neighbors, but she had chosen the language and he went along rather than call her "something or other."

"What are you going to do?"

Tuffy sniffed at the woman's feet and circled back to Mason's side. Mason held on to her collar. "About what?"

"About all of this?" she answered. "About all of us. I'm afraid to let my children out of the house. We want you to sell your house, move away, and leave us alone!"

Mason sighed, looking up and down the street. "Who, exactly, is the we you are talking about?"

She wrapped her hand around the end of the rolled newspaper, taking a defensive step back. "Why, all of us," she stammered. "The whole block would be better off without . . . without all of this."

"And what if I'm innocent, Mrs. Irwin?" he asked her. "What then? If I let you run me out of the house I've lived in all of my life and I'm innocent, what will you tell your kids? Who should they be afraid of then?"

She sputtered for a moment, backing up more, turning away. "I'm calling a lawyer today!"

"Let me know if you need a referral," Mason said.

Judith Bartholow lived in Leawood, a suburb that hugged the Kansas side of the state line with Missouri. Originally conceived as an exclusive enclave with restrictive covenants in deeds that would have prevented Mason or any other Jew or any African American from buying a house, it had grown into a prosperous municipality with demographics that made retailers foam at the mouth. The restrictive covenants were in the city's dustbin, though there still wasn't much color in the cul-de-sac.

An hour after Mason's chat with his neighbor, he turned onto Judith's block, cruising past large Country French and Tudor spreads with well-manicured lawns all being watered with carefully choreographed sprinkler systems. He wanted to get a feel for her before he decided what to do. Seeing where she lived was the best he could come up with on a Saturday morning, except maybe summoning the nerve to knock at her door.

He imagined her sitting at her kitchen table, having breakfast, opening the door when he knocked. She would greet him with open arms, apologizing for lost time, making up for it with answers to his questions. He knew it never happened that way and wouldn't this time, assuming he knocked at all.

Her subdivision was fairly new, carved out of a farmstead owned by one of the city's blue chip families that cashed in on the insatiable demand of people who wanted to live large. Built close to I-435, it was a magnet for the wealthy and those who thought they should be.

He parked in front of the house next to Judith's two-story beige Country French stone and stucco, its front windows catching the morning sun, bouncing the light back like diamonds. Multicolored summer flowers bloomed along the precisely landscaped perimeter shaded by mature trees the developer had been careful to preserve when the house was built.

Mason had a view of the driveway and three-car garage on the side of the house. The garage was open and empty except for a fleet of bicycles that occupied one of the three bays. A Mercedes SUV was parked in the driveway where a blonde, athletic-looking woman who he guessed was near his age was loading kids into the middle row of seats. Golf clubs, swim toys, and tennis rackets were loaded into the rear.

Mason double-checked the address Harry had given him. He had the right house, but he doubted that Judith

Bartholow was the right woman. The woman he was looking for had some connection to his parents. That's why she had visited their grave and that's why she had to be older than the soccer mom he was spying on.

He was about to give up when an older woman came running out of the garage carrying another tennis racket, handing it to the younger woman who rewarded her with a kiss on the cheek before gunning the Mercedes down the driveway and past Mason like he was invisible. The older woman stood in the driveway, looking directly at Mason and not at the SUV disappearing behind him. She covered her heart with her hand, her shoulders drooping as she turned and quickly went back inside.

Nothing about the woman was familiar to Mason, though she acted as if she had recognized him. All he could tell was that she had dark hair, a slender frame, and a family. She could be anyone, but she wasn't, not if she had visited his parents' grave more often in the last two weeks than Mason had in the last two years.

The garage had room for another car that wasn't there. Mason assumed that the younger woman's husband was not at home, leaving the older woman alone in the house. He sat in his car debating whether to leave or knock on her door; the issue settled when he realized he was massaging the scar over his heart. The ache he felt wouldn't go away that easily.

The older woman opened the door almost the instant he knocked, as if she had watched him walk from his car to the house. Mason looked over her shoulder into the wide entry hall, a spiral staircase leading upstairs, the marble floor gleaming beneath a shiny brass chandelier. There was a long, low table along the wall behind her, a plant set in a clear glass vase, smooth stones like the one on his parents' grave lining the bottom.

The woman's oval face was troubled, her cheeks drawn;

her deep brown eyes stretched open, darting glances to the street. She was taller than she'd looked from a distance, though half a foot shorter than Mason, and old enough to have known his parents. She was wearing khaki slacks and a white blouse open at the neck; a simple gold chain was her only jewelry. Her hair was too dark to be natural at her age, but apart from that concession to vanity, she'd trusted the years to treat her fairly and she wasn't disappointed. Even without makeup on a Saturday morning, he sensed a woman who'd turned heads in her youth. She straightened when she saw him, adding backbone to his instant image of her, though it wasn't enough to shake off her anxiety.

"My name is Lou Mason."

The light went out of her eyes for an instant, the color in her face fading along with it. She started to close the door without a word.

"Please don't," Mason said. "I'd just like to talk with you for a few minutes."

"I know who you are. I watch the news and I've seen your picture in the newspaper," she said. "I should call the police."

"I do think you know who I am, but not because of that. You saw me in my car when you were on the driveway. I had the feeling you recognized me then even though I've never seen you before."

"I told you," she said. "I saw you on television."

"It's been hard not to," Mason said. "If that was all, you wouldn't have been waiting at the door when I knocked. You would have called the police if you were frightened or you wouldn't have opened the door in the first place. But you opened the door so quickly you must have watched me come up the walk. I think you were waiting for me."

"You're mistaken. I was on my way upstairs when you knocked. That's all," she said, edging back.

"My parents, John and Linda Mason, were killed in a car

accident forty years ago. You visited their graves and left a rock on their headstone like the ones in that vase. I'd like to know why."

The woman glanced over her shoulder, then back to Mason. "I don't know anything about that," she said.

Mason ignored her denial. "When a Jew visits someone's grave, they leave a stone behind to show that they remember the person who died. Sheffield Cemetery is a long drive from here. That's a lot of remembering after forty years."

The woman dipped her head. "I don't even own a car," she said, her denial weakening.

"The Mercedes you drove to the cemetery is registered in Judith Bartholow's name, but you don't look like the SUV type. Is Judith your daughter?"

"Leave me and my family alone," she said, closing the door. Mason propped it open with his hand.

"Please," he said. "I was only three years old when they were killed. It was a car wreck, but I know that it was more than that. You must have been close to them. You must know what really happened."

She studied him, giving nothing away, offering less. "I'm not what you think," she said harshly.

"You don't know what I think," he said.

"Oh, but I can imagine after what Claire must have told you all these years."

"She hasn't told me anything, not even your name, not even that you exist," Mason said.

The woman's eyes filled, her chest swelling as she twisted the chain around her neck.

"Then leave it that way. I don't exist," she said, closing the door.

Chapter 40

Claire had taught Mason an important lesson in the practice of law the first time a judge nearly held him in contempt for continuing to argue after the judge had ruled against him. There was, she said, a time to talk and a time to walk. He knew what time it was. If he knocked on the woman's door again, she would probably call the police.

It was also time to have another talk with his aunt. She had hidden the truth about his parents and hidden the existence of at least one person who obviously knew the secret she was determined to keep. Claire didn't respond well to demands, though she never hesitated to make them. Mason didn't expect this time to be any different.

Something else struck him about his conversation with the woman as he walked to his car. She was certain that Claire had told Mason whatever it was the two of them were keeping secret, and she was equally certain that Claire had vilified her in the telling. That Claire hadn't done so didn't surprise him. That wasn't Claire's style.

Nonetheless, the woman's comment raised two possibilities. The first was that Claire's secret was so awful that Mason was better off not knowing, perhaps meaning that Claire had done the right thing in keeping silent. The second was that Claire's secret was tainted by uncertainty, putting it in the category of things better left unsaid.

Weighing the two possibilities, it wasn't hard for Mason to conjure the easy outlines of what might have happened. His father and the woman, whatever her name was, had had an affair. His mother must have found out, leading to an argument in his parents' car in the middle of a summer downpour. His father lost control and that was that.

It made for a sordid, pathetic rendering of wasted lives, except that he didn't buy it. In the first place, Claire would not have kept it from him. Whatever shame the story bore would have been tempered with the passage of time. When he was old enough, she would have told him a sanitized version, turning it into an apocryphal lesson. In the second place, the investigating officer wouldn't have labeled the crash intentional. There had to be something more that Claire couldn't bring herself to tell him.

The heat was building, the day thickening. A crew of Hispanic men was working the yard of the house where he had parked, mowing the lawn, trimming the shrubs, and laying down fresh mulch mixed with manure in the flower beds that ringed the house. They had stopped for a break, cigarettes dangling from their lips, sweat dripping from their brown faces and necks. The blend of sweat, engine exhaust, cut grass, and manure gave the air a fetid, decayed taste.

He reached his car, opened the door, and turned back toward the house. He scanned the windows on Judith Bartholow's house for a glimpse of the woman, not finding her face pressed to the glass, betting she was watching him from the shadows. He passed on the temptation to wave good-bye to her and slipped into the driver's seat as his cell phone rang.

"Mr. Mason?" the caller said, his voice feathery and familiar, but not quite right.

"Yes," Mason answered, juggling his memory, finding a partial match. "Nick? Is that you?"

"Yeah, it's me. I don't sound so good, huh?"

"Good? You sound great, kid," Mason lied. "When are they going to let you go home?"

"I just got out of the ICU last night. The doctor says I've got to stay a few more days, at least until I can go to the john by myself," Nick said.

"Well at least you're moving in the right direction. I'll come by and see you. What room are you in?"

"That's why I was calling," Nick said. "Can you come right away? It's pretty important. I'm in 619."

The last time Nick had asked to see him was to hire him. "Why? Do you have another case for me?"

"No. The cops are here. They told me I don't need a lawyer, but I'm not so sure."

Mason shook his head. The day before, Whitney King had announced that he wasn't pressing charges against Nick. That let the cops and Ortiz off the hook since prosecuting Nick would have been a public relations nightmare. On the other hand, they could live with turning Nick into a witness against Mason, using the shooting to establish a motive for Mason to kill Sandra Connelly. King shot Mason's client. Mason shot King's lawyer. It smelled of a certain schoolyard even-Steven symmetry.

"Is one of the cops a woman?" Mason asked.

"Yeah. How'd you know?" Nick asked.

"Never mind. Just put her on," Mason said.

Mason heard voices in the background, then Samantha Greer saying, "Lou, don't get excited."

"Not another word, Sam. Get out of that kid's hospital room until I get there."

"Lou, let me explain," she said.

"Out! Now! And put Nick back on," Mason said.

"Hey, Mr. Mason," Nick said. "You really pissed her off, man. That was cool."

"She'll get over it. Don't talk to anyone not wearing a stethoscope until I get there. I'm only a few minutes from the hospital. By the way, how did you get my cell phone number?" Mason asked, pretty certain he hadn't given it to Nick.

"I called your office," Nick said.

"On Saturday morning?" Mason asked. "There's no one there on Saturday mornings. In fact, if I'm not there, no one is there. Who did you talk to?"

"Some guy named Mickey. I told him it was important and he gave me your cell phone number. Hey, you aren't mad I called you on your cell, are you?"

Mason smiled for the first time in days. "Not a bit. I'm glad you did. I'm on my way."

Mary was alive. Nick was out of ICU. And Mickey Shanahan was back. Three solid hits, even if none of them was out of the park. He was behind, but at least he had some base runners. It was enough that he was willing to wait to ask Claire about Judith Bartholow's mother.

He still didn't know where Mary was, whether she was okay or why she had disappeared. Nick was out of the ICU but, judging from the weakness in his voice, still at the beginning of a long road back. Mickey could have just dropped by for his paycheck and would be gone before Mason saw him, or he might be back for good. If he was, Abby might not be far behind. Mason decided to find out.

Mickey answered on the second ring. "Lou Mason and Associates," he said.

"Since when do I have any associates?" Mason asked, not able to keep the pleasure from his voice.

"From what I've been reading, boss, I wouldn't be too picky. You should be grateful somebody wants to associate with you at all."

"I am grateful, Mickey. Are you back or just passing through?"

"Back, if you've got room for me."

"Room I've got," Mason said. "Cash paying clients whose fees pay your salary—well, that's another story."

"Don't worry about it, boss. I'd rather you owe me than cheat me out of it."

"What about Abby? I don't suppose she . . ." Mason said, unable to finish the question, feeling Mickey's answer in the sigh on the other end of the call.

"Sorry, Lou," Mickey said. "The primary is in ten days and things are pretty crazy. They can always find someone else to get coffee. Abby is tough to replace."

"That I know," Mason said, Mickey not arguing. "Listen, the kid who called you is our client, Nick Byrnes. I'm on the way to the hospital to see him. Stick around the office. I'll be there in an hour or so."

Mason rounded the corner on the sixth floor of the hospital, and headed down the corridor for the general surgery patients. He swept past the nurses' station, building up a head of steam for Samantha Greer. Mickey's return had pumped him up. It wasn't only that Mickey would help. It was that Mickey had given up something important to come back. Though Mason had had good reasons to let Mary's and Nick's case slide the last few days, he was determined to come back to them.

It was the right thing to do and, he realized, it was the one thing he could do to help his own case without getting too much in Dixon Smith's way. There was another side benefit. Working Mary's and Nick's case would give him cover for checking up on his lawyer.

Samantha was waiting for Mason outside Nick's door. She was wearing bone-colored slacks and a matching short-sleeve jacket over a black top. Her hair was pulled back and her makeup was thin. She was all cop, the butt of her gun sticking out from the shoulder rig under her jacket. Her partner, Al Kolatch, was sitting in a chair, leaning back against the wall, tapping his feet on the floor.

"Over here," she said to Mason, pointing to an empty room across the hall, taking Mason by the arm, not giving him any chance to argue.

She closed the door, waiting for the slow moving hinge to seal them in. There were two beds, both stripped, a bulletin board above each, a forgotten get-well card pinned to one. Mason crossed the room to the window that looked north from the hospital. Samantha stood behind him.

Traffic on I-435 streaked past beneath them, glass and distance muting any sound. Treetops stretched beyond the highway, shading subdivisions. Thick white clouds with towering superstructures promising thunder and lightning hung on the horizon. Kansas City's summer weather had a predictable pattern. Heat and humidity built up to the break-ing point, erupting in violence, cooled by rain that stoked the process for another round. The same could be said for this case, the cycle stretching back fifteen years to the night Graham and Elizabeth Byrnes were murdered.

"This is complete bullshit. You know that," Mason finally said, forcing his voice to a low, hospital quiet octave.

"You don't know what you're talking about," Samantha told him.

"Never a bad bet, but not this time," Mason said, ratcheting up to street volume. "Whitney King shoots my client, and then graciously promises that he won't press charges against Nick. You and Ortiz aren't satisfied with that. No. You've got to jump on Nick the minute he's out of intensive care so you can turn him into a witness against me. I can't believe you were ever on my side. Ever!"

Samantha, arms folded over her chest, listened to Mason rant, chewing her lower lip. "Are you finished?" she asked.

Mason threw up his hands. "Yeah. I'm finished and so are you and your partner. You're not talking to my client."

"I don't want to talk to him," she said.

Mason looked at her, hands on his hips, squinting as if he wasn't certain who she was. "You don't want to talk to him," he repeated, Samantha nodding. "Then want do you want to do?"

"Protect him."

"From whom?" Mason asked.

"Whitney King."

Chapter 41

Mason narrowed his eyes and jammed his hands into his pants pocket. He studied Samantha, looking for signs that she was casting bait, reeling him in. She was wearing a cop's dead flat stare. Mason knew the look. It didn't mean she wasn't bluffing, but it meant he was rolling for high stakes if he took the chance she was.

"What happened?" he asked.

"We got a tip," she said, barely moving her mouth.

"Not good enough," Mason said.

"We don't need your permission to put a guard on your client," she reminded Mason.

"True enough," he conceded. "But if his life really is in danger, he's got a right to know the details. He doesn't have to talk to you, but you've got to talk to him, which means you've got to talk to me. Now would be a good time to start."

Samantha heaved a sigh, hands on her hips. "Okay," she said. "We got an anonymous threat on the TIPS Hotline. The caller didn't stay on long enough for a trace. The voice is disguised, probably using an electronic device you can get from a hundred Web sites."

"Male or female?" Mason asked.

"Couldn't tell for sure. Best guess is male."

"What did he say?"

"Kept it short and simple," she said, consulting a notepad she pulled from her inside jacket pocket. "The exact quote is 'Be careful. The Byrnes boy is next and last.' Not too original, but it makes the point."

"You must get the whack jobs leaving you messages on that phone line. What makes this a credible threat?"

"We do get all kinds of whack jobs," Samantha said. "It's not unusual in high-profile cases like this for us to get a raft of death threats and confessions. After a while, we can even recognize some of the callers' voices, they call in so often. But this message is different."

"Why?" Mason asked.

"It's the part about being the next and the last. Like killing Nick would be related to the murders of his parents and the jurors."

"What makes you think King made the call after he gave his cousin's speech today?"

"What cousin are you talking about?" she asked.

"You know," Mason said. "Rodney King, the hero of the LA police brutality riots. After the cops beat the crap out of him and he sued the city for a bazillion bucks, he said can't we all just get along? That was Whitney's pitch this morning after he testified to the grand jury. He said he forgave Nick and was ready to move on."

"That's your problem, Lou. You believe everything you hear."

"Which makes you my opposite since you haven't believed anything I've told you in this case, including that King is guilty and I'm innocent."

Samantha boosted herself onto one of the unmade beds. "You live in an upside down world," she said. "Whitney King is acquitted of murder and you want me to believe that not only is he guilty but that he's spent the last fifteen years knocking off the jurors who set him free. Then, you're found next to the dead body of King's lawyer holding your gun which just happens to be the murder weapon, and you admit that you shot Sandra Connelly, and you want me to believe that you're innocent."

"Look who's talking. You get an anonymous death threat against my client and that's enough for you to indict Whitney King. Welcome to my world."

"It's not just the phone call," Samantha said.

"What else?"

She took a deep breath. "We've been running down what happened to the jurors. It's got some people in the department nervous. Nobody likes the odds that all those deaths are unrelated. It would make that jury the unluckiest group of people in history."

"Can you tie King to any of the killings?"

"Eight murders spread out over ten years, some of them committed in different cities. The bullets recovered from the shootings all came from different guns. That's a lot of loose ends to tie up, but we're working on it."

"What about the last two jurors? Have you found either of them?" Mason asked.

"We're looking," she answered.

"But not in the right places," Mason said.

Samantha rolled her eyes. "Janet Hook was twenty-four at the time of King's trial. She was a single black woman who had dropped out of high school. Serving on that jury was the longest job she'd ever had. We found her sister, Shawana James."

"And I'm guessing Shawana doesn't know where Janet is, right?"

"Right or she's not saying."

"You got an address for Shawana?" Mason asked.

Samantha flipped to another page in her notepad, hesitating a moment. "Why not," she said, copying the address for Mason.

"What about the other one, Andrea Bracco. I think she was a secretary," Mason said.

"Twenty-seven at the time of the trial," Samantha said. "She worked for an insurance broker. A week after the trial she stopped coming to work. They never saw her again and no one else has either. She was single. No family we can find. It's like she never existed."

"Have you talked to King yet?"

Samantha slid off the bed. "Nope. We can't find him."

"That's what makes you nervous, isn't it?" Mason asked.

She opened the door, propping her heel against it. "Yeah. Now how about letting me talk to your client?"

"Me first," Mason told Samantha when they reached Nick's room.

"C'mon, Lou," she said, shaking her head and stepping between Mason and the door. "No more games!"

Al Kolatch rolled out of his chair, lumbering toward them, Samantha raising her hand and shaking her head again, this time at her partner. Kolatch shrugged his shoulders, stuck a toothpick between his teeth, and returned to his seat.

"Representing my client isn't a game, Sam. You forget. The first time I've spoken to him since he was shot was when he called me thirty minutes ago. I'll let you talk to him after I find out what he's going to say. Besides, it will be easier for him to handle the death threat if I tell him about it."

She drew a short breath, sliding out of Mason's way. "Fine, but don't take too long."

"Relax. You're talking to a guy who gets paid by the hour," Mason said. "Everything I do takes too long."

* * *

Nick Brynes lay on his back, his hospital bed elevated at a forty-five-degree angle, his depleted body looking like he had melted into the sheets. His blond hair was matted, his skin was the color of dirty water, and both of his arms were plumbed with IVs. Another tube draining his wound ran from his chest to a bag on the side of his bed.

A television tuned to MTV hung from the ceiling in a corner, the sound broadcast from a remote speaker pinned to the mattress next to his pillow. The music was harsh and tinny, though Mason couldn't tell whether that was the result of the poor speaker or whether it was supposed to sound that way.

Nick brightened when Mason walked in, aiming the remote control at the television, trading the muffled music for a blank screen.

"Hey, Mr. Mason. Thanks for coming," he said, his raspy voice the result of spending a week with a tube down his throat while he was in ICU. "Have a seat."

Mason pulled a chair toward the end of the bed so Nick could see him without having to move. Looking at the IV lines in Nick's arms, Mason flashed back to Ryan's execution, wondering if Nick had an appreciation for irony.

"How you feelin'?" Mason asked him.

"You want the answer I give my grandma?"

Mason smiled. "Nope. We'd both know you're lying and she probably knows it too. You feel up to talking about what happened?"

"Is that why the cops are here? Did they arrest Whitney King for shooting me? Nobody has told me anything. My grandparents told them not to, I guess."

"Where is your grandmother?" Mason asked, ducking Nick's questions. "I thought she'd gotten her own room here."

Nick said, "My grandpa made her go home after I got out of intensive care. She'll be back, but I wish she'd stay home. All she does is sit in that chair and stare at me like I'm dead and it's my fault. I can't stand it."

"Cut her some slack, Nick. She doesn't know what else to do."

"Well, it wasn't my fault."

"Whitney King says you threatened him with the gun and that it went off when he tried to take it away from you. Is that what happened?"

Nick's eyes widened. "Partly, but not really," he said, softly thumping the mattress with his hand. "I can't believe that guy gets away with everything. They didn't arrest him did they? They're going to let him get away with it again! I can't believe it!"

"Nick, tell me what happened," Mason repeated.

Nick closed his eyes for a moment, gathering himself, opening them again. He reached for the bed's controls, raising himself until he was almost sitting up straight.

"After I left your office that day, I was really hot. Mr. Bluestone made it sound like there was nothing I could do, not without taking the chance something would happen to my grandparents. I wasn't going to let King get away with killing my parents a second time. I went home and got my grandfather's gun. Then I just drove around and hung out trying to figure out what to do. I got King's home phone number from directory assistance and I called him. I told him I wanted to settle things with him once and for all. He told me to meet him at his office in thirty minutes. He was waiting for me outside when I got there."

"What did you do?"

"I told him I knew he killed my parents and he laughed and said what are you going to do about it, kid. He didn't even deny it. He said that since the jury found him innocent no one could touch him. He said I'd be sorry if I sued him. I got so mad," Nick said, his eyes filling, his face showing some color. "I pulled the gun out and he laughed again. We were only a few feet apart and the next thing I knew he grabbed it and shot me. I thought I was gonna die," he added softly.

"What about the priest?" Mason asked. "Father Steve said he saw the whole thing and that the gun went off accidentally."

"I don't know what you're talking about," Nick said. "I never saw a priest."

"Sure you did," Mason told him. "Father Steve. He was the priest at Ryan's execution. Short, kind of dumpy. Smells like an ashtray and wears a collar."

"I would have remembered, Mr. Mason," Nick said. "Honest. There was no one else there."

Mason rose, locked his fingers behind his head, and paced the few steps from the bed to the window and back again. Father Steve had corroborated King's claim of self-defense. The priest had explained to Mason that he had gone to King's office to ask for money for the church. Though it was possible Nick had simply forgotten some of the details of what had happened, this was too big a detail to forget.

"Nick, did you pass out after you were shot?"

Nick thought for a moment, forehead furrowed, scrounging his memory. "I guess I must have," he said at last. "I mean at first I didn't feel anything. It was like I couldn't even believe he actually shot me. I was lying on the ground and I couldn't move. Then, my chest started to burn real bad and he was standing over me, aiming the gun at me like he was going to shoot me again. I thought for sure he would. I don't know what happened after that. The next thing I remember, I was in the emergency room."

"Father Steve said he and King had just come from

King's office. You said you called King at home and he told you to meet him at his office in half an hour. King lives almost thirty minutes away. There would have barely been enough time for him to get to his office, meet with Father Steve, and then come back downstairs and wait outside for you. Even if there was enough time, how did Father Steve know King was going to be there?"

"Mr. Mason, I don't understand anything you're talking about."

"Neither do I," Mason said. "All I know is that it's time for Father Steve to make confession."

"You're Jewish, Mr. Mason. How are you going to get a priest to do that?"

"It shouldn't be too tough. I have a feeling Father Steve's collar is getting a little tight."

"What about Whitney King?" Nick asked.

Mason sat on the edge of Nick's bed. "That's why the cops want to talk with you," he said, repeating what Samantha Greer had told him, gauging Nick's reaction.

Mason gave the kid a lot of credit. He didn't fall apart and he didn't bluff that he wasn't afraid. He clenched his fists, the veins in his arms rising.

"Mr. Mason?" he asked. "Is it too late to file that lawsuit?"

Chapter 42

Samantha Greer questioned Nick about the shooting, flashing a look at Al Kolatch when Nick told her the priest wasn't there when King shot him. Kolatch left, and Mason was certain he was headed to St. Mark's for a private prayer with Father Steve. Mason knew there was no point in trying to beat Kolatch to the punch. If the priest had lied to the cops, Kolatch would help him renew his vows.

Mason called Mickey from the car, telling him to meet him at The Peanut at Fiftieth and Main for lunch. Driving north from the hospital, Mason could see a faint darkening of the sky on the far horizon.

In some parts of town, The Peanut would have been called a dive. Since it was on the east edge of the Plaza, its warped and worn hardwood floors, tables with uneven legs, and pool hall lighting qualified it for quirky cool, proving again that location is everything. The Peanut thrived by turning the BLT into an art form. Mason considered himself a connoisseur.

Mickey and Blues were waiting for Mason when he arrived at The Peanut. He blinked his eyes while they adjusted from the sunlight to the blue light, finding his friends at a table against the far wall. He hadn't asked Mickey to bring Blues and he knew Blues hadn't asked Mickey if he could come. Blues wasn't good at asking permission. He was much better at knowing when Mason needed him.

Mickey's idea of business casual had always been a shirt with a collar and jeans that didn't have a hole in the knees. He was wearing gabardine slacks and a linen shirt. The mouse he'd grown in the cleft of his chin was gone, his anarchic hair style subdued by a close cut. Mason took one look at him, glancing at Blues who turned his head, biting his lip.

"Don't tell me," Mason said. "You gave up politics for selling cars."

Mickey laughed, plucking the front of his shirt. "Sucks, huh? It's Abby's new man plan. She said that the staff is a reflection on the candidate. If I had stayed another week, she would have made me bleach my teeth."

"So you didn't come back to help me," Mason teased. "You just needed a change of clothes."

Mickey said to Blues, "And I'm getting paid to take this abuse."

"Don't count on it," Mason told him. "How's Abby?" he asked as he scanned the menu, doing a lousy impression of nonchalance.

Mickey nodded. "She's good," he said. "Fine, really. Busy as hell. The campaign runs twenty-four-seven and she's working twenty-five-eight."

"That's great," Mason said with a puckered smile. "She okay with you coming back?"

"What is it with the two of you?" Mickey asked. "You guys act like you're my divorced parents fighting over custody."

Blues explained, "They're not divorced, just separated. And, you're not their baby. They just think you are."

"Nice, very nice," Mason said. "Abby got you the job with Seeley's campaign to protect you from me. Coming back to work for me is not part of her new man plan for you."

"Why do I need to be protected from you?" Mickey asked.

"Because," Blues answered, "people like to shoot at Lou and his friends."

"Oh, that," Mickey said. "I get it."

"Don't let Blues kid you, Mickey. That's the straight story. Abby was doing you a favor."

Mickey looked at Mason, then at Blues. Their banter was a thin coat of armor. "I've been down this road with you guys before," he reminded them. "Maybe I'm the one doing you a favor."

A television hung from the ceiling in a corner above the bar, the early laps of a NASCAR race running silently, the sound muted. Looking over Blues's shoulder, Mason read the crawl running across the bottom of the screen. It included a notice that a severe storm warning had been issued for the greater metropolitan Kansas City area until ten P.M. Though the storm clouds Mason had seen a few hours ago were on the far horizon, he wasn't surprised by the forecast. In the course of a Kansas City summer day, weather bulletins could progress from watches to warnings, from thunderstorms to severe storms, and, finally, to tornadoes.

A watch meant maybe. A warning meant probably. A thunderstorm meant lights and action. A severe storm meant pay attention and a tornado meant take cover.

This warning meant the five counties on either side of the state line could get anything from a cooling summer shower to a force five tornado, depending on the alignment of the planets over the next ten hours. The pattern could move lazily through the day or turn deadly on a dime. It also meant that nothing could happen, some vagary in the winds shifting the whole system east where it would pound the daylights out of a trailer park.

Mason, like most people in Kansas City, treated severe weather warnings with the same nonchalance as Californians considered the threat of earthquakes. There was nothing to be done about either and the threats were almost always overstated. Some people even served as self-appointed, unofficial tornado spotters for local radio and television stations, as if standing outside during a thunderstorm in the hopes of spotting a funnel cloud was a less than extreme sport.

They ordered singles with extra bacon, Mason filling them in while they waited for their sandwiches. Blues leaned back in his chair, his face flat. Mickey fiddled with sugar packets, drumming his fingers on the tabletop until Blues made him put his hands in his lap. The food arrived as Mason finished. The conversation about murder was tabled while they ate.

"Why would Father Steve cover for Whitney King?" Mickey asked, picking a stray bacon crumb off the table when they'd finished.

"Money, I guess," Mason answered. "The church needed it and King had it. Father Steve's job was to get it."

"I don't buy it," Blues said. "He's a priest not a bagman. He's not going to take chances like that just so the church can buy new carpet for the rectory."

"Then what?" Mason asked.

"They must have some history," Blues answered. "Maybe King has pictures of the priest with an altar boy. Whatever it is, King's got Father Steve by the collar, but it's not about money."

Mickey asked, "So what do we do?"

"You"—Mason said, pointing at him—"check out Damon Parker's company, Golden Years."

"What am I looking for?" Mickey asked.

"Connections with the King family. King's father built Parker's nursing homes. Dixon Smith represented Parker until Sandra Connelly asked him to find out if King's mother belonged in one of them. Smith says he got fired for asking."

"And you don't think your lawyer is being straight with you," Blues said.

"Let's just say that I'd like a second opinion," Mason said.

"What else?" Blues asked.

"This case goes back to King's murder trial. Something happened in that jury room. If we don't find Janet Hook and Andrea Bracco, we'll never know what it was. Andrea Bracco disappeared the day after the trial." Mason handed Blues the piece of paper with Shawana James's address. "This is the address for Shawana James, Janet Hook's sister. When Samantha talked to her, Shawna practically denied even having a sister. Maybe you'll have better luck."

"What are you going to do?" Blues asked him.

"I'm going to ask Whitney's mother if she knows where her son is."

Blues drained the last of his beer as the waiter cleared their table. "You're chasing too many shadows, Lou."

"I don't have much choice," Mason said. "The shadows are chasing me too. At least there's some good news. Nick is going to recover and Mary Kowalczyk is okay."

"Because of her damn fish?" Blues asked. "All that means is that her fish are missing too. She's still disappeared and Nick wants you to sue Whitney King before Whitney kills him. Which might work out since the cops are rooming with Nick at the hospital and Whitney is in the wind. On top of that, you're chasing a priest that's walking on the dark side while you bird dog your own lawyer who's supposed to defend you when the grand jury indicts you for first degree murder on Monday. I don't know why you get out of bed in the morning."

Mason shook his head. "Sure you do. To see what happens next."

Chapter 43

Johnson County used to be referred to as Kansas City's bedroom, the state line an artificial stripe separating the two in a rapidly growing region that blurred geopolitical identity into a massive metropolitan statistical area. With more people and square miles in its thirty-eight cities, towns, and villages than the city had within its borders, Johnson County had moved out of that metaphorical house to become Kansas City's rival and sometime partner. Mason preferred the city to the suburbs, unable to shake the sensation that he was drowning in vanilla whenever he found himself surrounded by strip malls and office parks.

Golden Years called its locations campuses, each facility euphemized as communities. Mason had been told that Whitney's mother lived in both the nursing home and the psychiatric hospital on the Johnson County campus in Lenexa, Kansas. He doubted the she lived in both unless she kept one as her vacation home.

Golden Year's Johnson County operation had grown from the original single-wing nursing home depicted in the photo-

graph of the groundbreaking to a campus offering everything from town houses sold as condos, to assisted living
apartments and inpatient care with twenty-four-hour private
nursing. Mason turned in the entrance on the south side of
Eighty-seventh Street Parkway, slowing for a small flock of
geese that had chosen to walk across the driveway rather
than fly to the pond on the other side of the road.

The campus was laid out in a horseshoe configuration. To
his left was a cluster of attached town houses, all painted the
same subdued shade of taupe and connected by walkways
and parking lots. A four-story, two-wing assisted living
apartment building wrapped around the back of the horseshoe. The taupe stucco motif was carried through this building and onto the long-term care unit on his right.

He parked his car in front of the apartment building, getting out and surveying the grounds. The grass was mowed
with a precision that would withstand inspection by a drill
sergeant measuring the length of each blade. Shade came
from well-pruned maples, oaks, and cottonwoods that provided optimal light for the annuals and perennials accenting
the taupe walls and green lawns with riots of color. A sign
between the apartments and the long-term care facility
pointed down a tree-lined sidewalk toward the Golden Year
Psychiatric and Alzheimer's Treatment Center.

Another sign directed all visitors to the information center
inside the apartment building where Mason found an attrac-
tive brunette sitting at a desk in the lobby reading *Cosmopolitan.* Brochures describing Golden Years were displayed
in a rack on one corner of her desk; the rack was engraved in
gold with the words "Information Center." It wasn't much of
a center, but the brochures didn't offer much information,
relying on sunny pictures of healthy elderly people flashing
happy smiles and good bridgework.

To his right was a lobby furnished in brightly upholstered

furniture, pastel and floral fabric the order of the day. A large screen television was parked in one corner. It was tuned to a local station broadcasting a golf tournament. A weather alert ran across the bottom of the screen advising that the National Severe Storms Forecast Center had upgraded its earlier severe thunderstorm warning by adding a tornado watch for the next three hours. A blue-haired woman and a bald-headed man sat in front of the television ignoring the golf and the weather alert, preferring the card game they were playing.

An elevator bank was on his left. The floor was carpeted and the walls were painted in muted tones that made the furniture the dominant visual effect. It was comfortable, a cut above bland institutional and, Mason guessed, just the kind of place that made the tenants feel at home though it would drive him nuts.

There was an office behind the information center desk with a bank of video monitors displaying scenes from around the grounds and the lobbies of the other buildings. The technology was good but there was no one watching the monitors. The woman behind the desk was wearing jeans and a snug fitting bright purple tank top. She didn't look like security was part of her job description.

The magazine lay open on her desk. From his upside down vantage point Mason deciphered the title of the article she was reading.

" 'Ten Ways to Make Your Man Come Back for More,' " he read out loud. "What's number one?"

She looked to be in her thirties with the ready smile and practiced eye of someone who quickly evaluated a prospect. Her blue eyes took their time with him.

"Don't you want the whole list?" she asked.

"I was hoping number one would be good enough that you wouldn't need the other nine."

"Keep him happy but hungry," she read, closing the magazine, standing, and extending her hand. "Welcome to Golden Years. My name is Adrienne."

"It's a pleasure to be here," he said, shaking hers with his. His name hadn't opened many doors lately so he didn't offer it.

She held his hand for an instant longer than necessary, letting him go when he gave a gentle tug. "That's what our residents tell us all the time. What can I show you today? Town houses, apartments, or long-term care?"

"Don't forget the psychiatric hospital," Mason teased her.

"Oh, I'm a pretty good judge of people," she said. "You don't look crazy to me."

"Don't bet on it, Adrienne. I do a pretty good crazy."

"In that case," she said. "I may have to show you the room with the padded walls."

"As tempting as that sounds, I'm here to see someone but I'm not certain which facility she's in."

"That's too bad. I'm not allowed to give out any information about our residents. They're very big on privacy here."

Mason gave her the easy smile, the one with soft light and high voltage. "What's your last name, Adrienne?"

She put her hands on her hips. "Rubinkowski. And don't tell me that's a pretty name. I can't do anything about the privacy policy."

"I don't want you to break the rules," he told her.

An elderly man wearing a Hawaiian print shirt, Bermuda shorts, black socks pulled up over his calves, and shiny black loafers, and carrying a newspaper tucked under his arm walked in, stopping at the desk next to Mason. He dropped the newspaper on her copy of *Cosmopolitan*. It was the *Kansas City Star* and Mason's picture as he left the courthouse the day before was on the front page above the fold.

"Put this in the recycling for me, honey," the man said,

patting Mason on the arm. "Forget it, sonny. Medicare don't cover her and she don't come with the apartment," he added and left.

Adrienne's mouth widened as she looked at Mason's picture and reached for the phone on her desk.

"It's okay," he told her. "You don't have to call anyone," he said, covering her hand with his. "I just want a room number."

She looked at the newspaper again and then at Mason, shrinking from him. "It's you, isn't it? I saw it on the news. They said you killed that woman."

"It's a lousy picture," he said, trying to keep it light, "but I didn't kill her. She was my friend. I was set up. That's why I'm here. I need your help, Adrienne."

A tremor rippled along her arm as she tightened her grip on the phone, looking down at the keypad. Mason felt her shake as he held onto her. "I'm supposed to call if you show up here," she said. "He didn't think you would, but he said to call. Just in case."

Mason let go of her hand, tipping her chin up so he could look her in the eye. "Adrienne, who are you supposed to call?"

"You really didn't do it?" she asked, her eyes moist, "because I am a good judge of people and you don't look the type."

Mason shook his head. "I didn't do it, Adrienne. Help me out. Who are you supposed to call?"

She took Mason's wrist, lowering his hand, letting her fingers slide across his. She opened her desk drawer and handed Mason a business card. It was turned upside down. Mason flipped it over.

"That's who," Adrienne said. "Dixon Smith."

Chapter 44

"Call him," Mason told her.

"But I thought . . ." she began.

"It's okay. I don't want you to get in any trouble. Dixon Smith is my lawyer," he told her. Adrienne's eyes widened in disbelief until Mason picked up the newspaper, found Smith's quote that his client, Lou Mason, was cooperating with the grand jury process and showed it to her.

"I don't understand. Mr. Parker told me that Mr. Smith was his lawyer," Adrienne said.

"You mean Damon Parker who owns Golden Years?" Mason asked, Adrienne nodding. "Dixon told me all about that," Mason reassured her. "A lawyer needs more than one client, you know." He picked up the phone and handed it to her. "You better call him," he said.

"You're sure?"

"Positive. But you probably shouldn't tell him that you told me you were supposed to call him. He might consider that to be covered by attorney-client privilege. I'll square it with him later. Lawyer to lawyer."

"You can do that?" she asked.

"Sure. Especially since he represents me too. I don't want you to get caught in the middle. Tell you what," Mason said. "Is there another extension I can use while you call him? I've got a call to make too."

"Of course. There's one right over there," she said, pointing to a phone in the office behind her.

Mason looked at her phone. It had lights for three incoming lines, the buttons for each line marked one, two and three, none of which were lit. She hadn't selected a line yet and Mason bet she would pick line one when she made the call. He walked into the office, keeping eye contact to delay the start of her call. He picked up the receiver for the office phone, gave her a quick wave and turned his back, hoping his timing was good. He pressed the button for line one at the same instant she did, joining her call without her knowledge, listening to the electronic tones as she dialed. He hoped she was too distracted to notice that neither of the other two lines was in use.

"Dixon Smith," his lawyer said when he answered the phone, his tone flat, disinterested.

"Mr. Smith. It's Adrienne Rubinkowski from Golden Years. You said to call if that man, Lou Mason, came here."

"Yes, I did, Adrienne," Smith said. Mason squeezed the phone when he heard Smith's voice quicken. "Is he there now?"

"Yes he is."

"Where?"

"Using a phone in the office."

"What did he want? What did he say?"

"He said he wanted to see someone but wasn't certain which unit she was in. I did just what you told me. I said I couldn't give out that information for privacy reasons."

"And you can't," Smith said. "That's the law. Did he say who he wanted to see?"

"No, he didn't. Do you want me to ask him?"

"Yes. That's very important. I need to know who it is. Tell him you'll call and ask if the person wants to see him. Then call me back. Got it?"

"Got it," Adrienne said.

"Good girl," Smith said. "I'll tell Mr. Parker what a great job you're doing."

"Thanks," she said, hanging up.

Mason punched the button for line two, keeping his back to Adrienne a moment longer, watching the video monitors, his head buzzing. His suspicions of Smith had been confirmed. The wild card was Smith's comment that he needed to know who Mason wanted to see. The only person on Mason's list was Victoria King. He wondered who else Smith was talking about as he returned to Adrienne's desk, still smiling.

"Everything go okay?" he asked her.

"Fine," she said, smoothing her jeans.

"You see," he said. "I told you it would be all right. See you around."

"Mr. Mason," she said, stammering.

"Please, call me, Lou."

"Okay, Lou" she said, still flustered. "If you'll just tell me who you want to see, I'll call them and ask if I can give you that information," she said, picking up the phone again, twisting the cord through her fingers.

"You know what?" he said. "Turns out she's not even here. She's at Lakewood Gardens. That's why I made that call. I don't know how I screwed that up. Sorry to have bothered you."

Mason left her looking stricken, hoping she didn't lose her job when she called Smith back with the bad news. He'd come to Golden Years to see Victoria King. He drove away wondering who else was there and why Dixon Smith didn't want him to talk to them.

* * *

There was a mammoth strip mall on the north side of Eighty-seventh Street Parkway directly across from Golden Years. A Wal-Mart Super Center anchored the west end, a Home Depot matching it on the east. In between, the center boasted a sandwich shop, video store, dry cleaner, liquor store, sports bar, Chinese restaurant, veterinarian, Lasik surgery center, cosmetic dentist, tanning salon, office supply store, and half a dozen other businesses. A bank, a Mexican restaurant, a pizza joint, and a Starbucks occupied pads scattered across the parking lot. Collectively, the retailers offered everything needed for survival in the suburbs, including duct tape.

Mason parked in front of Wal-Mart. He wanted to take his own tour of the Golden Years campus but doubted whether he would be welcomed back twice in one day. He decided that a maintenance man would have an easier time prowling around than he would.

Twenty minutes and two hundred dollars later, Mason had a pair of pewter-colored work pants, a short-sleeve denim shirt, a white crew neck T-shirt advertising an herbicide company, a ball cap with a tractor on the front, a pair of work boots, and a pair of aviator sunglasses. At Home Depot, he picked up a leather tool belt filled with an array of screwdrivers, pliers, wire cutters, and a tape measure. He bought a clipboard and a pad of forms labeled WORK ORDERS at the office supply store, then stopped at the sandwich shop for a bottle of water. Finished with his shopping, he moved his car to a parking space in the middle row of the strip center parking lot between two minivans that afforded a view of the entrance to Golden Years.

He changed out of his chinos, polo shirt, and loafers in his car, the only dicey moment coming when a mother and her teenage daughter climbed into the minivan on his left.

He was just pulling up his new pants as the daughter glanced into his car and burst out laughing. By the time the mother looked over, Mason was dressed and waving pleasantly at her. The mother shrugged her shoulders as if to ask whether Mason would take her daughter off her hands.

Standing alongside his car, his denim shirt open over his T-shirt, he bent down and rubbed his hands on the pavement, then wiped them off on his pants and shirt, not wanting his outfit to look brand new. Unsatisfied, he shimmied against the side of his car, picking up more dirt. He scuffed his new boots and tool belt against the pavement and scrunched his cap between his hands, wiping it against his car and working dirt into the bill. He rubbed his dirty hands on his neck and face, splashing bottled water on his neck to add a sweat line to his T-shirt.

It was hot and muggy in the parking lot, the asphalt radiating heat and generating more sweat to bolster his working man look. The sky above half the city was now a low-hanging, billowing tarnished green. The sky over Mason's head was still pale blue with tracers of white clouds streaking past trying to outrun the rapidly moving front. The weather gods were about to turn the forecasters into prophets.

As he walked across Eighty-seventh Street Parkway, he wondered whether his first visit would spark any other comings or goings. Whitney King lived nearby, though Samantha Greer had said that King had made himself scarce. Mason didn't know where Dixon Smith lived but doubted he was the suburban type. If Smith showed up, it would take awhile. That didn't matter to Mason. He had an entire pad of work orders to fill.

A slightly undulating berm landscaped with tall evergreens marked the Golden Years' northern property line along the Eighty-seventh Street Parkway. Mason walked west on Eighty-seventh, crossing the street at the edge of the campus farthest from the entrance. A maintenance man walking in off the street would arouse immediate suspicion.

An eight-foot-high wooden privacy fence surrounded the property. Mason assumed it was to keep both the psychiatric and Alzheimer's disease patients inside the grounds rather than to keep intruders out since the berm sloped down to a point midway on the outside of the fence. Mason easily climbed over and lowered himself down the other side.

There was an expansive park with benches and a walking trail winding through the trees between him and the nearest building. Unlike the other taupe and stucco buildings, this one was built with brick and had a long center section with high windows that divided the patient wings.

The park was empty, the patients having at least enough sense to come in out of the rain before the rain began. Uncertain whether anyone had seen him, Mason walked along the perimeter of the fence, stopping every so often to test a fence post, the best impression he could give of a diligent maintenance man.

He didn't know whether Golden Years employed its own on-site maintenance crew or, if it did, whether the employees had uniforms with their names stitched over the shirt pocket. He didn't know if anyone had called maintenance to fix an air-conditioning, plumbing, or electrical problem. If they had and he showed up, they would both be disappointed. Mason's handyman résumé began and ended with changing lightbulbs. The only thing he had going for him was the outfit and a purposeful stride.

By the time he reached the psychiatric hospital, the storm front had caught up to him, blotting out the sun and knocking the temperature back at least fifteen degrees. The trees swayed around him.

Mason made his way to an emergency exit at one end of the psychiatric hospital. He tried the door, not surprised that it was locked. Opening it would have probably triggered an alarm, a thought that made him quickly look up above the door for another security feature. There was a video camera aimed at his head. Just in case Adrienne was watching the video monitors, he gave a small salute, relying on his cap and dark glasses to conceal his identity, and continued around to the front of the building.

A heavy-set, elderly white man with hound dog jowls was hunched forward in a chair behind a counter in the lobby, switching channels on a portable television resting on a TV table. A football game replaced a commercial. Satisfied, the man leaned back, still unaware that Mason was standing on the other side of the counter.

To Mason's right, there was door to the patients' hallways with a sign that read "Authorized Personnel Only." A key card scanner was mounted in the wall next to the door.

"Who's playing?" Mason asked the man, sticking his sunglasses in his shirt pocket.

"Giants and Rams. Hall of Fame game. First exhibition game of the year. Been a long time since the Super Bowl and I am ready for some football," the man said, glancing at Mason long enough for Mason to read his name tag— Walt—before turning back to the television. The upper right-hand corner of the screen was filled with a weather map and a graphic announcing that the city was now under a tornado warning. "What do you need?" His question and his look said he hoped neither Mason nor the weather would interfere with the football game.

Mason tapped the clipboard on the counter. "Work order on the second floor. I forgot my key card. Can you buzz me in?"

Walt scooted his chair back, opened a desk drawer, and tossed Mason a key card attached to a coiled bracelet. "Don't forget to bring it back when you're finished," he said, his back to Mason, his head in the game.

In the same instant, the football game was interrupted by the Channel 6 weatherman who reported that a tornado had been sighted along a line stretching from Seventy-fifth and I-35 southwest to I-435. With a grim face normally reserved for wartime, he said the twister was moving toward the southwest and he warned everyone in its path to take immediate cover.

Chapter 45

"Son of a bitch!" Walt blurted. "That damn tornado isn't more than a few miles away and it's headed right for us. We've got seventy-five basket cases to get into the basement!"

As if to make the point, tornado sirens began to wail, mixing with the machine-gun splatter of rain and hail and wind that roared like a freight train.

"Where are the doctors and nurses?" Mason asked.

Walt snorted a laugh. "You got to be kidding, mister. There ain't no doctors on weekends and there's only one nurse on each floor and they gonna need our help."

"How can you run a hospital with one nurse on each floor?" Mason asked.

"Keep the patients doped up, that's how," he said. Walt bolted out of his chair faster than Mason would have thought him able. "You take the top floor, I'll take this one. Get everybody out of their rooms and downstairs to the basement."

The wind screeched and rattled the hospital like it was

made of tinker toys as a cataclysmic bolt of lightning arced across the sky, the blinding light feeling close enough to vaporize them, the trailing blast of thunder launching them toward the patients' rooms.

Mason swiped his key card over the sensor, yanking open the door to the hall. Walt shoved past him, banging on doors as he ran the length of the corridor. Mason took the stairs two at a time, bursting onto the second floor as people began to pour out of their rooms.

The stairs opened out into a sitting area in the center of the floor. The wall of windows that normally afforded a calming view of the pastoral grounds vibrated furiously with the beat of the storm.

A woman dressed in white pants and a white shirt stood in the middle of the room calling patients by name, motioning them toward her. She was middle-age, stout, had close cropped black hair, and was the closest thing to a nurse Mason could see in the growing crowd.

"Who are you?" she yelled at Mason.

"Maintenance," he said. "How can I help?"

"Get them out of their rooms. If we can get them under control, we'll take them downstairs. If we can't manage that, we'll have to put them in the halls away from any windows so they don't get hit by broken glass."

The lights began to flicker, adding a strobe effect to the keening and wailing of the frightened patients. A few ran toward him, hands extended like beggars, grabbing at his sleeves. Others pressed their backs against the windows, sliding down onto the floor, toppling over and curling into a ball. Down the halls, doors slammed as some patients retreated to their rooms, barricading themselves.

Two patients had latched on to him, one on either side. They were both older women, their faces slack, their eyes wide. They wore nightgowns even though it was the middle of the day. He led them to a sofa, easing them down. He gathered other patients, placing some in chairs, the rest in a circle on the carpeted floor.

As soon as he had them organized, they started to peel apart. The woman in white kept calling names. It took Mason a moment to realize that she kept repeating the same names and that no one was paying her any attention. The patients wandered past her as if she was one of them. Mason finally realized that she was when she extended her arms and began twirling slowly down onto the floor.

Crazy or not, she had the right idea. There was no way he could get the patients downstairs to the basement, so he had to get them into the hallway away from the glass. He had no idea how to get the holdouts to leave their rooms.

He grabbed two patients sitting on the couch, a man and a woman, and began leading them to the west wing. Hearing footsteps as he passed the stairs, he paused long enough to see Adrienne make the turn at the landing. She was soaked through, her tank top clinging to her in way that almost made him forget the storm.

"What the hell!" she said.

Mason shrugged. "You made the padded room sound irresistible. Welcome to the party."

She joined him, looking around the room where twenty people in pajamas were out of control, some crying, and some jabbering, some silently pressing their faces against the glass.

"Oh my God!" she said, drawing each word out like it was a separate paragraph. "We've got to get these people to the basement."

"There isn't time," Mason said. "This isn't all of them anyway. Some of them have gone back to their rooms. If they locked their doors, I don't know how we'll get them out. Our best bet is to put everyone in one of the hallways and ride this thing out."

Adrienne reached into her jeans and pulled out a key card. "Master card," she said. "Priceless. You get everyone into the west wing. I'll check the rooms on the east wing. Then I'll come back to help you."

The next few minutes were a blur, Mason shuttling patients into the west wing hallway. He couldn't separate the effects of their psychiatric condition, their fear, and their medication. All he knew was that any explanation he gave them could just as well have been in Chinese.

Adrienne led three patients from the east wing into his hall, then began checking each room. Satisfied that they had accounted for everyone, she stood at the entrance to the lobby, blocking anyone who thought about leaving while Mason patrolled the hall, reassuring the terrified patients that everything was okay.

There was an exit at the far end of the hall. Mason opened the door, making certain no one was hiding on the stairs. Satisfied, he noticed one patient, a woman sitting against the wall near the door, her knees pulled to her chest, her head pressed against her arms, hiding her face. She was small and had dark hair streaked with gray and was one of the few patients wearing normal clothes instead of pajamas. She was so silent Mason wasn't certain whether she was breathing. He knelt down, touching her shoulder gently.

"Ma'am," he said softly. "Are you all right?"

The woman stirred at the sound of his voice, raising her head. She blinked her eyes and then wiped them. "It's you," Mary Kowalczyk said.

Before Mason could answer, the building shook as if it had been ripped from its foundation and upended. The glass walls in the lobby exploded and tornado-driven winds screamed into their corridor, hurtling Adrienne over the bowed heads of the patients like she was a rag doll.

Mason flattened his body over Mary while the building continued to shake, not certain whether it would collapse around them. The wind howled down the hall like the devil giving chase, escaping with a painful groaning screech as the roof peeled off the hospital, tons of steel and concrete disappearing in the blackness.

Just as quickly, it was over, the winds dying, the rain easing to a mist, then stopping, the air chilled but clean. Sirens filled the afternoon, the sky lightening but still too dark for a late summer afternoon.

Mason lifted himself off of Mary. "Are you okay?" he asked her. He squeezed her shoulders when she nodded her head. "I'll be right back," he told her.

He found Adrienne sprawled on her back twenty feet from the doorway to the lobby. Blood oozed from a slice in her scalp and her arms were tattooed by a constellation of pinprick cuts caused by flying glass. He knelt next to her, glad that her eyes were open and not fixed.

"What hurts?" he asked her.

"What doesn't?" she said. "I can move everything and nothing feels broken. Help me sit up."

Mason motioned to two patients to move aside and make room for her. He was surprised at how calm the patients were. Either they were in shock or they were cured, Mason decided. He eased Adrienne into a sitting position and pulled off his denim shirt, giving it to her to press against the cut on her head.

"Easy," he told her. "You may have a concussion."

"I thought the person you wanted to visit was at Lakewood Gardens," she said as she took a deep breath.

"I took a wrong turn on my way over there," he said. "Good thing I did. Why did you come here instead of staying at the visitor's center?"

"I knew we were short-handed today. The nurse that's

supposed to cover this floor called in sick. When the sirens went off, I knew my dad would need help."

"Your dad?" Mason asked. "Was he the guy on the desk downstairs?"

"That's him. Walt. Boy is he going to be in a bad mood. He was really looking forward to that football game."

More sirens signaled the arrival of rescue crews. The first firefighters made it to the second floor lobby. Mason signaled them.

"The cavalry has arrived," he told Adrienne. "They'll take good care of you."

"Where are you going?" she asked.

"No place. I was never here. Remember?"

"Yeah," she said, nodding and pressing his shirt to her scalp. "Sure I don't. Never saw you after you left the Visitor's Center. How's that for a concussion?"

"Perfect."

He kissed her cheek as a firefighter reached them, while others attended to the rest of the patients. Mason stepped out of the way, returning to Mary who was standing at the end of the hall beneath the exit sign.

"You okay?" Mason asked her.

"At least I'm not crazy," she said.

Chapter 46

A tornado destroys with the whimsy and precision of a psychopath: vicious, capricious, and remorseless. It may choose to pulverize a house into sawdust and leave neighbors on either side untouched. If so inclined, it might scoop up a car from a parking lot and fling it like a Frisbee half a mile down the street, indifferent to the makes and models not to its taste. It might uproot a stand of trees as easily as a gardener plucking carrots from the ground, save one lone survivor unable to explain its luck.

The tornado that struck Golden Years was such a killer. It peeled the roof off the psychiatric hospital like it was an aluminum pull tab, the swirling wind turning up its nose at the patients, taking none of them. A slab of roof rocketed down Eighty-seventh Street Parkway, pierced the windshield of a tractor-trailer rig, and killed the driver. The unfortunate man was the only fatality of the storm.

Mason held onto Mary's arm as they walked down the stairway at the end of the hall. A platoon of firemen had hustled by them on their way down. None of them questioned

Mason's assurance that they were fine. The stairs quivered beneath them, Mason not certain whether it was the aftershocks as the building calmed itself or whether it was their own trembling. They came out the door that he had tried to get in earlier, the video camera dangling from an electrical thread as they passed beneath it.

They walked along the sidewalk toward the Visitors' Center, sidestepping fallen limbs that had been ripped from their trunks. Mason's arm was around Mary's waist, her arm stretched across his back. Her feet, unsteady at first, settled into a confident, short stride and she pulled away from his support. She offered no explanation for her presence at the hospital and, as anxious as he was to know, he let it ride for the moment.

Remnants of the roof littered the grounds along with furniture, bedding, and clothing that had been sucked into the whirlwind before drifting to earth. They stopped for a moment, looking back at the hospital. Shorn of its roof, its windows knocked out, it looked like a punch-drunk fighter.

A fleet of fire trucks, ambulances, and police cars, their lights cascading red, white, and blue, were making their way around the cars that had been in the parking lot when the storm hit. Many of those vehicles had overturned, smashing into one another like a demolition derby. The back end of a Mazda Miata stuck out of the front seat of a Lincoln Navigator, the storm tossing the coupe like a dart into the SUV. The air reeked of gasoline, a stench that warned it was too early to sound the all clear.

Sirens continued to blare in the distance as more rescue units raced to the scene. Uniformed men and woman rushed to the aid of residents and patients, corralling them for triage. Some residents wandered about in a daze. Others sat on the ground, nursing cuts and bruises.

All of the buildings on the campus had suffered some

damage, none as severe as the psychiatric hospital. The tornado had struck like precision guided meteorological munitions. Its target had been the hospital. Everything and everyone else was collateral damage.

Mason led Mary through the chaos, waving off inquiries and offers of help. She was, as nearly as he could tell, unhurt. He wanted to get her out of there without answering questions from someone checking names off a list to confirm who was a victim and who was not. And he had questions of his own that would have to wait.

He caught a glimpse of Adrienne's father, Walt, cutting through the crowd. Mason wasn't certain whether he was looking for patients that were still unaccounted for or whether he was looking for Mason and Mary. Any doubt vanished when Dixon Smith ran up to the man, poking him in the chest with his finger, gesturing wildly. Walt brushed Smith's hand away. The two men nearly came to blows until Walt saw Adrienne being helped by a paramedic to an ambulance and left Smith to argue alone.

Mason unhitched his tool belt, dropping it on the ground along with his ball cap. A navy blue windbreaker had blown across the grounds, lodging against the heel of a bench. Mason snatched it and slipped it on, ignoring the snug fit. It was all he could do to change his appearance. Placing his hand on the small of Mary's back, he urged her to pick up the pace.

They walked down the long drive toward Eighty-seventh Street Parkway through a growing crowd. Once the storm had passed and news of its attack on Golden Years was broadcast by radio and television, people came to offer help and to witness the destruction firsthand. The police were busy directing emergency vehicles in and out and hadn't had time for crowd control.

A police officer directing traffic from the middle of the

street held up his hand, signaling them to wait. Mary stood quietly on his left as Mason shifted his feet impatiently.

The traffic cop finally motioned them to cross, a new companion lagging a few steps behind but otherwise keeping pace. When they reached Mason's car, he opened the passenger door for Mary, closing it as she slid in. Walking around to his door, he found a woman standing in front of his car.

"Can I help you?" Mason asked.

"I want to go home," the woman answered. She was near his height with a slender frame and erect bearing. She was wearing a raincoat over pants and sneakers and a floppy hat pulled down low on her pale checks

"Where do you live?" Mason asked.

She hesitated and pulled her cap off, her tangled blonde hair pressed tightly against her head. Twisting the cap like it was a wet cloth, she looked around. "It's been so long," she said.

Her face was drawn, her eyes hollow but alive, not drugged. She was old enough to live at Golden Years, though he couldn't guess at which facility.

"You followed us out of Golden Years. Is that where you live?" Mason asked. He was sure she did and was equally certain that he didn't want to take her back and that he couldn't leave her in the parking lot, her uncertainty convincing him that she shouldn't be left alone.

"That's not my home," she answered. "I want to go home."

"Can I call someone for you?" Mason offered.

His question provoked a panic as her lips quivered and her eyes widened. She raised a hand to her mouth. "No calls," she said. "No more phone calls."

"Okay, okay," Mason said, looking over the woman's shoulder at the traffic cop, deciding that he had to take her at least that far. "What's your name?"

"Victoria King," she said. "And I want to go home."

A car turned into the parking lot from Eighty-seventh Street Parkway, circling away from Mason. It was a black BMW sedan with tinted passenger windows, the same model as Whitney King's car. He caught a glimpse of the driver through the windshield as the car turned away but didn't get a good enough look to tell if it was Whitney, though the chill in his gut was confirmation enough.

Crafting a quick mental argument on the difference between giving someone a ride home and kidnapping, Mason said, "I'll take you," and ushered the woman into the backseat.

Glad that he had parked the car facing out, he started his engine just as the BMW screeched to a stop behind him, the passenger window sliding down. He looked in his rearview mirror as Whitney King stared back at him. King's lips were peeled back in a snarl and his eyes were blacker than the storm. Hearing the car, Mary and Victoria both turned around. King's face twisted with rage as he pounded his steering wheel.

Gunning his car, Mason raced toward the street. Whitney was out of position to maneuver through Mason's parking space and was forced to drive around the long line of parked cars. The added distance Whitney had to travel was enough to let Mason escape from the parking lot, cutting in front of another fire truck on Eighty-seventh Street Parkway as the traffic cop shook his fist at him.

Looking over his shoulder, he saw Whitney trapped by the fire truck and the angry cop. Mary gaped at Mason as if he was the inmate who had just escaped from the asylum. Before she could speak, he made the introductions.

"Mary Kowalczyk, say hello to Victoria King."

Chapter 47

Neither woman spoke. Mary stared at Victoria, her face filled with questions. Victoria gazed back at Mary, no hint of recognition in her blank expression. After a moment, Victoria looked away, finding the passing scenery out her window of more interest.

"She doesn't know who I am," Mary said softly.

Mason looked at Victoria in his rearview mirror. "I'm not certain how much she knows about anything. She seems out of it."

"Where are we going?" she asked.

"I'll know when we get there," he said.

Mason sped east on Eighty-seventh Street Parkway, cutting north on a side street, working his way through a patchwork of subdivisions to avoid Whitney King. The aftermath of the storm added its own detours. Some streets were closed due to downed power lines. Others were blocked by fallen trees. People were already out in their yards, chainsaws in hand, cleaning up. No one gave them a second look and no black BMWs suddenly appeared in Mason's rearview mirror.

As badly as he wanted to talk with Mary about what had happened to her, he didn't want to do it in front of Victoria. He assumed Mary hadn't checked in to Golden Years for her health, which meant that taking her home was not an option. He didn't know where Victoria lived before she was at Golden Years and didn't want to take her there even if he did know. She was his ace, though he couldn't decide how to play her.

Whitney King knew that both women were with Mason. King couldn't report Mason to the cops for kidnapping his mother without implicating himself in Mary's disappearance.

Better yet, King had some explaining to do about his mother. Sandra Connelly suspected that Victoria King didn't belong at Golden Years. If Sandra was right, Victoria wasn't crazy and Whitney King had bundled his mother into the loony bin for some other reason. Mason's best guess was that Victoria knew that Whitney was guilty of the Byrnes's murders. Proving that there's an ounce of good in everyone, Whitney couldn't bring himself to off his mother. Instead, he warehoused her.

One thing bothered Mason about his theory. Victoria was out of it, muttering about going home and not wanting any more phone calls. Mason was no shrink, but Victoria didn't look right to him.

King's other problem was that the cops were looking for him. If he wanted his mother back, he'd have to come get her. In the meantime, Mason needed a place where both women could stay while he figured out what to do next.

Mason introduced Mary and Victoria to Claire who said how pleased she was to meet them and didn't ask any questions. She knew enough to understand who they were and knew Mason well enough to know that he wouldn't have brought them to her house if he had had another option. Harry stood behind her in the front hall of her first floor office.

"This is Harry," she said to Mary and Victoria, offering no further explanation. "Let me take you upstairs."

Mason and Harry watched as they climbed the stairs.

"Where'd you find them?" Harry asked him.

"Golden Years."

"You were there when the tornado hit or did they just drop out of the sky like Dorothy and Toto?" Harry asked, keeping his voice level.

"I was there," Mason answered. "And so were they. I was looking for Victoria. Mary was a bonus."

"What was Mary doing there?" Harry asked.

"I haven't had a chance to ask her yet. We've been kind of busy."

"You suppose Whitney King is going to be looking for his momma?"

"I suppose," Mason said, giving Harry a quick rundown on what had happened.

"What do you have in mind?" Harry asked.

"Been a long day," Mason said. "I think I'll have a chat with Mary and then Victoria. After that, I'm going to take the rest of the weekend off. See what Monday brings."

"You stirred up the shit stew and now you want to see what happens. Is that it?" Harry asked.

"Sometimes I'm a lot better at stirring stuff up than I am at figuring it out."

"Well then, you better get upstairs. Claire's probably taken their orders for breakfast already."

"Does she offer rooms with the American or European meal plan?" Mason asked.

"Doesn't matter. You know the woman can't cook."

* * *

When Claire bought her house, she renovated the first floor into her law office, keeping the existing rooms intact. She knocked out every wall on the second floor, stripping the space to the exterior frame, and started over. She had liked the open feeling of the loft she had lived in downtown but didn't want as much space. Here, the kitchen merged with dining and living areas into a single room. There were two bedrooms, each with a bath, tucked at one end. The walls were white, the floors were hard, but Claire warmed the atmosphere with plants, primitive art, and herself.

Claire was alone, sitting at her kitchen table, catching the first sunlight to emerge in the aftermath of the storm as it shot through her window. It was late in the day and the sun was dropping, giving the light a burnished glow against the glass. The door to the guest bedroom was closed. Harry joined her at the table.

"Where are they?" Mason asked, standing in the center of the living room.

"In there," Claire answered, tilting her head at the closed door.

"I need to talk to them," Mason said, taking a step in that direction.

Claire raised her hand. "Not yet, Lou."

"It's important," he said.

"No doubt it is. It may even be as important as what they are talking about, but I doubt it. Leave them alone. They're not going anywhere."

Mason took a deep breath and a long look at the bedroom before letting out an impatient sigh.

Claire said, "You know, that deep breath thing you do is really annoying. Those two women have lived with what happened to their sons a lot longer than you have. I imagine that they have never talked about it with each other until now. From the looks on their faces when you got here, they need to. You'll just have to wait."

Mason shrugged in surrender, joining his aunt and Harry. "I can wait."

"Why did you bring them here?" Claire asked.

"I can't take Mary home until I know whether it's safe. As long as King and my lawyer are running loose, that's not a good bet."

"Your lawyer?" Claire asked. "Why should Mary be afraid of your lawyer?"

Mason shook his head. "I'm not certain. Sandra Connelly asked Dixon Smith to find out whether Victoria King belonged at Golden Years. I'm guessing that Sandra had a good reason for asking. Victoria may have known that her son was a killer. Whitney may have put her in Golden Years to keep her doped up and quiet."

"A man who loves his mother is man enough for me," Harry said.

"But how could Whitney get away with that all these years?" Claire asked. "Too many people would know that she was there. Doctors, nurses, social workers. It would be impossible to keep that a secret. The insurance company that paid the bills would get suspicious after a while."

"Hard, but not impossible," Mason said. "Whitney may have paid the freight himself. Golden Years is a little short of medical supervision. Plus, the whole place was built by King's construction company, which Whitney owns. That would give him an in with Damon Parker who owns Golden Years."

"So why not talk to Parker?" Claire asked.

"If Sandra thought of that, she must have had a reason not to," Mason said. "Instead, she asked Dixon Smith to check into it since she knew that Dixon represented Parker and Golden Years."

Harry asked, "What did Dixon find out?"

"According to Dixon, not a damn thing. Plus, Dixon says that Parker fired him for asking."

"Why would any of that make you think your lawyer is a threat to Mary?" Claire asked.

"I went to Golden Years today to talk to Victoria," Mason said. "Dixon Smith had left instructions to call him if I showed up. Turns out, he lied to me about Parker firing him. He was running around at Golden Years after the storm acting like a tornado was the least of his worries. I think he was looking for Mary and me."

"He's supposed to be defending you," Claire said. "You should fire him!"

"Not yet. He doesn't know that I'm on to him. I'll learn more this way."

"Aren't you forgetting the small matter of the murder charge against you?" Claire asked. "You need a lawyer you can rely on."

"Maybe not. Maybe all I need is a lawyer I can prove killed Sandra."

Claire said, "You think it was Dixon?"

"Sandra was killed to stop her from telling me something about Whitney King or his mother. She was about to tell me when she got a phone call from Dixon Smith. Sandra must have told him we were together. She may have even told him we were meeting King at King's office."

Harry said, "Whitney says he didn't know anything about meeting with you and Sandra, plus his mother is his alibi. Dixon is the only other person who knew where you and Sandra were going to be."

"Exactly," Mason said. "Plus, there wasn't time for anyone else to do it."

"But how do you explain the phone call?" Harry asked.

"Why would Sandra tell you King had called and told you to wait there if the caller was Dixon?"

Mason frowned. "Maybe it wasn't King. Maybe it was Dixon with a bad cell phone connection or a disguised voice. I don't know. Dixon told me that there are no records of a call from Whitney to Sandra. There is a record of a call but no originating phone number."

Claire said, "Then it couldn't have been made from Dixon's phone. That number would appear in the records."

"If," Harry said, "Dixon was dumb enough to use his own phone. More likely he stole someone's cell phone."

"If he did, that stolen number would show up and lead us back to the owner of the cell phone. Dixon told me that all the numbers in Sandra's records checked out except for the one that's unidentified. Dixon wouldn't lie about that since he knows I'll see the records."

"I'll tell you what," Harry said. "You better find out who placed that anonymous call or the jury will think you made the whole story up."

"No plan is perfect," Mason said, pushing back from the table, casting another long look at the closed bedroom door.

"Go home," Claire told him. "Leave them be. Come back in the morning and bring a bag of bagels and cream cheese."

Mason nodded and stood. "Okay," he said. "We've got some things to talk about too."

"I know," she said. "It's time."

Mason looked at her, not certain if the light was playing tricks. A sadness he'd never seen crept into her eyes and spread across her face. He turned to Harry.

"You staying?"

Harry said, "I'll be here."

"Feel better?" Claire asked. "And no speeches about Whitney King looking for Mary and his mother. We'll be fine. Harry keeps a gun here that I'm not supposed to know about and I've still got the bulletproof vest he bought me for Valentine's Day," she added, patting Harry on the thigh.

Mason looked at them. His aunt was defiant. Harry was a rock. He doubted that King would think to look here. It was more likely that he'd wait for Mason to come home. Even if King showed up at Claire's house, he liked their chances.

"See you in the morning," Mason told them.

Chapter 48

On his way home, Mason called Samantha Greer and told her where he'd seen Whitney King.

"That's where the tornado hit," she said.

"Close. The heavy damage was across the street at Golden Years."

"I saw the news," she said. "What were you doing there?"

"I was picking up some things at Wal-Mart."

"And in the middle of a tornado, you just happened to go shopping at a Wal-Mart that's twenty miles from your house, right?"

"There aren't any Wal-Marts in my neighborhood," Mason said.

"Yeah, but there's a Costco at Linwood and Main that's less than ten minutes from your house. And I suppose it's just a coincidence that your favorite Wal-Mart is in Whitney King's neighborhood if I'm reading my street map correctly."

She didn't repeat Patrick Ortiz's theory that Mason had intended to kill both Sandra Connelly and Whitney King, but the accusation hummed in the background.

"So you want to convict me based on my shopping habits," Mason said.

"No. I want you to stop peddling this crap to me," Samantha said. "The night Sandra was murdered, you told me that she had doubts that Whitney's mother belonged at Golden Years, so I checked it out. Victoria King had a breakdown after Whitney's trial and her husband's death. Been there ever since. Satisfied?"

"I am if you are."

"Then why were you poking around out there and how did you just happen to run into Whitney King when we've been dogging him for the last three days without getting a sniff of him?"

"Why are you cross-examining me instead of thanking me for the tip on Whitney?" Mason asked.

"Because your lawyer is up to his eyeballs in a federal investigation of Golden Years and because you are the master of the omitted. If you just happened to be shopping at that Wal-Mart and Whitney King just happened to wave to you in the parking lot, then that damned tornado was airmailed special delivery to kick your ass. There's only so much Lou Mason bullshit I can shovel in one day!"

"I'll show you my receipt from Wal-Mart," he offered. "In the meantime, you might want to double the coverage on Nick Brynes. Whitney didn't look too happy when I saw him."

"I'm going to hang up so you don't have to tell me any more lies," she told him.

"Hang on a second," Mason said.

"What?" she asked, her voice vibrating with exasperation.

"Earlier today, when we were at the hospital, Nick told you that Father Steve wasn't a witness when Whitney shot him. You sent your partner Kolatch to talk to the priest. What did he find out?"

"Al talked to him. Father Steve is sticking to his story."

"You buy that?" Mason asked.

"It's an easier sell than your story of suburban adventure, but thanks for the tip on Whitney," she said, hanging up.

The more easily a story fits into someone's world, the more likely they are to believe it. Mason knew that. That's why primitive people worshiped the sun—making a star into a god fit with their limited knowledge of their world.

Mary believed her son was innocent because she couldn't imagine him being guilty and because she hated rich people like Whitney King. Samantha dismissed Mason's story about seeing Whitney and bought Father Steve's story about Nick's shooting because it fit with the case she had put together against Mason.

Cops, Mason decided, loved easy solutions that answered the most questions. Like sun-worshiping primitive tribes, cops looked for things that fit together. Mason looked for things that didn't.

Mason stopped at home long enough to pack clean clothes and Tuffy into the car. He'd typed some notes about the case on his laptop and tossed it onto the front seat of his car along with the files he'd brought home on King and the pictures he'd printed from the Golden Years' Web site.

Mason didn't know where or when King would show up, but he was confident that King would come after him. If he was right about King's mother, King would have no choice. Mason's house was too vulnerable. His office was easier to defend, especially with Mickey and Blues.

He found them both at Blues on Broadway. Blues was tending bar on a slow Saturday night, which was a bad thing in the bar business but understandable after the storm. He poured Mason a beer and listened without comment as

Mason described what had happened since they'd had lunch at the Peanut.

"Harry's not as good as he used to be since his eyesight has gone to hell," Blues said. "You're taking a chance stashing Mary and Victoria over there."

Mason nodded. "Can't be helped. I couldn't think of anyplace else."

"What about Abby's place?" Blues asked.

Mason thought for a minute, swirling the last ounce of beer in the bottom of his mug. It wasn't hard to imagine Abby's reaction if he asked her.

"Bad idea," he said. "What about you? Any luck with Shawana James?"

Blues wiped a white dish towel over imaginary spots on the gleaming surface of the bar. "She's not going to be buying any tickets to the Policeman's Ball. It took a while to get past that I used to be a cop."

"Why'd you tell her?" Mason asked.

"Didn't have to. She knew by looking. Turns out we know some of the same people but from different sides of the story. She finally told me what happened to her sister."

Mason slid off his bar stool. "It's been a long day, man. Don't make it any longer."

Blues flashed a smile, enjoying the moment. "Easy, son. She's not going anywhere. Janet is living in a halfway house over in Kansas City, Kansas. She's doing the last six months of a seven-to-ten stretch for armed robbery."

Mason took a step back from the bar. "And Samantha couldn't find her?"

"Janet Hook got married and divorced since the trial. Her last name was Curtis when she was convicted. If Sam ran her maiden name through the system, it'd be easy to miss her. I checked out the halfway house. It's off Twenty-seventh and

Georgia. I talked to the woman who runs it. She confirmed that Janet is there. I'll talk with her tomorrow."

"Almost makes me want to pay for the beer," Mason said, grinning.

"I'll settle for you paying the rent," Blues said as Mason made for the back of the bar and the stairs to his office.

The door to his office was open. Mickey was using his computer, prowling cyberspace for the link between Whitney King and Damon Parker. Mason watched silently for a moment, feeling at last as if part of his life was coming together again. Mickey looked up from the computer screen, pivoting in his chair toward Mason.

"You spying on me, boss?" he asked, smiling.

"Just making sure you're not going to any of those must be over twenty-one Web sites. Find anything?"

"Not much. Whitney King sits on the Golden Years board of directors, but it's mostly a window dressing deal, an advisory board, not a governing board. Meets once a year so Damon Parker can tell them what a great guy he is, but Parker runs the show."

"What about money? Any off-the-books deals?"

"That stuff is harder. I've got to hack into the Golden Years accounting system, dig out bank account numbers, and chase the dough."

"And?" Mason asked.

"And I'm working on it," Mickey answered, flexing his fingers and cracking his knuckles. "I'm working on it."

Mason called Harry to tell him where he was. Harry reassured Mason that they were buttoned down for the night. All secure.

Blues, Mickey, and Mason divided the rest of the night into four-hour shifts, two of them staying up at a time so they could watch the front and back of the building. Nothing happened.

Mason was sprawled on the couch in his office when Mickey woke him at six on Sunday morning. He rolled upright, slumping against the cushions, rubbing the cobwebs out of his eyes.

"You're going to like this, boss," Mickey said, waving a handful of papers at him.

Mason flipped through the pages, getting lost in the rows of numbers, handing them back to Mickey. "Too early. You tell me."

"Damon Parker has a silent partner."

"Whitney King?" Mason asked.

"Nope. His mother." Mickey said. "She bought into Parker's company around fifteen years ago."

Mason pulled himself to the edge of the couch. "His mother? She's three bricks short of a load! She's been a patient there for fifteen years."

"I guess that's why Parker put her money in a special account," Mickey said. "He's been paying her like clockwork."

"Paying her? For what?"

"Her share of the profits, man. What else? She's an owner."

Blues had finished out a complete bath, including shower, on the second floor. Mickey took advantage of it to avoid renting an apartment, using his office as home. Mason was glad to use it to get clean, massaging Mickey's information while he showered. He wrapped a towel around his waist, using the mirror to take inventory. He hadn't shaved, and his dark beard coupled with the circles under his eyes and the still angry scar on his chest gave him the look of a person just one wrong step away from life on the street.

But it wasn't just the beard or the bags under his eyes. He was worn, the battles notching lines on his face. He didn't have to take on this fight, but he had. He'd deluded himself into thinking that this one would be different, more to convince Abby than himself. He'd dived into the dark water again and it was deeper than ever.

He let out a long, slow breath, taking his time as he went back to his office for the electric razor he kept in his desk. Mickey was sitting on the couch, holding a microphone that was plugged into Mason's laptop computer.

"Watch this, boss," Mickey said, tapping the keys. Mason's phone rang. "Go ahead. Answer it," Mickey told him. Mason picked up the receiver. "Come here, Watson. I need you," Mickey said, his voice coming through clearly on Mason's phone.

"How'd you do that?" Mason asked, putting the phone down.

"While you were sleeping, I signed you up for WiFi phone service with your laptop."

"Does that mean anything in English?" Mason asked.

Mickey grinned. "Making phone calls on the Internet is nothing new. Not many people do it because they're too used to regular phones. But it's free. No long distance charges."

"I've heard of that," Mason said. "I thought you had to use a phone line or a cable hookup to do that."

"That's the beauty of wireless Internet. You can get online without a cable or phone hookup and call anybody anywhere for nothing. I saw your laptop and decided to try it. Cool, huh?"

Mason stared at Mickey, then at the laptop, his mind focusing more sharply. "Maybe," he said. "How much does it cost?"

"Depends on the package you buy, but they're all flat-rate programs."

"Sounds like an overgrown cell phone," Mason said.

"Except it's got a security feature you can't get with cell phones," Mickey explained. "These calls can't be traced back to your phone number since the computer doesn't use one. It just uses an Internet service provider that bills everything to your account with no records of individual calls. You want to make a call to someone that won't show up on anybody's phone bill, this is the way to do it. The phone sex companies are pushing it big time."

"You mean," Mason said with growing interest, "the person you call gets a bill that shows an incoming call without any originating phone number?"

"You got it," Mickey said. "Cool, huh?" he repeated.

"Very cool," Mason said. His phone rang a second time. Mickey raised his hands in a not me gesture.

"Mason," he answered.

"You better get over here quick," Harry said.

"Why? What happened?"

"It's Mary," Harry said.

"What's wrong with her?" Mason asked.

"She wants to go to church."

Chapter 49

Mary and Victoria were sitting on the couch in Claire's loft when Mason arrived ten minutes later. Their backs were straight, their feet on the floor, ankles crossed. Victoria cast a questioning look at Mason as if it was the first time she'd seen him. Her eyes fluttered as if she was trying to clear her sight. Mary was edgy, kneading her hands, reminding Mason of the first time he saw her. When Victoria reached for Mary's hand, Mason was not certain who was comforting whom.

Blues and Mickey came up the stairs a moment later. Mason looked at Blues.

"All clear," Blues said, answering Mason's unasked question.

Mary tightened up when she saw Blues, clenching her jaw and squaring her shoulders. "I told you I didn't want him involved," she said to Mason.

"Mary," he said, "a lot has happened since then. We need him."

"No! Not after what he did to my Ryan."

Mary's eyes narrowed, flashing anger and hate that put

Mason back on his heels. He didn't blame her for the depth of her feelings, even if they were misplaced. Perhaps the strength of those emotions had sustained her all these years. One thing was certain. Mason wouldn't convince her otherwise. At least not yet.

"Blues," he said. "Take Mickey with you and go see Janet Hook. I want two witnesses to hear whatever she has to say."

The big man nodded, his face impassive. It was personal. He wouldn't pretend otherwise, but he was there for Mason, not for Mary who offered a grimly triumphant smile when they left.

Mason marveled at Mary, remembering the contradictions between his and Blues's images of her, concluding that Blues had at least a piece of her dead to rights. She was a woman with a gutsy, sharp-edged determination whose diminutive size was deceptive. Mason's rugby coach would have said she played bigger than she looked.

"Mass is at eight o'clock," Mary said. "I haven't been to church in days. I need to go."

Mason tugged at his chin, looking at his watch. It was almost seven-thirty. "It may not be safe, Mary."

She smiled at him, though this time it was with the warmth she'd shown him earlier. "I'll be fine. St. Mark's isn't far from here, though I'd rather not walk," she said, standing and brushing her hands across her pants, smoothing the wrinkles.

Mason knew she was telling him more than she was asking him. He couldn't stop her from going and he couldn't let her go alone. Hoping that Father Steve would be there, he said, "I'll go with you."

Mary looked him up and down. "It may do you some good," she said.

Ten minutes later, they were parked across the street from

the church. Mary had been silent during the short drive and started to open the car door.

"Not yet, Mary," Mason said. She looked at him then looked away, leaving the door open. "Don't you think we should quit pretending that yesterday was just your average summer day? How in the world did you end up in that psychiatric hospital?"

She rubbed her hands together. "I miss my rosary beads," she said. "They were in my purse." She studied her hands for a moment then slapped her open palms against her knees. "God forgive me! I'm such a fool!"

"Mary, you disappeared," Mason said softly. "You went to St. Mark's to help Father Steve and then you fell off the face of the earth. Father Steve was the last person I could find who had seen you. I searched your house. I even filed a missing person's report."

Mary drew back in surprise. "You were in my house? How did you get in?"

Mason grinned like a busted schoolboy. "I broke in. I'll pay for a new lock on the back door. I was afraid you were dead until I went back and saw that your fish were gone too. I knew they were important to you and that convinced me that you were alive and had arranged for someone to take care of the fish."

"No," she said softly, her eyes widening. "I don't know what happened to the fish. I couldn't take care of anything."

"What happened to you?" Mason asked. "How did you end up at Golden Years?"

Mary glanced at him, her cheeks coloring, shaking her head. "I spent fifteen years trying to save my son. Fifteen years and they still took him from me! Victoria King knew her son was guilty and she let my Ryan rot in jail until they killed him."

"Victoria King has been in a mental institution for the last fifteen years," Mason said. "What makes you think she knows Whitney is guilty?"

"A mother knows," she said, shaking her head to banish any doubt. "I know it's sinful, but I've hated that woman as much as I've hated her son. She helped him get away with murder! All these years, I've hated her. I couldn't stand it another minute. I had to make her tell the truth."

"You mean you went to Golden Years to confront her?" Mason asked.

Mary nodded. "That day at church, it was Wednesday, my volunteer day. St. Mark's does outreach at Golden Years. A shuttle brings people to the church for afternoon mass. I saw the shuttle and I just got on. I didn't even think about it. I just did it."

"What happened when you got there?"

She took a deep breath, letting it out slowly, rubbing the palm of her hand across the dash. Her hand was dry and didn't leave a trace. "I went to the information desk and asked to see Victoria King. A man came to get me and said he would take me to her."

"What did she tell you?" Mason asked.

Mary looked at Mason, her eyes blazing. "I never saw her until yesterday when she got into your car. The man took me to the room where you found me and locked me in. The food they gave me was drugged so I slept most of the time at first. When I realized what was happening, I tried one food at a time until I was sure it wasn't drugged. Then I wrapped the rest in a towel and got rid of it when that man took me to the bathroom."

"Was it always the same person?" Mason asked.

"Always. No one else."

"Did he tell you why you were being held?"

"No. He acted like I was just one of the patients. He'd take me to the bathroom and wait outside the door, then take me back to my room. There was nothing I could do," she added, shaking her head again, repeating the words as if she was apologizing to herself. "There was nothing I could do."

"That man," Mason said. "Was he an older, heavy-set white man? He might have had a nametag that said Walt."

"I never saw a nametag, but that's what he looked like. He had jowls like a bulldog," Mary added. "Do you know who he is?"

"I think so," Mason answered, remembering how Walt and Dixon Smith had frantically searched for them after the tornado. "Did you tell Father Steve that you were going to see Victoria?"

Mary was quick with her answer. "No. I was afraid of what he would say if he knew what I was going to do. I told him I was going to see my husband Vince in Omaha. He was inside the church when I got on the shuttle."

"Why were you afraid?" Mason asked. "What would be wrong with you going to see Victoria King?"

Mary looked at Mason again, her eyes black and her face brittle. "I tried so hard to do things the right way, Mr. Mason. I raised my son to know right from wrong, to be a good boy. I let the lawyers tell me what to do after Ryan was arrested and now he's dead. I came to you to put it right, to save his memory, even though I knew it would do no good. Memory isn't enough for a mother to hold on to. You can't touch it. You can't sing to it. You can't even hold it because it slips through your fingers like smoke."

"Coming to me was the right thing to do, Mary. It was the only thing you could do."

"No, Mr. Mason. It wasn't the only thing I could do, not if Victoria King wouldn't tell the truth."

"And if she wouldn't, then what?" Mason asked.

"Then, I was going to make it right," she said, clipping her words. Her jaw tightened, pulling her skin taut across her chin. "I couldn't tell Father Steve that I was going to kill Victoria King, could I? So now do you know why I have to go to mass?"

"To confess and to pray for forgiveness," Mason answered.

She looked him in the eye, her fire gone, replaced by ashen sorrow. "No more. I've lost my faith," she said. "Too many unanswered prayers. I'll just ask Ryan to forgive me for failing him again."

Chapter 50

Mason cupped Mary's elbow with his hand, as much to help her across the street as to keep her within his grasp. He didn't know whether she would have killed Victoria King had she had the chance at Golden Years. He didn't ask Mary how she planned to do it, if she had a gun or a knife or whether she intended to throttle Victoria with her bare hands. It was a picture that crept reluctantly into his mind, yet he couldn't ignore Mary's sturdy confession or her history.

Mary had taken a knife to Blues when he arrested Ryan. That was a spontaneous attack launched as a protective impulse. She'd had fifteen years to premeditate the murder of Victoria King, telling Mason that day at his office that she would do what needed doing if he couldn't deliver. Boarding the church shuttle may not have been the spur of the moment decision she made it out to be.

Mason wondered what had passed between Mary and Victoria when they were behind closed doors at Claire's. Did one confess? Did the other forgive? Did Victoria deny her son's guilt, taunting Mary with the loss of her son? He suspected that Victoria hadn't said a word or responded at all, the fog that had overcome her protecting her from Mary's inquisition.

Perhaps Mary's hatred had failed her. Bitter though it was, maybe it wasn't bitter enough to fuel the murder of a woman who may have forgotten the best and the worst of her life. Samantha had confirmed for him the story of Victoria's breakdown. Whatever Victoria had known, it was likely that she didn't know it any longer. Nonetheless, one thing was certain. Mason wouldn't leave the two of them alone again.

Mary shook herself free of Mason's guiding hand as they passed beneath the arched limestone entrance to the church, flowing among the many people who greeted her, hiding her apostasy and her darker self in the rainbow light that refracted through the stained-glass windows lining the outer walls of the sanctuary. The windows were tall rectangles of bold color depicting great moments of faith, saints and sinners immortalized in their triumphs and failures.

She took a seat in a pew near the front, wedged between two large, older women who sheltered her, their blue-white coiffed heads towering over Mary like sentries. Mason got the message. She didn't want his company while she communed.

Mason slid into a pew at the back of the church, an outsider looking in on a ritual that was foreign to him. Moments later, a priest led a procession into the sanctuary, making his way to the stage a hundred paces from the entrance. He was a couple of decades younger than Father Steve, his devotion to his faith evident in his sure steps and the certainty of his gaze as he made eye contact with the congregation, favoring everyone with a comforting, confident nod. They were all in the right place at the right time, he said without speaking a word. People beamed back at him, silently confirming their mutual bond.

Father Steve was a no show. Mason doubted that priests could take Sundays off without a note from God, but Father Steve had become almost as elusive as Whitney King. Though he'd managed to defy the long-standing practice of the diocese to rotate priests at least every five to ten years, holding on to his pulpit for more than thirty, Mason saw Father Steve's future even if the priest didn't. Father Steve was on his way out. There was a new priest on the block.

The priest ended his processional by taking his place behind the pulpit. There was a set of stairs at each end of the altar that allowed the priest and his parishioners to come together. Another stairway, nearly invisible descended from a back corner of the altar, providing a private passage for the clergy, though Mason couldn't tell where those stairs led.

He scanned the parishioners, looking for Whitney King, the only other person who would be as obviously out of place as Mason even though King belonged to St. Mark's. The sanctuary had three sections of seats divided by two aisles running from front to back, each section split in half by aisles running side to side. Though it was only about two-thirds full, the sanctuary easily held five hundred people. A sea of heads bowed in front of him, listening to readings from the Old and New Testaments, reciting prayers and singing hymns, rising for the Gospel and kneeling for prayers until, as if on cue, they rose and formed three lines to receive communion, one line on either side of the sanctuary and the third down the center aisle.

Mary's two protectors peeled away from her, taking up station in front of the altar at the head of the lines on the sides of the sanctuary, where the wafers that were supposed to represent the body of Christ were being passed out. The priest performed the same rite in the center aisle. People jostled for position, preferring the priest's line; stragglers grumpily gave way for the blue-haired ladies. Mary let the crowd sweep past her before slipping into the priest's line.

The low buzzing chatter of people waiting their turn burst into an astonished miniroar as Father Steve emerged from the stairs at the back of the altar and walked briskly toward Mary. He wrapped his meaty arm around her, leaning to her ear as he whispered and pulled her out of line. Mason stood, watching as Father Steve elbowed aside the stout blue-haired guardian blocking the steps to the altar, knocking the bowl of wafers from her hands, pressing his hand into the small of Mary's back, propelling her up to the altar.

Chaos broke out when the bowl of wafers hit the floor, congregants rushing to scoop them up. When Mary cast a backward glance searching for him, Mason began weaving through the crowd, picking up his pace as Father Steve reached the stairs at the back of the altar. Mason broke into open field running, catching falling worshipers as he brushed past them, cursing loudly enough for many to hear when Mary and the priest disappeared from view.

People yelled as he vaulted onto the altar, nearly tripping over an exposed microphone cord. Though their outraged voices mixed together making it difficult to understand them, he was certain that they weren't offering their blessings. The young priest tried to restore order, calling back two men who thought to chase Mason.

Mason stopped for an instant at the top of the back stairs to get his bearings, throwing a look at the men that told them to listen to their priest. The menace in his unshaven face and bullet-hole eyes persuaded them to retreat.

There was a short hall at the bottom and a door that was slowly closing as he took the stairs two at a time. That door led into another passageway that continued straight ahead a short distance before branching off at right angles in opposite directions.

Mason looked down both halls. He didn't hear voices or footsteps, but he saw a red-lighted exit sign at the end of the hallway to his right. He ran down that corridor, turning another corner, crashing through a door and into a concrete cavern at the bottom of yet another set of stairs, the morning sun casting a shadow at his feet. He had emerged from the church's basement on its back side after bolting up the stairs into the sunlight.

Clearing the top step, he stopped again. He was on the edge of an empty grassy quadrangle; the church was behind him, the high school to his right, and the street to his left on the far side of the wrought-iron fence that surrounded the grounds. Opposite him and set back a hundred yards was a small house buried in a stand of tall oaks, their broad leafy expanse serving as camouflage. Mason guessed it was the rectory, Father Steve's house.

He sprinted across the grass, barely slowing when he reached the front door of the house, not bothering to knock as he shouldered the door open. He skidded to a stop in the front hall, caught off guard by the unexpected scene in the living room to his left.

He found Mary and Father Steve staring at an aquarium sitting on a black metal stand, the price tag still visible on one leg, brightly striped fish happily oblivious to the humans who had invaded their space.

The morning was hot and the house was stuffy, a floor fan stirring up dust mites without cooling the clotted air. The living room was sparsely furnished, a wooden rocker with a flattened red pillow on the seat, a tired gray couch half-covered with a turquoise knitted afghan, and a low wooden table littered with magazines. The hardwood floor wheezed with each step Mason took. A fireplace dominated the outer wall, a black screen drawn across the grate, a brick hearth cut into the floor.

–

Mary and Father Steve whirled toward Mason, both clutching their hearts.

"You scared me!" Mary said.

"Makes us even," Mason answered. "You left in kind of a hurry and you didn't look too happy about it."

"I'm afraid that's my fault," Father Steve said.

"You won't get an argument from me," Mason told him. "But don't expect me to believe you hustled Mary out of the church just to show her some fish."

"They're my fish," Mary said. "Father Steve rescued them for me."

The missing fish and the abandoned deep sea diver in Mary's aquarium had convinced Mason that she was still alive, though she had denied knowing what had happened to them. That Father Steve had taken them, buying an aquarium for their foster home, was the latest paragraph in the indictment Mason planned for him.

He said to the priest, "Then you knew Mary wasn't coming back. Which is funny since you told me she'd gone to Omaha to see her husband."

Mary said, "That's what I told Father Steve. He had no reason to think otherwise."

"Sure he did if he went to the trouble of breaking into your house, stealing your fish and buying an aquarium for them. If he thought you were only going to be gone for a few days and he was worried about your fish, he would have offered to take care of them," Mason said. "Better yet, you would have asked him, but you didn't."

Mary stepped away from Father Steve, crossing her arms over her chest. "You knew what they'd done to me?" she asked.

Father Steve's round shoulders sagged, his arms at his sides, palms upturned in a supplicant's pose. "Not for certain, Mary. You must believe me. When Mr. Mason told me you were missing, I did think you were in Omaha until I called Vince and he told me that he hadn't heard from you."

"Then why didn't you tell me?" Mason demanded. "Or the police?"

He shrugged, tilting his head and dropping his palms to his sides. "I've been a priest for more than thirty years. I suppose I've heard tens of thousands of confessions in that time. Many of them are small sins. I listen, absolve, and forget. A few are truly awful sins. I listen to them as well, even if I can't absolve the sinner and I can't forget the sin. Sometimes the sin gets inside of me and eats away at me like a disease."

"Is that supposed to be an excuse?" Mason said. "Knowing that Mary had been kidnapped made you too sick to do anything about it."

Father Steve permitted himself a thin smile. "I imagine you're quite a good lawyer, Mr. Mason, to be able to twist my failings to make them worse than even I make them to be. I'm not sick. I'm just afraid of the things I know. My weakness, my sin, is not doing anything about it. My sin is the sin of silence as you guessed that day when we talked in the school."

"Then what is this all about?" Mason asked. "Stealing Mary's fish and snatching her out of Sunday Mass."

"It's about someone who is sick of his own weaknesses and is trying to atone for his sins. I took Mary's fish to save them for her. I prayed for her safe return. I called the police to warn them about that young man Whitney shot, your client, Nick Byrnes."

"Nick says you weren't there when he was shot," Mason said.

"He's telling the truth," Father Steve said, looking at the floor, locking his hands together, twisting his fingers. "I was inside. Whitney and I had just finished meeting about another donation to the church. I came outside after the shooting. Whitney told me what had happened."

"Then why not tell that to the police instead of lying?" Mason asked.

"I'd compromised myself too many times to be that virtuous, Mr. Mason. Whitney King knew that. He knew which button of mine to push."

"So why the anonymous phone call to the cops?" Mason asked.

"I didn't know for certain if Whitney had taken Mary, but if he had, it was logical that he would want Nick as well. It's the way he is. He's often told me that he'll take any risk to avoid a risk, though he never cared about the contradiction. It was how he justified the things he did."

"What did Whitney have on you?" Mason asked.

The priest drew a deep breath. "Silence that made me an accomplice."

"An accomplice?" Mary asked. "An accomplice to what?"

"Murder," the priest confessed.

Chapter 51

Mary reached out her hand, steadying herself against the fireplace, turning away from Father Steve, the enormity of his confession beginning to sink in. She staggered to the rocking chair, collapsing into it as the chair bobbed back and forth.

"Whose murder?" Mason asked.

The priest looked at Mason as if the question demanded he extract a chamber from his heart to answer it. Then he looked at Mary who was holding herself as she rocked.

"Whitney called me this morning and asked if I knew where you were. I didn't know whether that was because he wasn't involved in your disappearance or whether you had somehow escaped. I told him I hadn't seen you since you left the church that Wednesday. He told me he thought you would come to church today and told me to call him and tell him if you did."

Mason stepped to the front window, looking out at the quadrangle, having learned that Whitney usually made his phone calls when he was close by, the call giving the false impression that he wasn't.

"So he knows that Mary is here," Mason said.

"When I saw you come in this morning, I came back to the rectory to call him because I didn't think I had a choice. But I didn't call him."

"Why? So you could wait until you got Mary back here and she couldn't get away?" Mason asked, squaring around at the priest.

"No, Mr. Mason," Father Steve said, hanging his head. "I realized that if I called him, I would be crossing a line between hiding behind my vows and giving up someone to evil. I couldn't do that even though I'd spent the last fifteen years pretending there was a difference. I was afraid Whitney would come looking for Mary no matter what I told him. That's why I was in such a hurry. I decided to give Mary something to protect her. To do that, I have to break my silence and my vow to protect the sanctity of confessions."

Father Steve took off his coat, laying it on the arm of the sofa. He knelt on the floor where he pulled up four bricks from the middle of the hearth, stacking them next to the fireplace screen. He reached down between the floorboards into the crawl space beneath the floor and retrieved a tightly wrapped oilskin bundle tied at both ends with knotted twine. He slipped the twine off the bundle and unrolled the oilskin, spilling a tire iron onto the hard floor.

Mason knelt alongside the priest. Using the tips of two fingers like a giant tweezers he raised the tire iron up by one end and laid it back on the oilskin. Cradling it in the protective cloth, he picked it up for a closer look. The oilskin had saved it from rusting too badly. Freckles of orange rust mixed with dark splotches that were burrowed into the imperfect surface. Holding it to the light, he caught the reflection of what could be a hair embossed in the open cup that was used to grasp lug nuts on a wheel.

"Where did you get this?" Mason asked him.

"Victoria King gave it to me," Father Steve said as he stood. "After the trial."

"Why didn't you turn it over to the police?" Mason asked. "There could have been fingerprints or blood or tissue that would have proven Ryan Kowalcyk was innocent. How could you bury a murder weapon under your fireplace for fifteen years?"

"Do you have children, Mr. Mason?" the priest asked.

"No."

"Imagine that you had two children and they were both drowning, but you could only save one. Which one would you choose? It's an old dilemma, the stuff of a college philosophy course, until you actually are faced with it. What would you do?"

Mary came out of her chair. "You had to choose between my Ryan and Whitney and you chose him because his family had money and we had nothing! May you rot in hell!"

Father Steve's wide round face blanched at Mary's bitter curse.

"That will be for God to decide, Mary," he said, his crushed voice resigned to his fate. "Though I expect you'll get your wish. But it wasn't just about that. I didn't know whether this tire iron would prove that either boy was guilty or innocent. I convinced myself the jury had made that decision. My decision was about choosing between my vows and Victoria King."

"Victoria King is the only child in that moral dilemma," Mason said.

"That's where you are wrong, Mr. Mason. My vows, my faith, my church. That was my other child. That was my life. That's what I thought I was choosing by keeping silent about Victoria."

"I don't understand," Mason said. "Victoria had nothing to do with the murders of Graham and Elizabeth Byrnes."

"You're correct. She didn't," Father Steve said. He wrapped his hand around the cross hanging from his neck, closing his eyes in a moment of silent prayer, Mason reading his lips as he mouthed *God forgive me.* "Victoria King killed her husband. With this," Father Steve said, taking the tire iron from Mason.

"You mean this isn't the tire iron used to kill the Byrneses?" Mason asked.

Father Steve wrapped the tire iron back in the oilskin, holding it at both ends. "She never said, but I've always assumed that it is."

"Then," Mason said, pacing the small room, "Whitney had to have given it to her. He got rid of his bloody clothes at Ryan's house but hung on to the murder weapon. He must have given it to his mother. She kept it so that the prosecutor couldn't use it to convict her son. But why did she kill her husband?"

"Because my father was going to ruin everything," Whitney King said as he walked into the room.

King was wearing a black suit jacket over a shirt and jeans. The jacket was cut too full and hung unevenly on him. Mason finally recognized it as identical to the one Father Steve was wearing. The butt of a gun poked out of a side pocket. King held another gun in one hand, waving it at the three of them.

"Over there," King said, pointing them toward the sofa.

The priest sat in the corner of the sofa, moist half-moons of sweat under the arms of his rumpled white shirt. His face continued to pale, the pasty shade running through the fleshy folds of his neck, nearly matching the color of his collar. His eyes darted between King and Mason as he licked his dry lips, swallowing hard, his mouth involuntarily puckering for a smoke. Mary chafed at being so close to him, arching her back, setting her jaw with a stiff fury.

Mason didn't move, forcing King to divide his attention. It was a small advantage, but survival was often the sum of slim chances. He only had one card to play, but he waited, choosing the moment.

"Father Steve's clothes aren't a good look for you," Mason told King. "I'd stick to cross-dressing."

King laughed, his chuckle low and guttural. "The Catholic Church isn't known for its fashion sense. I'll give you that. And this rag," he said, sniffing the fabric, "smells like shit, but it was the best I could find in Father Steve's closet while I was waiting for you to get here. My luck, I had to pick a chain-smoking priest."

Mason put it together, shaking his head. "You were wearing Father Steve's jacket when you shot Sandra. Just to make me think it was him. What was the point? You were going to kill me too."

"I never plan on things going exactly like I planned. I just plan on winning no matter what happens," King said. "Turns out Sandra was right. You're a hard man to kill."

"Sandra figured out that your mother had killed your father. That's why she asked Dixon Smith to find out why your mother had been at Golden Years for so long. She was going to tell me and you couldn't let her do that."

"Sandra's firm has represented my family for years. One of the partners suspected that my father's death wasn't an accident. No one else at the firm would listen to him so he buried a confidential CYA memo in my father's files. Unfortunately, Sandra found the memo. Fortunately, when she told me about it, she also told me about the gun you kept in your desk."

"Using your laptop to call her was a neat trick," Mason said. "No phone records and you could call from anywhere. My backyard or the bike path behind your office building."

"C'mon, Mason. Give me some credit. You think I'm lugging around a laptop computer? Here," he said, pulling a palm-sized PDA from his jeans pocket, an earpiece with microphone wrapped around it. "WiFi. The future is now. Slick, don't you think? Besides, everything gets old after a while if you don't give it some flair," he added, stuffing the PDA back in his pocket.

"Even killing people?" Mason asked.

"Especially killing people," King answered. "The end is always the same. It's the journey that counts."

Mason's gut instinct that the Byrneses murders were a thrill killing was right. Whitney King had whet an appetite that couldn't be satisfied. "Is that why you murdered the Byrneses? For the joy of killing?"

"That's too easy an answer," King said. "When Ryan left to go find a gas station, I started talking to the wife. I came on to her and the husband didn't like it. He and I got into it. He came after me with the tire iron, but he slipped on some gravel and dropped it when he tried to catch himself. I picked it up and started swinging. I didn't even think about it. She froze. It was like chopping wood. I didn't appreciate the rush until it was over. Getting away with it was like coming in my pants all over again."

Mason forced himself to act like a lawyer, hide his outrage long enough to get the facts. "But why go after the jury? They acquitted you."

"Some of them said I was innocent because they believed it. Those were the ones I could trust. The others did it for money. I'd never trust someone like that. Give them enough time, and they'll come back for more."

"The jury was deadlocked," Mason said. "How did you get to them?"

"My family had a lot of money," King said with a shrug of his shoulders. "We found the weak jurors, the ones who needed the money badly enough. It wasn't that hard."

"You were only a kid," Mason said. "You couldn't have pulled that off. Did your father do it? Did he have an attack of conscience and tell your mother he was going to the cops? Is that why she killed him?"

King smiled at Mason, his lips flat and bloodless. "You are such a conventional thinker, Mason."

"Your father couldn't have gotten to all the jurors," Mason said. "That was too risky. Someone would have refused to go along or turned all of you in. How did he know which jurors to go after?"

King's smile faded. "It doesn't matter now."

"He doesn't know," Father Steve said, biting the words off as if each was dipped in poison.

"It doesn't matter!" King shouted at the priest, taking a step toward him, sweeping the gun back and forth between Mason and the priest. "So shut your fucking mouth!"

"You don't know, do you? You never knew!" Mason said with sudden understanding. "Your father died without ever telling you and you couldn't stand taking the chance that whoever it was would turn on you. So you started picking them off one by one. You had to stretch it out all these years so the cops wouldn't link the killings. You probably liked that part, didn't you, Whitney? It gave you something to look forward to."

"Like I said, it doesn't matter," Whitney told him.

"It does matter," Mason said. "You've been feeling the heat. That's why you took the chance of killing Sonni Efron and Frances Peterson so close together. That's why you took a potshot at my house and shot Sandra Connelly. You're coming unglued."

King wiped a trickle of sweat from his brow, forcing a smile. "Loose ends, that's all."

"In that case, there are two that you missed. Janet Hook and Andrea Bracco."

"Wrong again, Mason. Andrea's body has never been found. As for Janet, that bitch is a three-time loser no one will ever believe, especially while she's doing time. I'll clean up this mess," he said, pointing his gun at Mason, Father Steve and Mary. "And everything will be back on track."

Mason decided not to tell him that Blues was going to talk to Janet Hook. Her story might turn out to be Mason's epitaph. Instead, he played his last card. "We've got your mother," he told King. "You want her back, let us go."

King smiled again, this time like a child about to get his wish. "Give me that," he said to Father Steve who was still holding the tire iron. "I've been looking for this for a long time. My mother would never tell me what she did with it. Giving it to a priest for safe keeping; now that's brilliant."

He unwrapped the tire iron with his left hand, keeping his gun pointed at them with his right. Hefting it for a moment like a baseball player reunited with a favored bat, he suddenly swung it in a wide arc, smashing it against Father Steve's temple.

"Good as new," King said, as the priest crumpled to the floor.

Mason charged King who sidestepped him, slamming the tire iron into Mason's ribs, sending Mason rolling onto the floor, grabbing his side, his breath coming in painful gasps as his lungs pressed against broken cartilage. Before he could get up, King was standing over him, pointing a different gun at him. It was the one Mason had seen sticking out of King's jacket pocket.

"There's an old limestone horse barn at the south end of Penn Valley Park. All that's left are the outer walls. The city built some kind of theater inside the walls. Meet me there in thirty minutes or Mary dies. Any cops show up and Mary dies," King said, then fired the gun squarely at Mason's heart.

Mason's body went rigid with fifty thousand volts of electricity, shaking violently as the current dissipated. His jellied limbs were useless as he watched King grab Mary by the arm, squeezing until she cried out.

"And don't forget to bring Mom," King said as they left, the tire iron under his arm.

Chapter 52

Thirty minutes wasn't enough time. Whitney had seen to that. Penn Valley Park stretched from Twenty-seventh Street south to Thirty-first, one hundred and thirty hilly acres of prime green space carved out between Broadway on the east and the Southwest Trafficway on the West. He could get there in a few minutes. If he could stand without falling over. If he could leave Father Steve not knowing whether the priest was alive or dead. And if he could pick up Victoria King and convince Harry and Claire to leave the cops out of it.

There wasn't time to brief a SWAT team and put them in play. Instead, siren screaming squad cars would pour into the park like it was the Daytona 500 and Mary would get a bullet in her face. He would have liked his chances better if Mickey and Blues were in the mix, but by now they were probably interrogating Janet Hook at the halfway house in Kansas City, Kansas. It would take them more than thirty minutes to get to the park and take up positions that would provide him with badly needed cover even if he could reach them.

_Whitney's timetable was a deadly obstacle course mined with hard choices, any one of which could blow up in his face. Mason belly crawled toward Father Steve. The priest lay on his side, blood seeping from his wound, pooling beneath his head like an unholy sacrament. Mason felt for a pulse, finding a feathery beat.

Pulling himself to his feet, he glanced around the room looking for a telephone, his electrical hangover lifting when he felt the cell phone clipped to his belt. He pried the cover open and tried to punch the numbers 9-1-1 to summon an ambulance for Father Steve. His fingers were clumsy sausages, missing their mark.

"I already called the police."

Mason looked up, closing the phone. It was the young priest, his robe and collar cast off, his short-sleeve black shirt and pants giving him a more militant than religious slant. He was fit, with ropy muscles, his face slightly flushed, jaw set, and ready for whatever he would find in the rectory. He'd told his congregants to stay back, putting himself at risk instead.

"What did you see?" Mason asked, certain that the priest would accuse him of crushing Father Steve's skull.

"Enough," the priest answered. "Where's your car?"

"On Main, across the street from the church."

"You can't go that way. The police will stop you even if one of my congregants doesn't try to play hero. My car is parked behind the rectory. It's the brown Ford Escort. You better hurry," he said, reaching in his pocket and handing Mason the keys. Mason nodded, clasping him by the shoulder for a moments support. "Go with God," the priest added.

"Tell Him to meet there, Father," Mason said.

Mason shuffled through the kitchen, finding his legs. He hesitated a moment when he saw a paring knife lying on the counter next to the sink. Its three-inch blade gave him little comfort when he stuck it in his jeans pocket, hoping he didn't inadvertently stab himself.

He saw blood on the handle of the back door and wondered if King was hurt. He was careful not to touch the blood, realizing instead that it was probably Father Steve's, having splattered onto King's hands.

He ground the gears on the Ford, pulling into an alley behind the church grounds, then looping around to the east and north to avoid the sirens he heard racing toward St. Mark's. He called Claire, giving her a quick summary, extracting her promise not to call the cops and telling her to meet him in front of her house with Victoria.

"There isn't time," she said. "I'll meet you at the park."

"Don't be stupid!" Mason shouted before he realized she'd hung up. He called back, but she didn't answer, not giving him the chance to argue with her. "Okay," he fumed, slamming his palm against the steering wheel. "Be stupid, just not too stupid to live."

He tried reaching Mickey on his cell phone, knowing that Blues rarely carried one and even more rarely had it on when he did. He told Mason that he didn't need a damn buzzer on his hip that people could ring like they ring the bell for service at the butcher's counter. Mickey's phone rang twice before a recorded voice told him that the person he was calling was outside the cellular company's service area, which meant that the halfway house was in a wireless dead zone.

He turned onto Thirty-first Street from Broadway, driving past the edge of the park, straining for a view, immediately understanding why King had chosen the location. The barn was in a hollow just far enough north of Thirty-first and sufficiently below street level not to be visible to passing traffic, though there was hardly any this early on a Sunday morning. Trinity Lutheran Hospital, closed, empty, and abandoned, dominated the ridge above the ruins to the east. The view from there was blocked by tall trees lining the slope beneath the street that ran between the hospital and the park.

The barn was close to the church, which gave Mason a chance to be there on time, but not until after King had arrived and chosen his ground. There were multiple entrances to the park and King could easily approach the barn from another direction, keeping hidden until he was ready to reveal himself. Mason and Victoria would be forced to come down the curved circle drive and wait for King in the theater courtyard where they would be both hidden and exposed.

The theatre was called Just Off Broadway, an almost clever play on the name of the nearby street and the dreams of the actors. It was a square building constructed of redwood with limestone corners and a forest green–pitched roof, the entire effect more suggestive of a rustic mountain retreat than an urban oasis for the arts.

The remains of the barn were also made of limestone, all that was left of outer walls with arched doorways and narrow windows. With no structure connected to its walls, it reminded him of a Hollywood back lot rendition of the Alamo.

There was a short stretch of wall in the southeast corner interrupted by the paved parking lot for the theater and the entrance to a courtyard inside the walls. The western wall was an unbroken bulwark that wrapped around the north end where the ground rose into the back of a hillside. The top of that wall was at least twenty feet above the interior courtyard, windows filled with wrought iron bars like it had once been a Wild West jail though it had been built in the early 1900s to house city-owned horses and park equipment.

Turning the car around, Mason parked on the street running alongside the hospital near the top of the driveway that led down to the theater. A few other cars were parked to the north, none of them Whitney's. He glanced at his watch. Ten minutes left and no sign of Claire. He circled the car, walked back to Thirty-first Street to stare at the empty street, then back again to the car, repeating the process four more times.

With only five minutes to go, Claire's white Volvo sedan turned onto Thirty-first Street from Broadway, crested a slight rise, and glided to a stop half a block away. Harry was behind the wheel, which only surprised Mason a little. Harry still liked to drive and would fight Claire for the keys if the trip was a short distance over familiar ground with little or no traffic. This trip fit the bill and Mason guessed Claire was too nervous to fight with Harry. Claire and Victoria were with him, one in the front and the other in the back, though he couldn't see their faces clearly enough through the dirty windshield to tell which was which.

Harry got out, walked around the back of the car, and opened the rear door, helping a woman out of the backseat. Mason recognized Victoria King's hat and raincoat from the day before. She hesitated as if uncertain of her surroundings, walking slowly toward Mason, looking back at Harry who nodded encouragement. Harry got back in the car, gunned the engine, and turned around, disappearing as Thirty-first Street dipped back down toward Broadway at the same moment Mason realized the woman was Claire, not Victoria.

"Are you out of your mind?" Mason hissed as she reached him.

"I would be if I let you trade that poor woman like a side of beef," she said. "She doesn't know where she is or what she's doing. We're about the same size and with her hat and coat, Whitney won't know the difference."

"What about Mary?" Mason demanded. "Whitney will kill her if we don't deliver his mother."

"You and I both know he'll kill her if we do once he has his mother back."

"And you don't think he will if we don't?" Mason asked.

"What are you going to do? Adopt him so he thinks you're his mother?"

"We'll keep our distance so he won't know I'm not. You tell him that I won't budge until he releases Mary," she said. "I know it's not much of a plan, but it's the best I could come up with on short notice. Just keep us far enough apart that he can't see me clearly."

"Where did Harry go?" Mason asked.

"Far enough away that you can't make me change my mind. He told me to give you this," she added, handing Mason a gun. It was Harry's .357 magnum, Mason remembered how he used to tease Harry that Clint Eastwood's Dirty Harry had nothing on him, Harry grinning and saying the difference between him and Eastwood was that he wasn't shooting blanks.

Mason stuck the gun in the back of his jeans, pulling his shirt out to cover it. He had a gun and a knife, neither of which could offset the odds Whitney had in his favor except for one thing. Whitney would assume he was unarmed. It was a slender edge.

He checked his watch. They were out of time. He studied his aunt. Her slate eyes were clear and unwavering. Her mouth was firm. Her hands didn't tremble. She was magnificent.

"Well, then," Mason said, threading his arm around hers. "Let's go for a walk."

Chapter 53

Mason stopped at the edge of the courtyard, shielding Claire though she was nearly as big as he was. The raincoat added unexpected bulk to her frame. The grass was more brown than green, stunted by the summer's heat in spite of the recent rain. The sun had risen far enough to clear the hospital high on the ridge to the east, splashing the top of the raised north wall with a blinding glare, the courtyard still shaded. He held his ground, preferring to keep the open parking lot to his back rather than the claustrophobic ruins.

They stood there, not moving, the only sounds a stray cry from a crow drifting lazily overhead before disappearing into the trees. Minutes passed, Mason feeling King's unseen eyes on them waiting until he was certain they were alone.

"Mason!" King finally called out. "Don't be shy. Come a little closer. I want a good look at my mom so I know she's okay."

Mason shaded his eyes with his hand, scanning the ruins for King's hiding place. King's voice had come from in front of them, the most likely place being from behind the north wall where the sloping ground gave him added cover and a clear field of fire down into the courtyard. Sandwiched between the hillside and the limestone, the sun's glare provided added camouflage.

"Not until I see Mary," Mason answered.

Mason heard her before he saw her as King flung Mary against the iron bars filling an otherwise empty window next to where he stood hidden behind the wall. She grunted in pain, swallowing her cry. Mason squinted against the sun, finding Mary clinging to the bars, her face pressed against them. King's gun was flush against her head. Mason started to reach for his gun, stopping when he realized Mary would be dead before he could clear it from his belt.

"Closer!" King demanded. "Or she dies!"

Claire took the first steps, Mason quickly catching up to her. He grabbed her arm, stopping alongside her near the middle of the courtyard.

"This is as close as we're coming," Mason said. "She's not going any farther until you let Mary go."

Whitney shoved Mary aside, standing in the window, his gun hand extended between the bars. "That's close enough," he said and shot Claire, the bullet slamming into her chest, knocking her to the ground and onto her side.

Mason screamed as he saw the muzzle flash, unable to knock Claire out of its path or take the bullet for her. He dropped to the ground, blanketing her, tensing his muscles, expecting a second bullet to cut into him. When none came, he rose up and rolled Claire onto her back, stunned that she wasn't a bloody mess. He ripped open the raincoat, blessing Harry's Kevlar vest that Claire was wearing, the slug cushioned firmly against it, still hot.

Her eyes were closed and he felt her neck for a pulse, finding a strong one. The impact had knocked the wind out of her, the shock causing her to faint.

"Don't move, Mason!" King shouted.

Mason stayed huddled over Claire, closing the raincoat, turning her on her side so that King wouldn't see that she wasn't bleeding. He found the handle of the knife sticking out of his pocket, wrapping his fingers around it, drawing it out. He listened to King's footsteps as he got closer, watching as King's shadow cast ahead of him by the sun marked his approach.

"For God's sake, Whitney! You killed your own mother!" Mason yelled, still keeping his head down.

"Had to," Whitney said, now standing directly behind Mason, nudging him with his shoe. "Can't trust a woman who'd get in a car with you, now could I?"

Mason slowly stood, palming the knife in his right had as he turned toward King. He caught a glimpse of Mary lying on the ground, her eyes open. There had been no second shot so Mason assumed that King had dumped her there, leaving her too stunned to move.

King raised his gun, aiming at Mason's face. "Smile," he said.

Mason whipped his right hand up, stabbing the short blade into Whitney's gut, ripping through muscle, warm blood coating his hand. Whitney's eyes widened, his jaw slackened as Mason knocked the gun from his hand. Whitney grabbed Mason's wrist, struggling against the knife as Mason drove the blade higher into his abdomen and buried his knee into Whitney's groin.

Moaning, Whitney collapsed to his knees as Mason let go of the knife, throwing it on the ground out of reach. Whitney pressed his fingers against his belly, looking up at Mason, his face contorted, unable to speak. Mason clasped his hands together like a mallet, swinging down hard against Whitney's face, the blow spinning Whitney into a heap. Stunned and bleeding, he lay still long enough for Mason to remove his belt and bind his hands behind his back.

Mason dragged him across the grass, propping him against the limestone wall. Breathing hard, he pulled his shirt off and pressed it against Whitney's wound, slapping Whitney when he spit at him. He couldn't tell how badly Whitney was hurt, though he expected he would live.

Wiping his bloody hands on the grass, Mason knelt beside Claire, loosening her collar and lifting her head. Her skin was white though her breathing was steady. He patted her cheek, smoothing her brow.

"C'mon, Claire. Wake up. Show's over," he said.

Her eyelids fluttered then opened. She blinked at him and said, "Whew."

"My sentiments exactly," Mason said, grinning at his aunt.

She smiled in return as he helped her sit up. She supported herself with one hand, feeling her chest with the other. "Good old Harry," she said, stroking the bulletproof fabric.

A sudden gunshot stunned them both. Mason jumped to his feet, whirling around as Mary walked away from Whitney King, dropping his gun at his feet, Whitney's face dissolving in a crimson blossom.

Chapter 54

Crime scenes grow like tiny cities. The victim and perpetrator are the founders. The police and paramedics move in next, annexing a wide ring of land around the small plot where the crime takes place. News media arrive like they are on a mission of manifest destiny crowding the cops for elbow room. Bystanders who sniff out calamity as if it had the scent of freshly baked bread plant themselves on the fringes like suburbanites enjoying the view and glad that someone else is there to do the dirty work, though they still find time to bitch about high taxes.

After the ambulance leaves carrying the dead and wounded and the cops finish picking over the ground like a prospector panning for gold, the voyeurs pack it in. Yellow crime scene tape is all that remains of the ghost town.

The Penn Valley Park scene followed the same boom-and-bust cycle. Reporters from the local Fox affiliate claimed special squatter's rights since the shootout took place within a stone's throw of their studio at Thirty-first and Southwest Trafficway. It all evaporated by early afternoon, latecomers consigned to a picnic in the park kept company only by the squirrels.

Blues and Mickey caught up with Mason just as he was getting into the Ford Escort, ready to return it to the young priest at St. Mark's. Mickey, breathless, bolted from Blues's car, slapping his hand on the hood of the Escort.

"Son of a bitch!" he yelled. "We heard the story on the radio! You okay, boss? What about Claire?"

Blues parked along the curb in front of the Escort, sauntering toward Mason, his blank face giving nothing away.

"I'm fine, she's fine," Mason said. "I'm sorry I let Mary run you off," he said to Blues. "I let the tail wag the dog when I could have used your help."

"Not a problem," Blues said. "She's got her issues. They ain't mine."

"She's got more than issues since she killed Whitney King," Mason said. "Tell me what you got from Janet Hook. That might help with Mary's defense."

Blues leaned against the Escort. "You got a good reason to be driving this piece of shit?"

Mason smiled, "Yeah. I got a reason. You got a reason you're not telling me what Janet Hook told you?"

Blues said, "Yeah, I got a reason. You found out from Whitney that Ryan was innocent. I found out from Janet Hook. I know that doesn't mean I put the needle in that boy's arm, but it sure feels that way."

"You did your job, Blues. You didn't decide guilt or innocence. Did Janet take a bribe to acquit Whitney and convict Ryan?" Mason asked.

"She was bought along with some of the other jurors," Blues answered. "She says she didn't know which ones or how many. Says she needed the money and figured it was no big deal. One white boy gets it, one white boy doesn't. Made no difference to her."

"How much did Whitney's father pay her?" Mason asked.

"It wasn't the father," Blues answered. "It was the mother, Victoria King, and she paid her five thousand dollars."

By late afternoon, Mason had visited Mary at the Jackson County jail, assuring her that he'd push for a bail hearing first thing Monday morning.

"Don't bother," she told him. "I'm in no hurry to go anywhere, but I'd appreciate it if you'd take care of my fish. What did you find out about Father Steve?"

Mason had finally learned the name of the young priest. "Father Brian told me that he made it through surgery but it's too early to tell about anything else. The doctors say there's probably some brain damage."

Mary nodded though her eyes were somewhere on the middle distance. Mason wasn't certain if she had heard him. She was relaxed to the point of indifference, content with what the system would do to her, devoid of any regret for what she had done.

Patrick Ortiz had tracked Mason down on his cell phone, assuring Mason that he would not be indicted for Sandra Connelly's murder and promising a public statement on Monday.

"Have you called Dixon Smith?" Mason asked Ortiz.

"Not yet. I wanted you to hear it from me," Ortiz told him.

Though Ortiz had started out as the least political of prosecutors, the office and his ambitions were reshaping him. This grand gesture with its public relations tie-in was the latest example.

Samantha Greer had called him a short time later, adding her congratulations. Mason pleaded fatigue when he turned down her invitation to have dinner that night or any other. Samantha gamely said she understood, telling him to call if Abby's move to the campaign trail proved permanent.

"What about Phil?" Mason asked her, picturing her sleep-over guest scratching his ass as he walked up the stairs after Mason woke him in the middle of the night a few lifetimes ago.

"Phil," she said. "Right! Can you see me long-term with a guy who puts on a bathrobe and slippers every time he gets out of bed in the middle of the night?"

"Not hardly," Mason assured her.

"Me either," she said.

He brought dinner to Claire's. Another boxed Chinese feast. Claire was wearing a loose-fitting blouse, the top buttons undone so Harry could check the status of the bruise left by the bullet.

"Blood red today, black orchid tomorrow," Harry announced. He'd recovered from an initial outburst of panic when he learned Claire had been shot to brag about his knockout gal who'd taken a bullet, his pronouncements tinged with unexpelled nervousness for her condition and frustration that he'd not been there to protect her.

Claire tried to be angry with him for treating a tragedy like it was a cause for celebration, but she couldn't stay angry with him. It was Harry's way of thanking God she was all right and her way of telling him she loved him.

"How's Victoria holding up?" Mason asked.

Claire sighed. "She was taken to St. Luke's Hospital. The doctors there assume she has Alzheimer's, but they won't know until they run some tests. I suppose that counts for a lucky break on a day like this. She hasn't a clue about what happened."

"If that's the case, I doubt whether Ortiz will prosecute her for killing her husband. Either way, she'll end up in an institution," Mason said.

"That boy of hers had balls, I'll give him that," Harry said. "Checking his mother out of the hospital to use her for an alibi when he killed Sonni Efron, Frances Peterson, and Sandra Connelly. Samantha told me they checked the records at Golden Years and they matched up. It'll take longer to trace back the records on the deaths of the other jurors, but Sam says she's betting the pattern holds up."

"Yeah," Mason said, "but Victoria didn't have Alzheimer's when she first went into the psychiatric hospital and I'm not convinced she had a breakdown either."

"What are you saying?" Claire asked.

"She killed her husband but the cops bought that his death was an accident—that he fell down the stairs. My guess is that he found out she had bribed the jurors and he was going to turn her and their son in," Mason said.

"Makes her the ultimate in overly protective mothers," Harry said.

"If the cops were looking at her for killing her husband, faking a nervous breakdown and checking into a psychiatric hospital wasn't a bad idea. Especially if she never checked out," Mason said.

"That's a tough scam to pull off for fifteen years," Harry said. "Doctors have to sign off on a diagnosis; the hospital has to go along. How'd she make all that happen?"

"I don't know, but I think my lawyer does," Mason answered.

"Dixon Smith?" Claire asked. "I'd nearly forgotten about him. You tell him I want my retainer back."

"You'd think he'd forgotten about me," Mason said. "Everyone in town knows what happened this morning at the park and he's the only one who hasn't called."

Mason caught himself as he spoke, realizing that someone else had failed to call as well. He hadn't heard from Abby, knew he had no right to expect that he would, but still he couldn't swallow the lump in his throat. Though he'd managed to surface after another dive into the dark water, she would only see him dripping with blood and death after taking the plunge, counting Claire's near-death experience heavily against him.

"Maybe," Harry said, bringing the conversation back to Victoria, "she was afraid Whitney would turn her in to the cops or that he'd kill her. That would be enough to cause a nervous breakdown. Or maybe she just thought it was a good idea, her son killing the jurors to keep them quiet. Be real interesting to finally find out the truth."

"It doesn't really matter," Mason said. "Everyone is just as dead. Graham and Elizabeth Byrnes, Ryan Kowalczyk, the jurors, Sandra, and Whitney King. The truth won't change any of that."

Claire looked at him and he returned her gaze with a silent concession that he was willing to leave their old business alone if that's what she wanted. It was the least he owed her after today.

"I used to think that," she said. "But I was wrong. The truth gives us the ability to live with the past and learn from it."

Harry said, "What? Did you read that in your fortune cookie?"

"Something like that," she said.

Chapter 55

Mason worked late that night, banging away at his laptop, Tuffy curled at his feet. He was wrung out but too wrung out for sleep. He'd shut his practice down when he was arrested for Sandra's murder. Back in business a little more than twelve hours, he had two clients, Mary Kowalczyk and Nick Byrnes.

Mary was guilty of killing Whitney King. No one would dispute that. The line drawing would be over whether it was premeditated, a sudden impulse, or justifiable. There was a lot of room in the surrounding facts for him to maneuver. Patrick Ortiz, his political antennae tuned to the next election, would be wary of the land mines buried in her case.

Nick Byrnes had two days left before the statute of limitations expired on his wrongful death claim. Mason had called him earlier in the evening. Nick was more concerned for Mason than for his case. Mason explained to him about Victoria King and the law of civil conspiracy, how if two or more people conspired to conceal a crime, they could be liable in damages almost as if they had committed the crime themselves.

That's why Mason was working late. He was redrafting the lawsuit against Whitney King, substituting Whitney's estate as one defendant since Whitney was dead, and adding Victoria King as another. She had conspired to hide her son's crime, defrauding Nick Byrnes of his claim against Whitney. She hadn't pulled the trigger, but Mason was confident a jury would hold her liable even with her diminished mental capacity.

Still, that wasn't his only purpose in adding Victoria to the lawsuit any more than it was his purpose to line Nick's pockets with money Nick neither wanted nor needed. It was about finding the truth. All of it. Without guns, knives, or death. It was about the law and about justice.

He logged on to the Internet, punching in the Golden Years Web site. The truth was there. He picked up the phone and woke Samantha Greer again.

At eleven o'clock on Monday morning, Patrick Ortiz held a news conference in the courtroom previously used by the grand jury. The time was calculated to give the media sufficient notice to assemble their coverage, giving broadcasters a lead story they could run beginning with their noon broadcasts and print journalists an entire afternoon to write their stories for Tuesday's editions.

Ortiz had called Dixon Smith first thing Monday morning to tell him that the charges against his client were being dropped and that he'd like both Smith and Mason to attend the news conference. Smith asked if Mason knew the charges were being dropped, and Ortiz replied that he'd let Smith tell his client so he could take the credit.

"Get your suit out of the closet, Lou," Smith told Mason when he called him at home.

"I only wear a suit when I go to court," Mason said. "The trial is still two months off."

"Not going to be a trial, son," Smith said. "I talked to Ortiz this morning. After that heavy shit you pulled yesterday, he's agreed to drop the charges. Damn, boy, you are something. I go to the lake for the weekend and look what you do."

"You were gone the whole weekend, huh?" Mason asked. "You missed the tornado on Saturday and the shootout on Sunday. I hope you at least caught some fish."

"That I did, but I'm back now and Ortiz has invited us to his news conference where he's going to surrender and we're going to declare victory and go home."

"I can put on a suit for that," Mason said. "Tell you what, you figure out how much I owe you, take it out of the retainer, and bring me a check for the rest. I'll buy you lunch after the news conference and tell you what you missed."

"Can do," Smith said.

At the news conference, Samantha Greer and Al Kolatch stood to Ortiz's left. Mason and Dixon Smith flanked him on his right. Claire and Harry sat in the front row, Claire blushing at Ortiz's description of her courage as Harry beamed.

Invoking the power of the presumption of innocence, Ortiz declared Mason innocent of the murder of Sandra Connelly. Decrying those who sought to corrupt the system of justice, he offered a heartfelt apology for the execution of Ryan Kowalczyk, noting that mercy and sympathy would temper justice in his determination of what charges he brought against Mary Kowalczyk. He ended by announcing that the investigation into the murders of Graham and Elizabeth Byrnes, the jurors, and Christopher King was now officially closed.

Mason had reserved a table at the Union Café located in the center of Union Station. It was an open air restaurant with an upper level that afforded splendid views of the grand hall and the immaculately restored hand-painted ceiling. Seated at a table along the outer rail of the upper level, he and Smith could talk privately, their conversation shielded by the surrounding white noise of people passing through the station.

Smith handed Mason a check for seventy-five thousand dollars. "I didn't have time to prepare an itemized bill," Smith told him. "But, you and I know that twenty-five grand is a fair fee for where we were in the case."

"Fair is right, Dixon," Mason said. "Watching you tap dance on Ortiz at the arraignment was worth the money."

"You're the one who did the heavy lifting," Smith said. "You make the rest of us look like pantywaists."

"I'd just as soon do the heavy lifting in the courtroom. I'm getting too old for the cowboy stuff. I'll tell you one thing, though. I never would have figured Victoria King for a mother who'd kill her husband to cover up for her kid."

"Like messing with a momma bear's cubs, I guess," Smith said, stirring his cocktail enough to swish a few drops over the edge of the glass.

"Then she checks into the nut house to cover herself. Imagine that. Her dead husband is rich, which means she's richer with him dead, and she gives up life in the big mansion to hang out with the loonies."

Smith let go of his swizzle stick. "I thought she had a breakdown."

"Nope," Mason said, taking a sip of his beer. "Faked it."

"You're kidding me!"

Mason leaned forward. "Not one damn bit, Dixon. You know how your old client Damon Parker got into the psychiatric hospital business? He was a shrink. It's right there in his bio on the company Web site. Guess he figured out there was more money to be made running hospitals and nursing homes than in listening to people's troubles eight hours a day."

"I knew he had a medical degree, but I thought he quit practicing."

"He just had one patient," Mason said. "Victoria King. He signed off on her admission, her treatment—which was mostly to leave her alone—and the insurance claims filed to reimburse Golden Years for taking such good care of her. Samantha Greer told me about it this morning before the news conference."

Smith inched toward Mason, keeping his voice down. "Parker hired me to represent him in a Medicare fraud investigation. The feds want him for filing phony claims, shit like that. Victoria's was one of the claims. I probably should have told you about it, but it was privileged. You understand."

Mason took another sip of beer and stared hard at Smith. "No problem, Dixon. Don't worry. I didn't hear it from you. But you might be interested in knowing that I'm going to sue Parker and Golden Years for conspiring with Victoria and Whitney King."

"Conspiracy? To do what?"

"Conceal the truth about her son and keep Nick Byrnes from suing the King family for his parents' wrongful deaths. It's going to be a huge case. Frankly, I could use your help. You know what's going on at Golden Years. Now that you don't represent Parker any longer, I was hoping you might want to change sides."

Smith laughed. "Isn't there a small problem of ethics, Lou? I represented the man. I know his secrets."

"Compared to the money I'm going to get out of Parker, it is a small problem. You can stay in the background. I'll split with you fifty-fifty after I collect. As long as you really do know Parker's secrets."

Smith rolled his cocktail glass between his hands, set it

aside, absently picked up his knife, tapping the blade against the table as he studied Mason, finally chuckling again. "I told you that you and I were a lot alike, Lou."

"Black or white, Dixon, we're all about the green underneath, man."

"How much green you figure is underneath us in this case?"

Mason pursed his lips. "I figure compensatory and punitive damages could go as high as fifty million. There's no jury that isn't going to be seriously pissed at these people. My fee is one-third. Half of that is yours. You do the math and I'll keep your name out of it. Parker will never know."

Smith cocked his head to one side. "When I get done talking to you, fifty million will be chump change."

"Then talk to me, baby," Mason said, grinning.

Chapter 56

Samantha Greer ushered Mason into Patrick Ortiz's office Monday evening after the rest of his staff had left for the day. Ortiz was leaning back in his chair, feet propped on his desk, glasses halfway down his nose, immersed in the typed transcript of Mason's lunchtime conversation with Dixon Smith.

"You're sure Smith didn't make you for wearing a wire?" Ortiz asked Mason.

"Positive. Why? Is it too good to be true?"

"It's better than that. Shows the power of the almighty dollar. You dangled enough money in front of him and he gave you enough to send Parker away for a long time, not just for Medicare fraud. Parker knew what Virginia King had done and he helped her get away with it. He must have been sleeping with her."

"If they were having an affair, that's not all there was to it," Mason said. "Parker was depositing money in an off-the-books account for Victoria every month. They were covering for each other. When she really got sick, Parker had to deal with Whitney."

"So why did Smith lie to you about Parker firing him?" Ortiz asked.

"Sandra Connelly found the memo in her firm's files from the partner who originally suspected Victoria had killed her husband. She knew Dixon represented Parker and asked him to check it out. Smith told Parker and Parker told Whitney. Smith told me he'd been fired because he was hoping to keep a line of communication open with me that he could use to feed information back to Parker. I went him one better when I hired him to represent me."

Ortiz dropped his feet to the floor. "Too bad he's such a damn good lawyer. He worked me over pretty good."

"Smith also incriminated himself on that tape. He was as much a part of it as the rest of them. Have you picked him up yet?" Mason asked.

"My partner, Al, just brought him in. He's screaming entrapment and every other damn thing, but I don't think he's going to return the favor," Samantha said.

"What favor?" Mason asked.

"I don't think he's going to hire you to represent him."

Tuesday morning was August 1, the last day Mason could file Nick's lawsuit. It was also the day of the primary election and the fortieth anniversary of his parents' deaths. The combination was a trifecta he would never have bet on.

He stopped at the cemetery just as the sun was rising over the hillside, the first light glancing off his parents' headstones. The grave diggers, Albert and Marty, watched him as he placed a stone on the graves. Afterward, Mason shook their hands, making good on his promise of fifty dollars.

He was waiting when the court clerk's office opened at eight o'clock, handing the lawsuit and a check for the filing fee to the woman on the other side of the counter. She stamped the papers with the date and time, gave him a copy and a receipt for his check, and told him that the papers would be served within the week.

He'd given the story to Rachel Firestone the night before and the morning paper carried it above the fold. Nick's grandmother called Mason to thank him, telling him that Nick was at physical therapy and making great progress.

He spent the day fielding congratulatory phone calls and welcoming back his old clients. He and Mickey were going over their files when Claire appeared in his doorway. Mickey looked up, saw the storm clouds on her face, and left, files under each arm.

Claire sat on the sofa, patting the space next to her. "Come sit," she said.

Mason joined her. Her color was a bit off, her gait a step slow.

"You don't look so hot," he said.

"I'm at the age when looking hot is not a good thing," she said, brushing off his concern. "Didn't take you long to get back in business," she added.

"There's no shortage of human suffering or people willing to add to the misery," Mason said.

She didn't say anything else for the moment, looking around his one room office, taking in the barely controlled chaos, the lived-in look of a life and a law practice that had no line separating one from the other.

"I was wrong," she said.

"Why? Because you were trying to protect me," Mason said, knowing that she was talking about his parents.

"When you were too young to understand, that was a good reason. But that was a long time ago. No, I was wrong to keep using that excuse to protect myself."

"From what?" Mason asked.

"From pain, more than anything else. I didn't want to deal

with what happened to your parents. It was all I could do to take you to that cemetery, but I did it because I had to. I owed you that much."

"The car wreck," Mason said softly. "Was it an accident or did my father kill himself and my mother?"

Claire reached over and rested her hand on Mason's cheek, angling her head slightly, taking him in with tears in her eyes.

"There was a group of us," she began. "Your parents and me and eight or ten others we got to be very good friends with at the synagogue. All of us full of faith and fury. You know social action is one of the most important things to the Jewish people. Heal the world. That was our motto. We studied Torah and we worked in inner city soup kitchens and we marched against the Vietnam War and we had a grand time."

"The woman I talked to, the one whose daughter is Judith Bartholow. She's the one who left the rocks at the cemetery. Was she in your group?"

Claire nodded. "Her name then was Brenda Roth. She was married to Frank Roth at the time. They eventually divorced."

"He was one of the pallbearers, right?"

"Yes he was," Claire answered. "And he was your father's best friend until your father and Brenda . . . well, until they . . ."

"Had an affair," Mason said, completing the sentence. "I thought it might be something like that. So, my father was unfaithful to my mother. I imagine that was a big deal in the sixties, especially in a group like that. Everyone reciting the Ten Commandments all the time," he said, the words coming in a rush.

"Don't you dare trivialize your faith," she snapped. "You don't know anything about it!"

"Because you never taught me!" he said.

"I didn't teach you but I didn't teach you to be a lawyer

either. You learned that on your own. Quit using me as an excuse!"

Mason rose, walked to his refrigerator, and popped the cap on a bottle of beer.

Claire said, "I'll take one if you've got another."

Mason brought it to her, both of them drinking in silence, Mason sitting in the chair next to the sofa.

"I'm sorry," he said at last. "I was out of line. It just seems like it had to be more than a simple affair to have ended the way it did."

"There's no such thing as a simple affair," she said. "Nothing that begins with betrayal is simple or ends well."

"What happened?" Mason asked.

Claire set her bottle down on the table in front of the sofa. "Brenda said that she tried to break off the affair but your father wouldn't. She says they fought and that he raped her. Your father's lawyer told him he was going to be arrested and charged with rape and that he should turn himself in to avoid the embarrassment of being taken away in handcuffs. He agreed to turn himself in the next morning."

"The accident happened the night before he was supposed to turn himself in?" Mason asked. Claire nodded in reply. "That's why the police said it was intentional?"

"There was more. Brenda said that your father called her and begged her to drop the charges. She said he was hysterical, yelling that he'd kill himself."

Mason slumped in his chair. Claire's words rang off him like hammer blows. "Was it true?" he asked. "Did my father rape that woman?"

Claire looked at him with anguished eyes, her face mottling with bursts of red. "I don't know."

Mason bolted out of his chair. "How could you not know? Didn't you ask him? Didn't you ask his lawyer?"

"I was his lawyer," she said. "And I did ask him and he denied it."

Mason circled around the office, stopping behind the chair, gripping it with both hands. "You didn't believe him, did you?"

"I was his sister. I knew him better than anyone. He admitted the affair. He said that he was the one who wanted to end it, not her. He admitted they fought, but he denied the rest."

"What about the woman? How soon after did she report it? Did she go to the hospital? Was there evidence of rape?"

"She told the police a month later. There was no physical evidence."

"Then she's a liar!" Mason said. "She said he raped her to get back at him!"

Claire said nothing, letting Mason wrestle with it as a lawyer and a son the way she had wrestled with it as a lawyer and a sister. Mason stared out his window, looking for answers in the traffic on Broadway, turning back to his aunt. He threw a dart so hard at the wall that the shaft shattered.

"How could Frank Roth have been a pallbearer for my father after what happened?" Claire didn't answer, Mason finding his own answer. "He didn't believe her either. Two people died because of an accusation that could never have been proved."

"Two people died. Our group of friends fell apart and I never went back to the synagogue."

"And the woman," Mason said, unable to speak her name, "leaves stones on their grave so she won't forget them! If that's not an admission of guilt, I don't know what is."

"But guilty of what?" Claire said. "If I was certain, perhaps I would have told you sooner."

"The accident happened forty years ago today. Why was she out there two weeks ago?"

"It was your parents' *yahrzeit*. The anniversary of their deaths on the Jewish calendar."

Mason came back to the sofa, taking his aunt's hands in his, shaking his head. "It's just like Ryan's Kowalczyk's case. He told the truth and still ended up dead."

Chapter 57

Josh Seeley won the primary. It was close, the networks not calling the winner until early Wednesday morning. Mason watched the returns until it was over, flipping between the cable and broadcast networks, hoping to catch live reports from the hotel ballroom in St. Louis where Seeley and his supporters had gathered to await the results.

He was channel surfing in the hopes that he wouldn't catch a glimpse of Abby. While the talking heads dissected exit polls, he played out his fantasy that she had left the campaign to come back to him—that she would ring his doorbell any minute, throw her arms around him, and whisper *for better and for worse* in his ear. He could practically feel her touch and taste her skin against his.

Since Sunday, he'd reached for his phone more than once to call her, stopping each time. She'd left him a voice message at home on Monday, picking a time she knew he wouldn't be there. She said that she was glad that he and Claire were okay and that she was sorry he wasn't home when she called. She said she would try again but things were crazy and not to miss her too much. He replayed the message just to hear her voice.

When Seeley finally appeared for his victory speech, Abby was on his left, Seeley's wife to his right. Seeley held both their hands, raising them high in victory, then turned to embrace each of them. Seeley's wife was more than gracious when he hugged Abby hard enough to lift her off the stage. The camera captured Abby's exhausted exhilaration. He did miss her—too much.

He waited an hour for things to calm down before calling her on her cell phone. It rang five times before she answered.

"Congratulations," he said.

"Lou? Is that you?" she shouted over the din of celebration.

"I saw you on TV," he shouted back. "You look great."

"Hang on a sec," she said. "Let me get somewhere quiet." He paced as he waited. "Are you still there?" she finally asked.

"Never left," he said.

"It's three o'clock in the morning, for God's sake," she said.

"You know how these election returns are. Once you start watching, you're hooked."

"You didn't have to call," she told him. "You could have waited."

"Not me. I wanted to talk to you, not leave a message."

He heard Abby catch her breath. "I called. You weren't home."

"I'm never home on Monday. Especially after I almost get killed on Sunday."

"Is that why you called? To tell me that I shouldn't have ducked you. I'm sorry if that upset you."

"I think that's called an apology with a tail."

"Don't do this, Lou. Please."

"You're right. It's your big night. I'm sorry. No tail." Neither of them spoke for a moment, though Mason thought he heard Abby crying softly. What's next for the campaign?" he finally asked, hoping to salvage something from the conversation.

Abby took a deep breath. "Washington. We leave in the morning to meet with the national campaign people. They think Josh can win in November and they're going to put a lot of money into the election."

"I guess you'll be living out of a suitcase for a while."

"Maybe longer," she said. "Josh wants me in Washington if he wins."

Mason thought about the way Seeley had embraced Abby. "I don't blame him."

"I've got to get back," she said. "I'll be in and out of town. I'll call you. We can have dinner."

"I'd like that," he said, and let her go.

He woke Tuffy, the dog coming alive when he picked up her leash.

"Yeah, I know," he told the dog. "It's three o'clock in the morning. Who goes for a walk at this hour? You and me, buddy," he said, clipping the leash to the dog's collar.

They took a lap around the block, Mason opening the car door instead of the front door when they got back. He rolled the windows down as he pulled out of the garage, Tuffy sticking her nose into the warm, moist night air. He hoped a drive into his past would get his mind off his uncertain future with Abby.

The drive to the suburbs flashed by, some of the traffic lights blinking yellow in deference to the late hour. He turned onto Judith Bartholow's cul-de-sac, parking across the street from her house, dousing his headlights.

The house was dark, the answers to his lingering questions tucked away in the mind of a woman who may have condemned his parents to death. Though he knew that harsh appraisal was less than fair. His father was to blame as well. He knew that but couldn't focus his raw emotions on his father as clearly as he could on the woman. She was an easier target since she was still alive; his father was a remote memory.

Mason thought about the woman's daughter, Judith, how she'd appeared to be close to his age, perhaps a few years younger. The math and the story played tricks with his mind, conjuring more fanciful complications of an incomplete story. Guilty of what? Claire had asked the question, Mason willing to let it go unanswered for now.

A security patrol car turned onto the cul-de-sac. Mason started his car and headed for home with the bright headlights bouncing off his rearview mirror. He waved to the rent-a-cop as he drove by.

It was just as well. He had to be in court first thing in the morning.

For a special preview of Joel's Goldman's
next Lou Mason novel, *Final Judgment*—coming soon
from Pinnacle Books—just turn the page. . . .

There was a dead body in the trunk of Avery Fish's Fleetwood Cadillac. Not that he didn't have enough problems already. He was late for a meeting with his lawyer, Lou Mason, and the assistant U.S. attorney, Peter Samuelson. They were negotiating a deal for Fish's body and soul like they were haggling over a used car, both sides selling him "as is." He had to be there to sign. Even deals with the devil required observance of legal formalities.

Fish knew how it would go. Mason had briefed him the day before, telling him he had better be on time.

"Why not just strip me down to my shorts and check my teeth like I was a slave being sold by the pound?" Fish asked.

"Because you're too old and ugly," Mason answered, grinning. "The feds wouldn't buy and I'd be stuck with you."

"So what kind of deal am I going to get?" Fish asked, waving his hand at Mason's joke.

"You're charged with mail fraud. I'll offer twelve months, which is a downward deviation from federal sentencing guidelines, and a hundred thousand dollars in restitution for the people the government says you swindled."

"Like I've got that kind of money," Fish said.

He didn't deny his guilt. He just wanted to know what he owed, figuring he was negotiating with his lawyer as well as with the Justice Department. Mason ignored Fish's complaint knowing that Fish had the money or could get it, just as he had gotten the money to pay Mason's fee.

"This is your first conviction. You're not a young man. Samuelson will want eighteen months and more money, maybe two hundred and fifty grand, plus a fine. Probably the same amount, maybe a little less. We've got a shot at probation if you agree on the dollars and offer to cooperate with other investigations."

"What other investigations? I'm not in any other investigations."

"Doesn't matter," Mason said. "Samuelson has hinted that he may want you to work for the feds. Use your contacts to get involved with other people they'd like to nail."

"Such a future," Fish said, rubbing the top of his bulging stomach. His indigestion steadily stoked heartburn that would eat through sheet metal. He appreciated Mason's precise explanation. First conviction. Not first indictment. He shouldn't complain. Not at his age. But he couldn't help it. "Spending my golden years as a bankrupt federal snitch. Acch! What a life."

"Beats the hell out of stripping to your shorts and having your teeth checked by some Aryan Brotherhood inmate who thinks you remind him of the uncle that molested him when he was a kid," Mason had told him.

Now this, Fish thought to himself, as he stood in the parking lot of his synagogue, the weekday morning service just finished. The air was damp and cold, the day raw and typical for February in Kansas City. The pavement and the sky were the same flat gray, just like the body in the trunk. He should have gone to Palm Springs for the winter like everybody else.

The dead man was naked and wrapped in a sheet of clear plastic that made him look like a prehistoric hunter left frozen in ice a thousand years ago until some modern day farmer dug him up. The limbs were tight against the torso, the skin unblemished by any visible wounds.

Fish's briefcase was in the trunk. He didn't need it for the meeting with the lawyers. In fact, there was nothing in it besides the latest issue of *Fast Company* with an article he wanted to read, especially now, titled "How to Make Your Own Luck." But, carrying the briefcase gave him a more substantial look. Like he was a businessman, not some *gonif* caught with his nuts in the wringer.

Which he was. *Gonif*, Yiddish for thief, defined itself as much by its pronunciation as its meaning. He liked the guttural way the word rolled off his tongue, straight from the back of his mouth, like he was throwing it at someone.

His briefcase was tucked underneath the dead man and Fish worried that the poor bastard had bled onto it even though the body was wrapped in plastic. He didn't want to walk into a meeting with the U.S. attorney carrying a briefcase with a bloodstain painted on it like a bull's-eye. He left the briefcase where it was and closed the trunk.

He was seventy-three years old. He had a wife who referred to herself as his ex-wife on the slight technicality that they'd been divorced for twenty-five years. Like that mattered. He had two kids who didn't talk to him unless they had to and four grandchildren.

He was thirty-five pounds overweight. He had plantar fasciitis in both feet and chronic pain in both hips that confirmed his doctor's diagnosis of arthritis. He had a lumbar disc at the base of his spine that bulged like a high school boy's dick at this first skin flick and chest pain that woke him at night like the devil was slipping a blade between his ribs. But he didn't complain. That was life. The odds favored a man like him having problems like these.

But a dead body in the trunk of his car on the day he was to bargain his life away in a comfortable conference room at the Federal Courthouse—that didn't defy the odds. It beat the living daylights out of them.

Fish didn't realize he was sweating until he slid into his car. Sweating and breathing as hard as a racehorse on the back stretch. Certain of what he'd seen, he still didn't want to believe it. It was too awful to be true, but it was. In spite of the cold, he turned on the air-conditioning, gripping the leather-wrapped steering wheel to steady himself until he cooled down and could breathe normally.

What are the odds? A dead body in his trunk. Blinking the sweat from his eyes, he squinted at the memory of when he'd last opened the trunk. It was the night before when he'd gotten home from meeting with Mason. The briefcase had been on the front seat of the car, the magazine already in it. His dry cleaning had been in the trunk. He'd taken the laundry out and left the briefcase in its place.

He'd stayed home the rest of the night. Gone to bed early. Slept all night except for the six times he'd gotten up to go to the bathroom. His car had been parked in front of his house because the garage was crammed full of junk he'd been meaning to throw away since his divorce.

Had to have been during the night. He lived on a quiet street. Hell, it was an historic district, that's how quiet it was. Most of the neighbors were old, like him, the houses even older. No young kids coming home late to interrupt some killer that had turned Fish's car into a drive-by drop-off for dead bodies. If the killer had bothered to ask, Fish would have told him that there was a twenty-four-hour Goodwill drop-off Dumpster a mile away.

During the night was a better bet than while he was in the synagogue, even if there were only a handful of cars in the parking lot belonging to the ten people who showed up for the morning service. It was still dark when he arrived a few minutes before seven that morning. The service lasted forty-five minutes. The rabbi had buttonholed him for another fifteen minutes afterward, making him late for his meeting with the attorneys, asking him how things were going with his case. His legal problems weren't a secret. The media and a city full of gossips had taken care of that.

He had to be downtown in fifteen minutes and he was thirty minutes away. The parking lot was across the street from the Courthouse. It was secure, regularly patrolled by the U.S. Marshalls officers who were responsible for Courthouse security. No one was going to break into a car in that lot. It was cold and the corpse was fresh enough that the body hadn't started to smell.

Mason had told him that the meeting with the U.S. attorney shouldn't take too long. The deal was pretty well fleshed out already, though he could expect some fireworks as the attorneys postured for one another, doing their peacock dance. Fish hoped the meeting was more a formality than anything else.

Good, he thought to himself. *Things work out if you give them a chance and work the right angles.* That had always been his philosophy. He took a deep breath, put the Cadillac in gear, and tried not to think about the body in the trunk.